imperfect match

ELIXIR BACHELOR BILLIONAIRES

VIKKI JAY

Copyright © 2024 by Vikki Jay

All rights reserved.

No part of this publication may be reproduced, distributed, or transmitted in any form or by any means, including photocopying, recording, or other electronic or mechanical methods, without the prior written permission of the publisher, except as permitted by U.S. copyright law. For permission requests, contact the author.

The story, all names, characters, and incidents portrayed in this production are fictitious. No identification with actual persons (living or deceased), places, buildings, and products is intended or should be inferred.

Book Cover and formatting by Qamber Designs

1st edition 2024

To all the girls who dare to make space for their own dreams: Tomorrow, you're going to look back and be proud of the little choices you're making, friend.

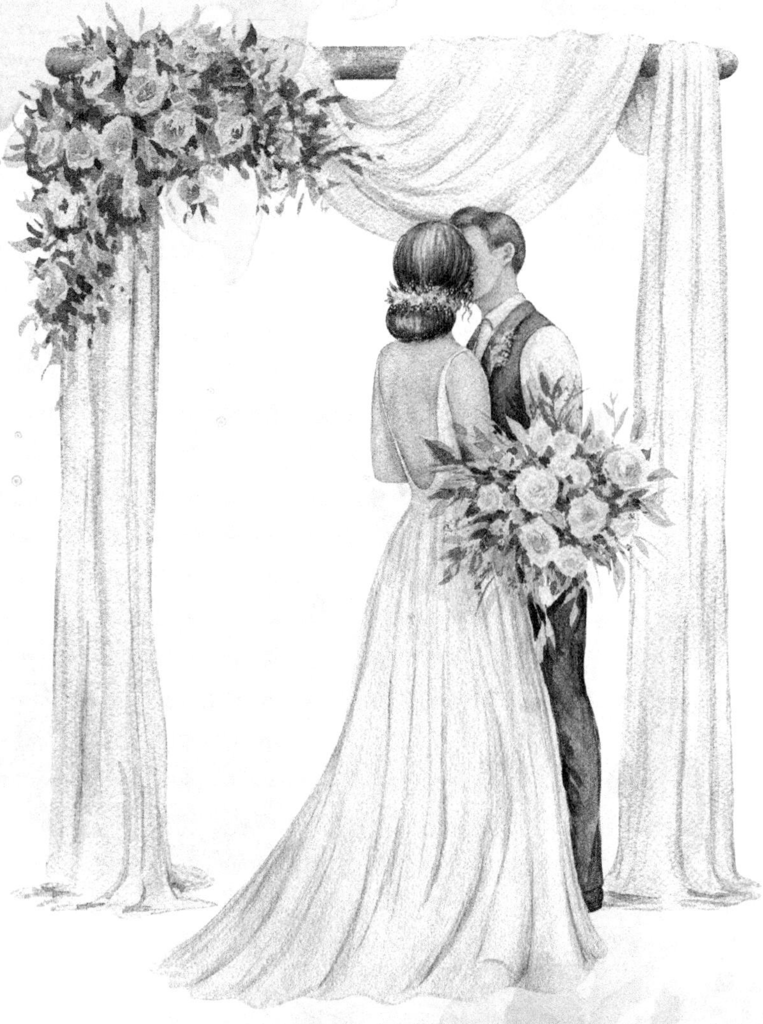

prologue

Three Months Ago

Charles

"No one is questioning your capability to run the business, Charles. Every board member believes there's no one more suited than you." Tim Baldwin takes a sip of his drink. He's not just the oldest board member of the Hawthorne Empire but also my late grandfather's best friend.

He knows what's at stake here.

Four years ago, I stepped up as CEO of Hawthorne Holdings, our sister company, and now, following the decades-old tradition, the board has to vote for the next official head of Hawthorne Empire.

Everything was going well until a few weeks ago, when a gossip column targeted my love for solitude. It's not the first time the media has pried into my personal life, but usually, they move on quickly to my professional work. That's always worked in my favor—until now.

There must be a lull in celebrity scandals or star-studded weddings for the page three reporters to stay focused on me. One piece of gossip led to another, and soon they were questioning my heavily guarded privacy, labeling me as some sort of modern monk or hermit.

"But we can't ignore your image the media has recently started to paint—a loner, a society-averse person," comments Ronald Grint, the latest addition to the board committee and someone who believes that gossip news is the most authentic judgment of my character. "Cherrywood is a close-knit family town. The residents want to know that their interests are safe and in good hands. With your family business being a pivotal part of the town's economy, your bachelor status, and more importantly, your detestation of social activities, raises a lot of eyebrows, son."

Tim gets up from his seat and pats my back before walking to his bar, providing me his silent support while Ronald's words feel like they've physically crawled under my skin, penetrating my fine Tom Ford suit and silk shirt.

"I was at the mayor's house for a dinner party last night," Ronald continues, "and someone brought up the topic of the next successor of the Hawthorne Empire. Even though everyone agreed you're the best businessman, there were several arguments that your image lacks the warmth that is essential for a town leader."

"I'm not running for a government position," I snap, clenching my fists painfully. "Hawthorne Holdings has done more for the town's economy under my leadership these last four years than in decades. I might not be the face of the business yet, but everyone knows I'm the one calling all the shots."

Tim returns and leans back in his seat. "When it comes to the head of Hawthorne Empire, it will never be just about the numbers. You know better than anyone the influence your family has in this town."

I stay silent because even though I hate his words, I know in my heart they are true.

"We wanted to give you a heads-up about the doubts the board members have before the official voting for the next Hawthorne heir." Ronald straightens his tie while a storm of thoughts whirl inside my mind, each one stoking the fire of anger.

"What are you suggesting, then? That I hand this empire my forefathers built from nothing over to a stranger?"

"No one wants that, Charles." Tim shakes his head subtly. "The easiest solution is to be more socially active. Or better yet, get married, or at least get engaged. You still have a few months. Find a nice girl if you haven't already and settle down. What's the problem with that?"

What he doesn't know is that my privacy, my solitude, is the one thing I've kept for myself. I want to be enough just on my own—for myself, for the family business, and for this town.

one

Job Title: A Perfect Bride

Charles

"Is Charles Hawthorne going to stay single forever?"

"Will the Hawthorne family line come to an end with him?"

"Is this the end of an era for the founding family of Cherrywood?"

Jimmy Garcia, the head of PR at Hawthorne Holdings slams his iPad onto the table with so much force that I'm shocked the screen is still intact. Spanish curses fly under his breath as he slides a plastic file across the surface. I don't need to glance at its contents to know what it holds.

Until a few months back, I had my suspicions that Jimmy was just making up stuff to either get a rise out of me or, worse, to manipulate me into becoming a PR puppet for the cameras. But that man has a sharper nose than a K-9 recruit's when it comes to sniffing out doubts. Now, every time he visits me, he's carrying a barrage of newspaper gossip-column clippings, which is enough ammunition he needs to blow up my day.

There are bigger problems in this world, yet they are after my personal life?

"Are you still not going to say anything?" Jimmy's face is flushed, his receding hairline growing every time we meet.

I feel for the man. I really do.

If I were him, working for me, I would have resigned already.

What can even the best PR team accomplish, when their client hates the limelight and media attention with a vengeance?

But this man is committed to the Hawthorne family. My family.

I head over to the minibar in my office and snag a water bottle. I'm about to turn around and hand it over to him, preferably before he explodes with all that suppressed tension, but my eyes catch sight of the unmissable pink paper napkins embossed with golden letters: Have a day that's as magical as a unicorn!

They clash against the sleek black surface like a glaring anomaly.

Damn this woman.

After grabbing the stack, I shove them behind the whiskey decanters. There's no point in tossing them out. It's not like I haven't tried that in the past. Within the hour, they'll magically reappear, courtesy of her relentless determination to annoy me.

How does she do it?

Maybe she keeps a secret stash of items she knows will get under my skin, just for the sheer pleasure of getting a rise out of me.

"If you're done admiring your posh bar, I'm eager to hear your thoughts, Charles." Jimmy's voice jolts me back to the present, away from my eccentric executive assistant, who occupies far too much of my mental real estate with her nonsensical behavior.

I hand him a bottle of water.

"What does the media think, I'm going on my deathbed tomorrow? I'm only twenty-nine, for Christ's sake."

"And in all these twenty-nine years, you've shown no interest in any woman. There haven't been any sightings of you at parties with potential love interests."

My teeth grind together. People pointing out my lack of a social life always hits a nerve. "That's because I don't go to those damn parties."

"And we need to fix that."

Completely undeterred by the murderous look on my face, Jimmy retrieves an envelope from the inner pocket of his jacket.

"This is an invitation to a social gala honoring your great-great-grandfather, the founder of the city hospital. As always, the Hawthorne family will match donations collected, but this year, you'll be there to personally hand over the check."

"If you think I'm even touching that thing, you're sorely mistaken. Plus, who even follows gossip news these days?" I sink into my chair and recline back, refusing to take my eyes off Jimmy.

He meets my gaze for a few more moments before his shoulders slump. Just as I release a pent-up breath, thinking this torturous meeting is finally over, Jimmy fixes me with a penetrating gaze.

"You can ignore me all you like, Charles, but your efforts in this office mean nothing if the board members don't trust you enough to vote you as the next head of family business."

My fists clench as Jimmy exits my office, his words echoing in my mind.

All my life, everything I've done is to be the best and be worthy of heading the Hawthorne Empire, but once again, I fail to be enough. A knock interrupts the silence that's slowly becoming unbearable.

Daisy Price waltzes in, dressed in a rose-gold circle skirt that grazes her knees, paired with a pastel blue top. She looks like she could be staff at an ice-cream parlor, *or perhaps, like an ice-cream cone herself.*

She glances straight to the minibar, undoubtedly catching sight of the crumpled stack of napkins peeking out from behind. She bites her lip, trying to stifle a smile and failing anyway. But I give her no satisfaction and don't even mention the color pop she attempted in my office.

"Jimmy didn't look very happy," she starts, gliding behind my desk and arranging pink Post-its on the glass wall in their order of priority.

I swivel in my chair, following her movements as she methodically scribbles the tasks onto the tiny colorful paper squares before sticking them onto the glass wall. Her heels, which are just an inch shorter than would be declared hazardous, match her skirt with a blue bow on the back, complementing the one on her hair clip. If there were an award for color coordination, my assistant would win it every day.

"He's not paid to look happy, but to do his job."

"He can't do anything unless you listen to him." Her hands halt, and she glances over her shoulder at me. Disagreement shines in those brown eyes, which seem to always speak volumes.

"Are you here to persuade me on his behalf?" If she thinks she can convince me to attend any social gathering, she can try at her own risk.

"How could I dare to do something like that?" The way she arches her eyebrow suggests she would dare indeed.

I motion toward the untouched invitation Jimmy so conveniently left behind.

"Send a reply a day before the event stating that, unfortunately, I can't make it due to an emergency. And for fuck's sake, if you make up an emergency like my pet duck's eggs are hatching and I have to be there to welcome them into the world, you'll find yourself without a job."

She spins around and doubles over, her laughter echoing throughout my office. I'm not sure what she finds funnier—my threat or the reminder of the feeble excuse she made last week for my absence at the town hall inauguration. Thanks to her, I'm still receiving congratulatory emails inquiring about my new chicks. But she knows all this since she's the one sorting them into the "NEED IMMEDIATE ATTENTION" folder.

"Do you think I won't fire you?" I ask a completely hypothetical question.

Despite all the nonsense I have to put up with, there's never been a more perfect assistant. She's not just the best, she's the best *for me*.

People call me a workaholic, but compared to Daisy when she started four years ago, I'm practically a slacker. She arrived at the office before me and left after me, never batting an eye when I asked her to rewrite the first client report five times over. Her only request was to work longhand for the first drafts.

What I didn't anticipate was how her love for paper and Post-its would one day devolve and become the bane of my existence.

She snaps her fingers in front of me. "Hey, you weren't even listening. I was just saying how I'd never do anything to upset you." She bats her eyelashes and pouts, which I find inconveniently attractive even when I tell her I don't.

"Stop with the pouting. You think you look cute, but you just look like a grinning Chihuahua."

Her response to my teasing is laughter.

As much as I wanted an assistant who wouldn't turn my office into a paper craft shop, and who feared me a little, every moment with Daisy is refreshing.

"If you're finished here, leave. And, Daisy…" I pause, waiting for her full attention. "Cancel my invitation. I'm not going."

This time, she huffs in seriousness. I know she wants to protest, but she also knows some things are nonnegotiable, and me walking into a room full of strangers is one of them.

My driver-slash-bodyguard, Steve, expertly parks the McLaren in my designated spot at Elixir Inc. before Dave, my second bodyguard, opens the door for me.

Leading Hawthorne Holdings and on track to become

CEO of Hawthorne Empire in the coming months, I already have my hands full with the family business. But Elixir is special. I'm proud to be on the board of directors in this company.

Years ago, my dad declared that he wasn't interested in running Hawthorne Empire and left it to my grandma. Instead, he helped his friends establish the Elixir research office in Cherrywood, which now serves as the company headquarters.

It was here that he met my *mom*, the woman who valued me and my dad over the family wealth, unlike my birth mother. This is also where I bonded with my cousins, who are more like brothers and now either run the company or serve on the board alongside me.

Honestly, I attend these meetings more to see them than the actual work. Elixir is in good hands with Alex as the CEO. As I enter the boardroom, I'm greeted by the familiar faces of the Teager brothers—Alex, Raymond, Rowan, and his fraternal twin, Archer.

"I thought this was a work meeting?" I comment, observing the lack of other important staff and take a seat between Alex and Rowan.

"We're all on the board and in a meeting room right now, so technically it *is* a board meeting." Raymond chuckles, placing a whiskey decanter onto the table.

"Then why does it feel like an intervention?"

"Not an intervention, more like a Charlie-got-a-new-label-and-Jimmy-is-on-his-ass meeting." Archer grins, waving his phone in the air.

"My ass is alright, brother. But tell me who I have to fire for this breach of information. Is it Jimmy, since sharing a PR manager clearly leaves me with no privacy? Or is this someone from my office?" I have my suspicions on my little secretary.

"Don't worry, no termination letters are going out today. Mom read some gossip column, and we expected Jimmy to come running to you first thing in the morning," Archer explains, passing me a glass of Scotch whiskey.

"So are you going to share some relationship wisdom with me?"

"You want relationship advice from us?" Raymond raises an eyebrow, flaunting a smirk the media has labeled a *killer smile*.

And he's not wrong.

None of us have had serious relationships, and we can blame our dads for that. They set the relationship bar so high that we'd rather avoid it than suck miserably at it. Besides, I'm certain our moms would never let us hear the end of it if we didn't meet their lofty expectations. So, we've gladly chosen to steer clear of serious commitments altogether.

But unlike me, my cousins don't have the media constantly hounding them about their bachelor status, treating it like a criminal offense.

"Why don't you hire someone?" Archer plays with the rim of his glass, the suggestion hanging in the air.

"What's that supposed to mean? He isn't hiring staff, Archie," Rowan signs while raising an eyebrow at his twin.

The day Rowan became selectively mute, his mom arranged extensive sign language classes for all of us. Eventually, we all became well-versed, and there hasn't been a day when Ro's unspoken words haven't been heard.

"But what's the difference? Charlie has to fill an open position in his life—a wife for the cameras. Just imagine if there was a way he could find the perfect woman, and she'd get paid well like any other working person for a job well done. Am I the only one who sees no wrong in this?"

I must be really insane, because Archer's idea doesn't sound so horrible.

No fear of feelings. No stress of attachment.

Everything professional, just the way I like things in my life.

"And what would be the job description for such a position, smartass?" Ray flicks a salted cashew toward Archie.

"Specific to the job and the potential husband." Archer grins, tapping away on his iPad. "So, for Charlie, we'd need a social butterfly, someone who not only tolerates people but thrives in the spotlight. She'll have to compensate for your lack of social skills, after all."

He's in the middle of typing when Rowan jumps in, apparently forgetting his initial opposition.

"She'll also need to have a thick skin. How else will she survive the shitstorm and scrutiny the media is going to throw her way? Everyone is itching to see Charlie tied down."

Yes, it's certified. I've gone crazy, because I start to feel bad for my fictional, fake wife.

"And don't forget about Grandma Irene Hawthorne's seal of approval." Ray grins.

"Not you too," I groan, shaking my head.

"I'm shocked that you still don't see the benefit of this process. Just imagine, you can find the perfect girl who fits all the bills." Archer gives me a look like I'm missing the obvious.

But what if I want the most imperfect girl and to watch her trying to fit all the bills not because I'm Charles Hawthorne but because I'm enough?

"Still not convinced?"

When I don't reply to his remark, Ray drawls, "Maybe Charlie is worried that she won't be pretty?"

"Enough about me, what about you? What would be on your list for a potential fake wife?" I volley his smirk right back at him. The thought of this perfect girl on paper is giving me a headache and false hope.

"Long legs, for sure. And a killer sense of humor. I can't deal with a girl who's too uptight."

The evening progresses until four printed papers grace the table, each listing the characteristics of the perfect fake wife for everyone except Alex. None of us would dare make such a list for him.

For one, we all know who's perfect for him. And secondly, if anyone can convince him of that, it's her. But she's chosen to move miles away to France.

I hate him for the pain he's causing her.

But at the same time, I admire him for standing up for what he believes is right, especially for her.

"So, when is the job offer going out for the new Mrs. Hawthorne?" Alex tilts his head toward the pages, flashing a dimpled grin.

"And here I thought at least you would behave like a grown-up and give some real advice."

"You're better off without my advice in this department, brother."

two

A Delicate Position

Charles

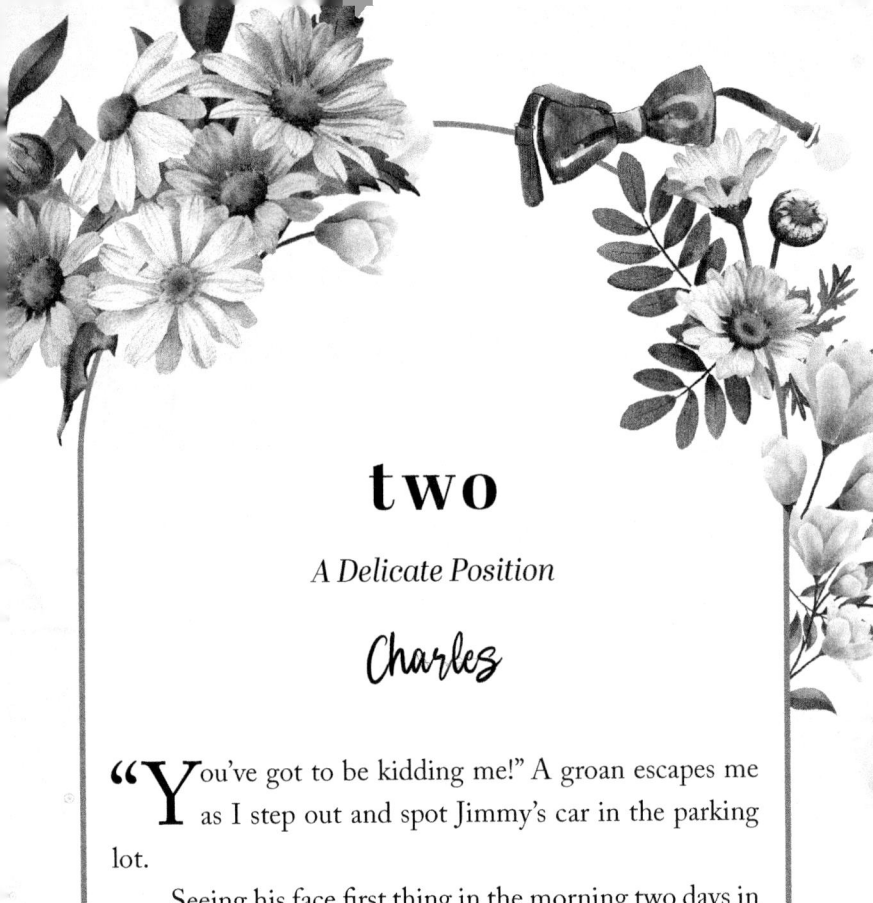

"You've got to be kidding me!" A groan escapes me as I step out and spot Jimmy's car in the parking lot.

Seeing his face first thing in the morning two days in a row couldn't make for a worse start to the week.

"Do you want us to turn around and drive back home, Mr. Hawthorne?" Dave raises an eyebrow.

"Tempting, but unfortunately, my house is not off-limits for Mr. Garcia." I give a parting nod to my bodyguards before stepping into the private elevator.

The tightness in my chest eases when I spot Daisy watering the two owl-shaped succulent pots on her desk, which she probably loves more than what's deemed healthy. I once caught her in a video consultation with the local nursery, asking how to ensure that her plants never die, *ever*.

Her words not mine.

Today, she's wearing a lilac circle skirt with a matching top, and there's a dainty purple flower hair clip secured in her hair. As she turns, the elephant-shaped, plastic watering can slips from her grasp, spilling water on the floor, including her feet.

Thankfully, I'm at a safe distance.

"What the heck?" She jumps from the mess toward her desk. "You scared me. Why are you secretly gawking at me like a lunatic?"

This woman has completely forgotten I'm her boss.

"I have better things to do in life than gawk at you." I step closer as she hastily covers the spill with pink paper napkins I left on her desk the previous evening.

She's still on her knees when my custom Tom Ford loafers stop right in front of her. Daisy looks up and grins.

"Are you avoiding going inside because you know Jimmy's here?"

She tips her head in the direction of my office. The mischievous glint in her eyes, her puckered lips, the tease of her cleavage as she's still bent forward, are a huge nuisance.

My heart rate picks up as I once again notice that my assistant sometimes looks beautiful in a way that makes it difficult to breathe.

My fists tighten around my laptop bag as, like always, I try to shut that crazy part of my brain off.

"Don't you know it's not wise to provoke someone when you're in a delicate position?"

Caught off guard, her almond-shaped brown eyes framed by thick lashes widen. I catch her subtle glance toward my zipper before she blinks a few times and rises hastily, cheeks flushed. Dumping the wet paper into the wastebasket, she avoids my gaze.

"What? No comeback?" I enjoy seeing her flustered, which is a rare sight in this office.

When she turns back to me, she's more composed, with a smirk tugging at her lips.

"Go into your office, Charles *A*. Hawthorne. Let's discuss delicate positions after Jimmy leaves."

Of course she'd bring out the big guns. Right now, that abbreviated "A" in my middle name sure as hell doesn't stand for Ashcroft.

But when I make no move to walk toward my office door, Daisy shakes her head.

"You can't avoid him forever, Charles. So instead of wasting time talking to me, go inside."

"You're coming with me." I grab the silk frill of her top resting on her forearm and tug her forward.

"You look mighty tough using someone half your size as a shield against your PR manager." Daisy giggles as if she expected nothing less.

"Yeah, I'll worry about how pathetic I look later. Right now, I have other priorities over self-pity."

She continues to laugh as we enter the room. Jimmy glances up from his iPad, his brows furrowed as he regards us.

"Thanks, Daisy, for finally getting your boss for me."

I glance down at my hand on her. "How does it look like she dragged me here?"

"Do you really think I can't imagine you debating whether to turn back when you saw my car in the parking lot, Charles?"

"You're not as hard to read as you think, boss." Daisy chuckles, slipping out of my grip with ease. It's like my morning misery is her personal comedy show.

"You're supposed to be on my side." I raise an eyebrow at her before settling behind my desk.

"Aww, I'm always on your side." She slips into the empty chair next to Jimmy.

"What now?" I turn to my PR manager, eager to get through whatever media nonsense he's brought today.

"Did you read the articles I sent you?" he inquires.

"You already know the answer to that. I'm not wasting time on gossip columns. I have a PR team and you for that job."

"Did you read them?" Unfazed by my words, Jimmy repeats his question to Daisy.

My assistant nods enthusiastically as if she's in a classroom and will be graded for her knowledge about some dirty gossip.

Satisfaction lights up Jimmy's eyes, as if Daisy's affirmation validates the value of those articles.

"I want to help you, Charles. I swear on my sweet dog that I want the announcement of your CEO position to be met with unanimous agreement, not just in town but across the state. I want everyone to see that there couldn't be a better person than you for this position."

His words tighten like a noose around my neck.

Isn't this exactly what I want?

I thought I had it all under control. How is the company's success and the growth under my leadership not enough? When did my personal life—or lack thereof—become the focal point, overshadowing everything else I've achieved?

"I know what you're thinking. But they call Cherrywood the Hawthorne town for a reason. You can never just be a businessman here, Charles."

"What does that mean? My life isn't mine?" I run a hand through my hair. I've heard these words before, but lately, they've been haunting me every waking moment.

"It is, but a part of your life will always be under scrutiny. I can help you balance it, make sure you're the one in control. If they want to talk about you, then we'll give them a slice of your life on your terms instead of being at their mercy. But ultimately, I can only advise you. If you don't act on my suggestions, it's better you let me go. I'd rather work for someone who values my input and doesn't see me as a nuisance."

The room falls into a weighty silence. It's the first time Jimmy has hinted at leaving.

"Are you threatening to quit?" I ask slowly, once the initial shock subsides. I watch Daisy in my periphery as she sits straight on her chair, her gaze fixed on Jimmy.

"Not yet. I'm asking you to listen to my advice for once. Instead of letting the media drag you down, leverage it to your advantage. Give them the real Charles Hawthorne, not the one they've conjured up in their minds."

"I won't—" I begin. Jimmy's about to interject when I halt him with a raised hand. "I can't handle social events."

The mere idea of being in a crowded room sends a

throbbing ache through my forehead. My collar feels too tight, and it becomes hard to breathe.

My eyes drift to Daisy, and there's a mix of seriousness and an emotion I loathe—pity—reflected on her face. I look away.

"What if it's a private event?" Daisy says softly, and I once again meet my assistant's gaze, finding a small encouraging smile on her lips.

In the four years we've worked together, I've learned to decipher the meaning behind the subtle movements of her mouth. The smile she's wearing now, directed at me, reassures me that everything will be fine.

"No crowd. Just a handful of reporters at *your* convenience." Daisy pauses, giving me some more time for her idea to sink in.

"Then make it an exclusive interview," I say, keeping my eyes locked on hers. If this is the only way, then I'll make sure to put a final stop on this social recluse nonsense. "Bring in the top reporters of the state—no, make it the top five in the country. Let's settle this once and for all. Pour a significant amount of advertising money into it. Let's market it as one of the biggest entertainment news stories of the year."

Daisy's smile widens with each word I speak, and I only tear my gaze away from her when Jimmy squeals.

"That's fantastic! An hour with Charles Hawthorne— raw, personal, and honest."

A wave of anxiety washes over me, but I push it aside, focusing on the reward and not on my fear.

"Where do you want to do this?" my PR manager asks.

I'm about to suggest my office, where I feel safest, but Daisy speaks up.

"How about the Hawthorne Heritage Room in the town hall?"

"That will do." I nod. At least that way, no strangers will be lurking in my office.

For the first time, there's a grin on Jimmy's face as he leaves the room. He pauses with his hand on the doorknob and looks back at me.

"You won't regret this, Charles. I promise."

"I can't believe I'm saying this, but I'm actually looking forward to opening our office in Cherrywood, Charles." Vincent Beaumont's smile widens on my computer screen.

"I'm thankful you gave Hawthorne Holdings a chance."

"Your sister didn't leave me much choice. She can be very persuasive, by the way." Vincent's gaze shifts to Daisy as she steps into the camera's view. "Where were you hiding, beautiful?"

My hands ball into fists at him referring to my assistant so informally. But Vincent is not just a client, he's also my sister, Chloe's, friend.

"Hi, Mr. Beaumont," Daisy responds with a giggle. "I was right here, listening to that cute French accent of yours."

My eyes narrow into slits as I focus on the woman beside me. But she simply shrugs while Vincent's laugh fills the room through the speakers.

"I'm sure you'll hear it in person when I visit Cherrywood, *ma belle*. Maybe I'll convince Chloe to join me."

"If you can bring my sister home, you'll be my favorite man." I forget my temporary irritation toward the man.

After the call ends, I pivot my chair to face Daisy as she efficiently moves the Post-it of CALL WITH VINCENT into the row of completed tasks.

"What the fuck was that?"

"What was what?" Daisy's eyebrow arches as she meets my gaze. The playful grin she wore during the call has vanished.

"Your comment about Vincent's accent. He's a client, not your friend. It's unprofessional."

"He didn't seem to mind."

"Of course he didn't. When you throw yourself at him like that, why would he mind?"

"Are you serious right now? I didn't throw myself at anyone. If I had, your computer screen might not have survived."

"You find this funny?"

"How dare I do such a thing?" When I don't respond to her dramatic gasp, she sighs. "I know he believes his accent is sexy, and I just complimented him on it so he leaves the meeting in a happy mood."

"His accent is sexy?" I lean back in my seat, and unlike hers, my surprise is one hundred percent original.

Daisy drops the papers she just collected, her palms flat on the glass table. Instead of backing away, she leans forward, looking right into my eyes.

"I said, he *believes* his accent is sexy. I know how much you love twisting others' words to your advantage, Charles A. Hawthorne. It might impress people in a boardroom, when you're winning an argument being like a bossy alpha book boyfriend, but don't you dare try that with me."

I file away her "bossy alpha book boyfriend" remark for later and mimic her stance. My hands are a sliver away from hers, and when I lean in, I catch a whiff of her delicate perfume, making my pulse jump.

"Are you secretly consulting with Vincent to learn his thoughts and opinions?"

She gulps, eyes widening. I hold her gaze as she struggles to put the smile back on her face, and finally, after a few successful attempts, she wins.

"Are you feeling jealous?"

The last word rolls in her mouth. She speaks it at a snail's pace, as if savoring it. I watch the way her tongue brushes against her upper lip before resettling at its place.

For a brief moment, I feel a pang of exactly the emotion she assumed—jealousy. I hate that she spent her time collecting personal insights about a client instead of thinking about me.

About the work, I mean.

But I refuse to give her any satisfaction.

"Do I strike you as the jealous type? If after all this time, you think so, maybe you should focus on getting to know *me* better before worrying about clients like Vincent."

I hold her gaze, but she starts to giggle, pulling back and taking that enticing scent with her.

"You're definitely the jealous type, Charles. But just so you know, I've got my hands full with you. I don't have time to learn about our clients, French or otherwise. Your sister texted me this morning that if the meeting goes sideways, I can always compliment Vincent's accent, as it seems to uplift his mood." With a playful grin, she snatches the pages from my desk and plops down in a nearby chair.

Irritable relief hits me at her comment, but I ignore it and arch an eyebrow at her instead. This time when she leans forward with elbows on the table, her expression is all curiosity.

"I have a question," she begins, confirming my suspicion. "Feel free to skip it if you'd rather not answer. No pressure."

"Spit it out. I have a lot of work, and so do you," I reply, my interest piqued.

She straightens up, a spark in her eyes. "Do you think there's something going on between Chloe and Vincent? I mean, Vincent brings up her name in every meeting."

"What?" I blink. That was a total curveball. "Are you serious? There's nothing going on between him and my sister. Vincent's just a flirt, in case you haven't noticed, *ma belle*. And Chloe? She cannot fall for someone like him."

"Oh, so is it some kind of rule that Hawthorne girls can't date European men?"

A mix of emotions akin to surprise and humor locks inside me.

"What soap opera are you watching now, Daisy? Please stop because it's killing your brain cells. And if you've gossiped over my sister's love life enough, we both can go back to work."

"I'm not gossiping. I just think they'd make a cute couple," she mumbles, backing away from my desk.

"For your own safety, please don't share that opinion with Chloe," I warn, and a beat later, I hear her heels clicking away. But before she can leave, I remember something. "How are we coming on with the gifts for the hospital?"

Her pout melts into a broad smile, and she hurries back to my desk, flipping open her iPad and placing it before me.

"Look, this is my plan."

There are beautiful gift baskets wrapped in pink and blue cellophane.

Damn, she's good.

"What do you think?" Daisy asks carefully. She knows how much these gifts mean to me, and every year, she surprises me by doing a better job than the previous year.

"Looks great. You made sure everything is of the best quality?" I ask, even when I know she sure has.

"Absolutely. All baked goods are from Cherrywood's finest bakeries. I've personally verified them for taste, quality, and hygiene. The same goes for other gifts." Daisy nods, moving her stylus from one item on the screen to another.

"Sounds right."

"Can I say something, Charles?" Her words are slow.

"Can I stop you?"

She grins before the mood in the room turns too serious, and I know where this is going.

"What you do for the hospitals during the holiday season is amazing. I just wish you could someday see the smiles you bring to the faces of the people."

The pang of inadequacy returns, but I quell it. "It's for them, not for me to feel good. That's why it's anonymous."

A sad smile touches her lips before she straightens. "I understand."

three

Blind Date with a Kidnapper

Daisy

"I'm off to a meeting at Elixir." Charles' voice pulls me away from the monitor.

His towering six-foot-two frame dominates the space. Standing, my four-inch heels offer my poor five-feet height some reprieve, but seated, I'm completely dwarfed.

My gaze wanders upward, taking in his tailored Tom Ford slacks and sleek leather belt. Like every other day, he's wearing the cufflinks bearing the Hawthorne family crest. His crisp white shirt, tailored to perfection, and the Windsor-knotted blue tie peek out from under his impeccably fitted suit jacket, and my eyes draw up to his long, elegant neck. Charles' dark blond hair is neatly cut and styled back. In all my years of working alongside him, I've never seen him as anything less than perfect.

My heart, ever the stickler for color coordination,

doesn't lament the sea of black and gray suits, because Charles looks so utterly delectable.

And since I'm in charge of managing his wardrobe deliveries and security sweeps for any hidden cameras and microphones, I know everything is just as expensive as it looks.

Is my boss a tad paranoid?

Well, I used to think so, until about two years ago when there was the final negotiation round during an acquisition deal at Elixir Inc. The security team overlooked inspecting a champagne bottle brought into the room for the after-party. The next day, Elixir lost the deal, and upon inspection, a hidden microphone was discovered in the bottle. Ever since that incident, everything within Charles' two-millimeter radius undergoes my thorough pat down and scan.

As a side benefit of the activity, I know that beneath his dark suit, my boss is wearing a pair of XL gray boxers right now. He always buys the same brand, color, and fabric—soft silk cotton that glides like a dream in my hand and probably feels just as smooth against his tight a—

"Why is your face all red? You feeling sick?" He leans in, reaching out with the back of his hand, and instinctively, I roll my chair back, the wheels coming in handy.

"Daisy?" He quirks that cocky eyebrow. As much as I hate to admit it, he looks super sexy doing that, especially with his furrowed forehead.

Stop thinking about him and sexy in the same sentence.

"I'm fine, I'm fine." I get up from the chair and immediately realize my mistake when a grin spreads on Charles' face.

"I sometimes forget how tiny you are." He doesn't have

to bend much to look down at my feet, clad in silly plush slippers. "Are those raccoons?"

"I'm not tiny. I'm five feet tall." *Barely.* "And that's a normal height for women. You're just a giant!"

"Of course, Daisy."

The way my name rolls over his lips gives me goose bumps. How does he do that? Say the same word but evoke a different feeling depending on his mood and our surroundings.

"Don't make fun of things you don't understand, Charles A. Hawthorne. You don't even know the pain of running around in four-inch heels." For some unknown reason, I'm suddenly too sensitive.

Liar. You know well. It's because of the text you received half an hour ago.

Charles' smile drops.

"Hey, seriously, you okay?" His gaze flicks to my desk, littered with numerous Post-its. "You plan to do all of this today?"

"Not *all*." I throw a glance at the wall clock. "I need to finalize contracts for Vincent's company and then contact the town hall about reserving the Hawthorne Heritage Room for next week."

"I'll ask Steve to drop you home." Charles knocks on my desk. "It's freezing outside, and I'm not going to have you sick next week."

All the humor leaves his face, and I catch the sheen of fear that surfaces whenever there's a possibility of Charles being in a crowd. His aversion to the media confuses me. Charles is not a weak person. In fact, he has the power to make men cry in the boardroom with just an icy stare. So what happens when it comes to crowded places?

"I'll drag you from your bed, cough, snot, sweat, and everything included, but I'm not going to that fucking interview alone." His words bring my attention back.

"Thank you for painting such a beautiful picture and making me feel so special."

When he doesn't smile or comment that I look like a lunatic as I bat my eyelashes, I sigh.

"I won't be needing the driver tonight. Sh—" I interrupt by extending my hand, capturing his serious gaze. "I'm going out for dinner."

Charles' forehead creases once again, and he bites the inside of his cheek once, a tiny indication of his disapproval. "Going out? Now?"

"When else would I go out for dinner?"

He ignores my comment and talks right through it. "With whom?"

"What?" His sudden interest in my personal life takes me by surprise.

"I'm asking if I need to send a bodyguard, just in case there's even a one percent chance that your date turns out to be a kidnapper."

Given my luck with men, the possibility of my date being a kidnapper, or worse a murderer, is unfortunately not far-fetched.

"I'm not some magnet for crazy guys, okay?"

My words immediately remind me of the infuriating text and the asshole who dared to ask for forgiveness after what he did.

Forget it, Daisy.

"I'm just going out with my girlfriends. Willow is going to pick me up in an hour."

Charles shakes his head, setting his laptop bag down on my desk, and I know what's coming.

"Don't start with the speech now."

"It's not a speech. But do you know how insane it is that you don't drive at twenty-three?"

"And who in God's name is afraid of crowds at twenty-nine?" I fire back.

As soon as the words escape, Charles winces, as if I've struck him with a whip.

Crap!

It's been four years, and I've never once questioned his eccentricities when it comes to anything with the word social in them. On the day of my interview, he mentioned he doesn't do crowded places. I assumed he simply avoided them when possible, not that he detested being in a room with unfamiliar people with the same intensity I reserve for having a plate of cockroaches for dinner.

But that's none of my freaking business.

"Charles, I'm so sorry. It just slipped out. I didn't mean it." I feel a pang in my chest as he looks away, a forced smile on his lips.

"I'd say it was called for."

"God, no. I was just being a bitch because of something else, and I took it out on you." The words slip out of my mouth before I can control them.

His entire demeanor shifts as expected, and the sharpness returns in his gaze. "What happened?"

I shake my head. I don't want to drag him into this mess. It'll just confirm his suspicions like I'm that lame girl who dates kidnappers. "It's nothing like that. I'm just tired."

Charles circles my desk and swivels my chair to face him. He shuts off the PC and is about to swipe his hand on my neatly placed Post-its, when I throw myself onto the table.

"What are you doing? That's my work!"

"Okay. I'm not touching anything." He promptly takes a step back. "But let's call it a day. Start fresh tomorrow." His gaze softens, hands held out in front of him, signaling he won't disturb anything.

"Who are you and what have you done with my demanding boss who expects me to work like a robot and never leave this office?"

"Don't worry, he's not far. As soon as we get over next week, he'll be back." Before he can turn away and leave, Charles meets my eyes. "I'll have Steve on standby. If you need anything, just call him."

"Are you ready to place your order, ladies?" A waitress walks over as Willow and I take our reserved seats in Giovanni's, Cherrywood's famous pizza joint and family restaurant. Christmas lights twinkle in every corner, and there's a towering fir tree near the entrance. There's a warm, cozy feel, with candles burning at every table next to a small orange flower arrangement.

My best friends and I have come here almost once a week since we were in school.

"Oh, we're still waiting—" I start, but my words halt as Violet and Elodie stroll over.

After sharing a hug, we place our drink order and settle

into our chairs. So far, I'm clueless about why we're meeting in the middle of the week, especially when the holidays are just around the corner.

"I love our town this time of year." Elodie sighs, echoing my emotions as she pulls her auburn hair into a scrunchie.

"I love this town all year round. We do know how to celebrate," Willow chimes in, and we all give an agreeing nod.

"Speaking of celebrations, did anyone read Willow's interview in the local travel magazine this week?" Violet grins, her eyes gleaming behind her golden-rimmed circular glasses, and I can't help my nod. I'm so proud of my friend as she takes another step closer to her dreams.

"How's that, speaking of celebrations?" Willow giggles, then shrugs. "I just thought it would be good for the inn's publicity. But tonight, we're here to discuss something else."

"We are?" I raise an eyebrow.

"I ran into Jax." Willow's lips twist, and my groan is loud enough to rattle the whole restaurant.

"Please tell me he didn't talk to you."

"Oh, he did more than that. He gave me something for you." She pulls out an envelope from her handbag and places it on the table.

Oh my God, he didn't.

"What the hell? I had no idea Jax was still around." Violet's gaze darts from me to the envelope.

"Me too," Elodie adds.

"Me three—until this, of course." Willow jerks her head toward the envelope. "That jerk said he's sending you messages but you're not responding. Is there still something between you and him, Daze?"

Okay, so now I know why we're here.

Maybe it's not so bad. I know I can confide in my friends.

"After catching Jax with his pants down and his dick in another woman's throat, I have no desire to go back to him." My face contorts at the memory, and I feel stupid that I ever wasted tears on such a jerk.

"And you're okay with that?"

"Give me some credit, Willow. It's not like Jax was a gift to womankind. Even before he decided to cheat, he was barely a decent boyfriend. I was just too scared to see it clearly. Forgetting my birthday every year. Showing up past midnight at my apartment, totally drunk. I'm not asking for the moon and the stars, but he could've made some effort, right?"

My best friends nod, and I feel like I'm finally ready to open up and get it all out of my system. Since I caught Jax red-handed, I've fried my brain wondering where I went wrong in our relationship, until the truth became clear—it wasn't me.

I grab my kombucha tea and take a sip.

"The worst part is, I wasn't even surprised when I caught him in the act. It's like I knew deep down he was cheating, but I just wasn't ready to face it. Does that make me a coward?"

"No way!" Elodie squeezes my hand on the table. "We all have to kiss a few frogs before finding our prince."

"If finding a prince means dating more guys like Jax, then no, thank you. I'd happily skip the whole fairy tale. Do you know he's texted me more in the last few months than in all the years we were together?"

Willow wrinkles her nose. "Men are idiots. Where are those movie-worthy guys? You know, the ones who are handsome and sweet."

"Jax wasn't even handsome," I mumble, placing my glass back onto the table.

"But the guy with whom you spend most of your day is so hot." Violet gives me a sly grin, tucking a curl behind her ear.

"Who are you talking about?" The words have barely left my mouth when she points to the window behind me.

"Isn't that Charles Hawthorne?"

It takes me less than a second to spot my boss sitting in his car. With his window down, I have a clear view of him absorbed in his phone.

"What the heck is he doing here?" I gasp in shock. As if he heard me, Charles looks up, his brow still knitted as his eyes find mine. He looks so out of place outside a family restaurant.

Recognition sparks in his ice-blue gaze before drifting to my surroundings and immediately returning to me.

Maybe it was the previous discussion of my jerk-supreme ex, but I can't help comparing Charles' disinterest in others to Jax's habit of focusing more on my friends whenever we were with anyone.

"God, he's gorgeous," Willow mumbles. "Those Hawthorne genes must be magic."

My friends don't even realize they're leaning on the table, their elbows resting over the wooden surface and their faces cradled in their hands, completely taken by my boss.

"And you call him an asshole," Willow adds in the same stunned voice.

"You call him what?" The horror in Elodie's voice can't be tamed as she gapes at me.

"Not to his face. I just stick with Charles A. Hawthorne."

"Yeah, Charles Asshole Hawthorne," Willow comments without looking away from him.

"Daze, that's genius. He can't even object, since you could always explain that you meant Charles Ashcroft Hawthorne." Violet beams as if I've discovered the cure for world hunger and not just nicknamed my boss.

"How did you find out his full name?"

She scoffs. "Come on. There's news about him in the gossip columns every day. Half of them are made up, but half are still kind of true."

"Vi, gossip columns aren't even real news! As a graduate in journalism, aren't you supposed to only publish and support the truth?" Elodie lightly taps on Violet's arm, who just shrugs in return.

Slowly, the attention of my friends returns back to our table as a staff member carries two pizza boxes outside and hands it to Charles' bodyguard. Of course that's why he's here. He must have lost some bet with his cousins, and it's his turn to get dinner.

Before his car pulls away, Charles nods at me, and I respond with a silly wave like a five-year-old. A corner of his mouth quirks up, and before I can further embarrass myself, my boss is gone.

"Have you ever seen Charles with someone?" Violet turns in her seat to face me.

"Vi! I'm not going to spill my boss' personal life to a gossipmonger like you."

"Hey, I'm not going to share it with anyone. It's just for my own curiosity."

"Forget it! And if you think Charles Hawthorne doesn't

have NDAs signed by everyone within a ten-mile radius, you know nothing about him. Breathing the same air as him practically requires an NDA."

"Yeah, yeah. I'm not asking for his jacking-off schedule."

"You're nuts. How would I even know any of that anyway? Do you think Charles is some kind of perv, getting off behind his desk?"

Great, now I can't get that image out of my head! Not just the act but the way his face might look—serious, maybe a curl fallen onto his forehead from his otherwise perfect hair. A bead of sweat travels down my spine, and I attribute it fully to the burning fireplace beside our table.

"Just tell me, how many girls have visited his apartment or his office? In four years, you might have seen a few." Violet's insistence snaps me out of my daydream about my boss, which is totally unprofessional with a capital *U*.

"Um, none," I reply.

"Really?" Elodie interjects. "But he's so secretive. Never seen in public much without his guards. I always thought he had a secret service on speed dial for hiring girlfriends."

Before I can respond, Willow leans forward. "But I wouldn't be surprised if Charles already has a secret fiancée or wife—maybe a daughter of some equally rich family, if not European royalty."

My heart sinks a little at her words and the thought of Charles with some rich snob.

I know he doesn't have a steady girlfriend. With the detailed information I have on his daily schedule, it'd be impossible for me to not know if he were in a relationship.

But it won't be like this forever, Daisy, especially given all the heat the media is sending his way about his bachelor status.

I rub my temples, imagining Charles with anyone else.

I don't know why, but suddenly a feeling of possessiveness rolls over me. Maybe because I've seen him with people he allows in his life. Despite being a demanding boss—hence my nickname for him—he's one of the kindest people I know. I still can't believe how much money he secretly sanctions every year for anonymous Christmas gifts at the hospital without a second glance. But more than that, he's so personally invested in all the donations.

"Okay, enough about Daisy's untouchable boss. We're here to talk about this." Willow nods toward the envelope, and I grimace.

"I hope it's not another picture of his dick," I say softly.

Elodie's hand, reaching for the envelope, freezes midair. "Why would you say that?"

"Because I received one this afternoon. I think he believes I was with him because of his dick and the service it provided." My hands cover my face, muffling my groan, as I remember the picture that ruined my mood and day.

"Were you?" Violet asks in a squeaky voice.

"If the service was to sleep on top of me as soon as he finished, then yeah, he was on top of his game."

My friends shudder, mirroring my emotions.

"I sometimes wonder what the heck it was that made me stay with him for so long." My eyes fall shut until Willow nudges the envelope against my arm on the table.

"Open it. This is the last time we waste our precious

moments talking about that loser, Jax. I'll make sure he doesn't make me his messenger pigeon again."

"Me too." Violet throws her lavender-dyed hair over her shoulder, while Elodie nods animatedly.

Looking at the supportive smiles of my friends, I take a deep breath.

What the hell? Why am I embarrassed? It should be him.

"Okay. Let's finally tear away Jax's name from my life's book once and for all, even if it means staring at his stupid dick pic one last time. Be prepared," I announce, ripping open the envelope and spilling its contents onto the table.

"Eww." There's a collective sound of disgust from all four of us.

I was only partly right. There isn't just one, but several pictures taken at different states of undress. I should have just thrown the envelope into the fireplace.

"Did he really think he'd win you back with this?" Elodie points, her finger a good distance away from the picture where Jax is sporting a neon pink brief with sparkles all over.

"What does he think I'd do with these?"

"I know the perfect thing we can do!" Violet throws her hand up in the air. "A cleansing ceremony. Burn the pics and stop this jerk-boyfriend curse that's been hanging around you."

I groan. "You really need to stop reading nonsense, Vi."

"What's the harm? You're going to throw these away anyway, right? Or do you have a secret Jax box where you are collecting his things?"

"Please. I've seen enough." I grab the pics, hide them back in the envelope, and sanitize my hands with my pocket sanitizer.

"Then let's do it." Violet rises from her seat and informs the waitress that we'll be back soon.

That's how the four of us find ourselves outside the back door, next to a large trash can.

"Crap! I forgot we need fire," Violet exclaims, looking around for assistance.

"Great! My jerk-boyfriend purging ceremony is off to an amazing start. Maybe even God doesn't want me to get rid of them. Let's just throw them into the trash."

"Stop being so dramatic, Daze." Willow opens the sling bag dangling from her tattooed arm before producing a dollar store lighter. When we look at her in surprise, she replies with a grin, "I've got all sorts of things for emergencies at the inn. Lighter, candles, sewing kit, you name it. It also comes in handy for surprising others."

"Now, girls, focus. Take out the cringiest picture, Daisy." Violet nods toward the envelope in my hand.

"Can we not just burn the entire thing at once and be done with it?" I'll do anything to skip Vi's theatrics, especially when I'm at the center of it all. Plus, she's just getting started.

"Be done with it? This is important, Daze. You clearly don't believe in this power, and I'll happily make you a convert tonight. But, girls, you all need to trust this process before we start. So, do you all trust this process?"

"Yes. We trust the process, Vi," we three reply in unison. I'm sure Elodie and Willow just want to get back inside too.

"Did you just roll your eyes, El?"

"I didn't, and just get on with it, Vi. It's freezing out here." Elodie runs her hands over her arms. Like me, she's also without her coat, since we were marshaled outside in a rush.

"We invite the great spirit of Mother Nature and goddesses all around the world to this jerk-boyfriend purging ritual."

My gaze flies to Elodie and Willow, and we share a look that is somewhere between amusement and shock, as if we all want to say, "What the heck is she doing?"

I bite my lip to stop my grin as Violet stands before us with her eyes closed, looking like a shaman invoking spirits and goddesses. In her defense, she looks pretty sincere.

"We give you this jerk today," Violet continues, opening one eye and extending her hand toward me.

I take out the neon-pink-brief picture.

I don't believe for a second that this stupidity is going to erase any bad luck out of my love life, and I'm here only for Vi and all the crazy things she does out of her care for us.

"Dear goddesses, please bless our Daisy so she no longer has to deal with stupid losers, and instead, ensure a handsome prince walks into her life. One who doesn't use his dick as a prop for photographs and knows how to satisfy all her sexual needs in bed. Amen," Violet chants.

My cheeks are burning red. I look once to my right and once to my left to make sure no one overheard her, and Vi ignites the lighter and brings the flame to the edge of the picture.

"Should we burn these too?" I wave the remaining pictures, when suddenly, a familiar throat clears behind me.

Crap! Crap!

"Daisy?"

four

Jerk-Boyfriend Purging Ritual

Daisy

"**D**aisy?"

His voice cuts through the silence again, but I keep my eyes tightly shut. Maybe, just maybe, if I wish hard enough, this will all turn out to be a dream, and my boss won't actually find me standing next to a trash bin holding nude photos of my ex.

But when have any of my wishes come true?

My friends exchange pleasantries with Charles, oblivious to my silent plea for the ground to swallow me whole in my moment of mortification.

"What are you all doing out here in this chilly weather?" Charles' voice holds a hint of both amusement and surprise.

You can't remain frozen like a statue forever, Daisy. You'll have to confront this embarrassment head-on.

As I slowly turn around, a momentary relief washes

over me when I notice his bodyguards. Thankfully, they're far enough away not to see the details of the pictures in my hand. So while they might still consider me crazy, at least they won't peg me as a pervert.

When my gaze lands on his face, he's biting the inside of his cheek, trying to stifle a laugh. *Asshole.*

His eyes flicker between me and the photos in my hand before I quickly tuck them behind my back. There's no way he missed them. I curse the overly bright festival lights that seem to illuminate every hidden corner tonight.

"We were just about to head in," I manage, slipping the pictures back into my purse. There's nothing I can do to wipe that smug grin off Charles' face tonight.

My friends head into the restaurant, and before I can follow them, Charles gently grasps my elbow, halting my movement.

"You girls don't plan to get drunk in addition to this, right?" He tips his head toward the dumpster without his gaze leaving my face. "If you are, I'll send the driver."

"Of course you will. Heaven forbid I fall sick before your interview, right?"

For just a second, his forehead puckers as if in confusion, but before I can make anything out of it, his face once again has that smirk.

"Absolutely. So keep yourself safe, Daisy Price. You're extremely valuable to me until next week."

As Charles saunters off, his grin lingering, I storm back into the restaurant. "You are so dead, Vi. How am I going to go back to work tomorrow and face my boss?"

"What do you mean?" Violet's jaw slackens as she stares at me in disbelief. "Did you miss what just happened? We asked for a prince, and Charles strolled in. Who else is more princely in this town than Charles Hawthorne?"

"Holy crap!" Willow gasps.

"I can't believe it!" Elodie's voice is filled with awe.

"Are you all out of your minds?" I throw my hands into the air. "Charles is the furthest thing from *my prince*, if I even have one!" I sink into my chair. "He saw those pictures in my hand. He probably thinks I'm some kind of pervert." I groan, banging my head against the table.

I imagine every possible scenario where Charles won't be ridiculing me tomorrow, but short of getting hit by a truck and ending up in a coma, there's no escape.

Dragging my feet, I enter the office building.

As I pass through all the security protocols to reach Charles' floor, I earnestly pray for a glitch to keep me outside, away from my boss. But of course, everything runs smoothly today like every other day.

I don't even bother swapping my heels for comfy fur slippers this morning, knowing he'll summon me soon enough.

And have I ever been wrong when it comes to my boss?

Logging in to my computer, I find his email on the top of my inbox.

> **From:** CHARLES A. HAWTHORNE
> **To:** DAISY PRICE
>
> I would like to discuss something urgent with you. See me in my office as soon as you get this email.
>
> - Charles A. Hawthorne

**CEO, Hawthorne Holdings &
Board of Directors, Elixir Inc.**

Urgent, my foot.

Ignoring the message, I focus on the *real urgent* emails in my inbox until my desk phone buzzes.

"Daisy, can you come in here, please?" His voice is a blend of honey and wine, a sweet and dangerous combination. The *please* sounded less like a request and more like a demand.

"If it's not urgent, I'd like to go through my emails first."

"Did you miss my message? As I mentioned, this is extremely urgent."

"I didn't see it. It must be buried in my unread emails."

Charles chuckles, sending goose bumps across my skin.

"You know I get read receipts on my emails, right?"

Asshole.

"Don't waste time, Daisy. Come in."

I end the call, my shoulders slumping with resignation. There's no escape.

Grabbing a pen and a Post-it pad without worrying about the color, I drag my feet toward his office. Knocking once on the door, I enter to find Charles leaning back in his chair, his smug smile intact.

For a moment, I'm starstruck, forgetting I'm annoyed with him. He's wearing one of my favorite ties, dark purple, with a sleek black suit and a crisp white shirt. He brings his pen closer to his lips, golden metal gleaming against pink, the diamond-studded H of his family crest sparkling.

But when he curls his lips, clearly relishing in my discomfort, the veil of lust drops from my eyes. Straightening my shoulders, I meet his haughty grin head-on.

I slam the Post-it pad onto his desk with force and plant my hands firmly beside it. "Let's hear it. You want to make fun of me? Go ahead."

His smile falters, his gaze finally falling, and I follow it to the standard yellow Post-it pad—the one color I barely use. But I'm like a wild, untamed spirit right now. I've had enough of men mistaking my politeness for weakness.

"What? No words? Let me help you, then. Yes, I'm crazy. Yes, I was outside a family restaurant holding a bunch of almost nude pictures. And no, I don't have an explanation for my behavior." My throat tightens, and I avert my gaze, unable to meet his eyes.

A heavy silence hangs between us until Charles rises from his chair and strides over to the minibar. He returns with a water bottle, a glass, and one of the pink-and-gold unicorn napkins I've been keeping there all week. After carefully filling the glass halfway, he places it on top of the napkin.

A sad chuckle, which sounds more like a cough, escapes me. He arches an eyebrow, and I offer a shrug.

"You're such a control freak," I mutter. "I'm sure someone like you would never find themselves in such an embarrassing situation."

"And what situation are we talking about here?"

"I didn't know you were such a dense man, Charles." I narrow my eyes on him, which of course doesn't work with my boss. "The one where I come off as a prev. Happy?"

I divert my gaze to the table, fixating on the sleek surface even when he leans against its edge.

I can see from the corner of my eye the smooth fabric

of his pants clinging to his thighs like a second skin. They scream wealth and power.

"I never took you for a pervert. If I had to guess, you and your friends were performing a jerk-boyfriend purging ritual."

What the heck?

"How do you know about that?" I gasp. "I thought it was something Violet just made up to cheer me up."

"You do know I have a sister, right? I've done all sorts of crazy stuff *for* her, including summoning Mother Nature and the Supreme Goddess to a bonfire."

"Holy crap! I can't freaking believe it."

Could this man get any more perfect? Suddenly, I'm jealous of Chloe and whatever heiress Charles is meant to marry.

"One thing I didn't understand, though. Why were you burning pictures of him without his clothes on? As far as I know, the goddesses aren't biased on the level of nudity."

"You're definitely more informed on the subject than I am." I cross my arms. But when he waits for my reply to his question, I sigh. "It's not like I went around with a camera, desperately trying to catch him naked. He sent them to me."

"He sent you his pictures of his junk? Including the one in a pink brief?" As usual, Charles' way of showing surprise is just a raise of an eyebrow, but I don't miss his clenched jaw.

"So you saw that too?"

"It was quite…unmissable."

Contrary to how I thought this morning would go, I suddenly feel much better. But then I remember Jax's text from this morning with the subject "WOOD MORNING." There was a matching picture, thankfully with his dick hidden behind white briefs this time.

"He sent more?" Charles doesn't wait for my response and extends his hand. "Show me."

"I'm doing no such thing." I'm not going to embarrass myself further.

"You think I'm interested in him?"

"Are you?"

"What?" He blinks rapidly, as if in shock.

"Are you interested in him? Because since I've worked here, I haven't seen you interested in a woman."

"No, Daisy Price, I'm not interested in your ex or any other man, and I'd rather not have this conversation ever again. But when my assistant burns faceless pictures of a man's junk in a public trash can with her friends, I have to be a little concerned. What if the media thinks it's me in those pictures?" His icy-blue eyes narrow on me as my stomach drops.

"W-what?"

I'm lost for words. Could that happen? Absolutely. But instead of worrying about Charles and my potentially ruined reputation, I'm wondering just how different his pictures would be. I'm sure there's a pretty "decent" package hiding behind those gray XL boxers.

Before my eyes can drift up to his groin, Charles clears his throat. His amused grin makes my cheeks flush. It's as if he knows what I'm thinking.

I take out my phone from the pocket of my jacket, unlock it, and cringe at the sight of yet another text from Jax. I don't even bother looking at it and place my phone into Charles' waiting hands before flopping down on a chair.

Every trace of amusement drops from his face, and his

fingers swipe the screen. His jaw tightens as he places the phone onto the table after initiating an outgoing call.

"Charles, what the heck? I don't want to talk to Jax." I jolt in my seat, my hands going to hit the end call button, but they're stopped in midair by his.

"And you won't have to," he grinds out, moments before Jax's voice fills the air.

"Daisy, is that you, babe? Finally! Thank God you contacted me. I knew you could only resist my charm for so long. You, my sex-crazed nymph—"

Before I can scream at Jax to shut the fuck up, Charles leans forward. "You better stop right there." His voice is sterner than I've ever heard it. It has the strength to silence a room full of people, and my ex is no exception.

When Jax finally finds his voice, it sounds irritated and whiny. "Who the hell are you?"

"None of your fucking business. But if I catch you contacting Daisy again, those nude pics you're so proud of will be plastered all over town, and this time your face will be on them."

"How…how do you know about my messages?" There's shock and even underlying fear in his words.

"Remember what I said—you in those pink briefs on every damn billboard in this town."

With a decisive click, Charles ends the call. He circles the desk, and when he perches back on his chair, he's once again the same composed person who rarely loses control.

There's no doubt in my mind that what just happened was a rarity. And I don't know how I feel about it—flattered, embarrassed, shocked, or maybe a cocktail of all those emotions.

"Thanks, but you didn't have to do that. I could have handled Jax," I say.

His gaze flickers to my face. "I never questioned your ability to handle him. But only a sexist man sends pictures of his junk to his ex. I wouldn't be surprised if he causes a scene when it finally gets to his thick brain that you're not taking him back. That's the intention, right? Or…" His voice trails off, lower than usual.

"Absolutely not. Jax and I are over. We've been over for a long time. This just makes it official. I'm a proudly single girl."

I might be much more distracted by Jax than I thought. Why else would the emotions on Charles' face look like relief at hearing my single status unless I'm hallucinating?

Before I can read further into the foreign expression on my boss' face, he averts his gaze.

With a key from his wallet, he unlocks the confidential top drawer of his desk. There are very few things in Charles' world that are off-limits to me, and this drawer is one of them.

Am I curious? Absolutely.

Do I have my suspicions? Certainly.

Anything from baseball cards to porn could be hiding in there. He's a man, after all, even if this town likes to think otherwise.

But today, he pulls out a pink Post-it notepad and pushes it toward me across the table. "If we're done sorting personal affairs, let's get down to some actual work."

five

Order for a Barbie Bride

Charles

As the car pulls into the family estate, my fists clench. It's been ingrained in me since childhood that I'm destined to be the next leader of the Hawthorne name. Not accepting my fate was never an option for me, and I never questioned my destiny, which was set in stone before my birth. This estate is my heritage, a legacy passed down through generations.

When my forefathers built this town, they had a vision—bringing prosperity while keeping traditions alive. And I want to be a part of that legacy and make my contribution to leave a mark. I was ready to work hard and give my everything, but I didn't know it'd demand the only thing I'm scared of—intimacy, allowing someone to get close to me and giving them an opportunity to hurt me.

The car comes to a halt, and I'm snapped out of my

thoughts. Steve opens the door, and I step out to find my mother waiting for me at the entrance. Kristy Hawthorne, dressed in a casual chiffon dress and high heels, her red curls resting over her shoulders, looks as stunning as the day Dad and I proposed to her together. While she may not be my birth mother, I know she loves me just as much as she does my half sister, Chloe, and worries about me probably more.

"Mom, you really don't have to wait for me at the door every time. I always feel like I'm late for an appointment." I inhale her floral scent, which is synonymous with home to me.

"I love waiting for my son. Don't you even dare ask me to change my habit, Charlie." She pats my cheeks like I'm four.

"If it makes you happy, I won't." With my arm around her shoulders, I guide us inside. A house staff member takes my coat and laptop case before we enter the dining room. My great-grandmother, or GG, my grandmother, and Dad are already seated at their places.

I make my way to GG, who's sitting at the head of the table, ready to win the award for being the best-dressed person. Her short white hair is styled to perfection. Her huge black frames hide her small eyes as they crinkle with warmth. I'm enveloped by the puff of the oversized sleeves of her yellow pantsuit when I hug her, and her many bracelets jingle when she pats my cheeks.

"How have you been, peanut?"

"I stopped being a peanut long ago, GG."

"Oh, you'll forever be my peanut." Her beaming smile radiates as she adjusts her necklaces. "How do I look today?"

"Stunning, as always. I'm surprised you don't have fashion reporters after you. You'd go viral in a heartbeat."

Her eyes shine as she mashes her lips together to hold back that wide grin and leans in. "Don't tell your grandmother, but Chloe is already talking to *Vogue* about my interview. Do you know I have a fashion portfolio now?"

I chuckle. Chloe and GG have been partners in crime since my sister was a kid.

"If you need any help or want to speed things up, just give me a call. I'll make it my top priority."

Her smile widens as she pats my cheeks once again before I move over to my grandmother. As opposed to GG, she's dressed in a burgundy dress and a matching jacket.

"Charles." She kisses both my cheeks. "How have you been?"

"Can't complain, Grandma. How are you?"

"I'm okay. Had some meetings this week with our trust fund managers. My team will email you all the information tomorrow." Grandma Irene has always cared about the Hawthorne name and its glory, sometimes even over her own children's interests.

I'm both intimidated and awed by her determination. After Grandfather's passing and my father's decision to officially step back from the family business, she became the face of the Hawthorne family, and she excelled at it. I know I have big shoes to fill.

"I look forward to it, Grandma."

Finally, I reach Dad, and we share a hug before I take the chair beside him.

"How's it going, Ace?" he asks.

"Can't complain. How about you?"

"All's under control." My dad rarely discusses work at

the table, perhaps his way of ensuring no one catches wind of his involvement with Hawthorne businesses or how deeply he's immersed behind the scenes.

As we eat, conversation flows about upcoming town holiday events, with GG reminiscing about how she and Great-granddad used to dress up and attend the local Christmas market in disguise. I welcome the distraction.

"By the way, did any of you catch *E! News* this week?" GG grins, directing her gaze at me, and I groan.

"Not you too."

"You know the media won't relent until you give them what they want." Unlike GG, Grandma Irene's tone lacks playfulness.

"Irene, the paparazzi just want to boost their own ratings. I'm curious what they'll spin about my *Vogue* interview."

"Mom, we need to discuss this beforehand. You can't just say anything on camera." Grandma Irene sets her fork down, fixing her gaze on GG, who simply shrugs.

I know well that GG brought up her interview to shift focus from me, but before I can relax, Grandma Irene's eyes flicker over to me, proving she's not someone who can be easily distracted.

"I know much of what's been said is nonsense, but some people genuinely wonder if this is the end for the Hawthorne family. The easiest solution would be for you to marry, Charles."

I wring the napkin on my lap as my teeth grit. "I'm not going to marry because the media believes that I'm more fit to run the family business with a woman beside me. I'm not going to be played like this, Grandma."

"I'm fully behind you, Ace." Dad gives my back a reassuring pat, but any relief is short-lived as Grandma clears her throat.

"It doesn't matter what we support, Oscar," she interjects, tapping a button on her phone before placing it in front of me.

On the screen, a news reporter stands beside an elderly gentleman, framed against the picturesque backdrop of the town square's gazebo. Beyond them, the Christmas market twinkles with holiday lights and cheer, while part of frosty Lake Cherry glistens under the wintry sky. Everything is nestled by surrounding hills, guarding our town like a medieval fortress.

"How long have you lived in this town, sir?" the reporter asks.

"I was born here seventy years ago and never left." The pride in the man's voice is hard to miss.

An outsider wouldn't understand it, but I do, because I feel the same emotion rising in my chest. It means the town my forefathers built is enough for people to not leave their homes, their roots, in search of something more lucrative outside.

"Not even for school or work?"

"No, never." The gentleman shakes his head. "This town has everything, and a large part of the credit for that goes to the Hawthorne family, who are dedicated to making Cherrywood one of the best small towns in the country."

"So you're optimistic about the town's future?"

"I am, but I'm also a bit concerned. We all love Charles Hawthorne. He took over the family business from his grandmother without a hitch. Even though he's media-shy, we know he has everyone's best interests at heart. But his reluctance to settle down worries me."

"But he's still young?" the reporter asks, and my mood has taken an unexpected detour down Disappointment Lane.

"He is. But instilling the same sentiment of responsibility to his kids won't be an easy job. Charles had great role models in his family who mentored him from a young age. He learned early what this town means to his family and how much the Hawthorne family means to us. Every Christmas, my family says a prayer for the Hawthorne family. I know a lot of other people do too. Charles needs to settle down and have a family so his kids can get the same education he did."

Did he just say kids?

"I'm not having kids because of some interview, Grandma."

"I'm not suggesting you rush into having children," Grandma says cooly before leaning back in her seat. "I'm simply saying you can't dismiss people's concerns just because you're high up in your office tower and have made yourself nearly inaccessible. Just get engaged, Charles. Give them something else to talk about, and buy yourself some time."

"And you don't think it'll look like I'm playing right into the media's hands if I suddenly show up with a fiancée who didn't exist until yesterday?"

"You're known for being private. People hardly know anything personal about you. We can always spin a story, how you didn't want to share her with the press, but with all the uncertainty in everyone's minds, you changed your mind. I can find a perfect match in just a week."

My muscles tense, coiling like a spring ready to snap. Before I can rush out of the room, my stepmother throws her napkin beside her plate on the table.

"Mom! Charles might already have someone he likes.

Isn't it bad enough that we're pushing him to announce his personal life on a billboard, and now we want to get involved in who he marries?"

The whole conversation must have pushed her limits because, in general, she avoids getting confrontational with Grandma.

"He'll have a choice, Kristy. I won't just bring up a girl out of thin air and announce her as his wife. I never planned on doing it to any of my children, despite what they might think."

Before this dinner completely unravels, I place my hand over Mom's on the table beside me. It's enough to draw both her and Grandma's attention back to me.

"I know this is important, Grandma, and I promise to think about it. Just give me some time."

The dinner ends, and before I can escape the stifling atmosphere and take away all the suffocation that will stay with me the whole night, Dad invites me into his study.

He lights a cigar and pours whiskey into two glasses, then hands one to me before sinking into his cherished wingback chair, casually draping one leg over the other. His brown Bontoni shoes catch the light of the chandelier.

"I understand you're in a tough spot, Ace. But I don't have any advice on how to navigate it."

"It's okay, Dad. With everyone in town offering their opinions on how I should proceed with my personal life, I'm glad you're not pushing pictures of potential matches my way."

He groans. "God, no. I'd never do that. I'm sure you're much better at hunting for a bride than I am."

"Please, let's keep that between us. I'm not sure we'll like the consequences if Mom hears you." It feels good to smile.

Dad snorts, placing his glass onto the corner table before taking off the silk cravat from his neck. "I'm thankful it was Kristy who came looking for me. If I had to chase after her, I'd have probably messed it up somehow."

"Nonsense, you would have been just fine. Remember, I was on your team. I did my best to charm Mom whenever I could." I walk around the room, looking at the several pictures hung on the wall. Dad with his gang, the first Teager brothers, popping a champagne bottle after Elixir won a big deal. Mom and her gal pals, who are basically Teager women, at a girls-only trip to Egypt. My dad, much younger in this one with his sisters, Aunt Clementine and Aunt Florence.

I've never seen a businessman like my dad. He should be teaching a course on how to place family above everything and still be on top at your work.

"You certainly did that," he says, throwing his head back in laughter. "Those were easier days, huh?"

"Definitely." I breathe freely for the first time since dinner, the anxiety momentarily fading away.

"But I'd still like to tell you two things, if it's okay?"

I turn around and give a nod, my curiosity piqued. He's always been the kind of father who allows us to navigate our own paths, only stepping in with assistance when he deems it's truly going to make a difference.

"Number one, your first personal responsibility is to yourself, Ace. You can't help anyone unless you are happy with your own life. Until you decide what you want to do at every step, people will decide for you. But as soon as you take a stand, everyone will have to accept and live with it. Never let go of *your* control over *your* life."

"And what's the second?" I ask, because I feel I'm already failing at the first one.

"Never marry the wrong person or for the wrong reason. It's not just about what you do to each other, but also what you do to yourself. A toxic relationship brings out the worst version of yourself, and a good relationship allows you to grow. I understand there's immense pressure on you, but the Hawthorne name isn't bigger for us than you and your happiness."

As I hit the treadmill in my home gym the next morning, I flip on the TV. The business news segment wraps up after twenty minutes just as I finish my last lap. The credits roll in and Cherrywood's town center fills the screen, festively decorated for the upcoming holidays.

A surprised smile tugs at my lips. Our small town on the news should be some sort of lucky omen for the day.

After stepping off the treadmill, I grab a towel from the rack and wipe the sweat from my neck and shoulders. As I reach for my water bottle, a gravelly voice saying my name on the TV catches me off guard. The news reporter, clad in a cheap charcoal suit, grins for the camera.

"Is Charles Hawthorne finally sharing his love life? We've just received word that Mr. Hawthorne is about to give an exclusive interview to a select news network. Unfortunately, we're not part of that exclusive group, but we won't let that stop us from digging into what he might reveal," the reporter announces with a sly grin.

What the fuck?

I quickly crank up the volume as the reporter continues his stroll through the streets, eventually pausing outside none other than my most cherished spot in town, Hawthorne Bakery.

"I'll be speaking with some locals to see if we can uncover any hints about what Charles Hawthorne has up his sleeve."

This man's fucking nerve! He's chosen to set up camp right outside GG's beloved bakery.

The towel that was draped around my neck just moments ago is now balled up tightly in my fist.

I reach for my phone, ready to dial security, but before I can, the reporter accosts a man in his sixties who's emerging from the bakery flanked by two kids on either side of him.

"Hello, sir, I'm from Channel Nine. Would you be willing to answer a few questions for our viewers?"

The man seems uncertain, glancing behind him before offering a hesitant smile. "Sure."

After the usual pleasantries, the reporter gets to the point. "Have you heard about Charles Hawthorne's exclusive interview?"

The man's smile immediately fades, and he shifts uncomfortably. But the reporter presses on, determined to get answers and aggravate me in the process.

"It could just be hearsay," the old man finally mumbles.

"No. It's absolutely confirmed news. What do you think Charles is announcing? He's kept the media at arm's length for so long. But now, an exclusive. A day with Charles

Hawthorne—raw, personal, honest. There has to be big news that he's ready to finally share. Don't you agree?" The reporter's free hand flails around.

"I...I don't know. Maybe," the man stammers.

"My bet is Charles is announcing his engagement or introducing us to the lovely woman he's kept hidden from the media all these years. With him taking over the Hawthorne business soon, it has to be it. The media's going wild," the reporter speculates, feeding off the excitement.

The man's nod is hesitant, a blend of agreement and uncertainty.

"So you don't care what the Hawthorne family does or if Charles is the last direct heir?"

"Of course I care." The gentleman's demeanor shifts suddenly, and the reporter can barely conceal his sinister smile. He's got the interviewee exactly where he wants him—talking.

"The Hawthorne line won't end anytime soon. This town needs the founding family. I'm sure Mr. Hawthorne will do what's best for all," the man says, his words igniting a warm surge in my chest. Validation and praise from those I intend to help and support feel more rewarding than any business deal.

"Absolutely. Charles Hawthorne's a savvy businessman, no doubt. But shouldn't he be more open about his personal life?" the reporter presses.

"Mr. Hawthorne doesn't owe anyone explanations. We'd be glad if he shared that he's found someone special. Life in those tall towers must be lonely, and we all want him to be happy. But I'm sure he'll share it with us when he's ready." The man doesn't even wait for the reporter's next question and grabs his grandkids' hands before walking away.

"As you can see, there's a special unspoken bond between this town and the Hawthornes."

My vibrating cellphone draws my attention from the TV, and a groan slips my mouth at the sight of Jimmy's picture flashing on the screen.

"Hello."

"You can't deny you saw it. I know Channel Nine is your go-to, especially during the business news hour."

"And people call me private."

"Now's not the time to grow a funny bone, Charles." His breath sounds rushed, as if he's in a hurry.

"Relax before you give yourself a heart attack. If you're referring to the reporter outside Hawthorne Bakery, yeah, I saw."

"And?"

"And what? Besides being inches from suing that asshole for setting up shop outside GG's bakery, we're doing the exclusive interview. That's enough."

"Not quite. You need to hint that you have a romantic life, even if you're living like a hermit. You need to tell them that you have a sweet, funny, and cute girl with long golden hair and a matching personality."

"And where are we going to put in an order for her? A Barbie shop in heaven?" My teeth grit to the point of pain. Why do my actions always seem to fall short?

"We'll cross that bridge when we come to it. For now, let's stop all of this about the Hawthorne line ending. If one reporter showed up today, I guarantee the streets of Cherrywood will be flooded with them in the coming weeks. And trust me, not all townspeople will be as friendly as today's gentleman."

"This is nonsense." I run my hands through my hair, almost pulling at it in frustration.

"Listen to me, Charles. Extinguish this flame before it turns into a wildfire."

"I'll think about it." I end the call, Dad's advice from last night echoing in my mind.

I need to think about my own happiness and not be with someone for the wrong reason. What's the point of being one of the most powerful people in the state when I have no control over my own life?

Before the unease consumes me entirely, I shake my head.

What the heck, Charles? Since when do you wait for things to happen? That's an act of a loser. Life always becomes what one wants only when one is willing to take action.

It's time to take charge and nip this problem in the bud.

Dressed and ready, I grab my laptop from the desk, spotting the paper Rowan printed a few nights back. It even has a title.

Perfect Match for Charles Hawthorne.

What was I even thinking?

I shove it into my laptop bag, fully intending to feed it into the shredder by day's end.

six

Where's the Monster Repeller?

Daisy

Double-check the security at town hall—we don't want any uninvited guests sneaking in.

I mark a check on my to-do list, before proceeding to the next item.

Make sure there's water ready for Charles.

Just imagining Charles' parched throat as he's facing the camera makes my own throat go dry.

This isn't the time to start feeling sympathy pains for your boss, Daisy.

He's probably nervous enough as it is, with the whole town watching.

Unlocking the door, my hand lingers on the key fob.

Do I need to use the restroom again?

You're not trekking through a desert, there are bathrooms at town hall, girl!

imperfect match

Right, let's go. I head down the stairs of my apartment building and am not surprised to find Dave, one of Charles' bodyguards, waiting for me on the street. On special occasions like today, I'm sure my boss doesn't want me to take a chance with a cab.

"Hey, Dave. Thanks for picking me up."

Slipping into the back seat, I pause. The faint scent of Charles' Tom Ford cologne, a mix of vanilla and tobacco, still lingers in the air. I take a deep breath before noticing the car freshener on the dashboard. Vanilla and pine.

Dammit, Charles, your nerves are rubbing off on me.

Flipping through my notes, I circle the most urgent tasks in red when my phone interrupts with a ring.

"You don't have to start a new habit of calling me instead of sending your pointed texts, Charles. I promise, everything's going to be okay."

"I'm not Charles, hon."

"Aunt Mel?" I glance at the caller ID and groan. "Sorry, it's a big day and I'm a little stressed. You might have already seen on TV—"

"You need to come home, Daisy."

"Yes, I will. I promise. These last few days have been crazy with work, but I'll be there on the weekend."

"No, honey. You need to come right now. We can't find your dad."

My fingers pause on my colorful notes as all air leaves my lungs.

"I saw him in the morning through the kitchen window, picking up his newspaper. But when I went to check on him after breakfast, he wasn't in the house. His sneakers were gone, and his furry house slippers were still at the entryway."

My stomach rolls. Dad and I bought those matching reindeer slippers last month while shopping for new Christmas tree ornaments. He promised to wear them all season, and to make sure he doesn't forget, he placed them near the front door.

"He left the home unlocked. The coffee pot was on the stove. I was just in time to prevent any accidents in the kitchen. Fred and the neighbors are looking for him now. I don't think he's gone far, but he'll be scared and disoriented when we find him. You need to be there for him, kiddo."

My fingers clutch the edges of my skirt, memories of the last time Dad vanished like this flooding my mind.

"Did he take his jacket?"

"No." That single word is wrapped in sympathy and pain.

How does he remember to change his shoes but forget the jacket right above them? But who knows what Alzheimer's does to a brain.

"I'll be right there."

As I end the call, negative thoughts swarm like a thick tornado, threatening to engulf me. Where could he have gone? Even though Cherrywood is a safe place, accidents aren't completely unheard of here.

I shake my head immediately. *Stop it, Daisy.*

"Dave, can we please reroute?"

The driver's brows furrow, but he nods as I relay my dad's address.

Next task, Call Jimmy.

"Hi, Daisy. I can't believe we're actually doing this. Thank you so much for getting Charles to agree to the interview."

"Jimmy, I won't make it to the town hall in time."

"What?" His exuberant speech falters. "No! You have to be here before Charles. He's gonna flip if he doesn't see you. We can't turn back now after coming this far."

"I can't, Jimmy. It's my dad." My throat tightens. "Everything will be okay. Just tell Charles I'm in the next room or something. I'm sure he's not going to be there even a second early. I'm sending you my notes. Please make sure everything's set up in a way that makes Charles comfortable. At least as much as he can be." My stomach churns, twisting into knots while I imagine Charles facing the press.

"I can't believe this. You're serious."

"I'm sorry. I'll be there as soon as I can."

I hear Jimmy's sigh through the phone. "Okay, you take care, but I hope to see you soon."

My relief is muted, covered in worry and anxiety both for Dad and Charles. My hands shake as I end the call and open the texting app.

Me: Best of luck.

Boss aka Charles Asshole
Hawthorne: I don't need luck. I just need to get through this. Are you on your way?

Me: Almost there.

Cold sweat breaks out on my forehead as I text the lie, but it's better if Charles doesn't know beforehand about my absence. He will create a scene, or worse, he might not arrive at the venue.

Boss aka Charles Asshole
Hawthorne: See you then.

As Dave turns onto my block, my phone buzzes.

Aunt Mel: Fred and his buddies found Jason at the cemetery. He's disoriented and doesn't remember how he got there.

A pang hits my chest as I step out of the car.

Uncle Fred, Aunt Mel's husband, is waiting for me on the curb, a weak smile lifting one corner of his lips as I approach.

"He's safe," he whispers as I hug him. "I'm sure he'll relax when he sees you."

I take the porch steps two at a time, and my chest clenches as I find Dad in the living room, staring at the blank TV.

"Dad."

He turns toward me, confusion clouding his brown eyes. "Um, Daisy?"

His doubtful tone squeezes my heart, but I muster fake bravado and walk inside.

"Of course it's me, Dad. Your Doodles." I kneel before him. "Or do you have any more secret daughters I don't know about?"

My joke only makes Dad think harder.

Stupid, Daisy!

"I don't think so," he says carefully.

"Me neither. Mom would have kicked you out if you tried that."

"I totally agree with you on that, Daze." Aunt Mel brings Dad tea as she tries to hide her worry behind a forced smile. "I'll leave you two alone. If you need something, just holler." She kisses my forehead, holding my head a bit tight before leaving.

Dad and I sit by the fireplace for several seconds, until he finally breaks the silence.

"I forgot why I went there." Dad's low voice trembles, creating a matching shiver in my heart.

"It's okay, Dad. You're safe, and that's what matters."

His grip tightens on my hand. "It's not okay, kiddo, and it won't get any better."

I swallow the lump in my throat. "Days like today might not get better, but all the others will be extra fabulous. I promise you that, Daddy. Do you trust your Doodles?"

"I trust you completely. But I also trust myself to be a bigger burden each day." His words are laced with pain.

"You could never be a burden to me." Placing a kiss on his hand still holding mine, I rise up. If we stay like this, we'll never get out of these sucky talks. "How about I make us some pancakes?"

A genuine smile spreads across his face. Mom used to joke that Dad would sell us both for his favorite peanut butter pancakes. Of course, that's the first thing I learned to cook, and they came in handy for getting special permissions.

As I set the large glass bowl for preparing pancake batter onto the counter, my phone buzzes.

Jimmy: The media is already here and setting up. Charles is leaving in five mins. Since he isn't flipping out, I'm assuming he doesn't know his Monster Repeller isn't here.

Me: I thought it was better this way.

Jimmy: Let's see. Because I completely trust your boss to storm out of a room full of reporters just because he can't find his assistant.

God, I hope not.

Please, Charles. Just for once, be a gentleman for the cameras.

I return to the living room with pancakes and tea. Since Dad's diagnosis, we've swapped his coffee for green tea entirely.

"Isn't that your boss?" Dad points toward Charles' photo on the TV screen, and without waiting for my response, he cranks up the volume.

"It's a special day in Cherrywood. Heir to the famous Hawthorne family, Charles Hawthorne is doing his first exclusive interview for a select group of news channels. Charles has been leading Hawthorne Holdings for four years and is soon to officially inherit the family business and empire from his grandmother. With significant shares in businesses like Elixir Inc., Charles ranks among the richest men in the business world. Yet the reclusive tycoon has always kept his personal life shrouded, so what's changed now? There are speculations about Charles finally coming out about his love life, which is talked about as much as his work." The female reporter grins, tipping her head toward the town hall building behind her.

"Aren't you supposed to be there?" Dad points his finger toward the screen.

"I'm right where I need to be, Dad. Don't worry—" My words are interrupted by the vibration of my phone once again.

Calm the heck down, Jimmy.

"Charles Hawthorne just arrived at Cherrywood Town Hall," the reporter exclaims.

My head feels like it's in a blender right now, swinging from Dad's confused face to my phone buzzing angrily and Charles' face on the TV.

My boss steps out of his car, disregarding the numerous cameras pointed at him. Dressed in a charcoal-black suit paired with a navy-blue tie and white shirt, he truly looks like he owns even the air that flows in this town. I can't believe he's the same man who I bother with silly pink napkins and a sillier nickname.

Somehow, I snap out of the trance that Charles Hawthorne weaves around people.

I pass a plate to Dad, whose gaze is fixed on the TV like the entirety of Cherrywood, and then check my phone.

My knees wobble, a rare feeling akin to fear settling in—fear of Charles' reaction.

Boss aka Charles Asshole
Hawthorne: Where are you?

Before I can reply, another message pops up on my phone screen.

Boss aka Charles Asshole
Hawthorne: Reply to me, goddammit.

My heart squeezes. I can't even call him an asshole right now. He has every right to go ballistic on me. I was the one who pushed him to do this interview and promised to handle everything. And then, at the last minute, I bailed on him as he faced what's probably the hardest task of his life.

The TV volume lowers, and when I turn to face Dad, he's looking at me.

"Go to work, Doodles. I'll be fine." When I don't respond, he adds, "I won't leave the house, I...I promise."

But we both know there's a good chance he'll forget he even made that promise.

"I'll do my best," he adds sincerely, his forced smile squeezing my heart even more. "After today, I might consider extra locks so it takes longer for me to leave the house, giving my memory some time to kick in."

"No! Please don't do that, Dad. If we ever need to enter the house forcibly, it'll take too much extra time."

His eyes widen. "I didn't consider that."

I return to him and hold his hands. "We'll find a way, Dad. Maybe I can move back home." I'll give up anything to make sure he's safe right now.

"You can't be with me twenty-four seven, kiddo. No one can."

But that's not entirely true. An idea sparks in my mind, tingling my skin. Since Dad's first time getting lost, I've been thinking about it.

"But a full-time nurse can."

"I—I don't think I can afford that, Doodles." Dad's response is bland compared to my excited squeal.

"Let me worry about something for once, Dad." I smile. I know it won't be easy or cheap, but I've saved enough over the years. And I can always take out a loan.

Yes, everything is going to be okay.

Half of my chest breathes in relief while the other half braces itself for Charles Hawthorne's impending wrath.

Focus on what you can control, Daisy. Your boss and his behavior are definitely not one of those things.

I'm mentally listing nearby hospitals to inquire about a full-time nurse when I hear a noise in the kitchen.

"What are you doing, Dad?" I rush to him as he's transferring pancakes from my plate into my childhood Barbie lunch box.

"I'm not an invalid, kiddo. Plus, you need to be there." He gestures toward the TV, where the camera shows a live feed of the town hall, with Charles' picture inset.

"I can't leave you right now."

"Your life can't come to a halt because of me, Doodles. I'll try to make sure stuff like this happens less." His smile doesn't reach his eyes, and we both know it's beyond his control. "Now, go."

"But, Dad—"

"I'll call Mel, and she'll check on me a few times. Is that better?"

I'm grateful every day that Aunt Mel and Uncle Fred live right next door to Dad.

"Only for now," I reply after a long pause. "But we still need to talk about a full-time nurse."

He simply smiles at my words, and I know it'll take some convincing.

"I love you, Daddy."

"I love you too, kiddo. Now go. Your boss needs you."

Stepping out of the house, I find Aunt Mel walking toward Dad's wrought iron gate.

"How is he?" she asks carefully.

"He's better. Can you please stay with him today?"

"Of course, hon. But he needs someone with him more often." Aunt Mel's eyebrows furrow. "I'll ask Fred to spend more time with Jason, and maybe take a sabbatical myself."

My chest squeezes in gratefulness at her concerned voice.

"You're the best sister in the world. Do you know that?" I throw my arms around her. "I have a plan. I'll tell you more about it in the evening. Right now, I have to reach the town hall."

"Is Mr. Hawthorne really announcing his fiancée's name?"

"What? No! Why would you ask that?"

"He's doing an exclusive media interview for the first time. Isn't it being called raw, personal, and honest? What's more personal than that for him?"

"No, Aunt Mel. He's definitely not doing that."

"Are you sure?"

"One hundred percent. If he were doing such a thing, I'd definitely know it." She doesn't know that my boss is so precise and perfect that he's rehearsed each of his statements for today more than a dozen times, and we've gone over them together more than that.

"Oh, really?" She shrugs. "What a shame, then."

I understand that people are curious about Charles' single status, but these days, everyone is a second away from being a reverend and marrying him off.

Leaving Aunt Mel with her disappointed thoughts, I slip into the back seat of Charles' limo.

"Did Charles call you, Dave?" I ask as the car begins to move.

"You know him well, Daisy. He certainly did. But I told Mr. Hawthorne you were at your folks', and it looked urgent,"

Dave replies, meeting my gaze in the rearview mirror for a second.

"And?" My heart races with anticipation.

"He said not to disturb you."

"Oh." I'm a mix of confused and relieved at Charles' unexpected understanding behavior, though concern for Dad quickly replaces every other feeling.

My fingers race across the phone screen as I search for the cost of a full-time nurse.

What on earth?

Aren't there a few too many zeros on this figure?

I use my nail to trace along the digits on the screen, hoping I'm making a mistake in reading them, but the numbers stubbornly remain unchanged. My shoulders slump in defeat. Even with a loan and draining my savings, I wouldn't be able to afford it for long. The figures stare back at me like an unsolvable puzzle, mocking my efforts.

Dad's confused gaze and his uncertain voice saying my name flood my mind. Today, he recognized me, but I know someday he won't.

My hand clutches at my chest, fingers gripping the fabric of my shirt. I blink rapidly, willing the tears away, but they refuse to listen. A droplet falls onto my hand, still clutching the phone.

Could this day possibly get any worse?

And within the hour, I receive my answer—a big blaring yes!

seven

Cake Catastrophe

Daisy

I hover outside Hawthorne Heritage Room, pressing my ear against the door in a futile attempt to catch any whispers from within. Charles' stoic bodyguards show no reaction as I awkwardly drop to all fours, trying to catch a glimpse through the small gap at the bottom of the door.

We all know today is freaking important.

"Daisy? I knew I'd find you here."

No, God no. Not today and definitely not right now.

"You can't pretend to not hear me, Daze."

My arms feel like they're carrying a ton of bricks as I try to rise up. I'm still kneeling when I face Jax, and I immediately cringe, coming face-to-face with his belt buckle. All his texts from the past days fill my head, making me want to retch.

His lips curl on one side, letting me know he's

thinking the same thing. How did I never notice before that Jax resembles a character from a zombie movie when he smiles like that?

I straighten up, taking a step closer to him. He needs to leave, and fast.

"Jax, I'm working. You need to go."

He responds with a deep chuckle. "Not happening. We need to talk, and I'm not budging until we do. Who answered my call that day, anyway? Did you hook up with someone in our off time, my bad girl?"

Was I seriously with this man all these years?

"Jax, this is not the time for this!"

"Was it the guy from your office reception? Or the coffee machine repairman? I've seen how they look at you."

He doesn't even consider it could be my boss, the person I'm closest to at work.

But shouldn't I be relieved? Isn't it a good thing he doesn't suspect Charles?

My thoughts whirl like a blender at full speed. Dad, Charles, and now Jax.

"I'm not having this conversation here, Jax. Actually, I'm not having it at all." I pull on Jax's arms, but he remains stubbornly in place.

"Do you need some assistance, Daisy?" Steve takes a step closer to us.

"Assistance?" Jax's eyebrows nearly reach his hairline. "What are you going to do? Drag me away? This is a public place, dude."

"Jax!" My teeth grind together. "Don't cause a scene here." This time, when I pull on his arm, he surprisingly relents. I continue until we reach the entrance of the building. "You and I are finished."

"Like hell we are. I made a mistake."

"A mistake?" I scoff, though my heart aches with pain and anxiety. "Which part was a mistake? Letting someone give you a blow job or being too lazy to find a discreet spot instead of the office coffee corner?"

"Daisy, you don't get it. You were working nonstop those days. You had no time for me, and I needed someone." Jax's words sear like acid through my ears.

"How dare you try to pin this on me?" I hiss.

"I'm not putting all the blame on you, but it wasn't entirely my fault. You were never around, and Marcy reminded me so much of you when we first met."

"Are you kidding me? Do you honestly think that makes it any better? You need to go, Jax, and I never want to see you again—"

My words are cut off as I'm blindsided by a door from the right, sending me careening into a massive three-tier cake. I hit the ground, bringing the cake down with me, until I'm left sprawled on the floor, covered head to toe in icing. My hair, face, and the purple silk top I bought just for today are all coated in the sticky mess.

I feel a prickling sensation behind my eyes, the tears threatening to spill over.

God, why are you being so cruel today? What have I done to deserve this punishment?

Instead of offering me a hand, Jax stands there looking at me as if I've committed the biggest crime of the century.

"Dammit, Daisy. What the hell did you do? You wrecked the poor guy's hours of hard work in an instant."

"I...I'm sorry." My throat tightens as I struggle to rise, the buttercream frosting making it difficult. Thankfully, my skirt is long enough to spare me from flashing anyone as I try to find my footing, feeling like a newborn baby goat.

"My chef will kill me!" The young server snaps out of his shock and dashes back through the door he came out of.

I grapple to rise up unsuccessfully, while Jax is fully immersed in conversation with the man who threw the door open carelessly, without bothering to check if anyone was standing on the other side. My ex, of course, has lots to say about how clumsy I am.

Right now, I want to hurl all this icing on him.

Did he really come here to patch things up between us?

"Let me help you, Daisy." Like a gentleman, Steve extends a hand, pulling me up. "Mr. Hawthorne has reserved a room for himself. There's a bathroom in there." He hands me the key card, gesturing to the right.

"Thanks, Steve. Could you please also make sure that this man is no longer here?" I nod toward Jax, who finally pays me some attention.

"You got it!"

As I exit, I catch a proud smile on the bodyguard's lips. Jax calls after me, but I tune him out. I was afraid he'd make a scene, but nothing could top what just happened.

I quickly locate the bathroom upon entering Charles' lounge. Glancing in the mirror, I realize I look even sillier than I imagined. Pink glittery frosting clings to my forehead and the left side of my cheek.

I run my tongue over my lip, and a groan leaves my mouth as the delicious buttery cream dances on my palate.

So, so delicious.

I feel bad for the baker and her hard work, and all the people who will miss out on this slice of heaven.

After shedding my icing-covered shirt and skirt, I hastily text Willow.

Me: How quickly can you get to the town hall?

Willow: How soon do you need me?

Me: I'd have preferred if you were already here. But I'll manage if you can make it within the next fifteen minutes.

Willow: You got it. Anything else?

Me: Yes, please bring me a change of clothes.

Willow: What are you doing naked in the town hall?

Me: I'm not naked. I got caught in a cake catastrophe—a door slammed me into a cake. Now I'm covered head to toe in icing.

Willow: Yikes! I feel for the baker.

Me: Me too. I'll apologize once I'm properly dressed.

Willow: Where are you now?

Me: I'm in Charles' lounge while

> he's at the interview. I should
> have been in that room with him
> an hour ago!

Willow: Got it. I'm wrapping up a
shoot. Will be there soon.

> **Me:** You're a lifesaver, Wills.

After resolving my clothing crisis, I rush into the shower to scrub away the clinging cream frosting from my hair and face. I step out from the glass door, then slip into my undergarments and immediately realize there's no bathrobe and the only towel isn't big enough to be wrapped around a human body.

They probably weren't expecting a cake catastrophe like yours, Daze.

When I return to the room, my gaze lands on Charles' laptop bag on the coffee table. In the middle of a white table runner are two water bottles symmetrically placed. The half-visible water ring clearly indicates that the flower vase has been recently adjusted to be at an equal distance from the two glass bottles.

Oh, Charles. You and your OCD tendencies. How are you holding up in that room?

The thought brings up a fresh wave of anxiety, prompting me to grab my phone.

> **Me:** Everything okay in there?

Jimmy: Thank goodness you're
here. Your boss is about to lose it at
any second.

> **Me:** What? Why?

Jimmy: Just join us and see for yourself.

Me: I can't. I'm in Charles' lounge. I'll explain later, but I can't step out of here.

Jimmy: Dammit! Then I'll have to wrap up this interview.

Me: Why? Don't we have half an hour more?

Jimmy: Trust me, the media won't survive. Charles Hawthorne is on the verge of exploding.

Me: I don't get it.

A second later, my phone rings, with Jimmy's name flashing on the screen. I pick up and hear an unfamiliar voice.

"Mr. Hawthorne, what about your personal life? We've spent the last hour discussing your plans for the town's future, and we believe in your vision. But people want to know more about *you*, the real Charles, the man behind the future leader of Hawthorne Empire."

"Being a Hawthorne is who I am. Since I can remember, I've known I'd be leading the family business someday. Every decision I made, from my studies to my university choice, was geared toward leading the company, growing Cherrywood, and serving my legacy."

Silence stretches in the room before a female reporter says, "Everyone in this town admires your dedication, but this is the first time we've had direct access to you. I hope you understand our curiosity about the real Charles Hawthorne." Her voice dips low, invoking an irritated vein in my temple.

"I don't think even I know everything about myself, so I'm afraid I can't share." Charles' serious and clipped response is met with her giggles.

Seriously, woman. Get your hormones in control! You're exhibiting unprofessionalism of the highest order!

"Okay, then give us something," she probes further. "What does Charles do to destress?"

Easy. Organizing stuff to precision.

My chuckle stops short when Charles replies, "Aikido."

What the heck?

Keeping the phone on speaker, I quickly search Aikido on the internet. As opposed to my thinking that it might be some sort of computer game where you get badges and money for cleaning, images of people in martial arts uniforms—white kimono-style gis and black loose-fitted hakamas—fill my screen.

"Wow! That's completely unexpected." The woman's surprise is genuine, and my initial annoyance toward her subsides.

She's definitely onto something. After all, in the past four years, I had no idea how my neat-freak boss spent his free time.

As if everyone in the room shares my feelings, no one interrupts her when she asks, "What is the most important thing in Charles' life?"

Work and Hawthorne Holdings, of course.

"My family," Charles replies instead.

0 for 2. Do you even know your boss, Daisy?

"What is Charles looking forward to the most right now?" the rapid fire continues.

This interview being over.

"Getting out of this room, preferably within the next second."

Finally! 1 for 3.

The interviewer giggles once again, drowning my own chuckles. She genuinely sounds fun and competent. If there was a romance movie about a hot billionaire and a sexy reporter falling in love during an interview, I'd definitely watch it. But somehow imagining the same situation with my boss doesn't leave me with happy feelings.

"We all love seeing this secret funny side of your personality, Charles," the interviewer remarks.

"He's not being funny, lady," I mumble to myself, flopping flat on the couch. "Plus, it's Mr. Hawthorne." With the phone resting on my chest, Charles' voice rumbles against my heart.

"I wasn't trying to be funny."

2 for 4.

Even my inner voice has lost its excitement, and I'll never admit it out loud, but right now I share Charles' abhorrence toward the media and reporters.

"I meant, what's Charles Hawthorne looking forward to the most in the near future?"

Becoming the CEO of Hawthorne Holdings.

I'm one hundred percent sure that's the only thing on his mind these days.

"Visiting my sister at the end of the year. Since she's in France, I spend every Christmas with my family here and every New Year's Eve with her."

"What?" I jump in place. How did I not know this?

Because your boss gives you a break once a year, and you'd rather worry about your own fun than wonder what he's up to. You wouldn't even think about him if there was a chance your thoughts would call to him and remind him that he has an assistant he can boss around.

"That's really sweet of you. Speaking of your sister, it's been years since Chloe Hawthorne has set foot in Cherrywood. The whole town is dying to see our local heiress in person. She's certainly taken Europe's fashion industry by storm."

"I'll give you anything if you can motivate her to come back," Charles says in his no-nonsense voice.

"Oh, Mr. Hawthorne, that's a risky thing to say in front of a camera. In case you don't know, there are many people in this town who would take this challenge seriously, including me." The reporter giggles, but Charles responds with a light clearing of his throat.

"On that note, we can close the interview."

"Oh no! You've just started telling us the good stuff. You have to give us something more. Please, Charles, we insist."

There's a collective hum of other reporters.

I can imagine Charles biting the inside of his cheek before he says, "I'll give you one more question."

"One? No! At least three, please."

"One is my final offer. You can take it or I can leave."

"You're a tough businessman, Mr. Hawthorne."

"Believe me, I don't feel like one right now."

"So since this is the last question, I have to be very careful. Does Charles Hawthorne have a special woman in his life?"

My grip around the phone tightens and I sit straight. I'm one hundred percent expecting a "Not at all," but still, this is the first time someone has asked this question to Charles directly.

"Yes, I do. And thank you so much, everyone, for coming here." Charles' words are drowned out by the loud gasps.

Holy freaking hell!

Before I can process Charles' bombshell declaration, my phone pings with an incoming text.

Willow: I'm here.

Thank goodness.

I end Jimmy's call right when there's a knock on the door. I rush to the door and swing it open.

"I love you the most."

I'm about to throw my arms around Willow, only to realize it's not her.

No, it's my boss on the other side, with an unreadable expression on his face. I'm held in stunned captivity under Charles' penetrating gaze. Moments roll into one another until I'm blinded by the flashing lights of a camera, reminding me that I'm just in my undergarments. Cold sweeps over me as more cameras whir, and finally Charles steps forward. He shields me from the intrusive lenses before guiding us back into the room and closing the door behind us.

"Daisy? What the fuck are you doing here?" His brows furrow and stay on my face for another second before his gaze slides lower.

Heat blooms in my stomach, spreading like wildfire across my skin under his weighty scrutiny.

"Where are your clothes?" His usually composed voice is nothing but a growl right now.

"I...had an accident," I stammer.

Charles' hands grip my shoulders, their warmth searing into my bare skin. Despite the heat, a shiver runs down my spine.

He's worried about me?

"With a cake," I quickly add.

"You were hit by a cake?" His jaw tightens, a flicker of emotion breaking through his indifferent expression, and the next instant, he withdraws his hands and removes his jacket before handing it to me.

"Thanks," I mumble, slipping it on and inhaling the scent of pine and tobacco that envelops me.

"So what happened?"

"I was hit by a door, which sent me crashing into a cake."

I wait for him to scream at me any second. This would definitely be a first time, but I've never ever fucked up like this before. As his assistant, I should have been at the town hall hours before anyone. I wasn't just late, but I also ended up in his room in my underwear. I messed up big-time and would completely understand if he fired me right now. But instead of reprimanding me, he surprises me once again.

"Are you hurt?"

A lump forms in my throat at his soft foreign concern. I shake my head, both in reply to his question and as a reminder to my own erratic heartbeat to settle down. This unfamiliar caring version of Charles is giving my poor heart tiny jerks, as if alerting of an imminent heart attack.

"I thought you were Willow. She's bringing me a change of clothes."

Before he can say anything, there's a knock on the door. I take a hesitant step forward, then glance back at Charles to find his gaze fixed on me. I used to think I've learned to read his every expression, but the way he looks at me today is completely alien.

"I'll get it," he says finally, striding away to answer the door.

"Someone's here for Miss Price, sir," Steve's voice rings out from behind the door.

"It's alright. You can send her in."

A second later, Willow breezes past Charles as he holds the door.

I rush to her. "What took you so long? You said you were here like ten minutes ago."

"It hasn't been ten minutes, Daze. Plus, I was at the light when I said I was almost here."

She never mentioned "*almost.*"

Willow hands me a shopping bag from one of the fancy shops outside of town, and I slip into the bathroom.

The soft fabric of the white silk dress glides over my skin like butter. When it finally hits my legs, I realize it's much longer than I expected. Not quite floor length, but close. I open the door to ask my friend why she brought what feels like an elegant wedding dress.

"Hello, Mr. Hawthorne," I hear Willow's sultry voice—the one that used to make the boys in school squirm and follow her like lovestruck puppies.

A foreign uneasiness settles in me as I watch my friend

grin at my boss, who, as usual, couldn't appear more bored. Willow is beautiful in every way. Unlike my unruly hair, which often looks like I've just been electrocuted, her long, silky red strands are pulled up in her usual bun. She's wearing a black crop top paired with frayed jeans. Even in sneakers, she reaches Charles' shoulders; unlike me, who looks like a dwarf even with suicidal four-inch heels.

"Miss Pershing, I hope you're doing well?"

"I'm always well. I was doing a wedding shoot for a newlywed couple who got married at my family's inn. Speaking of weddings, when are we seeing yours? The whole town is dying to meet the next Mrs. Hawthorne, even though no one has any idea what you really like in a woman."

I can almost picture the way her tongue hits her upper lip when she emphasizes the word *like*.

"Willow, did you bring me the bride's wedding gown?" My voice is accusatory without trying as I step back into the room.

"Of course not. It was the dress she wore to the venue before getting ready. You are just so tiny, Daze." My friend shrugs before walking over to me. "But it does look like a wedding gown on you."

All the playfulness disappears from her face as she walks closer and fixes the strap hanging from my shoulder. "But as your future bridesmaid, I'd kill anyone who suggests a boat neckline for you. No, we need a plunging sweetheart or a Queen Anne neckline. You need to flaunt these girls." Her eyebrows dance as she nods toward my boobs.

"My girls thank you for the compliment." I smile. Over the years, I've grown to love my body. It might not be perfect, but I find it beautiful. And whoever doesn't, including Jax, who tried to make me eat kale salad once a week, can go to hell.

A throat clears, slicing through our laughter. "You remember I'm here, right?"

Holy crap.

Willow and I turn to face him, and is it my imagination, or did he really, for a fleeting fraction of a second, stare at my chest?

I can't miss the fluttering sensation in my stomach, a mix of foreign nerves and excitement.

"I'm sure what you're discussing is *extremely important*, but I'd rather leave this place fast. Miss Pershing, can we drop you somewhere?"

"No." Willow shakes her head. "My car is parked outside. I can't wait to read your interview, Mr. Hawthorne."

"I'll return the dress to you tomorrow after getting it cleaned. Thank you so much once again, Wills."

"Don't worry, the couple is already on their way to their honeymoon in Hawaii. I'm sure clothes are the last thing on their mind." She winks before sauntering out.

Once Willow leaves, Charles loosens his tie and lets out a deep breath. Perching on the couch, he pours himself a glass of water.

"You really don't like people." Even though my voice is free of accusation, the words sound strange. Charles' gaze slants to me, but before I can apologize, he tips his head toward the room.

"It's not just the people, but also the place."

"What do you mean?"

"It's unfamiliar and unknown."

A chuckle escapes me as his pout deepens the frown lines on his beautiful forehead.

"Life is nothing but an unknown, Charles. You can never guess what's coming next."

"But I can prepare for possible scenarios."

"And what about enjoying the surprises?"

"Good for those who feel that way." His lips twist as if he just tasted sour milk.

"Alright, Mr. *I'm-Prepared-For-Everything*, what's going to happen next?"

Charles effortlessly fixes his tie in a single tug. "We're leaving this place and forgetting about interviews for the next four years."

"I hate to burst your bubble, boss"—my grin couldn't be wider, especially when his irritated frown is back—"but you are one of the media puppets now. There's no way they'll let you off that easy."

"I'm nobody's puppet. I'm serious, Daisy. Let Jimmy know we are not doing this nonsense again. Once was more than enough."

eight

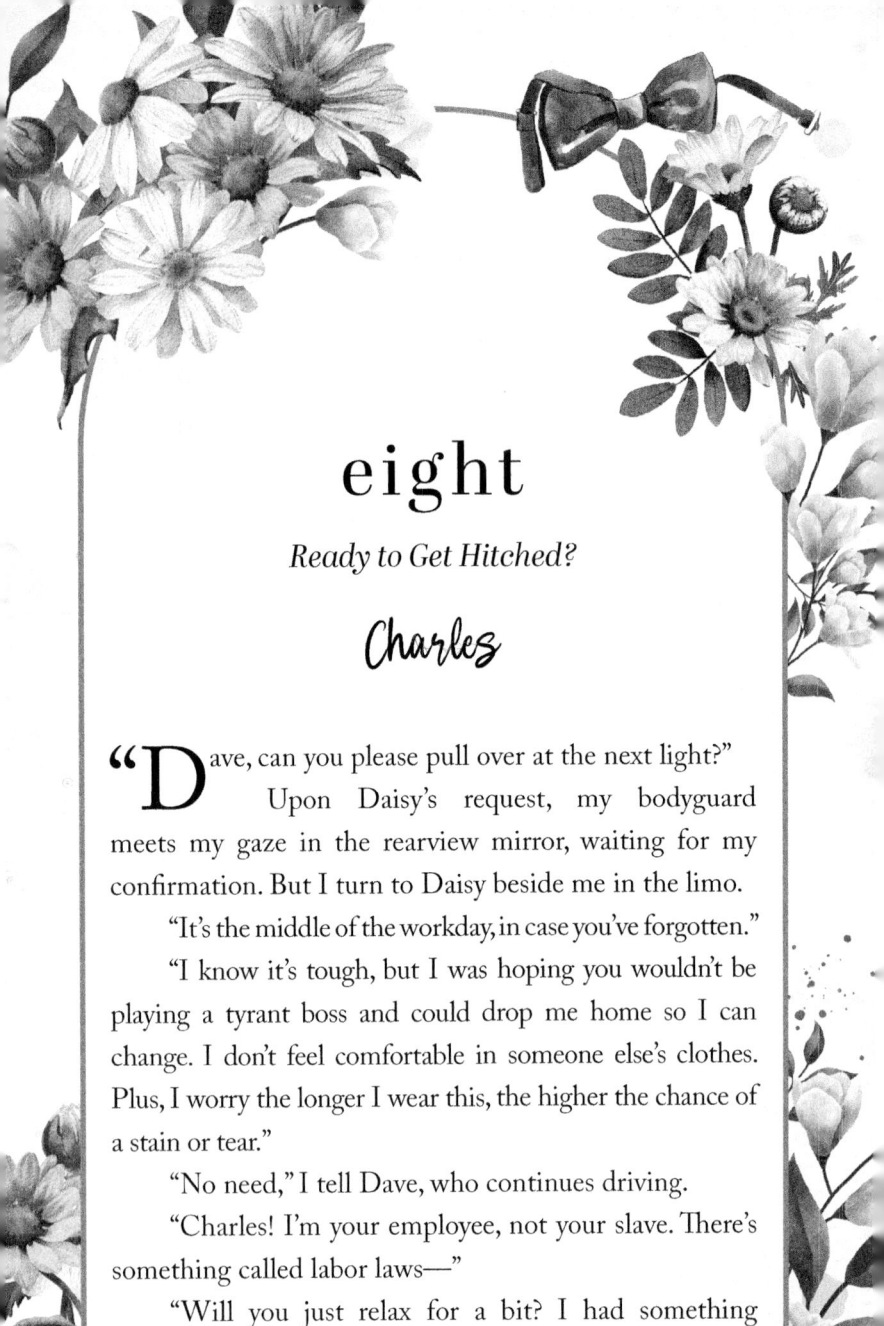

Ready to Get Hitched?

Charles

"Dave, can you please pull over at the next light?"

Upon Daisy's request, my bodyguard meets my gaze in the rearview mirror, waiting for my confirmation. But I turn to Daisy beside me in the limo.

"It's the middle of the workday, in case you've forgotten."

"I know it's tough, but I was hoping you wouldn't be playing a tyrant boss and could drop me home so I can change. I don't feel comfortable in someone else's clothes. Plus, I worry the longer I wear this, the higher the chance of a stain or tear."

"No need," I tell Dave, who continues driving.

"Charles! I'm your employee, not your slave. There's something called labor laws—"

"Will you just relax for a bit? I had something delivered to the office for you."

This dress is all wrong on her. Not because of her friend's stupid remark about the neckline, but because my assistant looks best in the usual soft colors she prefers to wear. Pink, purple, blue—that's Daisy. White is just too bland for her.

She gasps. "You did what?"

But instead of looking her way, I turn my head, focusing on the passing scenery outside. I catch a grin on my reflection in the window and kill it immediately.

"I've already wasted half my day with this ridiculous interview. I have no desire to waste the rest."

She falls silent for a moment and then asks slowly, "How did you even know my size?"

"I didn't." *But I'm sure my guess is fairly accurate.*

Growing up with a sister who was crazy for fashion design is definitely paying off for once.

"This is so…"

"Thoughtful?" I raise an eyebrow. "You're welcome."

"I was going to say weird, but sure, whatever feeds your already inflated ego."

This time, I have to bite down on my lip to stifle a smile. After the stressful morning and the soul-sucking interview, my heart rate is finally finding its normal pace.

After another second of pause, Daisy says, "I heard part of your interview. Jimmy turned on his phone for me. I think it went very well."

She trails off as if there's something more she wants to say but is holding back, and I absolutely hate that she's keeping her thoughts away from me. Despite my aversion to unnecessary talks, Daisy's chatter, sometimes teasing me and other times subtly trying to fix my life, has become an indispensable part of my life.

"What happened this morning?"

"I already told you about the cake—"

"I am not asking about your grand accident, Daisy. Why the hell weren't you at the town hall early like we planned?"

Even though I know there must be a very good reason for her absence, I'm unable to hide my irritation. I remember the moment when I found myself wedged between Jimmy and the mayor, facing ten unfamiliar faces all eager to dig into my personal life. My chest tightened to the point of pain, the air around me seeming to thin.

Daisy's eyes blaze with a fire I've always admired, yet she remains silent, her lips pressed tightly together.

"It was personal," she finally whispers.

I reach for the button next to my seat, raising the privacy shield.

"What the heck?" She jumps in her seat. "Since when has that thing been there?" She points at the black screen as if it's a piece of forbidden witchcraft.

"Since always."

"Why the heck do you need it?" Her eyes widen as she shifts her gaze between the screen and me. "Oh my goodness! Please don't tell me this is where you're hooking up with your special someone."

"What?"

"In the interview, you mentioned there's a special woman in your life. Is this where you *meet* her?" She wrinkles her nose, her hands lifting from the leather seat as if she's just touched something gross.

"I meant GG, my great-grandmother. Do you think I have the privacy screen so I can fuck women in the back of my car?"

If only she knew.

"Well, not exclusively for that, but I guess...if someone wants, it could come in handy." Her words finally slow down, as if she's struggling to keep up with her wild thoughts.

"I'm shocked and worried about the way your mind works sometimes. No, Daisy, the privacy screen is for times when I need to have private conversations—private *business* conversations that my driver and bodyguard don't need to hear."

She releases the bottom lip she's been biting, unknowingly distracting the hell out of me, and finally, a smile spreads across her face.

"It fits, you know. Private screen for a private, complicated man like you."

I didn't know she thinks of me as complicated. At least around her, I feel like my life is uncomplicated.

"Not so private, it seems, since you're sitting on this side of it and not the other."

She grins, but it immediately drops when I ask, "Now, if you're done irritating me, I'll ask again. What happened this morning? Jimmy and Dave told me you were at your parents' place."

All the playfulness disappears from her face, replaced by something akin to pain.

"Daisy?" I'm about to reach out to her and hold her hand fisting the silk of the white dress, when Dave's voice fills the cramped space.

"We're reaching the parking lot, sir."

The moment breaks, and Daisy puts on a smile that is as bad as a high school musical performed without a single rehearsal.

"It's nothing, and I'm so sorry, once again, for being late."

Before I can tell her to cut the bullshit, the car stops. She's already sprinting toward the elevator when Dave opens my door.

"There's a delivery coming in for Daisy. Please make sure it reaches her." I'm about to walk away but stop. "You were with Daisy this morning, correct?"

Dave gives a confirming nod, prompting my next question.

"What happened at her parents' place?"

My bodyguard's gaze moves from me to my assistant, standing in the open elevator waiting for me, one hand probably on the button to keep the door open.

"I believe it has something to do with her father. I'm sure she'll have more details for you, sir." Dave's tone is earnest and respectful.

I linger for a moment longer, in case he has something more for me, but when that seems to not be the case, I reply, "Very well. I'll check with her."

With a parting nod to Dave and Steve, I walk away and slip inside the elevator. As soon as the door closes, my phone springs to life with Jimmy's face flashing on the screen. My groan resonates in the metal enclosure.

"What's that for?" Daisy punches in the code for our office floor, where only a select few have access. When I show her the screen, a slow grin pulls on her lips. "He might be calling to tell you how amazing you were today."

"That would be a refreshing change. Finally, after four years, I've made the head of PR happy," I quip, tucking my phone away. "Dave will bring your clothes shortly. Once you're ready, let's go over the day." I hope to finally get answers about her unexpected absence this morning.

As I step into my office, Jimmy's call rings through once again, and I answer. "Contrary to what you may think, I don't spend my days sitting around waiting for your calls like some lovesick teenager. I have a business to run." I sink into my chair, which groans under my weight, mimicking my voice.

"Have you seen the news?" Jimmy's tone lacks its usual agitation.

"No, thank you. I've had my fill of entertainment for the day. Besides, the TV in my office is reserved for business news, not media gossip."

"Just turn it on, Charles. Trust me, you don't want to miss this."

An uneasy feeling starts to churn in my chest at Jimmy's flat voice. I reach for the remote and switch on the TV, but the ground beneath my feet shifts the moment I see my back, clad in the same black suit I'm wearing now, and hear Daisy's voice. "I love you the most."

"Does Charles Hawthorne have a secret love interest?"

My jaw tightens as a reporter narrates the circus of speculations.

"Charles Hawthorne hinted today that he has a special someone in his life. We all thought it was a joke—"

Because it fucking was.

"—but our sources have shared that a mystery woman dressed in a peach bikini—"

It was so not peach.

"—opened the door to Mr. Hawthorne's suite at the Cherrywood Town Hall today. She jumped right into Charles' arms as he walked in."

She fucking didn't.

"Sometime later, Charles Hawthorne left town hall with the same woman, now dressed in a long white dress. Is the most talked about bachelor finally ready to get hitched?"

Jimmy's aggravated voice rings through. "Why the hell wouldn't you say anything to me? Do you know I've been almost on the verge of a heart attack, planning ways to distract the media from your bachelor status until you officially inherit the family business?" Jimmy doesn't even pause to calm his rapid breathing, while my gaze is fixed on an unrecognizable image of Daisy on the TV screen, her words echoing in my mind.

I love you the most.

My phone chimes, alerting me of an incoming text. I put Jimmy on speaker as he rambles on and on about his recent visit to his cardiologist.

Ronald Grint, Anti-Charles Board Member: I'm impressed with how you managed to keep such big news under wraps, Charles. But with the media's fixation on the Hawthorne family, I completely understand your need for privacy. I want to invite you and your lovely fiancée for dinner at my home, to formally apologize for my behavior at the last board meeting. But I still maintain my stance. Cherrywood is our charming

> family town, and only someone who desires to raise their own family here will be able to understand the real needs of the townspeople. But now that we know you clearly are that person, you have my full support as the next CEO of Hawthorne Holdings.

What the fuck?

There are so many things in this text that demand attention, but my gaze can't move away from the word *fiancée*.

> **Grandma Irene:** Charles, my assistant's phone is ringing off the hook with calls from the board members. They want to reconvene to discuss their preferences for the CEO position. Do you know what prompted this change?

"Hawthorne, are you even paying attention?" Jimmy's bark snaps me back to reality.

"No. What did you say?" I run my hand through my hair, feeling the weight of the situation.

How did a simple interview spiral into this chaos?

But isn't this what I wanted? For the media and board members to see me in a new light?

But this is a lie.

Not really. It's just a misunderstanding that seems to have worked in your favor.

What the hell are you thinking, Charles? In a few hours, the truth will come out and everything will go back to how it was.

"I asked, who's the girl?"

"Who?" I absentmindedly run a hand over my jaw.

"Your special someone. Who else?"

"It's Daisy." And not anyone special.

"Daisy," Jimmy repeats slowly.

The word, tinged with awe, sends a zing of uneasiness my way.

"It all makes sense now. How did I not see it before? You and Daisy? Of course. She's funny, intelligent, and beautiful. She knows how to handle you and keep your tantrums in check. You're so different around her. There's no one more perfect for you than her."

"What the hell are you saying?"

My tantrums? Daisy handling me? What am I, a dog?

"You've never been seen with anyone because you spend all your time hiding away from the media *with her.*"

Jimmy's words slowly start to sink in as my phone continues to buzz incessantly with sounds of incoming texts. Shareholders who were reluctant with me taking over as the CEO of Hawthorne Holdings are inviting me and my imaginary fiancée to dinners and charity balls.

There's a knock on the door, and I swiftly turn off the TV.

"Jimmy, I need to end the call."

He responds with a hum, possibly still in shock, but I have bigger things to address right now. Like my assistant poking her head through the door after another knock.

"Are you on a call?" she whispers, eyes wide, and I shake my head slowly. She's dressed in a sky-blue skirt and a matching silk blouse. "Thanks for these, by the way."

Daisy motions in the general direction of her body, and my gaze momentarily drifts to her *girls.*

Focus, Charles.

"I was going to pay you back immediately, but after seeing the price tag, I realize I might have to sell my soul in order to do so. If it's okay with you, I'm going to pay you back in installments."

"I'm not asking you for your money." I amble back to my chair.

"No, you're not. But I can't just randomly accept clothes from my boss, right? It would be wrong and unethical on so many levels. And why would you pay for my things anyway? I am your assi—"

"Daisy, stop." I hold up my hand. "I'm not taking your money, period."

"Why not?"

"Because I don't need your money." This woman can be so infuriating sometimes.

Are you seriously considering doing this?

"Then can't you say it's a gift?"

"What?"

She tweaks her nose in pure annoyance. "*It's a gift, Daisy. How hard is that to say?*"

"Is it your birthday? Or some National Assistant Day?"

She crosses her arms over her chest. "It's not my birthday. But you don't pay someone for a gift. If you say it's a gift, I know you don't expect me to pay you." She looks at me with blazing eyes, as if I'm the one at fault here. Me, the person who bought her clothes and is refusing to take any money for it.

"Daisy, my competent and cherished assistant," I begin, but she snorts, those squinted eyes crinkling as she smiles. Something zaps through me like a lightning strike. Outside of my family, she's the only one I'm this comfortable with.

"There's no one in the world who can replace you in this office. And for everything you've done for me and this business, I'd like you to keep these clothes as a thank-you."

"They aren't *that* expensive, especially if we're talking about *everything* I've done for you." She grins wide.

Guilt slithers like a serpent inside me, realizing how much I'll be asking of her if we go ahead with the plan slowly forming in my head.

"But since you asked so politely, I'll accept it graciously." She pinches the corners of her skirt and curtsies. As she bends forward, her sky-blue rhinestone hair clip catches my eye.

"How many of those do you have?"

"You noticed my clips?" Her hand moves to her hair.

"They're hard to miss," I admit, fighting the urge to shift on my feet, feeling like a young boy caught with a hand in the cookie jar.

"These were my mom's. She loved hair jewelry, and my dad gifted her a new piece every year on their anniversary and her birthday. She had one in every color imaginable." Daisy's face flushes with warmth, a mix of awe and longing shadowing her expression.

I know she lost her mom a few years ago. Before I can offer my apologies or sympathy, she changes the discussion.

"Did Jimmy call you? I thought I heard him." Her downturned lips lift slightly, though sadness lingers in her eyes, and for a moment I feel a pang in my chest as if I feel her pain.

"Did you see the news?" I ask instead, ignoring the strange emotion. Why else would she not be freaking out?

"Um, no." Her head turns toward the black TV screen,

and slowly her eyes widen. "They are already showing your interview. Wasn't it scheduled for the nightly news?"

As she reaches for the remote, I lunge forward, placing my hand over it.

Daisy arches an eyebrow. "Um, what are you doing?"

"Has anyone called you?"

"Um, no. My phone battery just died. I've plugged it in to charge. What's going on, Charles? You're seriously weirding me out right now."

"Can you do me a favor?" I ask, and before she can say anything, quickly add, "And I really want you to do it." I'm not above begging at this point.

She nods, her eyes still wide.

"Don't turn on your computer, TV, or phone. Basically, don't go online."

"What? How will I work?"

"Do anything that doesn't involve going online."

"But—"

"Don't argue, Daisy. Just do it," I insist, but she doesn't budge and keeps staring at me, questioning my sanity. "I'll explain everything in an hour. I promise."

"Fine," she finally huffs, squinting at me. "You've got an hour. But I better hear the full story after that."

nine

I Don't Have Cooties

Charles

Daisy leaves my office and I immediately loosen the tie squeezing my windpipe. Collapsing onto the leather couch, I scroll through the messages from the stakeholders. Every fucking one of them has replied about how they're eagerly looking forward to the next Hawthorne wedding and hinted how they support me taking over as the CEO of Hawthorne Holdings.

Is it really that simple?

A fabricated media story about me and a mystery woman, and suddenly everything I've strived for in the past four years falls into place.

This doesn't even make any sense.

I throw my head back against the headrest, the news video replaying in my mind like a relentless loop. Daisy's honey-dipped voice, confessing she loves me, echoes in my ears. In the quiet of the room, my pulse quickens in a foreign beat. My fists clench as I struggle to maintain clarity and push aside the memory of her voice—a little out of breath and a whole lot excited.

Fuck!

The media won't stay quiet for long. I've got to give them something before their imagination spirals out of control and they start hunting for my imaginary girl.

But there's no one other than her I can trust with this. She's safe, familiar, and even though she's a whole lot of crazy, she's my only hope. Over the years, she's proved her loyalty and discretion. My family likes her, and even Jimmy believed in the story of our secret romance.

But will she agree?

Making people agree to your terms is the one thing you're best at, Charles. Work your Hawthorne magic and make her an offer she can't refuse.

This might be the biggest fucking deal of my life.

A knock startles me, and for the first time, my heartbeat accelerates in uncertainty and something weird like heartburn, at the anticipation of seeing my assistant.

But instead, Raymond enters holding two boxes of pizza, followed by Rowan and Archer with root beer. Alex saunters in empty-handed behind them.

"I knew you were going to be the first one among us to get hitched, brother." Ray slaps my back before plopping down on the leather chair beside me.

"Fuck off."

"Can we please start at: who's the lucky girl?" Archer raises an eyebrow.

"You mean the one who loves Charlie the most?" Rowan signs, his mischievous eyes and smile speaking his emotions.

"Feel free to throw in whatever punch line you've been saving." I motion toward Alex. "But when you're ready to hear the truth, I'd like your opinion on something."

"Go ahead. I'll survive without mocking you for today. I have a feeling there'll be plenty of chances in the future." Alex grins and all the Teager boys chuckle.

"Very funny. But if my plan works, I might be able to put an end to the nonsense of today and turn things in my favor." It's probably the gravity of my words or my tone that draws their attention, as they all sit straight.

"We're listening." Rowan passes me a can of root beer.

"The woman on the TV is Daisy. She was expecting her friend at the door."

"Fuck!"

"Jesus!"

"Holy shit!"

"That makes so much fucking sense!"

I give them all a minute.

"Here's the catch," I say, placing my phone onto the table and showing them the flood of texts. Congratulations, dinner invites for me and my lovely fiancée, and even speculation on how cute the next generation of Hawthornes is going to be.

"They want to vote in your favor." Alex says what they're probably all thinking. His usual calm voice has a touch of surprise.

I nod.

"But you know the media is not going to stay quiet.

I'm sure they're already snooping around." Archer throws a glance at me before tearing off a slice of pizza.

"Exactly. It won't take long before they piece it together." Ray takes a swig of his beer.

"I know, and that's why I have a plan."

Rowan tips his head to the side. "It must be something, because I've never seen you smile so big, Charlie."

"This is what I want to know from you all. What if this wasn't fake?"

"What do you mean?" Alex asks, leaning forward.

"What if Daisy is what the media says she is." My throat dries and I take a sip of my drink. "The next Mrs. Hawthorne. Jimmy buys it, by the way."

"If there's any woman you spend time with, it's her." Ray leans back. His eyes are intense and laser-focused, as they get when he's working on the ins and outs of a deal in his mind. "You don't even need to make up a story about how you met or fell in love. She's been with you for four years. That's more than enough time to fall in love with someone."

Rowan lightly knocks on the table to get our attention. "But isn't she seeing someone?"

Of course, my sweet cousin would know that detail.

"She broke up with that asshole."

"And you swooped right in to take advantage of the breakup?" Archer, being his usual self, doesn't mince any words.

"I'm not taking any advantage," I seethe before turning to Alex. "I suppose you think the same way?"

"It doesn't matter what we think, Charlie. Have you spoken to her?" Alex's voice is calm and collected, not giving away anything.

"Not yet." Suddenly, I feel like an asshole. Should I have talked to her first? Archer's jab rings in my ear. My cousin sure knows how to get inside someone's head.

"If you plan to find a fake bride, there's no one more perfect than her," Rowan signs, giving oxygen to my dying hope.

Ray nods. "That's true."

"So should I ask her?"

"Can I please be there?" Archer raises an eyebrow. "I've never seen a man proposing for someone to be their fake bride."

They all chuckle, but my heartbeat races to the highest degree.

Proposing? Fuck.

My cousins are eating pizza, coming up with ideas for my fake proposal, and each of their suggestions sound horrible. I'm about to tell them to stop when the door to my office opens and Daisy storms in, fuming with anger.

"Can I talk to you, Charles? It's urgent."

My cousins couldn't spring from their seats any faster, snapping the pizza boxes shut and snagging the drink cans from the table.

"Best of luck." Alex gives my shoulder a reassuring pat.

"You still want to stay?" Ray snickers at Archer.

"No, thanks." Archer winces and mouths a "Good luck" before they all file out.

"They knew."

My gaze returns to her fuming face as she walks closer.

"They knew it was me?"

I nod carefully.

"You consulted with them before you told me?" Daisy's cheeks flush.

I realize I've never seen my assistant pissed. She's never been so incensed, not even when I made her work overtime or redo tasks because they weren't up to my crazy standards.

"I know they're your cousins and you trust them much more, but this is about me, Charles." Her throat chokes, and it makes me feel worse than before.

"I told them only because I was in an ethical dilemma."

"Of course you did! Why would you talk to me about ethics? Since I don't have any."

She's about to turn around and storm out of the room, when I tug on her forearm, pulling her back. I didn't anticipate the move, and she smacks right against my chest.

A puff of her breath lands on my neck, and it sends a pulse shooting down to my cock. I immediately pull back, dropping my arms from her body as if touched by fire, and for a second it feels like so.

She feels like fire, igniting all the unfamiliar emotions within me. But I realize my mistake the moment I look at her wide eyes.

"I don't have cooties that you can't be near me."

"I didn't mean—"

"I don't care what you mean." She stomps.

"Daisy, wait." This time, I carefully hold her hand, keeping a safe distance between us. "You're misunderstanding me." She's about to say something, when I add, "Sorry. I mean, I'm not explaining it right. Just hear me out for a second. Please."

"Are we in one of my dreams where you behave like a gentleman, since you're apologizing and saying sorry and please all in the same sentence?"

My lips twitch. I stow the information that she dreams about me for later, even if it's not the real me in her imaginations.

"Unfortunately, it's all real."

"Why hasn't Jimmy released a press statement, then?" She perches on the edge of the couch.

I hate that my palms turn clammy. This is the first time I've been in a meeting without preparation. In this moment, I miss the pink Post-it notes that she attaches to meeting files, scribbling details about clients in her flowy handwriting. They always come in handy when I want to turn a meeting going south in my favor.

"Why do you leave me Post-its with personal notes about the clients? I don't remember asking for that." The question escapes my lips before I can fully process it.

"What?" Her dark brows pull together.

When I don't say anything and simply wait, she shrugs.

"When I joined the company, I noticed you get tense on the first meeting with a new client, so I started researching them online and making notes for you. They seemed to make you calmer, and since you never objected, I assumed you found them helpful."

My head hangs low before I look back at her. "I...I can't believe I never said this until now. Thanks."

Her eyes widen to a concerning degree before she says, "Can you just stop being this polite? You're weirding me out!" Her gaze flies to the blank TV screen. "Plus, what does that have to do with all that?"

I shake my head and take a deep breath. This is Daisy. The person I've spent most of my time with in the last four years. I don't need notes on her. I should fucking know her already.

"Is your mental monologue over?" She tips her head to the side, and I can't keep my lips from twitching.

"I didn't know you know me so well."

"Unfortunately, more than I want to, boss."

"Okay, here it goes. You've already seen how the media believes you're either my secret love interest or fiancée?"

"But I am neither."

I'm hoping you'll be much more.

"But everyone else, including the board members of Hawthorne Holdings, thinks otherwise. In the next board meeting, they all want to vote in my favor for the next CEO position. It seems my committed status has much more value to them than my capabilities as a businessman."

Daisy leans back in her seat. If anyone outside my family understands the significance of this for me, it's her. She's worked with me all these years, making sure all the business deals have been successful, inching me a step closer to take over the family business. And now it seems everything is within my grasp, but only when I'm reaching out to get it with her by my side.

"Wow. I…I can't believe this. This is huge, Charles. This is what we've been wanting for…forever."

Warmth courses through me at her use of *we* instead of *you*.

"It couldn't have been without you."

"Now isn't the time to be freaking modest, boss. You need to think about how we can fix this." She rises from her seat and paces back and forth.

"I do have a plan. But I need your help."

"What is it?"

"Marry me."

ten

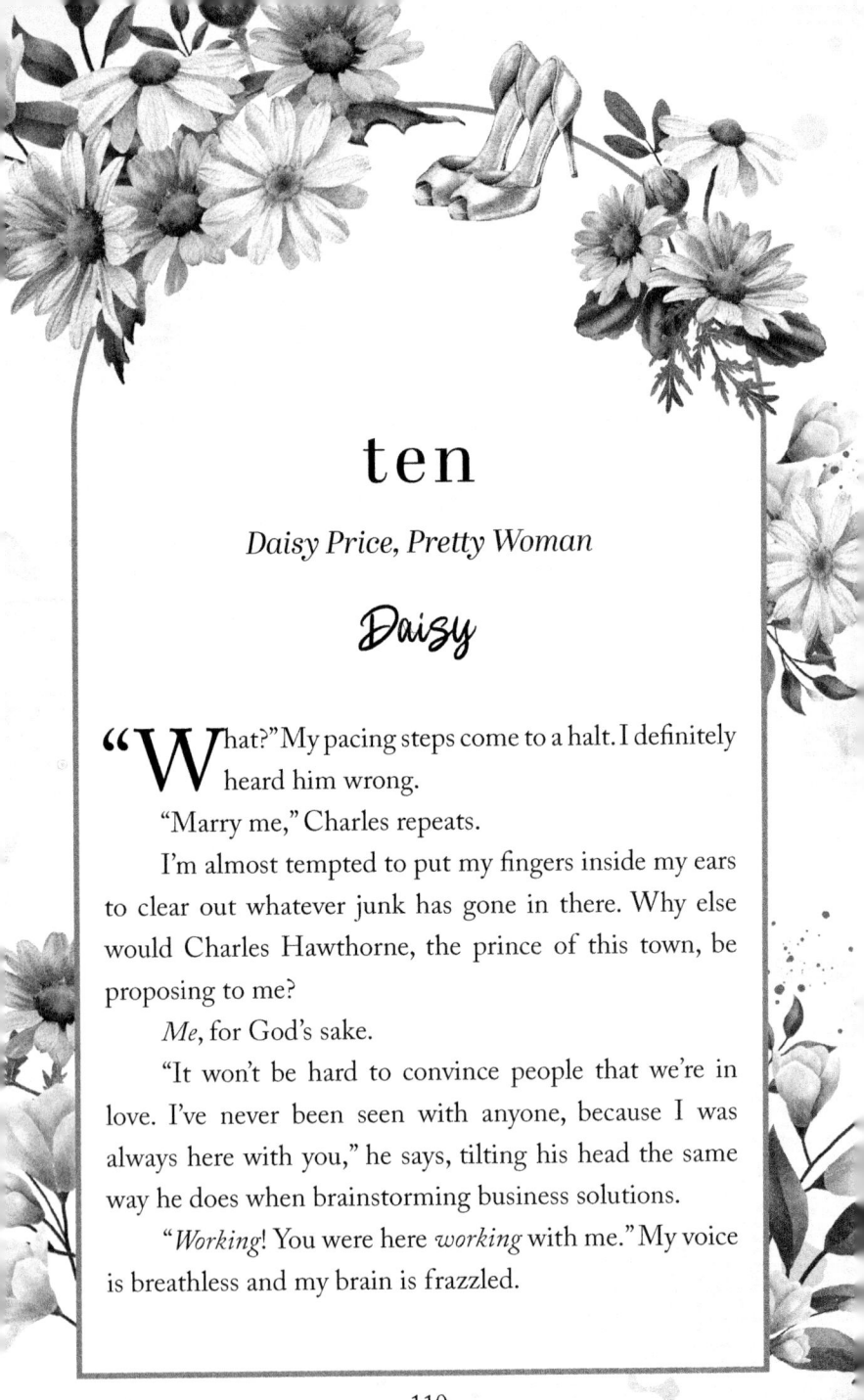

Daisy Price, Pretty Woman

Daisy

"What?" My pacing steps come to a halt. I definitely heard him wrong.

"Marry me," Charles repeats.

I'm almost tempted to put my fingers inside my ears to clear out whatever junk has gone in there. Why else would Charles Hawthorne, the prince of this town, be proposing to me?

Me, for God's sake.

"It won't be hard to convince people that we're in love. I've never been seen with anyone, because I was always here with you," he says, tilting his head the same way he does when brainstorming business solutions.

"*Working*! You were here *working* with me." My voice is breathless and my brain is frazzled.

How are the words *we are in love* rolling so effortlessly out of my stuck-up boss' mouth?

"I'm aware. I was there too." His tone is clipped, as if I'm the stupid one here.

Just thinking about how absurd this all is, a giggle escapes me.

"What are you laughing at?" His annoyed expression only makes me laugh harder. "Just stop it."

But when I still can't control my emotions, Charles pulls me closer. And the moment he tugs me by my forearm, not just my laugh, but everything, stops. My breathing, my heart rate, and my erratic pulse. The entire world comes to a standstill the moment Charles Hawthorne, the most coveted bachelor in town, places his hand over my lips.

"I've been telling you for years that you need to learn when to stop your laughing and to think before speaking, Miss Price."

My eyes widen at his slow words and the sight of him so close.

He's never been so freaking close that I can spot the flecks of silver, like distant stars embedded in a midnight sky, in his sapphire-blue eyes as they catch the ambient light in a dance of shadows and reflections.

And I have no choice but to nod.

When he finally removes his hand from my mouth, I take a few moments to calm myself. I can't let him know how much he's affecting me right now, and only when I'm sure my voice is going to sound sensible enough, I state, "It'll never work."

"Says who?" His jaw twitches as if my statement is almost offensive to him.

"Me." I finally find my bearings. "*I* am saying that. No one will believe we're together." Has he not looked in the mirror?

"Jimmy did."

"Jimmy what?" I gasp. "You…you told Jimmy? How many people have you shared this crazy plan with?" My gaze lands on the tissue papers with Giovanni's red, white, and green logo, and I gasp. "You told your cousins too? Didn't they tell you it was nonsense?"

"Not really. They said it was perfect."

"Did they now?" My eyes narrow on him, but instead of squirming in guilt like I expected him to, he flashes me his perfectly white teeth.

Is there anything that's not perfect about this man?

"Yes. Of course they mentioned my biggest challenge would be to convince you, and I think they were right."

There's something in his voice that makes me shiver.

"You're not joking, are you?" I ask carefully.

"In all these years, have you ever seen me joking, Daisy?"

"I—I suppose not. But this still isn't possible."

"Why not?" His voice is calm, in contrast to my insides, which feel like an overinflated balloon on the brink of bursting.

"For a hell of a lot of reasons, Charles!"

"Give me your number one."

"Forget Jimmy. The media will never believe you fell in love with *me*." Not just because he's *The Charles Hawthorne*, but because I'm me, someone with crappy luck when it comes to men, who have done nothing but hurt me.

"You think I can't be a good husband to you?"

All my female organs raise their hands. Okay, not just their hands, they do cartwheels at the word *husband*.

"Charles, this is not a competition, and I'm definitely not a prize."

He takes a step closer, and his gaze drops, those smoldering orbs locking on to me and holding me captive. I can't move, even when he lightly grazes the side of my cheek with his index finger. His eyes, never leaving mine, hypnotize me in their spell.

"You don't realize how special you are. But I'll spend every moment proving it to you." His low voice has a throaty, sexy lilt that seems straight out of a romance novel.

My eyes don't know where to look, until they decide to settle on his full lips, which look much too pink up close.

"Do you have any more questions about us?"

I nod slowly, still staring at his lips.

"What is it you want to ask, Daisy?"

I feel a flutter in my chest at the way he says my name.

"Do you wear some sort of manly lip color, Charles?" The question slips out, and Charles' laughter fills the room, his eyes sparkling with amusement.

Instead of replying in words, he holds my shivering hand in his and brings it closer to his lips.

My eyes fall closed, and I don't see the first time Charles Hawthorne kisses me. His soft lips seem to create a direct connection from the back of my hand to the core of my body.

"See for yourself," he murmurs, and I open my eyes.

My senses return when I find Charles smiling at me, and I immediately take a step back.

Holy freaking crap!

"What the heck was that?"

"You said no one would believe it, but I just showed you that I'm not that bad. And with the way you reacted, I'd say we'd have no problem making everyone believe we're in love."

With all the smiling my boss is doing today, he could be compensating for the past four years. And if this is how he's going to behave, I have zero doubt we'll make this believable. But what about me? How will I remember that this version of him is just a charade?

"I still can't do it." I fold my arms over my chest, even when it's an ordeal to pull away from Charles' magic.

"Why not? Tell me your second reason."

"Charles, stop counting my reasons and think carefully. What will happen after you become the CEO?"

"I'd like to get the position first before I start making grand plans for the future. But I guess for us, we should stay married for some more time to avoid any unwanted suspicions. So I'd say we remain married for a year or maybe even two."

"Then what? Have you thought about the media, which is constantly running behind you with a camera? Do you think they won't be interested to know why Charles Hawthorne is all of a sudden wifeless?"

"Couples divorce all the time, Daisy. Especially rich ones." He pauses as if his crazy thoughts are interrupted by some bigger annoyance. "Will it be okay for you?"

"Let me see. Was it in my life plan to get divorced before I'm even twenty-five? No, not really." I huff. "You know, I won't even be able to live in this town, *if* I agree to this madness."

He pauses for a second as if he hasn't considered

anything beyond us getting married, and then he asks in a low voice, "Is there anywhere you've wanted to live outside of Cherrywood?"

My mind immediately goes to all the postcards Mom and I used to collect of Italy. Our small family had big plans to travel around the world once Mom and Dad retired, but none of those came true. If I had the chance, would I leave Cherrywood? A year before, I might have considered it. I've lived all my life in this town, and as much as I love its charm, I know there's a whole world beyond these majestic mountains that protect Cherrywood.

But today, there's nothing more important than Dad.

"I can't leave Cherrywood, not for the foreseeable future."

"How long is that? Five years? Ten?" Charles asks sincerely, unaware of what he's really asking me.

How long will my dad be around to need my support?

I swallow back the lump in my throat. "I…I don't know, and I don't like this question. Please."

I swing my gaze away from his face. Silence lingers between us until he clears his throat.

"I didn't mean to disturb you. But what if we don't put an end date to this marriage?"

"Why the heck would you want to stay in a fake marriage indefinitely? What if you're at some fancy party, sulking at the bar, and you meet a pretty girl who's just as stuck-up as you? You click instantly, but oops! You can't do a thing because you're 'married' to your assistant." My voice takes on a growl. I equally hate the scenario and also the fact that I'm the one reminding him of it.

"Number one, I don't go to parties." He raises one finger up, his face bored, as if I'm wasting his precious time. "Second, I don't believe in the soulmate bullshit."

"What if I do?" I seethe. "What if I go to a party and meet my soulmate, only to realize I'm married to my superrich, dense boss?"

His nostrils flare as if he's daring me to even think about someone else, but the next second, he looks away and the spell breaks.

"How about we discuss the ending of this relationship after I've taken charge as the CEO? We'll keep everything low-key, including our married lives. I'm sure in a few months we'll be old news, and when we decide to separate, we can do it silently."

"I…I still can't do it, Charles."

"I'll buy you a house anywhere you want. Hell, I'll get you three. You'll receive a million dollars for every year we stay married, and every year after that, you'll get a hefty alimony—"

"Stop! Please. I'm not an auction piece you can keep raising your bid on." I place my hands over my ears.

Shame washes over me like an acidic downpour. I hate that even after knowing Charles' proposal is completely insane, my brain can't stop crunching numbers. That would be more than enough to cover Dad's extra medical bills and anything else he might need.

"Fuck. I…I didn't mean to be a total asshole, Daisy. I'm just desperate." Charles' face is sincerely contrite.

"I know, and if I could, I would help you, Charles. I know what's on the line here. But I can't marry you." He's about to say something, but I hold my hands forward. "Despite you having answers to all my reasons, there's one even you can't solve."

I admire his one raised brow as if silently grumbling, "Bring it on, Daisy."

"I want to marry for love. I watched my parents together, so in love that it was impossible to even breathe without the other. I want that for myself. And as much as I respect you, I don't love you. I'm sorry, but my answer is no."

This time when I storm out of his office, Charles doesn't stop me.

I reach home and start calling the hospitals once again. I increase my search area after every half an hour on the app and call the hospitals who provide in-house nursing staff. But so far, the lowest budget I got is still so far beyond my reach. With every phone call, my confidence dwindles and Charles' words, the money he promised, flash before me like golden stars.

"Shut the fuck up!" I close my eyes.

I'm not going to look at the imaginary golden money stars.

I cannot marry Charles for his money. It's the twenty-first century. Women don't need men for financial support. Yes, it would have been easier if there was someone in my life to share this anxiety with, but that someone is certainly not Charles Hawthorne.

Those gorgeous blue eyes, which I now know have silver flecks in them, don't belong to me, and neither do those soft, full lips. I bring my hand close to my face, and for some reason it smells of Charles' cologne. As much as I hate myself, I haven't been able to wash my hand since I stormed out of his office after telling my boss I don't love him.

I wrote Charles an email that I was leaving for home, and even though he didn't reply back, Dave was waiting for me as I stepped out of the elevator.

I take another whiff of my hand when my doorbell rings, making me jump.

Crap! Is that him?

No, Daisy, you haven't suddenly mastered the art of conjuring people with your thoughts. If you had, Charles would have appeared much earlier, considering you can't stop thinking about him.

I slowly inch toward the main door, and a pang of unexpected disappointment washes over me at the sound of Willow's voice.

"Daze, it's us. Open up. It's freezing out here."

I swing open the door to my apartment, and my three friends file inside, along with the rich aroma of Mexican food. My stomach rumbles, reminding me that I haven't eaten the whole day. Closing the door behind me, I return to the couch in my snug one-room apartment.

My friends have already set everything up. There are four glasses beside an uncorked bottle of wine, and paper napkins neatly arranged next to the sky-blue china plates I bought from a garage sale.

"Did we have plans that I forgot?" I flop down beside Willow on the floor, who finally looks up from her phone.

"No. This is an emergency meeting."

"And what's the—"

My words stop inside my mouth as she turns the screen of her phone toward me.

"I love you the most." My breathy voice fills the room as I fixate on Charles' figure, draped in a sleek black suit.

Until now, I haven't seen the video clip properly. I stumbled upon it by chance when I went down to the café at the ground floor of Hawthorne Tower. A group of employees had their heads grouped above the iPad sitting before them on the table. I fled before anyone could question me about being Charles' mystery woman.

"That's your voice," Willow says before swiping the screen and pointing at the second clip of me and Charles leaving the town hall and getting inside his limo. "And this is definitely you!"

"We have questions. So many." Violet's eyes are wild.

"But first, why was your phone switched off? We were worried," Elodie says as she holds the wine bottle. Unlike Willow and Violet, who are so loud they could be heard on the other side of town, she's thankfully much more relaxed.

"Charles asked me to."

He did ask me to be offline for the first hour, and I chose to stay that way in case he decided to contact me again and throw that ridiculous offer at me once more.

"Your boss told you not to talk to us? Your best friends?" Violet gasps, rising on her knees.

Elodie tugs Violet down. "Calm down, Vi. I doubt Charles Hawthorne had us specifically in mind."

"He didn't want me to see the video." I fidget in my seat, wondering if I should share what all happened today with my friends. Charles never said this was private, and he consulted his cousins.

"Because..." Violet drawls.

"Because my boss was planning to propose to me!" I throw my hands up in the air.

Looks like my brain has already made its decision.

"I knew it! Your boss is secretly pining over you. Why else would someone as handsome and sexy as Charles still be single, especially when women practically throw themselves at him?" Violet squeals, her pupils dancing like a puppy who just saw his favorite treat.

"Where is your calm-down button, Vi? No one is pining over anyone. He thinks marrying me will get the media off his back."

"And what did you say?" Willow asks carefully, curiosity shining in her eyes as she leans forward.

"No, of course! I can't say yes to this madness, can I?"

They all remain silent, looking at one another, until Violet breaks the quiet.

"If you say so. But he's going to have a hard time finding a more perfect bride."

"That's true. How can he be sure the woman he's marrying isn't after his money?" Elodie shrugs before passing me a glass of wine, unaware that her words hit me right in my chest.

If I go ahead with this plan, I'd be doing the same thing. Marrying him for his money.

"Plus, there are people in this town who would do anything to see Charles Hawthorne fail," Violet adds. "So what if the stranger does worse, like sabotage his business or ruin his image?"

My hand grabs the edge of the table at her crazy insinuation.

"Can we please talk about something else? I'm glad to see you worrying about my boss this much, but I've just spent half the day trying not to think about him or the video."

They all nod, and thankfully, we get back to the food while talking about our town's Christmas celebrations.

Willow is wiping the counter, and Elodie is loading our plates into the dishwasher. My hands are still in soapy warm water as I rinse the last wineglass, when Violet gasps.

"You all need to see this *right now*!" Her wide eyes, filled with excitement and a hint of worry, lock on to mine.

"What is it?" Willow plucks Vi's phone and sets it onto the counter.

The foot I've just placed forward retreats, and I feel a sudden urge to retch. The video of Charles and me leaving town hall is on the screen, with my photo inset beside Charles'.

I don't even notice which of my friends turns up the volume.

"The mystery woman is finally found, and despite what we all thought, she's not a royal princess but a local girl. Yes, you heard right! The woman who confessed her love to Charles Hawthorne today is none other than his executive assistant."

The clip of Charles' back and my "I love you" is playing on the screen.

"Once again, Charles Hawthorne has surprised everyone, and we all can't help but wonder if there's a *Pretty Woman* situation going on here."

I'm torn between feeling flattered by the comparison to *Julia Roberts* or offended because of the character's profession in the movie.

"How the hell did they find you so easily?" Willow wheezes.

Before my frazzled brain can even process her question, Jax appears on the screen with a reporter, standing outside town hall.

The room spins around me, and I feel dizzy for a second.

"Everyone, meet Jax Mendes, the man who confirmed the true identity of the mystery woman," the reporter announces, as Jax grins and waves to the camera, and I recoil watching his smile. "So, let's start from the beginning. What's the name of the woman in the video?"

"She's Daisy Price, Charles' executive assistant for the last four years. She has access to places in his life that no one else does." Jax's eyebrows lift in a lewd way, making me almost gag.

"I'm sure she does." The reporter grins back. "And how do you know her?"

"She's my ex."

"Charles Hawthorne's current girlfriend is your ex?"

The shock on the man's face can't be more fake and practiced. How did he end up in television?

"When did you find out about them? I hope she didn't cheat on you."

"What the hell? Show some decency, you jackass."

Willow's teeth grit, and every muscle in my body tenses, coiling like the bunched cleaning rag in her hand.

But Jax simply nods.

"Daisy used to spend an awful lot of time 'working.'" That asshole makes air quotes for emphasis. "Weekends. Late nights. Sometimes she'd be gone for days before we'd see each other."

"That's just cruel." The reporter's downturned lips and pout remind me of the cool kids from my high school who never hung with us normal people.

Jax nods on the screen. "I tolerated everything because I loved her. But then I caught them together and decided to get out of the picture. I'm definitely no match for Charles Hawthorne. I'm sure Mr. Hawthorne is used to having women throw themselves at him with a flick of his wrist and maybe a few hundred dollars, but I hope he'll treat Daisy with respect."

Did he just say, caught them together? A few hundred dollars?

Is he really the man you've wasted your tears on, Daisy?

"We share your concern, Mr. Mendes. It was lovely talking to you." The reporter turns to face the camera. "You all heard about Charles and the mystery woman, and if, like me, you're wondering whether this is a whirlwind romance or just a fling, only time will tell."

"Okay, we've seen enough." Elodie sets the phone facedown.

My friends release a collective deep breath, yet I can't believe what just happened was real and not some bad dream.

"It's going to be okay, Daisy." Willow throws her arms

over my shoulders. "They're not only talking about you but also Charles. I'm sure his team will put a leash on Jax and this nonsense soon."

Oh my God, Charles!

In shock and self-pity, I momentarily forgot that *I'm* Charles' assistant. Instead of slowly turning ice cold, my job is to alert his PR team when something like this surfaces.

I grab my phone from the couch, and as soon as I turn it on, there's an influx of notifications, unread messages, and missed calls. Ignoring them all, I shoot a text to Jimmy, asking him to check the news.

I'm about to switch off my phone again when it rings. A shiver skates down my spine at seeing Aunt Mel's name and face on the screen.

How the heck did I not think about Dad before making myself unavailable to everyone? What if he had called, or worse, someone else had called because he was once again lost?

"Hello, is Dad okay?" My words tumble upon one another in fear.

"Yes, hon. Jason is asleep. I just came back from your parent's place and turned on the TV. Is it true? You and Mr. Hawthorne are together?" Her last question is nothing but a gasp.

I glance up at the ceiling, imagining the smirking faces of the gods, who have all ganged up against me today and decided, for whatever reason, I don't deserve a single moment of peace.

"Um, Aunt Mel, can I please talk about this tomorrow? I have to be somewhere urgently."

"Oh, yes. Of course. You must have to handle the press. Go." I'm about to end the call when she adds, "I just want to tell you, Daze, Penny would be so happy today. She always used to say, 'My Daisy will marry a prince,' and Charles is nothing but a prince in this town."

Something in my chest twinges as memories of Mom saying those words swim in my mind. Watching my parents, I dreamed of having my own family so often. A small house. Long nights spent beside a fireplace in the arms of my husband while it snows. Corralling my kids inside as the sun goes down on a Cherrywood summer day.

Yet, here I am, with my reality headed toward a fake marriage.

"I love you, Aunt Mel. But right now, I really have to go. I'll call you soon, I promise." I hit the end call button and put my phone facedown on the table.

When I turn around, my friends are watching me with concern and sympathy. They know well that this is just a beginning. Aunt Mel was happy for something that isn't true, but I'm sure there will be a lot more people who won't think the same way about this news and me.

I'm almost scared for tomorrow.

"One of us can stay with you tonight, Daze." Elodie grabs my hand and holds on to it, as if reading my thoughts.

"Or all of us!" Violet adds. "We can turn this nightmarish evening into a throwback of our teenage slumber parties."

"I'm scared of your plans, Vi." I narrow my eyes on her. "We did the jerk-boyfriend purging ritual, and see where it landed me? I'm now the town slut."

"Oh, Daze. To earn that title, you have to do much more

than say you love Charles Hawthorne the most." Willow grins, looping her arm through mine.

How does one gentle touch from my friends seem to calm down my anxiety?

"If you want to be alone, then we'll leave. You lock up after us." Elodie tips her head toward the door.

"But you can call us anytime if you want to talk," Vi swiftly adds.

"Thanks." I give her a tiny smile before grabbing her hand. "I'm sorry for being cranky."

"You have all the right to be cranky, but I still believe the ritual worked and landed you a prince. You're just scared to see it right now, Daze."

After my friends leave, I slip into bed. My thoughts drift to all the events of today: Dad's incident, Charles' interview, his outrageous proposition, and finally, Jax appearing on TV.

How freaking long was this day anyway?

It's like my wish for a day longer than twenty-four hours was finally granted, and in the process, reminded me that wanting more always has consequences.

My hands clench the pillow lightly, and without any warning, my mind goes to the texture of Charles' soft suit as he pulled me against his hard chest. Once that floodgate opens, I can't stop the torrent of thoughts about my boss and the side of his personality he kept hidden until today. It defies my every preconceived notion about Charles. He isn't as ice cold as I thought, because right now just the mere thought of him makes me burn and sweat.

The next morning, I wake up with a fresh feeling of

dread, my hands shaking as I go for my phone on the table. I swipe the screen to read the latest text.

> **Violet:** It's all gone, Daze. Jax's interview, the media report about you…nothing is online anymore.

What?

I quickly type Jax Mendes into the search engine, and there's only one listing—his social media profile.

I go for Daisy Price and *Pretty Woman*, but get nothing.

Holy crap! Did I just dream the entire thing, including standing before Charles in my underwear?

My gaze slants to the date on top of my phone screen. No, I am definitely not reliving the same day. Once that's confirmed, with quivering fingers, I type out *Charles Hawthorne and the mystery woman* before pressing enter.

There it is—the video clip of me and Charles leaving town hall.

I peek through the curtains to see if anything is out of the ordinary, like a press reporter lurking outside my apartment, but I've a bigger surprise, and thankfully, one not as nerve-racking. One of Charles' cars is parked right across the street, and Steve leans against the door, dressed in his usual black suit and sunglasses, looking the street up and down.

What is he doing here so early? Is there a new crisis that I'm unaware of?

I put on my boho poncho and slippers and rush down the stairs.

"Steve? Is everything alright?"

"Morning, Daisy. Yes, of course. I'm here as your chauffeur and will drive you to work." The big man smiles casually. As always, he's showing me a much more casual side of his personality in the absence of Charles.

"Um, but I usually leave at eight." I look at my watch, and it's only six fifteen. "Is Charles going in early?" I struggle to piece everything together.

Surprise flashes in his wide eyes for a fleeting second. "Mr. Hawthorne asked me to stand guard here last night. I thought you knew."

I shake my head slowly, unable to find words for several beats. "When did you get here?"

"Ten thirty."

Right after the video of Jax went out.

Everything inside me stills as I finally try to process all that's happening. Charles sent him for me, even after I turned down his insane marriage proposal.

"Thank you so much, Steve," I say, almost in a daze, and upon returning to my apartment, I send a group text to my friends.

Me: Did you see Charles' driver outside of my place last night?

Violet: Yup.

Me: And you didn't think of telling me?

Willow: It was such a sweet gesture. Just think, if you accept Charles' proposal, this will be one of those moments you'll share with your kids.

Kids?

A few willful butterflies take flight in my tummy. Charles proposed an indefinite ending to this marriage.

Did he forget that he's supposed to have kids and grow the Hawthorne line? The lack of his image as a family man is the reason stakeholders are opposed to him taking over. Or is my crazy boss under the impression that marrying me would mean we would automatically be sleeping together and raising a family?

Damn you, Charles.

eleven

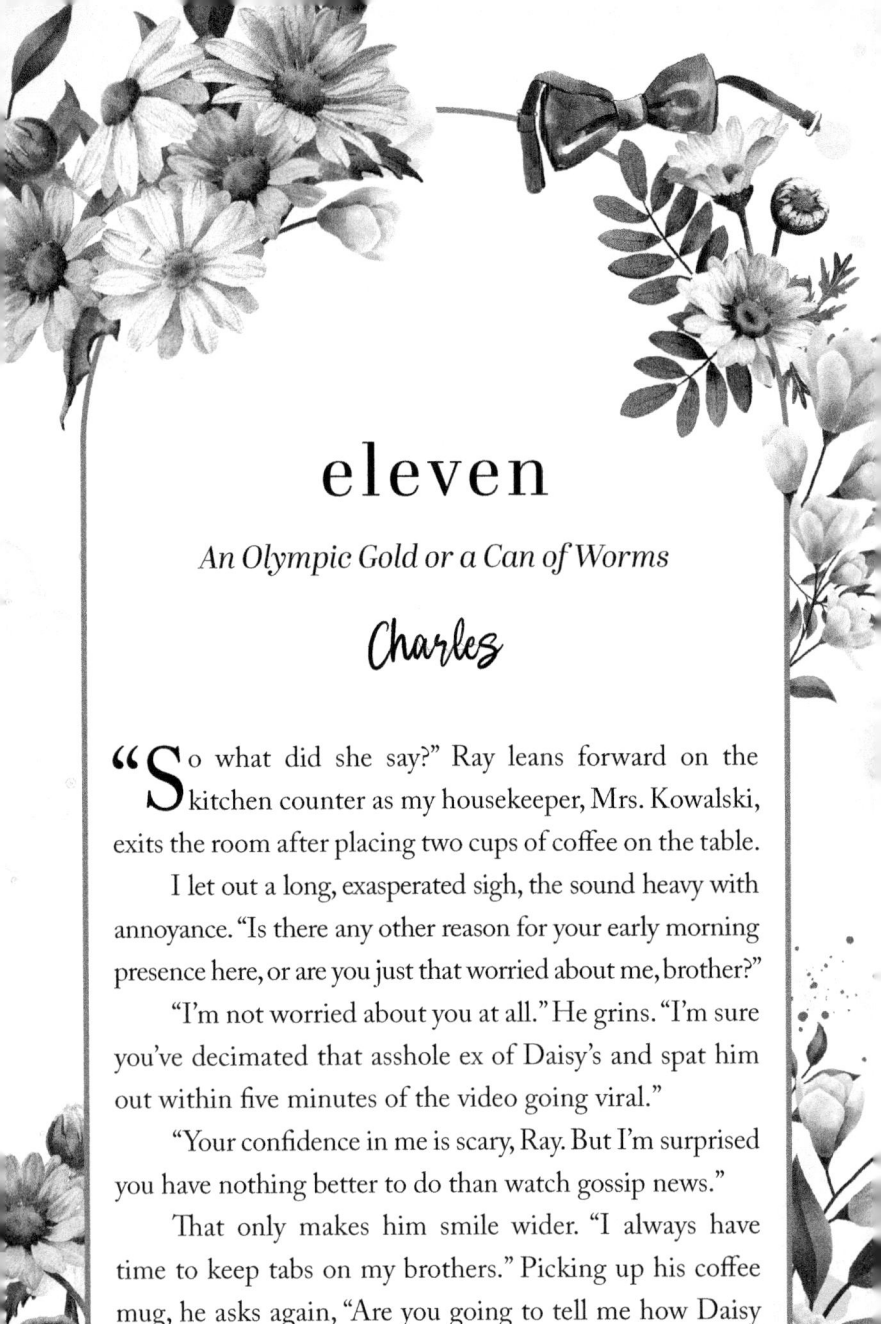

An Olympic Gold or a Can of Worms

Charles

"So what did she say?" Ray leans forward on the kitchen counter as my housekeeper, Mrs. Kowalski, exits the room after placing two cups of coffee on the table.

I let out a long, exasperated sigh, the sound heavy with annoyance. "Is there any other reason for your early morning presence here, or are you just that worried about me, brother?"

"I'm not worried about you at all." He grins. "I'm sure you've decimated that asshole ex of Daisy's and spat him out within five minutes of the video going viral."

"Your confidence in me is scary, Ray. But I'm surprised you have nothing better to do than watch gossip news."

That only makes him smile wider. "I always have time to keep tabs on my brothers." Picking up his coffee mug, he asks again, "Are you going to tell me how Daisy replied to your great proposal?"

"She's not going to do it," I state flatly, hiding away the tightening of my chest. The more I think about it, the clearer it becomes that there's no one more perfect than her for this job. If only I could prove it to her that this will work beautifully.

"So there's someone in Cherrywood who's not falling for your charms?"

"It seems so."

"Didn't you make a tempting enough offer? I don't think there's anything in this world you can't offer."

His playful joke hits the mark, because there's *something* I can't offer.

She wants to marry for love, and I've sworn off that feeble emotion from my life. Love only makes us weak, and weakness isn't something I can afford in my world.

"It appears there is," I drawl, losing interest in the verbal spar.

"And what's that?" Ray's smile drops immediately, as if he can read my locked emotions.

"Why don't I worry about that, and you can focus on the latest deal for Elixir Hotels?"

He pauses for a second, then rises from his chair. "I'm driving to St. Peppers to meet Mom and Dad today. Should I bring you something?"

I shake my head. "Not specifically, but I'm sure Aunt Hope will pack some of her baked treats anyway." Ray's parents, Zach and Hope, live in St. Peppers, which, until a few years back, was the headquarters of Elixir Inc.

"You bet she will." Ray chuckles, but instead of walking away, he saunters in my direction, and I lean back in my chair.

"Remember the golden rule of business, Charlie. It's not about what you're offering. It's about what the other party wants."

"And what if I can't give her what she wants?"

"Then offer what she needs." He looks me right in the eye. "Those aren't always the same thing."

I reach the office to find Daisy already seated behind her desk, staring at her black computer screen. Even when there are a few worry lines etched on her forehead, she looks her usual beautiful self. My knuckles tap against the mahogany table, and she jerks in her seat.

"Charles!" Her hands clutch her chest. "You're here?"

I raise an eyebrow. "It's *my* office. You should be surprised when I'm *not* here."

This is the first time I'm seeing her since she left through my office doors yesterday in a bewildered state. Despite her rejecting my offer, I got a sliver of enjoyment in making her speechless for a moment.

"It's not funny. I thought, given everything, you might be working from home," she rasps. Her gaze swiftly drifts away, and her fingers with purple nail polish play with the long sleeves of her matching silk blouse. Lightly squaring her shoulders, she looks up. "I mean, after Jax's interview."

I hate hearing that jerk's name from her mouth. How did she end up with that piece of shit?

"I can't run this company if I'm scared of assholes like him."

"I...I'm sorry, Charles. It's all my fault. I should have

been more careful. If I hadn't hit the cake—" She stops abruptly. "Oh my God! The cake. I had planned to call the baker, apologize, and even offer to pay."

Yes, no surprise there. I'm fully aware of my little assistant's need to make things right with anyone she inconveniences.

"Don't worry. I took care of it."

"You mean you paid?"

When I nod lightly, she makes a grab for her purse, but before she can open it, I place my hand above hers. A spark shoots down my spine at the contact, but years of practice comes in, and I don't let any emotion show on my face.

"I don't want your money, Daisy." *I want something bigger.*

A curl of hair falls in front of her eyes, and she tucks it behind her ear, as if hearing but choosing to ignore my unsaid words.

"Jax's interview is no longer available. Did you do something?"

I nod.

"But the other is still there?" She doesn't need to say which one explicitly—it's the one where she declared she loves me the most.

"It was up for a while and had already worked in my benefit with the shareholders. Temporarily, at least." Desperation furls inside me like a tightening coil. "What do you want, Daisy? Just tell me."

"I told you, Charles. I want to marry for love, and that's not a part of this proposal."

I run a hand through my hair. There's no hiding my

disappointment as I'm reminded again that our wants are completely opposites.

"Then there must be something you need. Something that will fix every problem in your life in this current moment."

She sucks in a breath. I'm finally fucking saying the right thing. The most important thing this business world has taught me is to read the person sitting on the opposite side of the table. And right now, I know there's something she needs that she believes I can give, even if it's not love.

But that relief in her gaze starts to fade.

"And what about the future? You don't think this"—she motions between us—"will create a new set of problems? In resolving what's broken now, we won't be opening a new can of worms for the future?"

My hands unclench and my fingers relax from the tense grip I didn't know I had. We are finally moving forward, even if she might not see it yet.

Time to seal the deal, Hawthorne. Fix the future problems she's imagining.

"Come with me."

I walk toward my office door and don't look back to check if she's following. As much as I hate waiting, negotiations only work when the other person arrives at the same point on their own.

I can only clear out the mental hurdles blocking her path, and luckily for us, I'm damn great at it.

Once we're seated on the couch, I turn to fully face her.

"What are you worried about? You won't have to do anything more than what you already do in the office. After we get married, your life will remain the same, but your bank balance will see significantly more zeroes. I'd say it's a once-in-a-lifetime deal."

"If you think a wife's job is to arrange your calendar, write emails to your clients, and make sure your coffee is exactly the way you like it, I feel sorry for you, Charles A. Hawthorne."

Despite her widening eyes, there's a slight twitch at the corner of her lips, a tiny reaction that soothes my own anxiety. She said wife, and she's still here.

"Don't for a second think that I'm not aware of why you deliberately use my full name when you're pissed off, or what the *A* stands for."

"I never tried to hide it, boss."

The grin that spreads across her face is wide, reminding me of how much I look forward to seeing her smile every day. A curl of those full lips and, bam, my day starts to look up.

"Say yes, Daisy. I swear you're not going to regret it."

"Charles." Her smile drops, surging my own anxiety. "Can't you see that this is never going to work? Despite this being equivalent to an Olympic gold for me, as you just stated"—her eyebrows rise—"I'm not one of the townsfolk who want to see me by your side. In case you missed it last night, I was almost compared to a slut in that interview."

A tight knot forms in my chest at hearing that word. Once I've convinced her, I'm going to hunt down the reporter who dared to compare Daisy with anything less than perfection. I ignore that pulse in my jaw and focus back on her.

"That's even better. It'd be like a fairy-tale love story."

"Hey! I was expecting consideration, not for you to agree to that nonsense." She throws her hands up in the air.

"Asking for sympathy is for the weak, and that's definitely not you."

Her lips curl up, and I go in for the final hit.

"Say yes, Daisy. Forget the media. The stakeholders believe it and that's enough."

"And what about your family? Your parents, Chloe, GG, and your grandmother? God, your grandmother! Have you thought about how Irene Hawthorne will react? The whole town has heard rumors about how she was upset with your dad and your aunts for not marrying into families of her choosing. And I'm the most imperfect match of all."

I shrug. "Then I'm keeping up with the family tradition."

"You're not even denying that I'm an imperfect match? Way to go in making a girl feel special."

Her accusing eyes squint, tracing my moves as I walk to my desk. I open the top drawer, and my hand hesitates as I grab the paper.

Do it, Charles.

Being upfront and honest is the only way to convince her that this will work.

"Remember, this is a special situation, and the only reason I'm sharing this with you is because we'll be able to fool everyone else as long as we're true to each other."

Daisy's eyes gleam with excitement as her gaze swings between me and the paper I slide across the coffee table. A second later, she picks it up and flips it side to side before reading through.

I watch her face, but she gives nothing away, and then finally, she bites her lip. I don't know if it's to hide her smile or if she's just thinking deeply.

"Please don't tell me this is how you spend your free time, Charles." Her wide eyes finally meet mine, making me *almost* squirm in my seat. "Making doodles with hearts and flowers with your crush's name on it would be better than dreaming about a fictional soulmate."

"I was at Elixir after the board meeting, pretty pissed that the members were using my single status against me. My cousins joked that I should just hire a bride. They wrote a list of characteristics for the job description and you…fit none." I trail off as her eyebrows rise and she opens and closes her mouth like a fish.

"Are you listening to yourself?" Daisy is already on her feet.

Dammit! I thought I was getting through to her. How did I screw this up already?

"If I was even considering being a part of this nonsense for a second, I don't any longer. We're doomed to fail from the start if *you* don't think I'm right for the job. So, Mr. Hawthorne, sorry, but I reject the offer to be your wife."

I'm stunned, rooted to my seat. But before she can make her escape, taking my dream of becoming the CEO with her, I discreetly lock the door using the safety button under the coffee table.

Daisy tries to force the door open, but it doesn't budge. When she turns back to me, her eyes blaze with fury, making her look sexier and hotter than ever.

There's only her and no one else—my *perfectly* imperfect match.

"What the hell, Charles? Open this door."

"Not until you say yes."

"Are you freaking hearing yourself?"

twelve

Better than Essential Oils

Daisy

I stand next to the door, stunned and unable to move as Charles leans back on the leather couch.

"This isn't funny, Charles. Open the goddamn door."

"Say yes and we can stop this useless discussion."

"Useless? I'd say this has been the most useful discussion of my life. Now I see how imperfect you think I am. Why are you even pushing this?" My eyes narrow at him as an uncomfortable feeling finds its place in my chest.

"Because I also know that you can rise up to a challenge like no one else." His penetrating gaze drills into me.

There must be something seriously wrong with me, because his praise warms my chest.

In my defense, Charles' habit of giving compliments rivals that of a grizzly bear allowing anyone near her cubs.

This is probably the first, and possibly the last, time he's openly acknowledged my work ethic.

"How are you not seeing the benefit here, Daisy? I become the CEO, while you can have whatever you need," he states matter-of-factly, his tone crisp and without a hint of hesitation, making me wonder if I'm stupid to even question his proposal.

"What is it that you need?" He approaches me with confidence, the kind that often signals he's not playing around and is here to seal the deal. "Whatever I promised yesterday is still on the table. Just tell me what I can add to it for you to say yes."

"I don't need your money. At least not for myself," I mumble. "Forget it, this isn't right."

Embarrassment floods me like a whirlwind, and I spin around, forgetting that the door is still locked. Before I can ask him to unlock it, Charles places his hand over mine on the golden knocker. A shiver races down my spine at the touch of his soft, warm palm against my ice-cold hand.

"Why are you so cold?"

"Because I'm nervous! It's not every day that my crazy boss proposes to marry me!"

His lips twitch. "See, you can call me all the names you think of out loud as my wife."

Every time he says the word *wife*, a tiny explosion goes off inside me.

"Don't worry, I get enough satisfaction when I'm saying them in my head."

He grins, and despite my best efforts to ignore it, I can't

miss the lazy circles he's tracing with his thumb on the back of my hand, still held in his grip, slowly warming up.

"Will you please tell me what I can do for you?"

All the butterflies drown in a storm of panic rising in my belly. The worry about Dad's care returns with unbeaten intensity. I've called more hospitals and care facilities, even outside of town, but none are within my budget. When I called Aunt Mel this morning, she told me Dad once again left the gas burner on after making his breakfast. We were lucky she was there in time to turn it off. I'm scared to even imagine what would have happened otherwise.

Charles' grip on my quivering hand tightens.

"Forget my proposition. What is happening that's troubling you this much? Is that asshole ex of yours texting you again?" His teeth grit, and I quickly shake my head.

"I blocked his number."

"Then what is it?"

"It's…my dad." I blink rapidly to dispel the burning behind my eyes. Apart from Aunt Mel and Uncle Frank, I haven't talked to anyone about the severity of Dad's condition. My friends know he's sick, but I've yet to tell them how badly.

Charles leads me back to the sitting area, and this time I go willingly. He guides me to the couch and settles down beside me.

"Tell me everything, okay?"

At hearing his featherlight, soft voice laced with concern, my tears threaten to make a reappearance.

I don't know why I choose to share this with him before my friends. Maybe I'm just tired this morning after calling all the hospitals and still being nowhere near a solution. Maybe seeing Charles struggling with his problems, I feel more comfortable in acknowledging my own.

"My dad was diagnosed with Alzheimer's a few months back. I thought I'd have a little more time to figure everything out, but he's already struggling, putting himself in life-threatening situations."

Finally, I look up at Charles as he leans forward, listening to me with rapt attention. His expressionless, stoic face is one I've known throughout the years while working with him, unlike the new, foreign side of his personality that's making my heart race a mile a minute. Right now, I can't even imagine that he's the same man who locked me inside this room, grinned, and made a crazy marriage proposition a few minutes ago.

"Yesterday, we couldn't find him. That's why I was late for your interview."

"Why didn't you call me, Dave, or Steve for help?" His voice maintains a calm cadence, which is both admirable and exasperating.

Do businessmen get some kind of special training on hiding their thoughts and emotions? If they did, I'm sure my boss was top of the class in the subject.

"My aunt's husband and his friends managed to find Dad at the cemetery, but he doesn't remember why he was there. He, of course, went to see Mom, but he left without a jacket and with the gas stove on." I clutch the edges of my skirt as fear gnaws at my insides like a relentless predator stalking its prey, consuming every ounce of courage and leaving behind a hollow emptiness. "I cannot leave him unattended. He's struggling to remember basic things. I need to find him a full-time caretaker, but everything is so freaking expensive."

My gaze drops with humiliation. What kind of child can't bear the expense of their parent's medical bills?

"Here."

I glance up to find Charles no longer perched on the couch but standing before me. He bends down and slides a check across the table.

"You should have told me about it sooner."

When I make no move to grab the check, he arches an eyebrow.

"So you're not going to accept my help?" he asks.

"I haven't decided if I'll accept your proposition," I murmur. Everything I need to take care of Dad is right here. I just have to give up a few years of my life, and that's all.

"Fuck the proposition. Do you really think I'd ask you to marry me in exchange for helping your dad? I'm not that much of an asshole."

I sit in stunned silence because, deep in my heart, I knew Charles would never add a condition if I ever asked him for help. I continue to stare at the zeroes on the paper. "This is too much."

"If it eases your mind, use what you need and return the rest," he says calmly, setting aside his own problems in light of mine.

When I remain frozen, Charles takes my hand and places the check in my palm. I don't think his fingers on my wrist miss my thundering pulse. The soft paper feels too heavy in my hands.

Are all my worries gone with a stroke of his signature?

"Your dad is with Cherrywood Memorial Hospital?"

When I confirm that, he gives me an inscrutable nod before pressing a discreet button under the table that I've never seen before, and the door clicks open.

"I'm sorry I did that." An embarrassed smile finally graces his lips. "This was installed for security reasons. In case I'd need to protect myself from something dangerous outside. I never thought it would come in handy for capturing something special inside."

Special?

If this is a dream, I want to stay in it for a little while longer. My problems with Dad's care might be gone, and Charles just called me special.

I return to my seat, unable to do anything but stare at the slip of paper with Charles' elegant signature sitting at my desk. I've been worried about Dad for so many weeks, and now, with a flick of his pen, Charles solved everything. I don't even know how much time has passed when the ringing of my phone interrupts my thoughts and I almost jump in my seat.

"How's my favorite girl?" The familiar voice calms my anxious insides.

"Since when am I your favorite girl, Jimmy?"

"Since the moment I learned that the easiest cure for my shortness of breath and chest pain was you, and I didn't have to waste hundreds of dollars on essential oils that don't even work. When Charles and you make your relationship public, all these media vultures will finally have something good to say regarding Hawthorne Holdings. I can't wait for these suckers to start a guessing game about the name of the

Italian town hosting your wedding or the French chef baking your wedding cake."

My stomach flips as I imagine the scene Jimmy paints in a chipper voice.

"Can you please tell that boss of yours that we still have to discuss how we're sharing the news with the media?"

There's a sudden pause in his excited speech, and Jimmy clears his throat once.

"Daisy, speaking of the media, don't you worry about that asshole Jax Mendes who was on the news for ten seconds last night. Charles sent a personal message to the channel who did that interview. If they ever think about showing it again, they'll no longer be in the entertainment business."

"He did what?" My gasp resonates in the office, but it's still not enough to put a dent on Jimmy's excitement.

"Isn't that romantic? The media will be eating from my hands if Charles continues to show this possessive side of his personality. Why is his phone busy anyway? What's more important than resolving the only problem standing between him and the CEO title? Can you please check?"

"Um, you mean now?" Only half of my brain is focused on Jimmy's instructions. The other half is still processing what he just told me about Charles.

"That would be good. I want to get the ball rolling on this news as soon as possible."

"Okay, give me a minute. I'll—" I'm about to knock when the door to Charles' office is pulled open. Just the sight of him makes my heart lurch.

"It's Jimmy," I whisper.

Charles' lips twist in their usual annoyance as he grabs my phone, still tucked to my ear, and ends the call.

"He wanted to talk to you!"

"Tell me something new. As opposed to what Jimmy thinks, I'm a businessman, not a celebrity. Besides, you need to leave."

"What?"

Is he firing me for not accepting his offer?

Stop being so dramatic, Daisy. He just gave you a check to cover your dad's expenses, why would he fire you?

"One of the best neurologists in the country is flying to Cherrywood Memorial today, and your dad has an appointment this afternoon."

"How do you know about the doctor?"

"Because I asked him to visit, and also because he's flying in the Hawthorne jet. Your dad's neurologist suggested it himself."

"You talked to my dad's doctor?" My voice rises in shock. On one hand, his action is a gross intrusion of Dad's privacy, yet on the other, I can't believe it. Charles has never taken a personal interest in anyone's life except his own.

"Not about the details of your dad's medical case," he replies in a clipped, almost offended tone. "I'm aware of the medical laws, Daisy. But a renowned neurologist visits Cherrywood Memorial twice a year. I just asked if we could make his visit sooner, and luckily, he agreed to my offer."

My lips quiver and I don't have the words or the strength to ask how much it costs to fly someone in a personal jet at one's command, but it looks like Charles isn't waiting for my question.

"You go now. Steve is already waiting for you in the parking lot." He even hands me my bag and leads me to the private elevator.

An hour later, Dad and I step into the neurology department, where a nurse is waiting for us. For the first time, we're not left waiting at reception. Instead, we're escorted immediately to the doctor's office. Dad undergoes a round of tests before the visiting doctor examines him. I'm still in a daze at how fast everything is moving, when his regular neurologist asks me to follow him into the lobby.

"Miss Price, we've received your application for a twenty-four-hour caregiver for your father. I've personally shortlisted three of our best candidates, and if you like, you can interview them today. This way, your dad can already have someone at his home by this evening."

"B-but I didn't fill out an application." The shake in my voice can't be tamed. All I can do is gape at him.

"Really?" The old man runs his fingers over his jaw as he looks down at the paper in his hand. "Perhaps Mr. Hawthorne did. Nevertheless, would you like to meet the candidates?"

I can only nod and follow him.

It's almost late afternoon when I drive back to the office after dropping Dad off at his home. His new caretaker, Kai, is already with him. After interviewing the three candidates, I arranged for Kai and Dad to meet, and as expected, they instantly hit it off.

Kai is the youngest of seven siblings, and in his free time, he performs with his band at local restaurants. I'm sure his fun and approachable personality comes in handy in his job as a nurse.

When I reach the office, I find Charles standing in front of my desk, or more precisely, in front of the purple tray holding several menus from restaurants on the approved list by his security team.

An unruly strand of hair drops onto his forehead as he looks between the two menus in confusion. I clear my throat and he looks up.

"Thank God you're here. How's—"

"I'm in, Charles. If your proposal is still open, I'm ready to be your wife."

thirteen

Fake Wife vs Lousy Assistant

Charles

"I'm in, Charles. If your proposal is still open, I'm ready to be your wife."

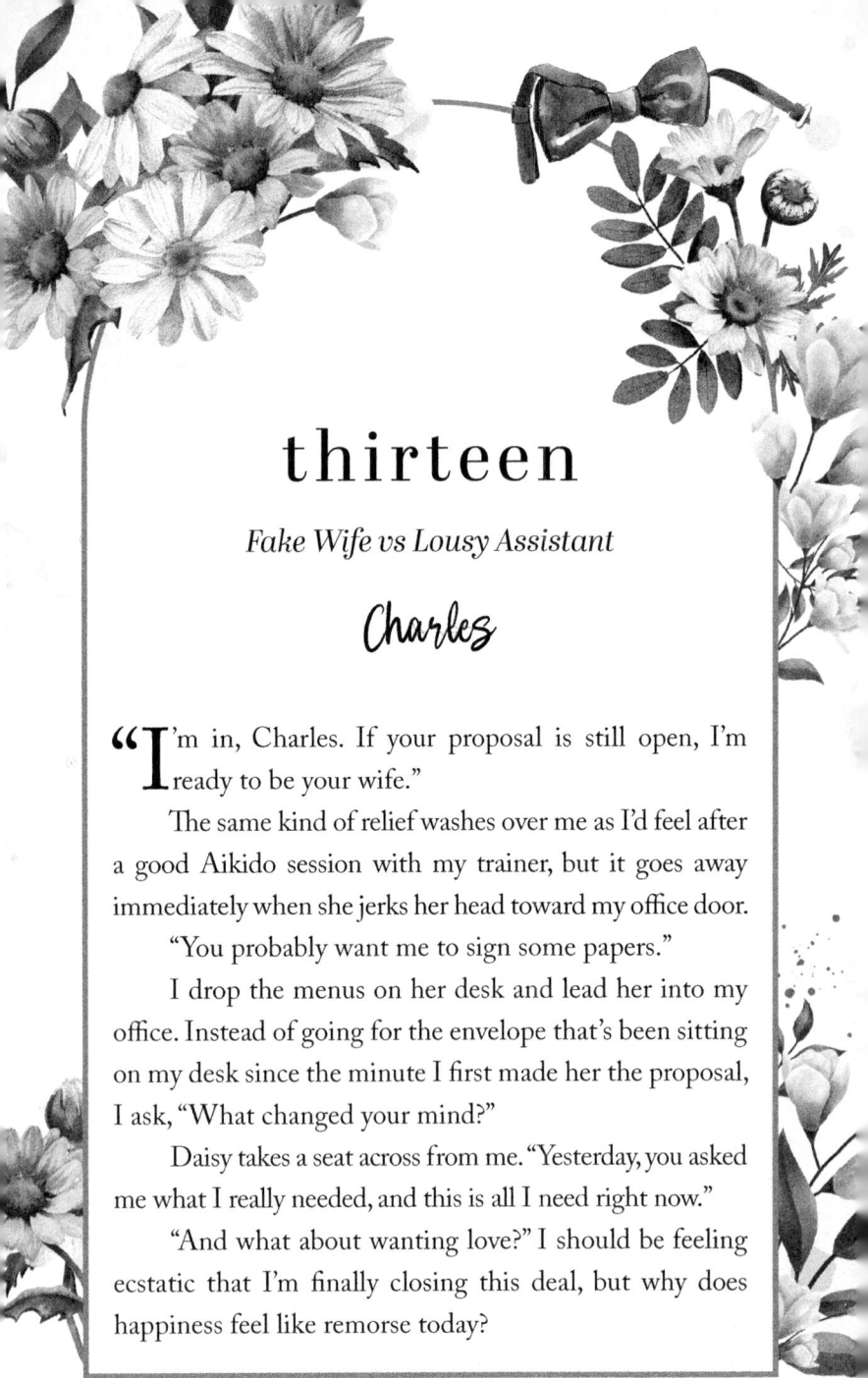

The same kind of relief washes over me as I'd feel after a good Aikido session with my trainer, but it goes away immediately when she jerks her head toward my office door.

"You probably want me to sign some papers."

I drop the menus on her desk and lead her into my office. Instead of going for the envelope that's been sitting on my desk since the minute I first made her the proposal, I ask, "What changed your mind?"

Daisy takes a seat across from me. "Yesterday, you asked me what I really needed, and this is all I need right now."

"And what about wanting love?" I should be feeling ecstatic that I'm finally closing this deal, but why does happiness feel like remorse today?

"If love is made of people like Jax, I think I'm better without it." A dry laugh slips out of her mouth.

"And what about having a marriage like your parents?"

She pauses until a painful smile tugs on her lips. It's uncomfortable to watch for some reason.

"I think one has to have wished on a dozen shooting stars to have that kind of love in their lives. Not all dreams come true, Charles, and I'm okay with that. There's a reason they're called dreams and not reality."

Those words hit a foreign nerve in my chest. In making my own dream come true, I'm ripping her away from any chance of finding her own.

I slide a paper across the desk and place my Hawthorne crest pen on top. "Since love is off the table, I want you to make a list of things I can give you. A lifetime supply of colorful sticky notes. Fur slippers in every imaginable animal."

"Don't tempt me, boss. You might end up regretting telling me that." She snorts, and I realize the absence of her smile affects me more than I thought.

"Do you have a minute? Because I'd like to seal this deal fast."

"A minute? How can I write all my wishes down in one minute?" Daisy lets out a whoosh of air.

"Chop, chop, Cinderella. You already lost a few seconds." I tap my wristwatch.

"Asshole!" she mumbles.

Since she's so busy scribbling, I don't have to worry about her catching my grin.

As the sixty seconds pass, I look up from my watch. "Time's up."

Daisy raises her head but then goes back to finishing whatever she was writing.

"Hey." I get up from my chair and circle around the desk until I'm standing above her. "That's not fair play."

"What can I say? I learned how to bend the rules from you, future husband."

The word *husband* rolls off her lips and hits me in the chest like a Cupid's arrow. I can't help but smile as I lean forward and her eyes widen.

"Good, but it's us against the world, future wife. Let's not forget that." My nose brushes against hers for a fraction before I pull back, the tiny contact registering in every cell of my body. "Now tell me how we can drop the word 'future' from our titles." I nod toward the paper.

She clears her throat and sits straight. "So, first, I'd like to leave at six every evening."

I return to my seat as she raises a second finger.

"And I'd like to not come to work any time before ten. From now on, I'll only work forty hours a week, as written in my contract. I'll also not work on the weekends, and definitely not on holidays. Do you agree?"

"Why don't I hear you out completely before I comment?" I fold my hands together, pressing my fingers against my lips.

"I need an hour lunch break, uninterrupted, and not one where I'm chewing and taking notes for your next meeting while sitting on that couch."

"That only happened once or twice."

"Twenty times in the last six months!" She throws up her hands, only bringing them down when I nod.

"You also can't ruin my plans with my friends because, just as I'm leaving, you remember something else for me to do. I won't leave movies in the middle just because you had an amazing idea and would like to get started right that second. I won't eat dinners in the office because you want to work late. I won't consult with any of your home staff. You have an excellent housekeeper for that. Lastly, I would like you to arrange for me and my friends to meet Minnie King, the Dreamcatcher. We're all big fans of her music, and I know you're close to the Kings." She finally takes a deep breath and looks at me. "I'm done. So, do you agree with everything?"

"Not at all. I'm not trading a fake wife for a lousy assistant. You'll do everything exactly as you do today. But I'll see what I can do for the last request."

When she sits there looking smug, I lean back in my chair. "You knew I wasn't going to agree to anything, right?"

"But it was *so* worth trying."

My emotions are in a much calmer place when I finally slide the white envelope toward her. Her secret talent to calm down my nerves with just a smile is both scary and unexpected.

"Now let's get to business. All the monetary stipulations I mentioned earlier are in here. In addition, I'll pay for your dad's medical bills. Anything that will ease his life and reduce your worry, we'll do it. The marriage has no official end date, but after me becoming the CEO and with the media's attention possibly elsewhere, let's talk. You'll always have a job with Hawthorne Holdings, even after we split up."

It feels strange to talk about splitting up before we've even started our married life. But this isn't a traditional setup, and ours is possibly the most imperfect match of the century.

"Charles, it's too much." She gnaws on her bottom lip. "You paying for Dad's healthcare is more than enough for me. I don't need anything else."

"In business, you squeeze the maximum out of a great opportunity, Daisy. You don't let your racehorse sit for seasons when it's in the best shape. Build a safety net for your future."

Her head hangs in embarrassment, but I'm certainly not letting her get into such a delicate situation ever again. She might not realize it, but the moment she signs the papers, everything between us will change. She'll be carrying my name. Like everything else that's mine, I'll protect my wife from all present and future problems.

"Charles—"

"Daisy." I lean forward. "This is nonnegotiable. There's an NDA. The fewer people who know the truth, the lesser chance it'll ever get out."

"But your cousins know, don't they?" Her words are flat, not meant to be accusatory, but they still hit me right in the chest. I'm being a hypocrite.

She doesn't need to say it out loud.

"But I trust them." I nod. "Is there someone with whom you want to share the truth?"

What the hell, Hawthorne? How can you even think of letting strangers in on this?

"My friends. They know you made a marriage proposal, but I don't want them to know the rest." She motions toward the contract papers. "I'd rather they think this is some sort of a fairy tale than constantly worrying if I made a deal with a handsome devil. Anyway, they believe you have a secret crush on me."

Secret crush?

I have *something* for my assistant.

I've been calling it momentary insanity, which hits me more than a few times every day when she's either making one of her hilarious remarks or just making me crazy by simply existing in my world.

Secret crush is a very simple description for it.

"I didn't know I was infamous as a devil."

"A handsome devil who would look amazing in a tux." Her brows wiggle, taking away some of the bite.

"So where am I standing while wearing this tux? City hall, a private garden with a small group of family and friends, or the wedding hall of a luxury resort?"

"I don't care as long as it's not city hall. My Dad would love to walk me down an aisle, even though he'll possibly not remember the moment for long." A sad smile brushes her lips, and I make a vow right then to make it the most fucking memorable wedding of the century.

"Noted. I'm sure Jimmy will have a blast in the next few days."

True to my words, within the next thirty minutes, my PR team has released the media packet with a story of how I fell for my assistant at first sight. It's complete with photos taken over the years, innocent when placed individually, but together with the story, they could convince anyone of our fairy-tale romance.

fourteen

Confessions of Undying Love for My Wife

Daisy

Kai: Hello, Daisy. Can you please come over? It's kinda urgent.

My mouth dries as I read the text. It's Kai's third day with Dad. What could have happened that he needs me already?

"What's wrong?"

The phone slips from my hand at Charles' voice. Before the glass and plastic meets a shattering doom, my soon-to-be husband takes a huge step forward and grabs it.

His gaze drops to the texting app, where Kai's message is still open.

"Let's go." Charles holds me by my elbow and turns me around toward the elevators.

"Charles, where are *you* going? You have a meeting"—I look down at my watch—"in fifteen minutes."

"Meetings can be rescheduled, Daisy."

Since when?

But my words remain locked in my throat when the elevator stops. Steve is already at the door waiting. With practiced ease, Charles and I enter the back seat of his Porsche.

This might probably be the first time we're driving together for something that isn't a business meeting.

And this won't be the last.

Before the thought and its reality sets in, my phone rings.

"Aunt Mel, please tell me Dad's okay." I hold the device close to my ear with both hands.

"Come fast, Daisy. There're reporters in your home, and your dad is—" Her voice gets a high-pitched tone I've never heard before. "God, Jason, no…"

"No, what?" I jump in my seat, but the call ends. I immediately turn around to face Charles. "There are reporters at my dad's place! He must be freaking out." Since his diagnosis, Dad has become wary of strangers, wondering if he should remember a face he doesn't recognize.

Before my tripping heart can combust in this cramped space, Steve parks the Porsche and I rush out. For once, I don't wait for my boss.

But my feet get stuck at the landing watching the scene before me. At least fifteen reporters are seated trying to fit themselves into a space that looks exactly like the times my mom would host a Christmas party and invite too many people. But instead of a giant Christmas tree, everyone is facing the chair at the center of the room, where my dad is seated with the widest smile on his face.

"So before we start, does everyone have their coffee?" he

asks, and when the reporters raise their cups, Dad continues. "Good. As I was saying, Daisy is my pretty girl with a heart of gold. I'm not surprised Mr. Hawthorne fell for her, but I think he should have asked for my permission. That's the right way of doing these things. What do you say, Kai?"

My dad's handsome nurse stands behind him in a plain white tee and black pants. Celtic tattoos cover his folded arms, and he gives Dad a confused nod before his gaze lands on me.

"Thank God," Kai mouths.

"Dad, what's all this?" I finally find my voice and take a step further in. All heads turn in our direction as I approach Dad while Charles remains glued to the doorway, his bodyguards right behind him.

"They all came to congratulate me, Doodles. On your engagement."

My legs almost shake as I walk toward him, looking at the wide smile on his face.

Oh my God.

Dad's gaze drifts from me to the doorway, and he slowly gets up. "Mr. Hawthorne. Please come in. This is your first time in our house."

Oh, Charles.

Unfamiliar place. Unfamiliar people. Unfamiliar situation.

His panic engine must be running at full throttle.

Before I can think of a way to fix this mess, which means getting every reporter out of this room, Charles into his car on the way back to work, and Dad preferably still with his smile, a throat clears beside me.

"You have quite a party going on here, Mr. Price." Charles plays with the knot of his tie as his assessing gaze flies to the cameras in the room.

He might be fooling everyone in this room with his smile, but I know it's his *I-can't-wait-to-get-the-hell-out-of-here* grin. But when his gaze lands on Dad, a foreign smile touches his lips. If it were anyone else, I might call his face friendly. But this is Charles, a man who doesn't quite know *that* f-word.

"I know this isn't the correct order." He takes a step forward, away from me, toward my dad and the reporters. "But I've been trying to convince your daughter about us for so long that when she finally agreed to my proposal, I forgot all the rules."

I don't know if it's just me, but Charles' honey-dipped words *almost* sound sincere. Almost.

"Nevertheless, I'd very much like to fix this. Would it be acceptable to you?"

A second later, Dad nods and takes his seat. One of the reporters vacates a garden chair for Charles. My fiancé of three days thanks the man and gracefully turns to face Dad.

"Mr. Price, my life hasn't been the same since your daughter walked into it, and I can't imagine doing this with anyone else in the world. Would you give me your permission to marry her?"

There's pin-drop silence in the room, and even my own heartbeat stops as Dad looks at me and then slowly back at Charles.

"You didn't mention the most important prerequisite for a successful marriage, Mr. Hawthorne. Do you love my daughter?" Dad finally asks, slicing the silence with his soft voice.

My heart jumps into my throat. A part of me doesn't want Charles to lie to my dad, but he's a businessman adept at closing deals, and this marriage is nothing more. While I expect him to profess his undying love for me, Charles runs a hand through his hair.

His gaze drops for a second before the smile returns. "I love her intense sincerity and absolute honesty. I love how she's not hesitant to call anyone out, including me, if her self-respect is threatened. I love how much she's willing to walk the extra mile for everything that's important to her, including you, and I hope me too."

Wow!

It takes a second of heart-attack-inducing quiet before a smile spreads on Dad's face. "You have my permission, but know that you are a very lucky man, Mr. Hawthorne."

I'm shocked to see Charles running a hand through his hair in relief. *He was nervous about my dad's response!*

"Please call me Charles, and you're one hundred percent right on that one, Mr. Price."

My dad's lips curl when there's a collective roar from the audience, and multiple camera flashes go wild as if we're on a red carpet and not in my parents' simple living room.

Dad's arm feels light when he places it over my shoulders. We're standing on the porch, watching Charles saunter toward his car, with Steve waiting for him outside, holding the door open. I decided to stay for another hour and make sure Dad's fine after the morning disruption.

"I'm no longer worried about you after I'm gone, Doodles. You've found the perfect husband, one who'll keep you very happy."

My heart stutters against my rib cage like a caged bird. There have been so few instances when I've lied to my parents, and this one is the worst of all.

"He's the Hawthorne heir, Dad. Everyone thinks he's perfect." I shrug, mustering up a smile and hoping it doesn't look too fake.

"He could be a handyman, Doodles, and if he looked at you the same way, I'd still say you found the *perfect husband*." Dad's eyebrows wiggle.

I feel a surge of electricity coursing through my veins while watching Dad, who's alert and happy. He's acting like his usual self from before the diagnosis.

"Now, come on. I need to show you something before I forget." He holds my hand and leads me inside, not stopping until we reach his bedroom.

A fresh wave of nostalgia hits me at the sight of the daisies by Mom's dresser.

"You bought Mom's favorite flowers," I whisper.

Dad looks up from his nightstand and slowly smiles as he glances between me and the white ceramic vase. "Kai asked me to do one thing I used to do regularly in the past."

"I'm so happy that we found Kai."

"Me too, kiddo. Now, come here." He pats the edge of the bed before perching on it himself.

"What is it, Dad?"

Instead of replying with words, he removes his wedding band from his finger and places it in my palm.

"Um, you want me to keep it safe for you?" My gaze slants between my dad's soft face and his bare finger with a clear discoloration from his missing wedding band.

He slowly shakes his head. "Your nana gave this ring to your mom after I proposed. This was your grandfather's. He made it himself in his metal shop, along with a matching band for Nana. I always thought Penny and I had such a happy married life because we had your grandparents' blessing. I'd like the same for you, Doodles."

My throat tightens uncomfortably, and I look away to avoid his gaze. The ring sears my skin as if it's on fire.

"I…I don't know, Daddy. Charles might prefer… something else." *Like not wearing a wedding band at all.*

In the last four years, Charles has never once changed his dressing style or accessories. I'm sure he isn't suddenly going to become a jewelry fan.

Dad's smile drops for a flash before he nods. "I understand. But why don't you ask once, for my sake?" He closes my fist around the ring, wrapping my fingers under his own.

"That, I'll do. I promise."

The next morning, I enter the office to find my desk transformed into a ring showcase from a jewelry store. I grab the pearly white notecard with a Hawthorne monogram at the bottom and read the words written in Charles' flowing cursive handwriting.

imperfect match

"Pick the one you like the best and we'll be engaged."

A feeling of remorse hits me like a heavy gust of wind, shaking me to my core. No girl would probably admit it out loud, but we all imagine that moment when, with hearts in our eyes, we'll find the right guy who will endure sleepless nights trying to come up with the perfect proposal and make all our dreams come true. And these monstrous rings are a far cry from my dreams, which never changed whether I was thirteen or twenty-three.

I dreamed of the day when someone would give me a ring because he couldn't wait to marry me and start our family. Like my dad, he would probably go to a thrift shop to find something within his budget that was meaningful to us. To me.

But here I am, standing before diamonds the size of my eyes, probably costing more than Cherrywood's worth, and still—

"You don't like them."

"Make a noise, will you?" I grip my chest. My gaze shifts to Charles, who simply shrugs, leaning against the door of his office.

"So…the rings. You hate them," he repeats, awaiting my confirmation.

Daisy, he's the same man who told your dad yesterday that he loved your sincerity and honesty.

But does he really?

So you're going to ask him that?

Of course not!

Instead, I grab the closest ring without a second glance and shove it in front of him.

"This."

"Really?" His eyebrows rise.

I look down and grimace. It's an obnoxiously huge diamond on a shining gold band.

This is so not me.

But neither is this marriage.

It'll work as a perfect daily reminder that everything is fake.

Before I can put the monstrosity on my finger, Charles plucks it away from my hand.

"There are no reporters around," I say. "I can put it on myself."

His lips twitch in response, only fueling my irritation.

Here I am drowning in lost dreams, and he's enjoying this.

"How about you try this one?" Charles takes out a blue velvet ring box from his jacket. When he opens the box, nestled in the soft white cushion, is the prettiest ring I've ever seen.

A daisy—circular yellow diamonds in the center with white shining petals.

"The jewelers sent it by mistake. It was custom made for someone, but the couple split up. Neither of them want a reminder of their failed engagement. The jeweler is going to split it and reuse the diamonds."

"They'll rip it apart?" The horror in my voice can't be tamed. "Why can't they sell it as secondhand?"

But my boss couldn't be more pragmatic as he shrugs. "It would be difficult to sell it as the promise of a lifetime when its original owners find it imperfectly misfortunate."

Imperfect.

There's that word again, which is the foundation of our relationship. "I'll take it." I grab the box from his hand.

"You don't want something with less bad luck?" He tugs on his tie, a telltale sign that he's skeptical, but I can't help my laugh.

"How can it be bad luck when we want this marriage to fail? I think it's perfect. Plus, it's beautiful." My hands stop before I can put it on my finger. "Should I?" I look at him to find his gaze fixed on my hand before sliding to my face. My breath hitches, and I know I'll never forget the way Charles is looking at me right now.

He slowly nods and I put the ring on.

The diamonds shine against the light as I move my fingers, admiring the ring. The feeling in my heart is almost indescribable. Almost like watching the last episode of your favorite show. You want to know how everything wraps up, but you also don't want it to end.

Charles clears his throat. "What are you thinking?"

"That I'd hate for this to be ripped apart someday."

"It doesn't have to be ripped apart." Charles' voice drops lower than usual. "You can always keep it. It would make a good investment for the future."

Of course, if there's anyone who would think of an engagement ring as an investment, it's my boss.

"I'll think about it."

"When you send these back, can you also get a wedding band for me?"

"You'll wear a band?" My question is laced with shock.

"How else will I flaunt my undying love for you, wife?"

His hesitant grin makes me shiver. "Nothing fancy. Just get something simple. Whatever seems okay to you will do."

While Charles stands there, the wedding band in my bag screams to be picked up.

Will I be cornering him by showing him Dad's ring?

But I promised Dad I'd ask. How can I ignore that, especially when Charles himself is asking about the ring?

"I...I might have something." I bring the golden band forward. "This is my dad's. He gave it to me yesterday. You can say no. I just promised him I'd ask you."

He looks between the ring and me for several seconds, his expression unreadable and stoic. My heart is almost in my throat, and I'm about to demand that Charles show some emotion so I can guess what he's thinking.

"It'll do," he says. "Now that we've gotten that out of the way, let's get some real work done. We're breaking ground on Vincent's showroom construction this afternoon, so make sure everything goes without a hitch. Don't forget your duties here, wife."

fifteen

Oh, Sweetheart

Charles

A week later, I'm dressed in a tux, standing under a wooden arch covered with white daisies and silky satin, my cousins behind me. My hands itch to tug on the white bow tie that suffocates the hell out of me, but I'm enduring it only because of the smiling faces of my family sitting in the first row.

All the women, including Daisy's three best friends and bridesmaids, are dressed in pastel pink. GG is rocking a matching feather cap and can't stop beaming. Even Grandma Irene's smile seems to be wider today. It's for them that I'm tolerating the crowd.

The guest list for today's party is longer than Mt. Everest. Everyone who's *someone* in this town is invited. Jimmy has even handpicked a few reporters who will get the inside scoop on the event. So, yeah, I have to act like the best fucking doting husband who is head over heels for his bride. This is a wedding for show, after all.

I'm stunned, a grimace on my lips when the music changes.

The white curtain lifts, and instantly, I feel a zip in my chest as Daisy walks in holding her father's hand. She's dressed in an ivory princess-style wedding gown. The off-shoulder frills rest on her breasts. It's modest for the most part, but the hint of her cleavage teases me today. The embroidered top fits her perfectly before flaring at her waist in a tulle skirt.

I've always been very careful with my thoughts when it comes to my assistant, because I worry how far and how fast that sequence will spiral. But once Daisy signed those papers, it was like my mind got a free ticket—or maybe a *signed* ticket—to think about her.

And God, do I think about her.

I thought of her running away from Cherrywood in a horse-drawn carriage, wearing a bridal dress with more features than a swan.

I thought of her saying *I don't* instead of *I do* in front of all the guests.

The human mind works in strange ways, and I guess in stranger ways when we're stressed.

But my mind and imagination were wrong about everything, including her running away *and* her dress.

She is the most beautiful bride to ever walk down the aisle, and I'm the luckiest man who gets to go home with her.

Her cheeks are flushed as she inches closer, which I can see thanks to the absence of a veil. My sister forced Daisy to swap it for a tiara with diamonds that match her engagement ring.

The same ring she chose as a reminder of what this wedding means, a time-bound transaction, has gained lots of attention from everyone—the media and our families. Mom and Chloe can't stop gushing about it and the fact that none of them knew I was such a romantic at heart.

Jason has told me more than a few times how Daisy's mom would have loved me for caring about her every small happiness. How the man, on the verge of losing his memory, keeps bringing his dead wife up in every conversation is beyond me.

A noose of guilt tightens around my neck when Daisy and her father stop a few steps away from me. Jason kisses his daughter's cheeks before placing her hand in mine. I've *touched* my assistant's hands several times in the past, but I've never felt the weight of it in my chest like today. The minister continues in a calm voice while my heartbeat skyrockets. I only hope Daisy remains unaware of the betraying organ.

The minister starts but his words are like the buzzing sound of a bee in my ears. I'm too distracted to focus on anything or anyone except Daisy. Until Ray, standing behind me along with my cousins as my best men taps my shoulder.

"The man asked you something, Charlie," Ray whispers in an overly polite tone.

Fuck, my cousins won't let this moment go.

"Do you, Charles Hawthorne, take Daisy Price as your lawfully wedded wife?"

"I do."

My bride lifts her gaze, and her hand trembles in mine as I hold it tightly in my grasp.

Focus, Charles. This is like any other business transaction you've been a part of.

She got what she wanted—or what she needed*—and you're getting what you need.*

But when she tries to place her father's ring on my finger, the feeling that hits my chest isn't the usual excitement of winning a deal. Her hands tremble and I fear she'll drop the golden band.

"Here, sweetheart." The endearment rolls from my lips as I hold the ring and help her.

Her kohl-lined eyes are wide as they meet mine before drifting to the minister. Those brown orbs return to me as if confirming she understands that everything happening this evening is fake.

I hate that once again I'm a clown in the hands of the public.

"You may kiss the bride."

It's not like I haven't thought of this moment in the last few days, but what I never imagined was the subtle hint of her familiar floral perfume as I leaned in, or the way her chest would rise and fall. Everything is a reminder that in this huge gathering at Hawthorne gardens, there's still *one* truth, and that's my bride.

Her love for her dad and her being worried about me enough to marry me.

And I can't fucking tarnish that.

My lips stop before they can make contact with her trembling ones. Eyes closed, Daisy looks like a sacrificial virgin.

Possessiveness roars inside my chest, and my usual instinct to find immediate safety extends to her. I want to protect her and keep her away from all the eyes that have been judging her for the past few weeks and will continue to do so after today, and even years later when we split up.

I tip her chin up and turn to the side. The back of my head covers us from prying eyes as I place a kiss on her cheek, right at the corner of her lips. Her eyes open, and instead of nerves, they now shine with confusion.

Of course she's confused, you fool!

It's not that I've given her many reasons to trust me.

But I'm not prepared for the blazing emotions that swirl in her gaze the next instant, as if she'd rather see me in a casket right now than next to her at the altar.

My cousins continue to hoot as I navigate my new bride along the dance floor. My palm grazes over the crystals on her dress, which shine as if stars have come down to earth tonight. When I tug her closer, she's stiffer than a washboard. Thinking she doesn't like the contact, I move away.

"You can touch me. I'm not *that* contagious." Her teeth grit.

That's the first and last thing Daisy says to me throughout the ceremony. She continues to smile for our families, the cameras, and even the creepy reporters, but it's me she has difficulty looking in the eye.

Is she realizing that this deal doesn't work for her?

Too bad. She's already Mrs. Charles Hawthorne.

When we're finally alone in the car and I have my chance to ask Daisy what's up with her mood, my sister slides in.

"Don't make such a sad face, Charlie. It's not like you

don't see Daisy every day in the office." Chloe wrinkles her nose playfully, giving me a mock-serious look.

My sister has had me wrapped around her little finger since the day she was born, and I'm more than happy to oblige to her demands, even if I don't always show it.

"Are you here because you expect me to thank you for coming home in a rush and possibly losing a hell of a lot of money for canceling contracts last minute?" I tip my head to the side.

There might be almost a decade age gap between us, but my little sister is an icon in the fashion world. What started as a hobby when she used to help my dad's sister, Aunt Clementine, at her work, transformed into a career.

Chloe Hawthorne isn't just one of the leading fashion designers in the world, but also one of the top models.

"I could go bankrupt, but I'd never miss my brother's wedding." She grins and even Daisy snorts at her.

"You are the last person who could go bankrupt, Chloe." My wife's smile is still in place, maybe because she hasn't looked at me, her happiness buster, since the car started. "I can't believe you made my wedding gown and bridesmaid dresses in such a short time."

"Don't worry. I had some excellent help. Plus, I don't plan to do anything except eat and sleep for the next week."

"And in which city will you be doing all this sleeping and eating?" I ask just before the car halts at the security gate of my property.

"Cherrywood."

Chloe's gaze drops, and Daisy finally looks at me, her teeth worrying her bottom lip. Since she moved out, my sister has avoided Cherrywood and anything that relates to it with a burning passion. I'm shocked that she came home the moment I told her I was getting married.

"Does that mean you're moving back permanently?" I keep my voice calm, burying the hope and confusion away.

"Let's say for the foreseeable time."

"What changed?" I ask carefully, the simplest and safest question I can think of.

"Maybe I did." Chloe gives me a conspiratorial smile that doesn't fully reach her eyes before stepping out of the car.

I help Daisy with the train of her wedding dress even when she's gone back to ignoring me. We walk along the pavement and I realize my safest place won't be just mine anymore.

I'm about to use my key card to open the door when Chloe shoves my hand away and shakes her head in resignation.

"I knew you would be this stupid, Charlie. That's why I'm here."

Now I've upset both my sister and my wife without having any fucking clue how.

"Please tell me my brother is a little more romantic."

Daisy snorts, and the two girls give me an irritated look before grinning at each other in total cahoots.

"I can be romantic if I want to be."

"Then can you summon that Romeo alter ego right now? Because I want you to cross the threshold holding Daisy in your arms," my sister quips.

"What?"

The single word leaves Daisy's and my mouth at the same time. At last, we're on the same page about *something* today.

"I want you to have the best married life, Charlie. If there's a zero point one percent chance that a marriage tradition is going to bring good luck, I'm not letting you ignore it."

Now, how could someone say no to that?

I take Daisy's silence as a yes and place my arm over her bare shoulder. Her skin is cold, and I don't know if it's because of the chill of the weather or if the goose bumps come to attention in response to my touch.

I bend to hold her in my arms. She's light and fits perfectly, even with the weight of her dress, as if she was meant to be here. Her gaze is fixed on my sister, and her expression hasn't changed.

How is she acting like being so close to me is completely normal for her, while my heart is pounding so hard I might have a heart attack?

Her indifference and not knowing the reason behind it frustrates the hell out of me.

I walk inside and place Daisy down in the living room amidst my sister's claps and the huge smiles of the waiting house staff. Daisy has already met my housekeeper, but today she meets everyone.

God, I didn't know we'd have this welcome committee. My sister must have arranged this, because there's no other reason why Mrs. Kowalski wouldn't run this by me first.

The staff welcomes Daisy and hands her a bouquet, a genuine smile on their faces, and for the first time today, I don't hate being the center of attention.

"My work here is done." Chloe hugs Daisy first,

whispering something in her ear that makes my new wife smile genuinely.

When she reaches me, my sister throws her arms around my neck. "I'm so happy for you, Charlie. I wish you the best married life forever."

Guilt settles on me like a heavy weight. I'll rot in hell for lying to my little sister, who wipes away the tears from the corner of her eyes, oblivious to my reality.

After Chloe sprints away, I guide Daisy to my bedroom with a hand against her back.

Our bedroom.

There's nothing in this house that's going to be just yours any longer.

She's stiffer than a board under my touch, but I get some relief as she looks closely at her new surroundings. The hallway leading to the bedroom is lined with decor items, though not handpicked by me, but it speaks of my taste.

"You and I will sleep here. I can't risk the staff knowing the truth about us." I nod toward the room as the door closes behind us.

"Of course you can't."

Her clipped words finally snap the tiny latch that's been locking down my anxiety for the past week.

"Is there a problem, Daisy?" I tip my head to the side and cross my arms over my chest.

"Not at all." Her irritated gaze drifts from the king-sized bed to me, and she plasters on a fake smile.

I'm still struggling with the right words to say when Daisy turns around, about to march in the direction of her bags, which were brought in earlier.

"I'm tired. If you would just let me know where I sleep, I'll stop being a nuisance to you."

I snag her elbow, stopping her movement. "Nuisance? Where the hell is this coming from?"

"Oh, so you mean I misread your grimace when you saw me walking down the aisle? Or was it the fact that my husband couldn't kiss me because he's so much better than the rest of the world?"

Daisy doesn't stop for me to respond. Her free arm flails while the other still remains in my grip.

"I know this marriage is for show," she continues, "and you possibly hated everything about today, the crowd, the noise, but this was my first freaking wedding. A day that was supposed to be the most beautiful prelude to all my dreams coming true. Would it have killed you to pretend just for a few hours? Would it have killed you to kiss me and not pretend that I was—"

My lips land on hers before she can compare herself to anything less than perfection. I kiss her like I'd wanted when I saw her walking toward me.

Daisy grabs the lapels of my tux, and my hand on her waist pulls her closer to me. I don't stop until my arm around her middle is tight as a steel band.

She wants the real me? She'll get the real me.

I tug her hair back and she loses her balance, but I'm here—to hold her, to kiss her, to tell her without words that she can be a lot of things in my life, but a nuisance is certainly not one of them.

My palm wraps around the back of her neck and I kiss her senseless. We move to a rhythm. Her lips are soft, smooth like her skin, which rasps against my stubble.

For so long, I've seen her from afar, kept my brain from imagining anything that could really get me in trouble with labor laws, but right now, all that pent-up imagination has found an acting reprieve.

The world comes to a standstill as I kiss her in the middle of my room, a place that has always been my safest sanctuary. But tonight, I see her, feel her, taste her in every air molecule in here, and I *like* it.

Daisy's grip on my jacket tightens, moving to my shirt before her hands flatten over my chest. I hate that it's not my bare skin getting her touch.

"Charles," she breathes against my lips when we take a break for air.

But I'm not ready for this to end.

My mind, my body, hasn't gotten its fill. Will it ever when it comes to Daisy?

I don't speak a word but tug her hair harder, and once again my lips are on hers. Kissing, nipping, sucking, and bottling her inside me.

She stands on the toes of her high heels, and my grip around her middle tightens as Daisy's hand loops around my neck. She rakes her fingers through my hair, and I feel a pulse run throughout my entire body.

Next time when we break, my mouth is on her neck, breathing in that familiar flower scent. She makes a sound that is somewhere between a whine and a groan, and I know if we stay like this for any longer, I won't be able to hold back anymore.

My knuckles stroke her cheek, and I don't recognize my own growling voice in her ear.

"We've played enough for the camera. I thought you'd

agree. Does any of this look like I don't want to kiss you or that you're a nuisance to me?"

There's no way she missed my hard cock, which could be used in place of a hammer to stick nails into walls, or my pounding heart, which could break an echocardiogram machine right now.

Instead of replying to me, Daisy's eyes remain closed even when I take a step back. She inhales another deep breath and then finally lets go of my suit and opens her eyes.

"The groom doesn't have to empty an entire bottle of cologne on his wedding day, Charles."

I can't help my chuckle, the buried anxiousness from the day slowly finding a release. "How long were you thinking of that comment?"

"Since you leaned in to help me with the ring, *sweetheart*. I'm sure you shocked the minister with that endearment."

This time my laugh is loud, and I throw my head back. "Except for you wanting to kill me, I think the day went well. What do you say?"

Daisy is finally smiling her usual smile, where her cheeks turn rosy and her eyes crinkle. "I say you did exceptionally well, Mr. Hawthorne. Can you continue this stellar performance of being a gentleman and sit with me for a while?"

"And do what?" I raise an eyebrow.

"Talk, like normal people," Daisy replies as she flops onto the turquoise couch placed under the tall windows. Her gaze wanders to the multiple books about leadership and business on the table and bookshelf.

I didn't know my private reading nook surrounded by indoor plants would someday become a conversation spot.

But I didn't know a lot of things.

Including how it's impossible to look away from Daisy, still in her wedding dress, looking all-so mine, and not remember how her lips felt a few moments back.

"I can *only* offer to listen." I take a seat on the opposite side of the couch.

"That will do."

And then without any preamble, she demands what I didn't offer, like always—speaking.

"Your parents are so in love. Was it always like that, even when you were a kid?"

"Kristy isn't my birth mother." My straight reply causes her smile to vanish in an instant.

"Really? I'm sorry. I didn't know, Charles." Daisy's stricken face makes me realize that as much as I like silencing people in a boardroom, it's no fun with my new *wife*.

"That's because Kristy loves me a lot. And don't worry, the woman who gave birth to me isn't dead."

"She wasn't at the wedding. You don't talk to her?" Daisy gnaws at her bottom lip, as if it was her duty to ensure that woman's presence at the ceremony.

"Daisy, as soon as my dad declared he wasn't interested in the Hawthorne family money, a lot of people dropped out of our lives. I have no intention of pulling those selfish souls back in." My fists clench. I'm one second away from getting off the couch and walking away before horrid memories I keep locked away find their release, but then Daisy places her hand over mine.

Just her touch is enough to loosen all my corded muscles.

"I…I'm so sorry."

"I thought you wanted to talk and not interrogate." I tip my head to the side.

"Um, yeah. I'm sorry. Now I can't remember what I wanted to talk about." Daisy looks at me, her doe-shaped eyes marked with a touch of guilt.

"Maybe about *your* parents."

"Oh yeah! But first, thanks for joining me here anyway."

"You're welcome. It's not like I have a multi-billion-dollar business waiting for me outside this room."

"Charles A. Hawthorne! Did you just make a joke?"

"It wasn't a joke but sarcasm." I hide my smile from her twinkling eyes by ducking my head and swiping away an invisible wrinkle on my pant leg. "So what was it about your parents that needs discussing at ten in the night?"

"It's not the time but the day." She rolls her eyes and mutters a few expletives as she usually does when I'm being extra difficult. "Do you know my parents celebrated three anniversaries every year?"

"I don't understand."

"The day Dad saw Mom the first time—love at first sight. The day he took her out on their first date—finding their soulmate. And the day they finally got married—starting their happily ever after. They did that every year."

"It's...something." And too much work.

Is she expecting this from me too?

The day she nicknamed me Charles Asshole Hawthorne.

The day I made her the proposition of a fake wedding.

The day we fooled our family and friends.

"You can relax that tensed jaw, Charles. I'm just

remembering my mom on this day. Another interesting fact—my parents never had any meals without the other."

"And what if they were in different towns? Don't tell me that never happened."

"Of course not, silly. But there's something called the telephone."

"And what if one of them was invited to a lunch or dinner *individually*?"

Why the hell am I so adamant on proving to her that what her parents did or had isn't practical for most people?

As if the same question is running through her mind, Daisy raises an eyebrow. "Who knows better than you that invitations can be avoided or adjusted to what one wants?"

I can't hide my smile this time. "Touché, my dear wife."

Her eyes widen at the title that rolled off my tongue without a second thought, but when I make no big deal out of it, her smile slowly returns.

"What I'm trying to say is that I thought my life would turn out like theirs. I might not be the most professionally ambitious person in a room, but I wanted to be formidable in love."

My heart stops at the shine in her eyes. Her life expectations are completely opposite of mine. I'm downright scared of love, and since fear has no space in my life, I scraped everything away that ignited that feeling.

Once again, it becomes clear that ours is the most imperfect match.

"Thank you for coming to my talk and taking time away from your billion-dollar business." Daisy finally gets up from the couch, her wedding dress making a rustling sound as she moves.

"If I didn't have time for my wife on our wedding day,

I'm sure I'd top the Worst Husband of the Year list. I'm happy being in third or fourth place."

"So, there's somewhere Charles Hawthorne doesn't like being on top?"

"It appears so, my dear wife."

I stay on the couch, legs crossed, and enjoy the way her cheeks turn pink, the only indication she gives that the nickname affects her somehow.

"Good to know." Daisy's voice shakes before she clears her throat. "Since sleeping in separate rooms isn't an option, what's the plan, boss?"

"You take the bed and I'll take the couch." I've thought about this the whole week, and that's the easiest solution, even though allowing someone in my personal space is anything but easy. But this is Daisy, a person who has never been just *someone*.

"You'll hear no arguments from this obedient assistant." Flashing another smile, Daisy goes for her bags while I chuckle.

"Half of the closet space is for you."

Her brows pull together, and she discards the half-opened zipper of her bag and stands tall.

"I asked the staff to leave your bags as they were in case you don't like others touching your stuff."

"Of course you would think so."

Is she making fun of my habits?

What if she is? Why do I care? She knew what she was getting into.

Having no genuine reason to simply stare at my wife any longer, I get up and walk toward the closet.

I remove my gold cufflinks that are embossed with the

Hawthorne crest and place them onto the glass tray. After taking off my suit jacket, I'm removing the bow tie when a throat clears behind me. My eyes snap up to Daisy's reflection in the mirror. It's impossible to miss the warm tingling sensation that starts from my chest and radiates outward at the sight. Daisy has taken off her heels and she suddenly looks too small, too fragile.

"Is it okay if I use your bathroom? But be warned, I'll need at least thirty minutes since I have two dozen hairpins secured in my hair right now."

I leave the loose bow tie hanging around my neck and turn around.

"Daisy, this is your room, your home, too. You don't have to ask my permission for anything. Take the bathroom for as long as you need to. There are four bathrooms in this house for my use."

Her furrowed forehead relaxes. "On a scale of one to ten, how high is your panic meter at seeing me encroach upon your private space, Charles?"

I can't even help my grin. "I think you know the answer to that question, since you know me so well, Miss Price."

"I'm going by Mrs. Hawthorne these days, boss." She winks and turns around, escalating my heartbeat with her words.

Fucking hell.

Why the hell was it so hot to hear that title on her lips?

After taking a shower in the guest bathroom and changing into track pants and a T-shirt, I situate myself on the couch, sifting through my unread emails. I try to focus on the work, but my gaze keeps drifting toward the locked bathroom door, especially with Daisy's muffled voice coming through intermittently as she speaks to herself—which I verified when I heard her say her name a few times as I was near the door *by coincidence.*

Thirty minutes later, the door of the bathroom opens, and my pulse ricochets against my rib cage. Dressed in a silk white PJ set with colorful butterflies, Daisy saunters inside holding a hanger with her wedding dress. Her face is wiped clean of makeup, and her hair is pulled up in some sort of messy bun.

The thud in my chest intensifies as I watch her looking so beautiful without even trying.

"Charles!" Daisy waves her hands before me, and I realize I've completely zoned out.

"What?" I adjust my laptop, which is on the verge of falling, and also to hide the reaction she's having on me.

"I asked what the sound you made was?"

Fuck, what did I say?

"There was no sound. And if you don't mind, I'm trying to catch up on some work."

Her expression remains confused for a beat longer, until she shrugs. "If you say so."

I breathe freely only when she's on the bed, tugging the covers over her. Daisy turns off the lights and whispers, "Good night, Charles. I know how much you like your silence. I'll try to fall asleep quickly and quietly."

"Don't worry, Daisy. I'm considering your chatter a white noise to my silence these days."

I hear her snort and wait for some smartass one-of-a-kind comment, but what really comes forces me to bite my lip so as to not burst out in laughter and wake up my sleeping *snoring* wife.

Mrs. Hawthorne is a damn snorer.

sixteen

Be a Good Wife

Daisy

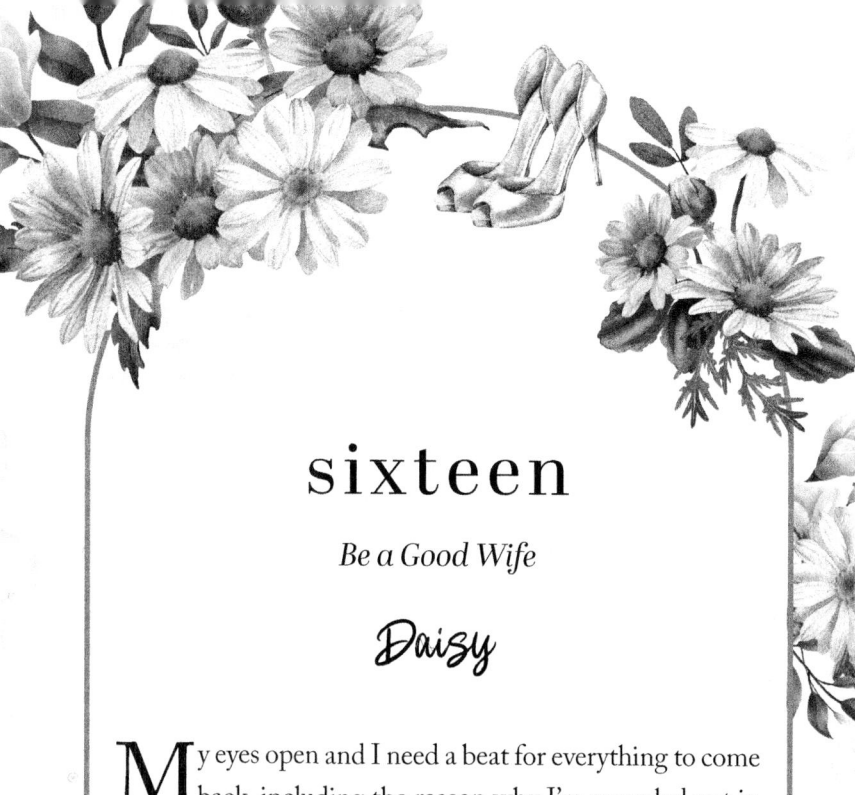

My eyes open and I need a beat for everything to come back, including the reason why I'm sprawled out in a room that looks fancier than a first-class hotel room.

It's no hard guess which side is Charles' on this bed. There are two leadership books neatly stacked on the nightstand, along with his notepad with an engraved Hawthorne crest and a matching ballpoint pen.

And of course it's also the one I claimed last night.

Did I do it intentionally? Of course not. I was too nervous to make all those observations yesterday.

If anything, last night was a gift of revelations in so many ways. For the last four years, I've wondered if my boss even sleeps in his expensive tailor-made three-piece suits, but God, those suits fade in comparison to how Charles looks in black track pants and a matching T-shirt. The corded muscles of his neck, his shoulder blades, and that broad chest that remains hidden was all there for my eyes and my eyes only. The time he spends in the gym is definitely worth it if this is the result, and for a change, I'm happy that Charles hides all this masculinity behind his suits.

His usually perfect hair was a bit amiss, one dark blond curl falling over his forehead as he read his emails, his forehead furrowing in the process.

I couldn't have spelled my name if someone had asked me, so noticing which side of the bed I claimed was definitely not in my focus.

But he didn't correct me.

Is he the same man who guards his private space tighter than the security at the Louvre?

I slowly rise, resting my weight on my elbows behind my back and peering at the couch.

But it's bare, without a trace of a pillow or the black duvet Charles had near his feet last night.

I glance at the clock, and it's been eight hours since the man whom I nicknamed asshole kissed me right in the middle of this room. My fingers involuntarily drift to my lips, but they weren't the only thing Charles touched last night. His grip was on my shoulders and my waist, and his fingers locked in my hair, tugging just enough to make me feel alive.

And then there was his unmistakable erection sliding against my stomach. Even through layers and layers of my wedding gown, I could feel it as Charles slightly rocked me, rubbing me over his hard length. I'm not a virgin, but Charles' touch was damn powerful in a way I've never been touched before.

"What the heck?" I almost lurch at the sound of the cuckoo bird call that is accompanied by the sound of a gong from Charles' wall clock.

My thighs jerk and I'm wetter than I've ever been, making me aware of new information—the memory of kissing my husband is my personalized and most potent foreplay.

I get out of bed and go in search of the man who's the leading star of my dreams and thoughts these days. It doesn't take much effort to find Charles, dressed immaculately in a fine black suit with a cup of black coffee before him. His gaze lifts from the tablet in his hand, where he's busy reading the morning business news.

How do I know this?

Because I'm the one authorizing the payments for all those annual subscriptions, plus I've memorized my boss' schedule by heart.

Yet, you didn't know a whole lot about him—like he can melt you like butter with just a touch of his lips.

"Good morning." I do a small wave when Charles simply stares at me for a beat. I wait for him to comment on me getting up so late and still being in my pajamas, but nothing.

Instead, Charles places the tablet back onto the table and rises from his chair. I freeze in place when he walks toward me.

"It's definitely a good morning. You are finally mine, Mrs. Hawthorne." His lips, which usually remain flat, curl to one side before he holds my face.

My breathing stops and my brain short-circuits when his thumb runs along my cheek before he leans in. My eyes fall closed as I wait for a peck like yesterday at the altar, because of course I know Charles losing control last night in his bedroom was something that happens probably once in a decade. But when his lips touch mine, fireworks go off in my head. His mouth, even though closed the entire time, works like magic.

When Charles finally pulls back, my hands are clutching his perfectly pressed suit jacket, leaving wrinkles in their wake. His one hand is still on my face, while the other is wrapped around my waist, supporting me in place.

"Definitely a good morning." He winks, and before I can ask him what the hell is going on, his housekeeper, Mrs. K, as she's called by everyone *but* Charles, clears her throat.

So much for not kissing for an audience. Hypocrite.

"Good morning, Mrs. Hawthorne. How do you take your coffee?" Her eyes crinkle with amusement as if surprised by this side of her boss.

That makes two of us.

"She'll have two sugars and half a cup of milk." Charles doesn't even bother looking at her as he leads me to the chair next to him, surprising me some more.

"How do you know how I take my coffee?" I hiss while he replies with a grin.

For someone who can't keep that perpetual scowl away for less than two seconds, he definitely met a happiness fairy and got dusted with some happiness dust this morning.

"What sort of husband would I be if I didn't know that about my dear wife?"

Every time he says those three words, *my dear wife*, I feel a small zing going through my spine.

"I was waiting for you to show up for breakfast," Charles adds.

"I'm not hungry this morning," I mumble absently. This new version of Charles seems to have stolen my hunger and thirst, at least temporarily.

"Oh." His grin slips but he recovers fast. "Then if you don't mind, I'll leave for the office. You can take the day off, if you'd like. You are a new bride, after all."

Take a day off.

He continues to fire the surprise cannon relentlessly.

You want acting? You got it, Hawthorne.

My hands find his tie and I tug him closer. His eyes flare with a foreign expression for a second, so fleeting that I might have just guessed it, until he smiles and leans further in, making me gulp. But I push away those butterflies that have started to take flight every time Charles is around me.

"I'll miss you too much if I stay home, husband. You can expect me at my desk in the next hour," I coo in a honey-dipped voice.

"I'll be counting the seconds, Mrs. Hawthorne." His smile is so wide that I almost die.

He kisses the tip of my nose, and I want to bawl like a child at the sweetness of it all.

How dare he act so well.

Charles grabs his bag and saunters toward the main door, which opens right on cue. Dave's hand stays at the knocker, and he speaks into his earpiece, alerting Steve about Charles' move.

But everything dies in the background when, just before leaving through the heavy door, Charles looks over his shoulder. His eyes meet mine, and I suck in a breath of air.

"You look beautiful in butterflies, Mrs. Hawthorne." His lips tip to one side, and then he's gone.

What the heck?

My gaze skids from the door to my PJs, which have colorful butterflies, until I close my eyes hoping my racing heartbeat will calm down.

Before that can happen, I hear Mrs. Kowalski behind me. "Are you sure I can't get you anything, Mrs. Hawthorne? Maybe some eggs or pancakes?"

"Please call me Daisy like you used to, Mrs. K. I don't want everything to change." Especially when my boss is filling every quota in that department.

I'm about to refuse the food again when my stomach rumbles loudly. In all my nervousness yesterday, I barely ate anything, and it seems the smell of coffee and the offer of pancakes is enough to bring back my lost appetite.

"My stomach likes the pancake offer." I smile sheepishly.

"I'm happy to hear that. Just give me a few minutes and I'll have your breakfast ready."

When she leaves, I send a text to Kai.

Me: Hi. How's Dad doing? Was yesterday too much exhaustion for him?

Kai: Not at all.

He sends me a picture of Dad focused deeply on his iPad.

Kai: He's searching the latest fashions for older men. To set his social media image right from the start.

I can't help my laugh.

Me: I don't know if I should be happy or bothered about my dad's newfound addiction.

Kai: Don't worry. I have it under control.

Me: Thank you so much. You're a godsend.

"Can I take my breakfast to the bedroom?" I ask Mrs. Kowalski as she gently places a plate of pancakes next to my coffee mug.

"This is your home, Daisy. You don't need anyone's permission here. Definitely not mine." She gives me that warm smile once again.

"Does Charles ever eat in his room?"

"I think you know Mr. Hawthorne better than anyone."

This time I match her grin with my own.

"So that's a big fat no. Then I'd like to show his room some change."

Your bedroom is no longer a breakfast spot virgin, my dear husband.

Mrs. Kowalski arranges my plate and coffee mug along with cutlery and a napkin on a wooden tray.

"In all the years of me working in this house, today is the first time Mr. Hawthorne acted out of his routine. He needed someone just like you in his life. I'm so happy to see you here, Daisy."

Guilt slithers inside me, but I keep my smile in place. "Thank you."

Once back in my room, I check my cellphone and

there's a missed call from Charles. I take a deep breath before pressing the green call sign on the screen.

"Wife." His voice is cool like a breeze, and goose bumps litter my skin in its wake.

"If you are in the limo and the privacy screen is up, there's no need for pretensions, Charles."

He chuckles, and for some absurd reason I like the sound of it.

"Every second, you continue to prove that my decision about this marriage was absolutely perfect."

"Your ego will someday kill you." I bite my bottom lip to hide my smile.

"My darling wife wanting me dead the day after our wedding? I must be a really cruel husband."

Gosh! Who the heck is this man?

I need some extra preparation to win against this version of Charles.

"What do you want, boss?"

"I want you to check that everything is okay for Vincent's project. There's an email about issues with the construction material. See what's going on there. Vincent is one of our biggest clients. His project takes priority over everything else."

"On it." I put the phone on speaker and open the email app.

"Also, there's a board meeting late this afternoon."

"But it wasn't on the schedule." I pause and jump into the calendar app while Charles hums in agreement.

"It appears that after seeing us yesterday, no one has any more doubts. I once again have you to thank for everything, my dear wife."

"I'd prefer a raise."

"Let's talk about that later."

Charles' chuckle ringing in my ear is so foreign. In this moment, I also realize he's rarely called me in the past, always preferring text to calls.

"Why did you call me, Charles?" I ask carefully.

He's quiet for a while and then says in that guarded tone of his, "I'll be getting home late."

"You could have sent me a text." Another long pause, but I wait, knowing well that pulling words out of his mouth is like pulling teeth.

"I won't be joining you for dinner at home. Don't wait for me."

It takes me a few moments to process his words, and finally it clicks.

I stare at the warm breakfast before me.

"Charles, did you—"

"I gotta go, Daisy. But I want the construction crew on Vincent's site today."

The call ends but the phone remains tucked against my ear. I grab the untouched breakfast tray and walk back to the kitchen.

Mrs. Kowalski leaves the carnations and scissors beside the vase and approaches me as I place the food onto the table. "Is something not right, dear?"

"Um, no. Did Charles eat breakfast this morning, Mrs. K?"

She shakes her head before a slow smile takes over her lips. "I think he was waiting for you."

Oh, my!

"I didn't know! He could have at least told me so."

"You and I both know Mr. Hawthorne guards his emotions fiercely. But don't worry, he'll probably eat something in the office."

Or he won't, because my fake husband seems to have taken my parents' story to heart.

"I hate doing this, but can you please store this for me in the fridge? I'll have it for dinner. Charles is going to be late and will eat out."

"Don't worry, Daisy. I'll send this plate for Steve. That man will eat anything with sugar and syrup. You just let me know in the evening what you'd like to have for dinner, and I'll make you something fresh."

"Thank you so much. You're the best."

I still can't get over the fact that Charles Hawthorne, the man who would rather cut off an arm than let go of his routine, skipped breakfast because of me.

By the time I reach the office, my brain is a hurricane of conflicting emotions. I'm almost tempted to give a name to this feeling that is equal parts attraction and irritation for Charles—*irri-attraction*.

My steps come to halt when I spot a gift box on my desk. With shaky legs, I approach it, and the thunder in my heart returns as I read the ivory paper engraved with a Hawthorne crest.

My dear wife,

This is your wedding present. It's not something from your list, but I think you will like it.

Your husband,
Charles A. Hawthorne.

My fingers brush against the letters, tracing the black ink.

Who knew you could be such an amazing husband, Charles?

Once I tear off the wrapping paper, I can't stop laughing. So hard that my belly hurts.

It's a pair of furry slippers with butterflies and *Best Wife* written on their wings.

It's cheesy, corny, and everything that my husband isn't. Or the man I knew until yesterday.

I slip out of my heels and put the slippers on. A groan slips out of me as my feet meet the plush fur. I snap a picture, making sure that my purple-painted toenails are clearly visible.

> **Me:** I give you 10/10 on your performance as a husband. In fact, I think you're even compensating for your asshole, bossy vibes with this new charm.

Boss aka Charles Asshole
Hawthorne: Don't worry, that asshole boss isn't far away.

While the three dots dance under his text, indicating he's still typing something, I change his name on my contact list.

Husband aka Charles Adorable
Hawthorne: This gift is also to remind you who you are, Mrs. Hawthorne. Now be a good wife and get to work.

This time I don't even try to stop the butterflies taking

flight inside my stomach as I imagine Charles repeating those same words, but we're talking about a very different type of work.

I fan my face and drop my phone on my desk.

You are going to hell, Daisy.

Get to work means get to work and not think about Charles' beautiful face graced by a five o'clock shadow, his pink lips, which are so soft and full that they make me jealous and hot at the same time, or his erection, which feels like it could take any girl on the ride of her life.

It takes another half hour for me to bring my focus back on the work at hand.

I sift through my inbox and move a ton of congratulatory emails to a separate folder so I don't forget to reply with a personal note of thanks later. Finally, I reach the email about Vincent's site and am shocked to find the construction union rep complaining about the weak infrastructure and unsafe working conditions.

I go through the reports and call the head of the construction company.

"Good morning, Mr. Buffay. This is Daisy from Hawthorne Holdings. What's going on with the new construction site? I thought everything was on track."

"Hi, Daisy. I mean…Mrs. Hawthorne."

We both pause until I clear my throat and smile, even though the older man can't see it. "Please call me Daisy. It's worked all these years."

"Sounds good. First of all, congratulations on the wedding. I didn't expect you to be back to work already."

"One day off for the wedding day was enough of a break

for Charles, and I didn't want my husband to miss his second wife—his work—too much."

He chuckles. "You're a funny one, as always. Regarding the construction"—his voice gets serious—"I have no idea what changed in the last forty-eight hours. Everything was going as planned until two days back."

"Can you meet me at the site and we can figure out what's going on?"

"Sure. If you like, I can pick you up at your office."

"Oh, that'll be good. Then I'll wait for your call when you're close to the Hawthorne Tower." It's not the first time I'll be riding with one of our business partners for work.

"You got it."

An hour later, Mr. Buffay and I are standing outside the building, if we can use that term for the four walls that sway with a heavy gust of wind.

I tug on the collar of my coat to stop my shivering in the cold. My teeth chatter as I turn to Mr. Buffay. "Let's get in and then we can talk to the workers and the supervisor."

But when we step inside, the place is empty except for one worker, who's also hurrying to the door.

"Hi, sir. Where is everyone?"

"Everyone's gone." The worker looks over his shoulder. "This place isn't safe."

"Wait, please." I run after him, which is a dangerous thing to do in heels in this place that's on the verge of falling any minute. "Where's your supervisor?"

"He was the first to leave once we found out that the

construction material is dirt cheap. It's unsafe and hazardous. This place will collapse any minute. If you're here for proof, you can check the super's office. There are some files and reports." With those departing words, the worker in blue overalls leaves without waiting for any more of my questions.

"It's impossible," Mr. Buffay mumbles, wiping away the sweat beads from his forehead.

He's right to be nervous.

If what the worker said is correct, Charles will not tolerate this. He'll want Buffay's head and maybe even mine for picking Buffay Construction for one of the biggest high-stake Hawthorne Holdings projects.

"I should go to the warehouse and talk to the person in charge." Buffay presses several buttons on his phone, possibly reprimanding his staff in text. "I'll drop you off first, and then—"

"No, you go. I'll call Steve, but first I want to gather all the paperwork from the super's office. If there's anything in there that can tell us what happened here, I'll find it out."

"Are you sure? I don't like leaving you here, Daisy. It's not safe." He grimaces as he looks around.

"Don't worry. If this place stayed for two days, I'm sure it'll stay for another ten minutes. I'll text Steve right now."

> **Me:** Can you come to this address and pick me up, please?

I show the text to Mr. Buffay.

"We need to figure out what the hell happened here by the end of the day. Believe me, Charles is not looking forward to hearing this, so I'd like us to at least have a plan for how we're getting back on track."

The old man cringes. "I understand completely. I'm going to leave now, but you call me when you reach your office so I know you are safe."

"I will."

After he leaves, I walk past the brick walls and finally locate a small makeshift office.

The walls in this room are plastered, and there's a small light bulb hanging from the ceiling. There's a chair that looks like it was delivered recently, with the untorn plastic still intact. I flop down on it and grab the manila folder on the table.

Everything clearly shows that whoever was put in charge by Mr. Buffay was not doing their job, unless it was to mooch money off their boss.

My gaze lands on my watch, and I realize it's already been forty minutes.

Where is Steve?

I grab my phone from my purse and realize two things—I never sent the text, and my phone is almost dead. Of course, with everything that happened last night, plugging my phone in to charge was the last thing on my mind.

The moment I hit send, my phone turns off.

Crap.

I grab the charger from my purse and find an electric outlet. Right when I flip a light switch on, a spark hits the bulb, which crashes down to the floor. A squeal leaves my lips when the wall next to the door collapses, and I find myself leaning against the only two walls that are still erect.

seventeen

Boner - A Bone or a Tissue?

Charles

It's five in the evening when I step inside the meeting room where the board members and Grandma Irene are waiting for me. I'm about to take a seat when my phone vibrates in my pocket. I look down at an unknown number and slide it back.

"Irene, Charles, thank you for making time on such short notice. But we would all like to fix something," says Tim Baldwin. He's one of the oldest board members, and also one of my granddad's closest friends.

"But before we do that, we have something for you." He grabs a huge bouquet of purple carnations decorated with paper butterflies. My mind immediately slips to the picture of Daisy's feet wearing the fuzzy slippers.

Chloe had been hounding me since the day our wedding date was finalized to buy something for my new bride. As much as I don't like to admit it, I've never been able to say no to my sister.

While scouring the internet for some expensive jewelry, I found an advertisement for unorthodox gifts and saw the slippers. The rest was easy.

What I didn't know was watching her wear them and the hint of her toenails, would affect my mind and body this way. But it's not just the picture.

It's her.

Everything about her since we returned home last evening is different.

The way she demanded my kiss.

The way she felt in my arms.

Her bee-stung, heart-shaped lips, which taste fucking delicious.

Her soft skin, which makes me want to never pull my hand away.

The scent of her perfume.

My fist tightens against my thigh.

This is not the time to be fucking horny, Charles.

I adjust my suit before I rise and accept the flowers. I've just taken my seat when the door of the meeting room pulls open. Something sharp digs in my chest when Dave's eyes find mine, and he walks in.

There has to be an emergency for him to interrupt.

"What is it?" I ask as soon as he's near me.

"It's Mrs. Hawthorne, sir," he whispers only for my ears.

"Mom?" I ask, my heart thumping hard.

Dave shakes his head. "It's Daisy."

Fear digs its claws into my chest, and I find my ability

to breathe becoming progressively more difficult with each second that passes.

"She went to the new construction site with a business partner, and he just now called to check if she's returned. Steve is on his way, but we're much closer to the site. I don't want to leave you, but—"

"Let's go." I'm already marching toward the door when Grandma calls my name.

"Charles? Where are you going?"

"I need to go. It's urgent."

Without a second thought, I leave the room. We step into the elevator, and Dave clears his throat.

"I know what this meeting means for you, Mr. Hawthorne. I can check up on Mrs. Hawthorne—"

"I don't like people questioning me, Dave, especially the ones I expect to be by my side. And I want to know what happened today and why the fuck Steve wasn't with Daisy."

The man nods and doesn't say anything further. I'll feel bad about barking at him sometime later. Right now, I want to bring my wife home, where I know she's safe.

My heart is in my throat at the sight before me. The building is partially collapsed, and I hope with everything in me that if Daisy is inside, she's safe in the only tower still standing.

I'm about to enter when Steve parks my McLaren next to the limo in a hurry.

"Mr. Hawthorne, I'm so sorry, sir." His face is pale, as it should be. "Dave and I will safely get Mrs. Hawthorne. Please wait here, sir."

"Do you really think I'm going to trust anyone after this? You better have a damn good reason for not being with Daisy, Steve."

Without waiting for his apology, I enter the building, my bodyguards following closely behind. The farther I walk inside, the more the lasso of fear tightens around my chest.

"Daisy." My panicked call for her is met with no response.

What the fuck are you doing here all alone, Daisy?

We split in different directions. I make a second left and continue to holler her name, until I hear a faint "Yes" in her soft, shivery voice.

Thank fucking God.

"Charles."

I rush in her direction as fast as I can, trying not to think about the debris crunching under my footsteps.

I finally reach what might have been an office. The door has collapsed, along with the neighboring walls, which have fallen on each other and closed the entire space.

"Daisy, I'm here."

Her low sniffles cut me raw. I try to ignore the grip of fear and instead focus on bringing her out.

Thankfully, Steve and Dave join me. The moment we pull away the door, my heart lurches in my mouth. Daisy is hunkered in the corner with a thick beam precariously hanging above her head, ready to fall any second. Her hands rest above her head, shielding herself.

"Charles," she whispers as if she doesn't believe I'm here.

"You're safe." My fingers tighten into a fist as I whisper, when all I want to do is scream at whoever is responsible for putting my wife in this situation.

Fresh tears run down her cheeks as she closes her eyes but makes no attempt to move.

"I thought I'd die tonight." Daisy hiccups. "I thought I'd never see Dad again, never see you." Her hands are still above her head, and she finally looks up at them. "I've been sitting like this for an hour in case the beam falls down, even though I know if it happens, I wouldn't be able to stop it. It'd probably crush my skull. I was so scared, Charles."

"I know, Daisy." *Who knows fear better than me?* "But you have to come out so I can take you home where it's safe."

She nods vehemently while tears continue to race down her cheeks. "I…I don't think I can move."

Fuck. My heart rattles against my rib cage.

Focus, Charles.

Be strong. She's here. You just have to get her out, bring her home, and then fucking destroy whoever left her here.

"Give us a minute," I instruct Steve and Dave without my gaze leaving my wife.

When they're out of earshot, I get down on my knees. But before I can say anything, she tips her chin up.

"What if everything falls down the moment I move, Charles?"

"Steve and Dave inspected the area, Daisy. It's safe for you to step out. I promise. I'm here and I'm not going to leave without you."

She nods and slowly gets on all fours before crawling toward me. My molars grind together when her palms land on the broken glass bulb. She yelps in pain but continues to move forward, her hiccups echoing in the space. The moment her knees land on the broken glass will be etched into my memory forever.

Whoever did this will have to pay for every one of her tears that fell on the ground today.

When she finally reaches me, Daisy throws herself into my arms and I catch her. She's like my oxygen right now, and without her, I can't breathe. I don't stop until we reach the limo. This evening is going to be the highlight of my nightmares for countless nights.

All my self-control snaps the moment I place Daisy into the rear seat of the car and she collapses against the seat and her eyes slowly close.

"Call the doctor, and then I want to know exactly what the fuck happened!"

I hit the privacy screen and help her rest against the back seat. Instead, Daisy falls over me. Her scraped hands grip the lapels of my gray jacket, leaving red marks on the expensive fabric.

After grabbing two paper napkins from the tray table and wetting them with water, I gently rub them against her tattered palms. Her head rolls against my chest, and I breathe in the floral scent of her perfume and shampoo.

Thankfully, there's no shards sticking out of her skin. I dispose of the soaked paper into the bin before tearing my handkerchief into two and use the scraps as a bandage on her hands.

I repeat the process and clean her knees. Daisy moans in pain, but the sound sends a jolt inside me. My free hand tightens around her naked thigh as her skirt rises up. Feeling like the biggest jerk, I push it down.

When we reach home, Mrs. Kowalski is already waiting with the doctor in the living room. Daisy rouses up slowly when I place her on the couch. There's a tense silence in the room when the doctor examines her. All my muscles tighten, and I feel there's a tornado rising inside me, struggling for release. I just need to be away from her when that happens.

"Charles?" Daisy's low voice torments me.

"I'm here, butterfly."

The nickname slips from my lips without thought. But I have no plans to take it back, especially after seeing a hint of color on her ashen face for the first time since she got home. I perch lightly on the oak wood coffee table before her and turn to her doctor.

"Why did she faint?"

"I think it's because of stress, Mr. Hawthorne. But I'd still like to run some blood work, just to be sure everything is okay and there are no surprises like any deficiencies or a pregnancy. I hope this is okay with you?"

The doctor awaits a response, but my brain hasn't processed anything beyond the p-word.

Is she goddamn pregnant?

"Mr. Hawthorne?" he asks, but I can't tear my eyes away from Daisy.

The pink on her cheeks is replaced by crimson, and it's certainly not because she's burning with anger like me.

Does she like the idea of carrying the child of that dick-pic porno star, Jax.

"Yes, it's okay with us," Daisy finally replies.

The doctor leaves, but I'm rooted in place because everything I've feared in life is knocking at my door with a roaring intensity. Silence stretches in the living room, but there's a raging tempest in my chest, ready to burst out.

"Charles." My name on Daisy's lips is a soft whisper, and when she gingerly places her hand covered in white gauze over my left knee, my control snaps.

I rise and in the next second, I've pinned Steve against the wall. "How the fuck was she alone in that hellhole today?"

The ex-Navy SEAL who scares everyone with his size and deadly looks gulps.

"Charles!" Daisy lets out a high-pitched scream while Mrs. Kowalski gasps.

But everything is white noise as my forearm digs into Steve's chest until Daisy limps toward us.

"Let Steve go." When she hisses in pain trying to push me away, I release my bodyguard and turn around in a flash.

"Will you get back on the couch?"

"No!" Daisy's eyes blaze, completely opposite to how I found her. "You need to listen to me."

"I don't need to do a fucking thing."

Especially if there's even a one percent chance that she's pregnant with that asshole's kid.

"Charles, it's not Steve's fault." As always, my assistant doesn't listen to me. "I decided to join Mr. Buffay at the site."

"Why didn't you take your own car instead of driving with a stranger?" My teeth grit.

"What?"

Daisy looks at me as if I'm speaking a different language, but I have nothing to add. My question was goddamn clear.

"It's not the first time I've accompanied a partner for work. What's changed?"

"This changed everything." I grab her hand, mindful of the bandage, where her engagement ring and wedding band shine under the bright light of the chandelier. "You are Mrs. Charles Hawthorne, in case you've forgotten."

She shoots me a withering look, but that only intensifies the fire inside me.

"And it seems there's a possibility we soon might be three."

I tug her closer, and she falls over my chest. My hand rests against her belly, and a defining thunder booms in my chest.

Daisy stiffens, and after a momentarily frozen pause, she intertwines our fingers, her trembling bandaged hands grabbing my cold ones. Her father's gold band on my finger clicks with her rings.

"Will you please give us a minute?" she mumbles to the staff and tugs me toward the bedroom.

I go willingly. I'd love to talk to her without an audience and false pretenses.

The moment the door shuts with a loud thud, Daisy jabs her finger against my chest. "You want to know why I accompanied Mr. Buffay? Because you asked me to."

Before I can call her out on this bullshit lie, she raises her hand.

"Not today. When I was first attending a meeting at the client site, I asked if your driver could drop me off, since he was already headed that way. But you refused. You said, and I quote"—she makes those stupid air quotes—"'Miss Price, the last time I checked, Steve and Dave don't receive their salary from you. You should manage like everyone else.'"

She pauses just long enough to suck in a breath. "The company policy is either I take the company car and pay for gas or take a cab. Many days, I have lots of meetings around town, and to save money, I started carpooling or taking lifts, but only after I know the person well."

"That was before I knew you couldn't drive, dammit."

She's throwing that in my face today?

Since I learned that Daisy can't drive—which is an entirely different stupidity of its own—I've made sure she has a ride always, even at the expense of me running late on some rare occasions.

"Sorry that my instincts are failing me and I'm not immediately on board like you in this marriage thing. I'm sorry that I didn't receive proper acting skills. I'm sorry that I thought I should say yes to the pregnancy test otherwise it might stir up a new set of rumors about this being fake. But you don't have to worry because I'm not pregnant. It's been a year since my jerk ex bothered to sleep with me while he was getting his dick sucked by other women. So, no, Mr. Hawthorne, there's no bastard coming to destroy your perfect plan."

Her finger jabs at my chest repeatedly with so much force that the bandage around her hand comes loose. She attempts to put it back in place but fails and gets more irritated.

I yank her closer, but she jerks out of my grasp. "I don't need your help."

But when she continues to fail, I tug on her wrist. "Either I'm doing it or I'm calling the doctor back." Before she can look away, I pin her with my gaze. "I mean it, Daisy."

She finally stops squirming, and I tie the bandage. Her rapid breathing subsides, and knowing she's safe and there are no surprises, my own heartbeat starts to settle to its normal pace.

"From this moment on, you'll drive with either Steve or Dave. I also don't want you running inside dilapidated buildings, wife."

Her pulse flutters under my touch when I call her that—*wife*. For someone who hated the idea of getting tied down, I'm enjoying riling Daisy up.

It's because you know this is temporary.

"I'll try not to make it a habit, husband." Her eyes are shining, gleaming with anger, but a slow smile finally touches her lips.

My gaze travels south from her face to her hands and scraped knees, until it settles on her bare feet. One of her purple toenails has broken.

"You hurt your feet too."

A shiver courses through her at my whispered words. Daisy's face pales again, reminding me of the moment I found her trapped under the wall.

"I...I was scared," she whispers, her eyes falling closed, and a tiny tear finds escape.

"Me too." My grip on her face is featherlight as I run my thumb over the teardrop.

Her eyes open, lips quiver, and the realization of what could have happened today brushes against me once again.

There's a reason I keep everyone at arm's length.

"Thank you for coming to save me."

Before I can reply and tell her that she never has to thank me, there's a small knock on the bedroom door.

When I open the door, Mrs. Kowalski is patiently waiting with a tea tray.

"Can I get you both some early dinner, sir? Mrs. Hawthorne hasn't eaten anything since last night."

Daisy is beside me in the next second. Without thought, I throw my arms around her waist for support.

"You didn't have breakfast?" I feel the irritation returning to my voice.

"You neither," she replies with equal fervor.

I'm not used to people butting heads with me at every step, but I didn't expect anything less from my wife. I can't stop smiling at my own stupidity.

"People call me competitive, Mrs. Hawthorne, but if they saw you, I'd easily be dethroned."

After giving me a satisfied smirk, Daisy turns to Mrs. Kowalski. "I'm not very hungry. But since I have to take the meds, can I please get a glass of milk?"

"Daisy—"

"No, you've said enough tonight, Charles. In case you've forgotten, you're not my master."

Once Mrs. Kowalski leaves, I shut the door and follow Daisy toward the closet. "I'm not trying to be difficult, but I'm not going to sit silent when I see that your safety is compromised. I can't let that happen."

Doesn't she know I'd sell my soul to protect her from any harm?
Did you *know this before today, Hawthorne?*

Daisy's irritated, furrowed forehead relaxes. "I know, and that's the *only* reason I listened."

After her dinner of a glass of milk and a quick shower she insisted on because she didn't want to smell like dust and debris, Daisy changes into another of her cute pajamas before slipping under the covers. When I step into the bathroom, next to my black towel on the towel rack is her purple one. Beside my toiletries in black packaging, her floral and colorful bottles stand out, making me aware of how much my life has changed.

I step into the shower and turn on the water, and for some reason the first droplet is enough to suck me back to when I found Daisy crammed in a corner with tears racing down her cheeks. My mouth goes dry, even as I'm surrounded by mist, and before my brain can freeze fully, I remind myself that she's safe and mostly unharmed. I crush my fists over my eyes, willing myself to stay with that emotion of relief and nothing else. When my heartbeat has finally calmed down, I step out, dry myself, and brush my teeth. I throw my toothbrush next to hers in the holder. The pink and gray bristles touch as I turn away.

Returning to the bedroom, my gaze slants to Daisy's small frame asleep on the bed.

I softly amble toward the couch and close my eyes. Images of her trapped under the rubble fill my headspace once again.

When I get up, my mouth is dry and my T-shirt is soaked in sweat.

What the fuck?

In a split second, I turn around to find Daisy safely sleeping on my bed. My hands fucking shake as I grab a glass of water before resting my head once again against the pillow.

Eyes closed, I try to think of something else, something where Daisy isn't at risk.

My wife in her wedding dress swaying side to side with her dad on the dance floor.

A zing zips through my chest as I remember the happiness on Jason's face as if right in this moment, every other problem of his life is insignificant.

You'll never get to experience that emotion, Charles, a tiny voice whispers, but I crush it before it has a chance to expand.

Instead, I remind myself that Jason might have enjoyed every part of Daisy's wedding, but he's not going to remember anything.

Next time I'm jerked out of sleep, it's not because of my dreams, but Daisy's wild cry.

I turn on the nightlight to find her thrashing, with the duvet thrown on the floor. I rush to her as tears continue racing down her cheeks, soaking the pillowcase and her hair in their wake.

"Daisy?" I call her name softly a few times, but it's like my voice doesn't even reach her.

When she moans in pain, I hold her shoulders and gently shake her.

"Daisy!"

She rises with a shriek leaving her lips.

"Hey, it's okay. You're safe."

"W-where am I?" Her teeth chatter, and I gently hold her face to find her frozen.

"You're home, butterfly. You're safe with me." I get beside her and pull her against my warm chest before bringing the covers over us.

"Can you p-please turn on the h-heat, Charles?" She continues to stutter.

"It's at max." I rub her hands against mine.

Her ice-cold cheek rest against my bare warm chest. Her breaths come in pants, caressing my skin.

My fists clench as I will my heartbeat to slow down the thrumming that has recently started to make an appearance every time Daisy is around. I hate myself for loving the way she fits against me and the way she affects my body.

My wife. Fragile on the outside, with nerves of steel. Mine to protect from every threat.

"Then the radiator must be broken. What's the use of so much money if you can't get it fixed?" Her chatter used to sound nonsensical, but now I can't get enough of it.

"Do you really think I'd let my beautiful wife sleep in a cold room?" I whisper against her ear.

This time when she shivers, I know it's not because of the cold, but me.

Daisy's Bambi-brown eyes wide with surprise slowly turn up to me.

"Save your charm for when there's an audience, husband."

"Don't worry, there's plenty where that came from." I hide my smile in her hair, inhaling her shampoo.

"Who knew you'd have a caring bone in your body?"

Her voice is no longer quivering as before, but goose bumps rise on her arms under my touch.

"I have enough bones you're not familiar with."

"Did you just make a dirty joke, Charles A. Hawthorne?" She squeals, turning around in a flash.

Ensuring she doesn't fall from the bed, I pull her closer, and that's how my wife lands smack right on my lap. Her face is an inch away from mine. Her feet are on either side of my hips, and her butt is right on top of my cock, which has become more and more aware of her presence.

"I pointed out the truth. Plus, the part you're referring to"—which now jerks its neck as if waving a hello—"is not really a bone but tissue."

"Then why is it called a boner?" she asks while the organ gets to full mast. There's no way she's missing it.

"Are you really asking me that right now?" I raise an eyebrow, and Daisy finally smiles for the first time since waking up from whatever nightmare hit her.

As if the same thought crosses her mind, her smile drops. "Can you stay here for a little longer?"

I nod. "I can't go anywhere anyway. My little wife has me captive."

Her grin is wide, warming my insides. Folding her arms over her chest, Daisy leans in. "Yes, I do. Who knew you could be so well-behaved!"

"Well-behaved? What am I, a dog?" Laughter spurts out of my mouth.

"No, you are my big, bad husband." Her jaw drops, because in the same instant, that *big* part of me jerks, once again making its presence known. "Sorry. I didn't think before speaking."

"That's fine as long as you can ignore a few things. I don't think I can control it."

And ain't that true.

As much as I like to control every aspect of my life, right now that word is far from my mind. Everything about her is driving me crazy.

Her soft voice.

The feel of her curves under my hands.

The light scent of her floral body wash, which I now know comes in bright red packaging.

"So there's something in this world that is out of *the* Charles Hawthorne's control?"

"I'm equally surprised." More from the fact that it's wrapped up in the tiny body of my wife.

Her fingers move over my chest, and color rises on her cheeks. My heart is thumping wildly against my rib cage.

"Where's your shirt?" Her words break my thoughts.

"I run hot at night," I reply without blinking, because it's the truth. Before her, I preferred sleeping in my boxers.

"Uh-huh. So you mean you don't even wear pants?"

Her face is serious, as if she's talking about the weather and not questioning about me being naked. I can't believe we're having his conversation, especially when she's made my lap her favorite seat.

I nod. "But since I didn't want to scandalize you too much, I decided to put some on."

"It would be too hard to ignore," she says slowly, her gaze moving up from my chest to my face. "You know what I mean?"

"Definitely," I reply, almost in pain.

"Want to talk about something else?"

"Definitely," I repeat, releasing a heavy breath.

"What happened in the board meeting today?"

All the roaring blood in my body traveling south settles down.

Everything I'd wanted was right in that room, but I rushed out like a madman without a second thought.

Do I have regrets? Hell no. I knew what was at stake.

Will there be a lot of answering to Grandma and the board? Unfortunately, yes.

"I don't know. I left before it started."

"You did what?"

eighteen

Safety Mummy

Daisy

"Why would you do such a thing?" I gape at Charles, horror lacing my voice.

"Because I'd just received a phone call that you were nowhere to be found, and since you were busy playing Wonder Woman, I had no way to know if you were even safe. And apparently, I was right to be cautious."

I'm quite familiar with this low menacing tone of Charles', but until today, I never noticed how his eyes narrow, his lips twist, and above all, how his heart rises and falls like a raging storm, each beat echoing his turmoil. With his face inches away from mine and my hands resting over his warm bare chest, I experience the complete package of pissed-off Charles Hawthorne.

"You left for me?" I ask slowly, unable to believe it.

There's a 99.9 percent chance that the board was

ready to announce that they'd vote in his favor. How the heck could he walk away from something like that, when becoming the CEO has been his biggest dream?

He freaking married me for this, and now he left it all like it was nothing.

"How much of an asshole do you really think I am?" He grits his teeth.

But right now, he doesn't look like an asshole. Sitting before me, he looks like a man pulled out of my every dream.

Caring. Loving. Protecting.

"We need to fix this, Charles." I jump out of the bed, forgetting the scrapes on my knees, and a hiss escapes my lips.

"You need to sit down."

He pulls me back, right against his chest. My lips brush the side of his neck.

The subtle foresty smell of his cologne and the feel of his prickling five o'clock shadow against my soft lips is enough to bloom heat in my stomach, spreading like wildfire across my skin. Everything about this moment feels unreal, including the man before me.

The way he's looking at me, talking to me, caressing my arms for Christ's sake—this version of Charles is almost like a familiar stranger who feels safe yet gives my heart those first meeting sparks.

But what curls my insides the most is the knowledge that he left something important…*for me*. I can't just sit here and let everything Charles has worked for over the years go down the toilet.

"We need to find out what happened in the meeting. I'll be damned if they don't make you the CEO. I'll threaten, beg, or kiss every board member if they don't give you what you deserve."

An amused grin takes over his face. I thought Charles Hawthorne had no facial muscles to smile, but right now, I'm thankful for the lack of it all these years. Because when those lips curl up, Charles is like my personalized wet dream.

"First, calm down. I'm going to call Grandma tomorrow morning. Second, I'll remember about your threatening capabilities should the need arise. Other than that, you're my wife. You don't beg and kiss anyone."

"Anyone?" I gulp.

Showing that killer grin once again, he grabs my hand so lightly that I almost want to die. Mindful of the gauze, he nods toward my diamond wedding band and the beloved daisy engagement ring.

"These give me the right to do some things that might involve begging and kissing. Don't you think?"

I'm not prepared for the quick kiss he places on my lips, and it takes me a few seconds to calm down my breathing.

"I hope it's on your part, because I'm not begging you, Charles A. Hawthorne."

The smirk that lights up his face gives me the same feeling as if I'm sitting beside the fireplace in my parents' home with a cup of hot cocoa on Christmas Eve. It's personal and a prelude to the best happiness.

"I can't wait to abolish these nonsense thoughts out of your mind, my dear wife."

I'm just about floating in a fluffy pink cloud, which is probably what heaven feels like.

"For someone who hated the idea of marriage, don't you think you like calling me that a tad too much?"

"Believe me, I'm equally surprised."

The clock in his bedroom hits as the hour completes, and a cuckoo comes out. Last night, every time it did that, I almost jerked out of bed.

"Why do you have it in your bedroom? Doesn't it disturb you repeatedly?"

I spot a familiar look of irritation on Charles' face, the one I've seen numerous times whenever anyone tries to get a peek of his private life.

"I'm sorry. I—" I pause.

I, what?

I'm sorry I intervened?

Yes, as his executive assistant, it's none of my concern. But what about his wife? The wife who, a few minutes ago, was sitting over his hard-on.

Um, and let's just say impressive wouldn't be enough to describe how he felt under me.

As if he's thinking the same thing, Charles gently runs the back of his hand against my cheek. "It also reminds me that I'm in my room, in my bed, and everything is okay."

Even though his words are simple, there's a raw honesty on his face, which resembles something like…fear.

That's nonsense.

Charles Hawthorne, the most powerful man in this town, isn't scared of anything.

"But you're no longer in your bed now that I'm here?" My fingers dig into his biceps.

"Then it tells me *you're* safe in my bed."

I don't know what changes in the air around us. The playful, sensual warmth morphs into something dense.

My heart says Charles just confessed something huge, and I know I'll spend countless minutes tomorrow dissecting his words to find out the hidden meaning behind them.

"But I don't feel safe tonight," I whisper. His earlier admission allows me to share my fears.

"I'm here. I promise I'm not going to let anything happen to you, butterfly." Charles' voice is so calm and relaxed, in a way I've never seen him before.

"I never thought there'd be a day when you'd call someone by such a cheesy nickname," I whisper again.

"Me neither." He smiles. "Guess I've made another exception for you."

"What's the first?"

"First?" He raises an eyebrow.

"You just said you've made another exception for me. What's the first one?"

"You can take your pick. You're the first person other than me who's sleeping in my bed. Today is the first time I've left a meeting before it even began. It's also the first time I didn't fire someone when they failed to do their job."

"Are you talking about me?" I ask, despite knowing that he's going to reply in the negative.

Charles slowly shakes his head.

"Steve's job was to keep you safe and he failed."

"I love Steve." I grab his hands as they hold my face.

"This is the last time I want to hear the word *love* and any other man's name on your lips. You are my wife now."

Possessiveness oozes from him like molten lava. On one

hand, my feminism is bursting to give him a fitting reply on claiming me like a possession, but there's also a part of me that loves every bit of this jealous side of him.

"You know I don't mean it that way."

"It doesn't matter, butterfly." He grins as if knowing well the impact his soft words are having on me. "Now go to sleep."

He places me back on the bed. The moment my head rests against the pillow, thoughts of being trapped under the rubble hit me like a tsunami. Before he can take another step away, I grab his hand.

He looks over his shoulder. Before tonight, I could say in a heartbeat that I've never met a more impatient man than my boss, but right now, his patience rivals that of the mom of a cranky toddler.

"You're safe, Daisy. I promise."

"I'm sorry for acting like a baby. But…will you please sleep here? On the bed?"

The smile on his face drops, and I know Charles is about to decline.

"Please. I promise I'll be good. I won't take advantage of you, Charles." I try to make a joke, but neither of us smile.

Comforting each other. Sleeping on the same bed.

These were not the conditions of our marriage contract. But I still can't ignore the fear in my chest.

"I swear I'll sleep on my side." When he just stands there, saying nothing, my voice cracks. "Are you really going to make me beg?"

"Fuck," he groans softly before pulling the covers down and getting in on the other side of the bed. "Are you done or are you planning on torturing me some more tonight?"

My lips twitch. "It depends. Do you consider my talking torture?"

"Does it matter? You're going to say whatever you want anyway."

"You know me so well." I pull the covers up to my neck, all the while thankful that I'm getting a front-row view of Charles' bare chest.

"What are you smiling at, Mrs. Hawthorne?"

"That I finally get to appreciate what you were hiding under those fitted suits all these years."

He laughs!

Charles Hawthorne, my boss and husband, the man who smiles so rarely that there's a better chance of seeing a shooting star, lets go of full-blown laughter.

"You're pulling no punches tonight. Are you, butterfly?"

My heart is so full that I feel it'll just combust.

"Based on how you felt under me, I think you can take a tiny person like me."

"You don't know the power you hold."

Over me.

I don't know if he said those two additional words or if it was my imagination.

"Now sleep. We both have work tomorrow. And remember your promise—no taking advantage of me."

"Pinky promise." I intertwine my pinky finger with his, completely oblivious to the fact that I'll not just break the promise but thrash it with my hands, legs, face, and body.

"How much longer are you going to pretend you're asleep?" Charles' voice is more like a groan.

I don't just hear his words but feel them moving in his throat where my mouth is pressed. It's not just my mouth, though—every inch of me is pressed to him.

His one arm is functioning as a pillow, taking the weight of my head, while the other is wrapped around my waist. My feet are trapped between his legs, and my thigh is over his erection, which has surged to life.

"Since when are you awake?" I ask, making no attempt to pull away.

"Since you started breathing hard and making tiny circles all over me."

My hand drifting over his stiffening nipple halts. "Sorry."

Charles pulls back, and with a single digit under my chin, tugs my face up to his. "That wasn't a complaint, butterfly. But sometimes even saints fail to restrain themselves."

"Charles Hawthorne! Whoever is accusing you of being a saint, please bring them to me. I'll fix their misplaced beliefs."

My hands, which were resting on his chest, now land on his cheeks. I have a faint awareness that this is Charles Hawthorne.

My boss, the man who I've nicknamed asshole.

But right now, as the morning rays filter through the tall windows and graze his face, it's so hard to see him as anyone but my husband, who left all his important work behind in order to save *me*.

"What are you thinking?" He caresses my cheek. Since last night, he's repeated the move so many times, as if he just can't stop touching me. "You're so flushed." His voice turns hoarse.

My eyes fall closed as Charles leans in. I wait for his kiss, but instead, his nose runs against the column of my neck. My world tips when he inhales slowly, his hot breath coasting my skin, leaving goose bumps in its wake. My whole body is on fire when his lips touch my bare skin, just a brush, but I can't stop my moan.

So far, Charles and I have only kissed, and this is the first time his lips have treaded below my face. I never knew my neck was such an erogenous zone.

"What are you doing?"

"I love the way you smell."

My head rolls back and my back arches as if offering more of whatever he's willing to take. But Charles pulls back. My eyes open to find him staring at my chest. I follow his gaze, and one of my boobs is almost falling out of my camisole top. When I removed my bra the previous night, I wasn't expecting to wake up beside Charles.

His hand lightly rests against my rib cage, the heat of his touch searing my skin through the silk.

His eyes meet mine, and my breath is almost in my throat when his thumb starts its journey upward.

I don't think I'm even breathing until his digit touches my nipple, a part peeking out, a part still hiding beneath the frill of my top's neckline. That's my undoing. I moan shamelessly.

"Fuck." Charles' curse echoes in the room.

I don't remember if I've ever been touched this way, where the other person is in no hurry. Jax's definition of foreplay was to kiss me for two seconds, and we were done with everything in the next sixty. But this is magic.

My nipple is so hard, it could be used to cut diamonds when Charles finally moves his thumb away.

"Do you know how beautiful you look right now?"

"Charles," I whisper, trying to free my feet still captive between his muscular thighs.

I need movement. I need friction.

But he doesn't budge. If anything, his grip on me tightens.

"I—I need…please let me go."

"Never." He grins and his thumb returns again.

How the heck is this simple graze turning me on so freaking much?

When Charles chuckles I realize I've said it out loud.

"For the first time, I'm grateful you don't think before speaking."

My eyes open, and even though I'm still a hot mess of hormones needing release, I can't help my smile.

"I told you someday you'd see the benefit."

"I definitely do now." He smiles back before letting me go and tucking me into the covers like a burrito.

"Um, why do I look like a mummy?"

"Because I can't think straight when you're lying down before me looking so pretty and so mine and so fucking turned on."

"And you need your brain to do the next thing?"

He smirks. "Mrs. Hawthorne, you'll be the end of me someday."

I love how my new name slips from his lips effortlessly.

"I need my brain and you do too, because I want you to think before we do anything." He moves his hand between us. "This was not what we agreed upon in the contract."

The light in my chest loses some of its spark at the mention of the contract.

But why am I surprised?

This man considers his every step, and us sleeping together was never a part of his plan.

Yours either, Daisy.

"And by this"—I repeat his action, *trying* to move my trapped hand under the duvet between us—"you mean sex. Right?"

"Yes, butterfly." He leans in and kisses my lips. So light that I want to cry. "I mean sex. You and me on this bed, not stopping until you're crying my name," he adds after pulling back and getting out of bed in a single move.

I lift my head. "Where are you going?"

"I need a long shower."

My gaze travels past his face, lower to his spotless skin, which glows under the warm morning light filtering through the curtains. There's not even a hint of hair on his muscular chest. I explore further down to his rippling abs, lower to his navel, below which rests the waistband of his track pants— the ones he put on for my benefit.

But they're more of an inconvenience now, and despite not being able to have my full fill of Charles Hawthorne, my pulse pounds at the sight of his erection proudly jutting out.

"Wow," I whisper, equal parts nervous and mesmerized.

"You're going to be the death of me, my dear wife." Charles chuckles, and this time when he turns around, he doesn't stop until the bathroom door shuts with a loud thud behind him.

I'm also tempted to follow him or push my hand under my shorts. Thanks to how wet I am, and with the light sound of the running shower, where I *know* Charles is jerking off, it'll take less than a second for me to experience the biggest orgasm of my life.

But suddenly I'm into delayed gratification, especially if the reward is Charles.

nineteen

Possession or Not?

Charles

"Can I still not convince you to stay at home?" I ask as Daisy joins me for breakfast.

She's wearing a sky-blue skirt and a white blouse that has pink peonies all over it. There's nothing unprofessional about her clothes, and I've seen them on her more times than I can count, but my body has never been so aware of her presence. My cock—let's not talk about that asshole, who seems to have a mind of his own around her these days. But how can I blame it all on him, when she's making no attempt to hide how she feels about me physically?

But did you expect anything else from her?

If I hide my feelings in a tight vault with numerous locks, she proudly displays every emotion on her face.

Just this morning when I stepped out of the shower, she was waiting by the door. She blatantly perused my almost naked body, focusing extra hard on the towel wrapped around my waist, which was doing a shitty job at hiding my erection.

As I walked past her, she groaned. "Somebody likes seeing me."

"Not at all." Daisy's words pull me back to the present. "I need to talk to Mr. Buffay about the updates on Vincent's site, and you, my dear boss, have to find out what the price is for you running away from the board meeting."

"I didn't run away. I ran to you, my dear wife."

"Cute, but too cheesy for you. Even Mrs. K thinks so. Isn't that right?" Daisy raises an eyebrow as my housekeeper places two cups of coffee onto the table.

Mrs. Kowalski pales, her usual small smile dropping the same instant. "I…I…don't—"

"Don't worry, Mrs. Kowalski. You'll get used to Daisy's natural talent of taking everyone by surprise."

"Don't complain, husband. Someone needs to keep you in check."

"And who's better for the job than you?"

Mrs. Kowalski sets down two plates of breakfast before disappearing. The moment we're alone, the air morphs into something thick and heavy. I pick up my coffee mug, and Daisy takes a bite of her croissant, but my mind is busy remembering how we were less than an hour ago. I can still smell the fruity scent of her perfume.

Have you thought things through?

Those words are on the tip of my tongue, because next time when she's in my arms begging with her eyes, I don't think I'll have the willpower to stop and walk away.

Her lips quiver as if she's about to answer my silent question, when my phone rings.

Daisy jerks in her seat while I splash the hot coffee over my hand.

"Fuck." I use the paper towel to wipe my hand before turning toward her. "You okay?"

Only when she nods do I grab my phone from the table.

Ashcroft Miller—my grandfather, Kristy's dad, and a man who gave new meaning to my middle name because he's the strongest person I've known.

"Good morning, Opa."

"How's married life, Charlie?"

"Full of surprises," I reply, glancing at my new wife.

"Happy ones, I hope." I can feel his smile through the line.

"So far, yeah."

"That's good, kid. You tied the knot so fast we didn't get to meet Daisy properly. Your Oma is inviting everyone home for dinner tonight. She wanted to know if you're available, but if you aren't, free up your calendar. No matter how busy a businessman gets, family should always come first."

"We'll be there." I could never imagine declining an invitation from him. I end the call and turn to Daisy.

"It was my grandfather. Mom's—I mean, Kristy's dad. They have invited us for dinner in St. Peppers. We'll have to leave early in the afternoon to be there on time."

That also means I have half the time to fix the mess of yesterday. Usually, I wouldn't hesitate to send a text to Daisy and ask her to reprioritize my schedule. But today, she's seated before me, her knees and palms covered in bandages while she's typing furiously on the phone, possibly checking up on her dad.

I'm still watching her from the corner of my eye when my phone vibrates in my hand. I look down to find my ten o'clock meeting has been shifted to tomorrow. Notifications continue to pop up until my entire calendar has been rearranged.

"I freed up your evening and also a part of the morning so you can talk to your grandmother and any other board members to explain why you left in a rush."

When I don't reply, she looks up at me and grins. But this isn't one of those that makes me want to put her in my pocket and never let go—like the one she gave me this morning, when her entire face beams. No, this is her professional smile.

"I haven't forgotten what you told me when we signed the contract, boss. I know you're not trading a wife for a lousy assistant."

Her mentioning the contract leaves a bad taste in my mouth.

But why? It's there for our benefit—hers and mine.

Even if we slept together, the terms of the contract will protect the future of our arrangement. No surprises. Clean separation. The idea, which was reassuring a few weeks ago, now makes me want to throw up.

What did Mrs. Kowalski put in the breakfast today?

"I thought you'd be pleased, but you're making that face where you want to murder someone." Daisy pushes a curl behind her ear, and I realize I'm scowling right at her.

"It's not that." I clear my throat, trying to come up with a sensible response. "I don't like the bandages. I was serious about you staying home."

Surprise colors her face. "I swear I'm fine, Charles. I

texted the doctor before changing the bandage this morning. He agreed there's no harm in going to work."

"And what about the blood work?" I ask carefully. Not that I'm worried about her being pregnant; I'm worried about *her*. "Is there any chance of you collapsing on the street someday due to a vitamin deficiency? Everything okay there?"

"Nothing out of the ordinary." She drops her gaze.

"And what's ordinary for my wife? Show me." I place my hand forward for her phone, where I'm sure she's received a digital copy of her blood work.

"Charles, that's personal! I'm not sharing my health report with you."

"After what I glimpsed this morning, I think your reports are safe with me."

Daisy flushes at the reminder. "I'll just tell you, okay. I'm vitamin D deficient, but every person has that. I'm going to pick up some supplements. Satisfied?"

Not at all.

"Only for now."

"If you're done being difficult, I want to remind you that we have half a day to handle everything at work." Daisy throws her hair over her shoulder and rises up.

Ten minutes later, we're seated in the limo like all the numerous times before. No words are exchanged, as she's busy switching between a tablet and a phone, typing furiously, while I go through a report on my laptop. We finally pause when the car stops in front of my private elevator at Hawthorne Tower.

Steve opens the door by my side, but before we can march toward the waiting elevator cab, Daisy stops.

"Steve, I'm sorry about yesterday. I shouldn't have accompanied Mr. Buffay instead of asking you to drive me."

"Please don't say that, Mrs. Hawthorne." The man shakes his head as his gaze lands on the bandages around Daisy's hands. "I'm grateful that you're okay and nothing major happened."

Daisy takes a step forward, closer to him and away from me, making my pulse jump.

"I'm still me, Steve. I'm not going to tolerate this Mrs. Hawthorne nonsense. You're calling me Daisy like you always did. You too, Dave." She looks at the other man. "How else will we continue to have our personal talks?"

Personal talks? What the hell is she talking to them about?

My bodyguards are right to look nervous, but my wife hasn't received the same memo.

"I cannot share with you all the evil but *true* things about Charles if you call me Mrs. Hawthorne, can I now?"

I'm about to ask Dave and Steve a question of my own, something along the lines of if they've forgotten who's paying them their salary, when Daisy tugs on the sleeve of my suit jacket.

"Aren't you going to say anything to Steve?"

I know she wants me to apologize, and it's *cute* that she thinks she can order me around.

"I definitely am." I turn to my bodyguards. "I don't want a repeat of yesterday."

They both nod, and I don't wait anymore, marching toward the elevator. Daisy huffs before trailing behind.

"You know that was not what I meant."

"Daisy, Steve made a mistake, and I'm not going to hesitate in reminding him of that."

It must be my serious, humorless tone, because she doesn't interrupt or add any playful comment.

We step out, and before she can say anything more, my phone rings.

Once I've seen the caller's name, I know it's not safe to take this call here. I wouldn't want the first emotion Daisy feels this morning to be guilt. So, I leave her at her desk and walk inside my office.

"Good morning, Grandma."

"Charles, what happened yesterday? You left the meeting without a word, and then you didn't pick up your phone. Is everything alright with you and Daisy?"

"Yes. She's fine now." I stand before the mirrored wall in my office. The special glass provides me a perfect view of Daisy's desk, while she can't catch me gawking at her.

"That's good to hear. But since you weren't there, the board rescheduled the meeting for after the holiday season. My assistant will send an email to Daisy, and I hope nothing comes up this time that is more urgent than the agreement on your CEO position."

I don't miss the hint of disapproval in her voice, but I have no regrets.

"I'm sure it was a one-time thing, Grandma," I reply, watching Daisy water the plants on her desk while slowly talking to them. My lips twitch as she prances around, from one shrub to another, tending to her kingdom like a queen.

She finally places the elephant-shaped watering jar on the floor under her desk and grabs the pink Post-its.

With hurried steps, I step away from the wall, and I'm leaning against my desk when she knocks.

I wave for her to come in as my call ends. She walks up to the glass wall behind my desk and removes the Post-its from yesterday. My gaze follows her moves as, like every other day, she throws them into the empty paper trash can.

"So, which organ do I have to donate to compensate for pulling you out of a board meeting?" she asks without turning around, putting fresh task notes onto the wall.

"All your organs are safe for now, but if you're planning to get kidnapped in the first week of February, I'd suggest postponing it for the following month."

"Two jokes in twenty-four hours. There must be a long summer in hell for so much ice to crack." Daisy looks over her shoulder and grins.

"Don't get used to it. Anyway, did we hear anything about Vincent's site?"

Daisy's face is serious when she nods.

"Mr. Buffay has sent us a new assessment report confirming the workers' observations. It appears that someone within Buffay Construction is exploiting the company by delivering substandard materials."

My muscles tense as I once again imagine yesterday. "Please tell me we've canceled all our future contracts with them."

Daisy stays silent, nervously biting her lips. I recognize the familiar expression—she's searching for the best way to admit that she hasn't done the job, and her reasoning likely involves something emotional.

But for once, I'm not feeling impatient or on the verge

of exploding. In fact, I find myself oddly content, relishing in the sight of her furrowed brows, the indent on her lips left by her teeth, and even the faint stain of her pink lipstick as it trails behind.

As she's busy sorting through her thoughts, memories of her in my bed flood my mind. I'm almost tempted to ask her if she's given *that* any thought. I didn't want us to have any regrets later, yet leaving her in that bed was without a doubt one of the hardest things I've ever done.

Nothing and no one has ever looked as enticing. This morning, Daisy was the ultimate temptation, and I should be awarded some grand prize for walking away. But now I can't wait to hear her decision, because in truth, I want her—my wife.

"Charles!" She waves her hand in front of me like an airport staff member directing traffic. "Did you hear what I just said?"

Fuck! "Of course I did," I lie through my teeth. "You want to give Buffay another chance."

"So you agree?"

"Not at all. I didn't marry you to become a widower before I could show you what it really means to be my wife."

Daisy sucks in a breath, and seeing the pink flush on her cheeks, I know for sure she's thinking about this morning like I am. I push away from where I'm leaning against the desk and approach her. Suddenly, our few feet of distance is too much.

"Mr. Buffay is a good man, Charles."

"Should I remind you that you're my wife?" I continue until I'm right in front of her. My wingtips align with the points of her heels, and even with those, she barely reaches my chest.

"I'm serious." Her voice wavers.

"And you think I'm not? I take my possessions very seriously, and you, my dear wife, are priceless."

"I'm not your possession." She wrinkles her nose in that adorable way that makes me crazy. "Besides, jealousy doesn't suit you, my dear husband."

Every time she calls me that, Daisy claws away some ice around my chest with her tiny hands and leaves a bit of warmth inside me.

"I don't know the meaning of that word."

"Of course you don't." As always, she calls me on my bullshit. "But Buffay is a good person—a loyal business partner to Hawthorne Holdings and a good family man to his wife and kids. Give him one more chance. Please, Charles."

"There are no second chances in business." All my life, I've followed this rule and it has served me right. Plus, Buffay not only caused me loss in business but also put my wife's safety at risk.

"This morning, you mentioned you've made exceptions for me," Daisy whispers, pulling me away from risky thoughts. "Can I not have one more?"

How the hell does one say no to that?

I fold my hands together, bringing them close to my face, my index fingers resting over my bottom lip. "Only if you promise to think about what we discussed this morning."

Her eyes flutter closed. "Believe me, I haven't stopped thinking about it for a minute."

twenty

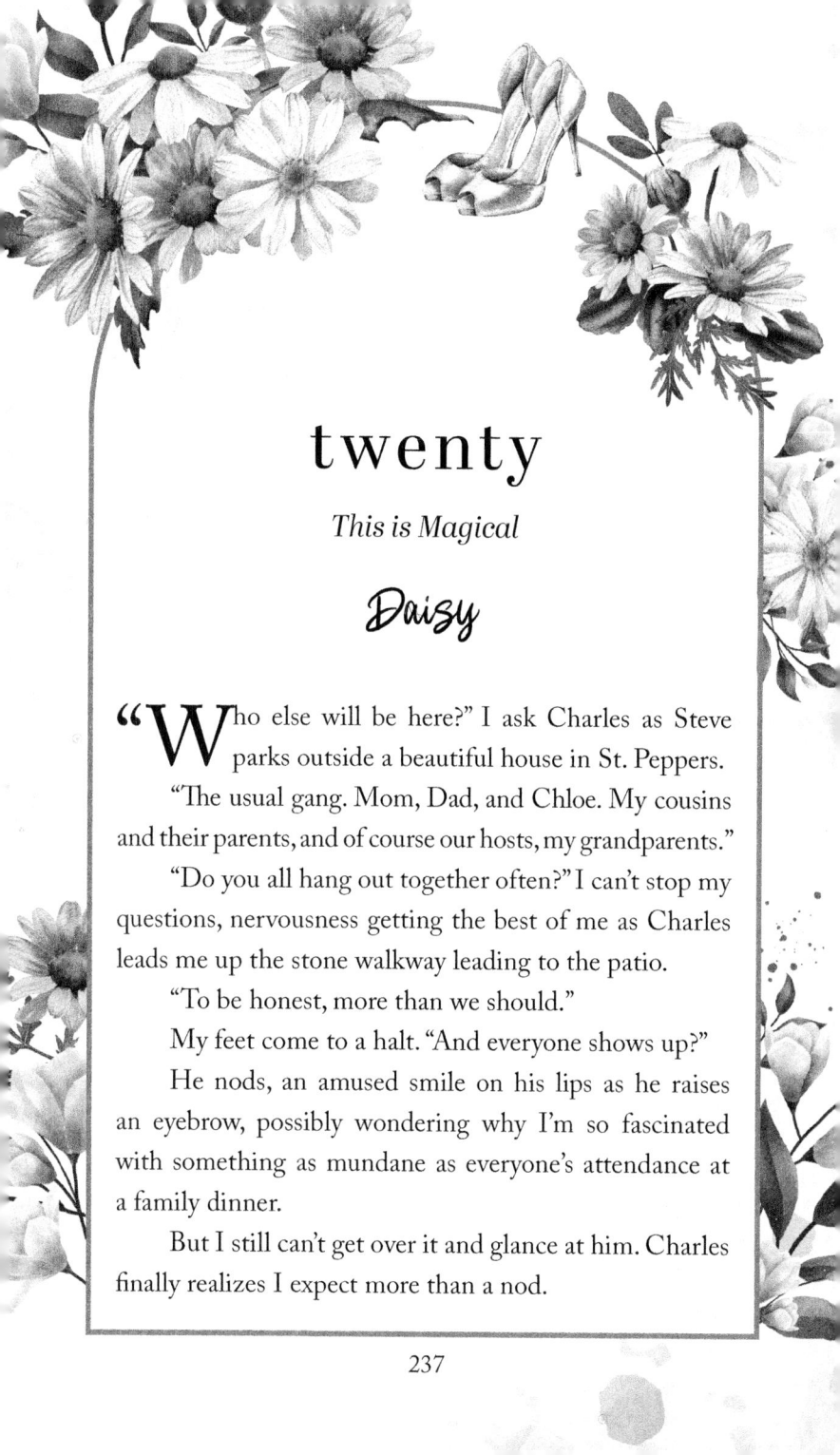

This is Magical

Daisy

"Who else will be here?" I ask Charles as Steve parks outside a beautiful house in St. Peppers.

"The usual gang. Mom, Dad, and Chloe. My cousins and their parents, and of course our hosts, my grandparents."

"Do you all hang out together often?" I can't stop my questions, nervousness getting the best of me as Charles leads me up the stone walkway leading to the patio.

"To be honest, more than we should."

My feet come to a halt. "And everyone shows up?"

He nods, an amused smile on his lips as he raises an eyebrow, possibly wondering why I'm so fascinated with something as mundane as everyone's attendance at a family dinner.

But I still can't get over it and glance at him. Charles finally realizes I expect more than a nod.

"My grandparents missed out on a lot in life due to misunderstandings, and now they want to embrace every bit of family love. They host weekly dinners whenever they're in town and not off globe-trotting."

"Wow! That's…so magical."

He raises his eyebrow farther, his grin deepening at my expense.

"Okay, so maybe not *magical*, per se. But for someone who never had much family except my parents, Aunt Mel and her husband, it's not normal." A knot tightens in my chest.

How was it to be surrounded by the love of such a big family?

"What about cousins?" Charles asks softly as we stand by the door, in no hurry to walk in.

I shrug. "I don't have any."

"I'd never admit it to their faces, but I can't imagine living without my cousins. They're my best friends, my biggest confidants, and I know I can count on them for anything."

"I understand completely. I think I cashed in all of my luck in the friends department. Even though we're not related by blood, Willow, Elodie, and Violet feel no less than sisters to me."

I'm interrupted when the main door opens softly.

"I thought I heard someone. Welcome, you two." A woman with shiny white hair and wrinkles around her eyes steps out and places a kiss on my forehead.

There's so much affection in her face that I feel a sting behind my eyelids as memories of Mom hit me out of nowhere.

"I'm Sophia, Charlie's grandmother. You can call me Oma like all the other kids in the family. We met briefly at your wedding ceremony, but I'm sure it was hard to remember every face from that evening." Her smile is so sweet and gentle that I fall in love with her instantly.

She hugs Charles before kissing his forehead and then holds *my* hand, leading us inside the house. Photographs of smiling faces and family dinners litter the hallway. I'm sure sometime later, I'll just stand here and spot the young Charles in these frames.

We cross a living room and step out of the glass door to the backyard. I almost gasp in surprise at the scene before me. There's a huge fire pit in the middle of a sitting area, above which solar lamps hang from the trees, casting a warm glow. There's a wooden bar in the corner and a huge man dressed in a three-piece suit manning it. In fact, every man is dressed the same way, proving they all came straight from work.

"You already know the boys." Sophia nods toward Ray, Rowan, Archer, and Alex, who are all seated on the barstools laughing. Right beside them, there's another group of a bit older but no less dashing gentlemen. I immediately recognize Charles' dad, Oscar, and his friends, the famous Teagers. Everyone in Cherrywood knows the history of Elixir, and what started as a pharmaceutical company has now grown as its own business empire.

"Come on. I'll introduce you to the rest." Sophia leads me to the circular sitting area.

"Finally, you're both here. What took you so long?"

"Chloe, as newlyweds they're entitled to be late. I'd be worried if they showed up early for family dinners." Sophia grins, and all the ladies snicker while my cheeks flame.

"Holy crap, Charlie!" Chloe squeals, pulling everyone's

attention to my husband. "I knew it wasn't that you didn't know how to smile. You just needed the right person to pull that out of you."

"We all know why you appointed Charlie as the judge of those beauty pageants you hosted with your friends since you were thirteen, Chloe," Archer quips as he arrives with a tray of cocktails.

"Yet he showed no interest in any of my friends, Daisy." As always, Chloe wastes no time in coming to her brother's defense. "For so long, I thought he played for the other team."

Didn't I, too? I barely hold back my snicker.

"Don't think for a second that I've forgotten about the time you invited your classmate Jacob over for a movie night and conveniently left us alone, sis. I still get teased mercilessly about those excruciating two and a half hours."

Charles motions toward the couch where Ray and Rowan flank Archer, before placing bowls of tortillas and guacamole onto the table. It's almost surreal to see these men, who are infamously shrewd businessmen, in such an informal setting.

"Okay, if you kids are done bickering, I want to introduce Daisy to my girl gang." Kristy motions toward the women seated beside her. "This is my sister, Rose. We both started at Elixir together."

"And can you imagine, it took *three* years before Zander fell for our nerdy Rose?" says the woman whose face seems familiar, yet I can't quite place her name.

"Like Aunt Hope pointed out, Uncle Zander and Aunt Rose had an office romance like you guys," Chloe quips.

I gasp. "You're Hope Teager! the owner of the coffee chain at our office and every other corner in the country!"

"Co-owner, dear. Vi and I co-own the business." Hope nods toward the other woman, Vienna Teager, who has long hair and colorful tattoos of four paw prints on the inside of her wrist.

"Yes, I'm aware. My friends and I used to follow your YouTube videos and have made several failed attempts at trying to recreate your food art."

Vienna grins. "You all are welcome to my kitchen anytime."

"I've never been a part of such a big family dinner," I blurt unexpectedly, my nerves and excitement once again getting the best of me.

"Then I hope we don't scare you, Daisy, because this bunch can set records when it comes to family dinners." Ray grins, getting a groan from everyone and a backslap from Archer.

"Don't pretend we don't know who baked Oma's favorite cookies, Ray."

My jaw drops hearing Chloe's words. Did Raymond, the so-called real estate shark, have time to make cookies?

"I don't think he made them because they are my favorite, honey." Sophia smiles, looking between Ray and Chloe.

"You made them for me?" Chloe gasps before rising from her seat and dumping herself next to Ray.

"Of course I did. We finally have you back, and if my baking is going to make you stay, I'll spend time in the kitchen daily."

Rowan leans forward and musses Chloe's hair before he signs something.

"Now all we need is for Rory to be back, and then the entire gang will be complete," Charles whispers for only my ears, interpreting Rowan's words for me. He adds, "Rory is Alex's sister, the kid of the house."

I'm suddenly so full of emotions. Everyone here is well-versed in sign language, but it's not just that. Charles, the man for whom you'd rarely use the adjective *considerate*, is thoughtful enough to make sure I'm included in the conversation.

The evening passes like a dream. After drinks by the fire, we all return inside to the dining hall, which is huge to accommodate everyone.

"You boys need to take a lesson from Charles and Daisy. Look how happy they are together." Sophia points her fork toward Charles' cousins. "I want you all to take a step back in business and work hard to find a soulmate for yourselves, like these two have."

Soulmate?

My breath hitches. Not only because I'm fooling these wonderful people but also because I know Charles' cousins are aware of the reality of this relationship, which to be honest, is slowly escaping my mind.

We aren't soulmates. We're two business partners who are mutually benefitting a partnership at the expense of the feelings of genuine people who care about us.

My spiraling thoughts come to a halt as Charles clasps my cold, shivering hands, which are folded together on my lap under the table. I glance at him, sensing another tempest brewing in my chest.

"In a few years, I want this table to have seats for all your brides and my great-grandkids."

This time it's Charles who goes rock solid next to me. I know it's not because he can't wait to produce some cute but scowling babies with me, but because he abhors the idea. His jaw pulses the same way it did the night the doctor suggested a pregnancy test.

"I'm sure the people of Cherrywood are waiting to see the next Hawthorne heir," Raymond drawls, leaning back in his seat as he takes a sip of his drink.

As always, he hits it right in the bullseye, a skill I admire in a meeting, but not so much at a family gathering, especially when Charles clenches his jaw so hard I think he'll lose a few teeth.

"That's nonsense. You kids need to do nothing because someone expects something of you. You write your own story with love, patience, and kindness." Sophia's words are like a little breath of relief.

"How did you flip so fast, Oma? One second you're preaching for them to get married, and the next you're telling Daisy and Charles not to listen to anyone and to follow their own hearts. This is hypocrisy of the highest order." Chloe tweaks her nose, but Sophia's eyes gleam as if she's prepared for the response.

"Don't think I missed you, sweetheart. Now that Charles has tied the knot, I'm sure the media is already snooping around for some dirt on your love life."

"Don't worry, Oma." Chloe places her cloth napkin

onto the table with a winning smile. "I'm ready for whatever the media has planned. In fact, I might introduce you all to someone special very soon."

There's a sound of shattering glass on the other side of the table, followed by a faint curse from Alex's lips. One of the house staff appears immediately, and the remnants of the broken champagne flute is taken away the next second.

"Don't play with fire, sweetheart," Sophia whispers softly to Chloe. "You might just burn yourself."

Since they're seated right in front of me, I don't miss the understanding that passes between them.

The rest of the dinner continues with lighter conversation, but my mind is stuck on one memory—Charles' expressions at the mention of a baby.

Is it because the concept is foreign to him, like marriage, and he needs to slowly warm up to it? Or does he simply hate the idea of being a father?

"Let me give you a tour of the house, Daisy." Sophia leads me out of the living room, where everyone is seated for a nightcap post-dinner.

A few steps in through the hallway, and we walk right into a huge guest room where the dark gray walls are decorated with superhero posters. There's a pirate tent in one corner and a small library with comic books right next to it. The whole space is complete with a bunk bed.

"This used to be the boys' room whenever they came over for slumber parties."

Adjacent to the kids' bedroom is the media room,

complete with plenty of couches and cozy floor seating adorned with throw blankets. There's also a fireplace, a small popcorn machine, and a bar. I effortlessly imagine everyone in this welcoming space.

"This is where Ashcroft hosts his famous movie nights."

"I'm so jealous," I whisper, and then add fast, "I mean not of the room and the amenities, but the idea of being surrounded by so much love and the safety it might provide."

Done with my small speech, I glance up and find Sophia smiling at me.

"I know what you mean, honey. I didn't come from a big family either." She holds my hands in her soft ones. "But now this is *your* family. Like all my kids and grandkids, this is your home too, and I'm here for you whenever you need me."

Tears threaten to make an appearance at her sweet words, and the emotion of guilt isn't far. I'm fooling these people who have welcomed me into their lives and hearts.

"I'm sorry," I blurt, as usual unable to put a lid on my feelings.

"Oh, honey. Why are you apologizing?"

"I...I come from a modest house, and Charles is like the prince of Cherrywood. I sometimes worry what everyone thinks of me." I make an excuse that also has some truth in it.

"I didn't come from money either, Daisy. In fact, I hated rich people because I thought they were total snobs." Sophia smiles, her fingers softly running over my hair. "To be honest, I still think a lot of rich people are total assholes. But in love, money means nothing. What's more important is how you make each other feel when you're together. And we'd have to be blind not to see how happy Charles is around you.

Since he was born, that kid had everyone watching his every move. People were either waiting for him to be a business marvel or a failure. My small boy never got a chance to live for himself. He was trained to hide his emotions and feelings, but for the first time tonight, his training failed him. His gaze couldn't stop following you, and his eyes sparkled whenever you smiled at him. I thought we killed my little Charlie's emotion while training him to be *the* Charles Hawthorne, but with you, he's just any other man in love."

My heart lurches as a thousand butterflies take flight in my stomach. "I...I don't know what to say," I whisper. Somehow, the tightness in my chest loosened at her words.

"I know." She smiles. "You just need to keep in mind that all these boys can be dense, especially when it comes to displaying their emotions, so you'll have to hold the reins in this relationship."

twenty-one

Ready to Beg?

Daisy

"Did my family scare you too much?" Charles asks as we both settle in the back seat of the limo.

"I'm not someone who gets scared easily, Mr. Hawthorne." I turn my head toward him with a smirk.

Reality? I might not have been scared, but God was I nervous when we got out of the car this evening. Yet the moment I stepped inside Charles' grandparents' home, it was like visiting old friends.

"Yes, you certainly aren't." After a moment's pause, he asks, "So, any questions about anyone or anything you found interesting tonight?"

"Charles Hawthorne! Are you a secret gossip connoisseur?"

"Hey, you dropped the A in my name."

"You don't behave like one anymore." I grin. "But I do have questions. Several, to be honest."

What's the deal with Alex and Chloe?

Even though I tried to keep my small-town gossip-mongering instincts down, there was no missing the sizzling tension between them.

Why was everyone so protective over Rory? It took me a while to put together that Rory is the mysterious Aurora Teager, Zander and Rose's daughter. There has never been a picture of her in the news, just her name.

But despite all those curiosities, I chose the one question that was making me crazy. "Promise you won't be upset."

"Out with it, wife."

"Who's going to take over the Hawthorne business after you?" I ask carefully, and the grin on Charles' lips drops faster than a popped balloon, as I expected.

"Already looking forward to my demise." Even though his words are light, there's no humor in his voice.

"After your outburst before the doctor last night and the way you behaved today when your grandmother mentioned kids, it's clear that you're not exactly eager to become a dad." It takes everything in me to keep that smile on my lips.

"No, thank fuck. I'm not."

My heart sinks like a pebble in a lake.

Stop it, Daisy. This is about him and not the time for your feelings.

"Since you're so committed to the Hawthorne name, I'm sure you have a plan in place for future."

Charles' lips twist, clear that he doesn't like my impromptu interrogation session.

"There's nothing to plan. Chloe and her future kids have the same rights as me to our family property and business."

I don't need to tell him that it'll never be so simple in this traditional town.

"But what if Chloe doesn't want kids either?"

This time the grin on Charles' lips is sincere. "Chloe loves kids. I'd be shocked if she doesn't produce a wailing, thrashing baby within the first year of marriage. She'll love that little devil despite the pain, vomit, and poop."

"You're definitely not competing for the favorite uncle trophy." An irritating knot of tension settles in my stomach, twisting uncomfortably.

"There're enough people who will give them love. I better do the things I'm good at, and love is definitely not my strength."

"You don't say." I bite the inside of my cheek.

Why the heck is my agitation rising with Charles' every word.

He's just being honest.

"Daisy—" Whatever Charles is about to say gets interrupted by the ringing of his phone. His gaze stays on me for a second longer before he tends to the call.

My head turns toward the window, staring at the moving traffic and streetlights. I hate the feeling of jealousy that creeps up in my chest as I imagine Chloe with her kids. They'd enjoy slumber parties and movie nights in Sophia and Ashcroft's home. Everyone would love them, and I know without a doubt that Charles would protect his sister's family and her dreams more fiercely than his own heartbeat.

If this isn't luck, what is?

Lost in my thoughts, I spot a streak of light in the sky and my eyelids fall closed, a wish taking shape in my heart.

If not in this life, please, Mother Nature, I want to have love of every kind in my next life.

But with my horrible luck at relationships, there's a massive chance that it isn't a shooting star and just the flashing headlights of a vehicle on the windy streets of the mountains.

When my eyes open, I find Charles' reflection staring at me in the mirror, the phone still tucked to his ear.

Standing in front of the mirror, I apply my night cream and stare at my reflection.

This is silly and borderline crazy, Daisy.

Why the heck are you upset that Charles doesn't want kids or a family?

He isn't your real husband. This is a contract marriage with an end date.

Plus, we haven't even had sex. I haven't even seen his dick for real. Maybe he doesn't know how to use it to make babies.

Yeah, now that's a whole other level of bullshit.

If he wanted to, Charles Hawthorne could get a woman pregnant with his statement scowling glare alone.

Like the previous nights, I'm not wearing a bra, and my nipples poke through the thin cotton of my panda T-shirt just at the thought of my husband.

My brain continues to be on a seesaw with this man—

one second, angry and upset, and in the next, remembering how he's started to act around me.

I'm still staring in the mirror when the doorknob turns and Charles walks in, dressed in low-hanging track pants and his chest bare in all its glory.

"Hey, you cannot walk in like that." All the butterflies in my stomach go crazy wild at his sly grin.

"Then you should have locked the door."

Good point.

But for someone who's used to living alone in my apartment, I'm still getting used to the idea of a roommate.

"What if I wasn't dressed or in the shower?"

"Then we would be having a very different kind of conversation," Charles drawls.

It's so easy to fall under the spell of this man, who's completely different from the one outside these four walls of his bedroom. Even though this version of Charles smiles and makes stupid jokes, he's still a pole apart from me.

Different needs. Different dreams.

"What do you want, Charles?" I ask.

"I wanted to offer something in return of a truce," he says patiently.

"I didn't know we were at war." I take a step toward the door, but Charles blocks me from leaving the en-suite bathroom.

"Okay, Daisy, then I would like to be where we were this morning. You trapped, at my mercy, and me free to do whatever I want."

"Whatever you want?" My eyebrows rise, heat crawling up my cheeks.

He *probably* could have done whatever he wanted and I *probably* wouldn't have complained.

There's no probably about it. It's all definitely.

"I have something to cheer you up. But you need to close your eyes."

"Are you going to take advantage of me?"

Would I mind? Not really.

I would like to get out of this depressive mood that has suddenly set upon me like a dark cloud.

"I told you already, when we have sex, you'll be begging me for it, my dear wife." Charles grins.

When and not if. Oh my!

"Uh-huh. Your overconfidence has always been scary, boss."

"Are you done being difficult, or will you just close your eyes?" He shakes his head.

Am I curious to know what Charles' definition of a truce is?

Of course, yes.

Do I close my eyes at his command?

Unfortunately, also yes.

But in the next second, Charles has thrown me over his shoulder and is walking out of the bathroom.

"Charles! Put me down."

"Shh, and remember, eyes closed."

"I'm not going to be shushed."

For some reason, I want to experience his surprise to its greatest extent, hence I keep my eyes closed, but that doesn't stop me from smacking his behind.

God, this man has a tight ass. He could even put Captain America to shame.

"Can you please not share everything you think?" Charles chuckles before placing me down next to the tall windows in the bedroom.

"I'm not going to apologize for admiring your ass. You should be happy."

"Thank you so much for objectifying a part of my body I don't even spend a minute thinking about."

"Don't worry, there are plenty of girls who spend an unhealthy amount of time thinking about it, so it's not getting left out."

"Does that mean my favorite girl thinks about it too?" He grins.

His favorite girl.

Oh. My. God.

I'm going to die from all of this swooning.

There's a ringing of his cellphone, but instead of reaching for it, Charles opens the window latch, and we walk to the patio.

"Ready?" he asks, grinning like a kid on Christmas morning.

"For what?" I'm unable to hold back my own smile.

He points his finger toward the sky, where fireworks go off one after another, resembling shooting stars.

My heart is beating so loud and fast right now I think I might just die of a heart attack.

"Make a wish fast, wife."

I wish there could be a world where this suffocating man standing beside me could want the same things as I do, and for whom my wishes and dreams, however silly they may be, mean the same to him as they do for me.

When the last firework goes up, I turn around and throw myself in Charles' arms.

He catches me immediately.

"How the hell did you do that? You are this broody, scowling man for the entire evening, and then you…you arrange fireworks like shooting stars for me. Do you suffer from multiple personality disorder?"

"Can I not be a simple man with a brilliant idea to make his wife smile?" He grins, looking me in the eye.

"You're anything but simple, Charles Hawthorne." My hands find their way to his hair.

I get to see Charles' killer smile for only one more second before his lips slam against mine. There's a buzzing electricity that sparks from my lips and travels throughout my body, leaving goose bumps in its wake. With me still in his arms, Charles takes a few steps forward until he has my back flat against the wall.

His chest presses against mine. His hard erection pokes at my center through our clothes, and slowly, his hand goes from my waist to the back of my neck. I have no clue how he's doing it, but Charles' touch is equally possessive and tender.

My arms lock around his neck like a lifeline. I'm completely lost in him, sensations drowning me in his spell.

We pull apart for oxygen only for a second before Charles' lips are back on me. This time, his forehead touches mine, and my heart catapults out of my body.

"Are you ready to beg, my dear wife?" His voice is hoarse, a tone I've never heard.

A part of me is about to scream yes, but my brain, which thankfully still has some cells working, is telling a different story.

My body has started to react around Charles in a way that is unacceptable. If I want to have any chance at keeping my heart safe from this man, I shouldn't forget the reality of this marriage.

I slowly shake my head.

Instead of being disappointed, a sly grin takes over Charles' face. "Then I'll be waiting for the moment you are."

It's been a few days since Charles surprised me with the fireworks. During this time, we've touched the flame of passion, but every time he asks, "Ready to beg, my dear wife?" I shake my head.

As much as my body is screaming at me to drop to my knees and pray at his pedestal, I know this would be the craziest thing I've ever done.

For the past thirty minutes, I've been doing nothing but staring at my computer screen as if it holds the answers to my questions.

How long will I be able to resist if Charles continues to tempt me this way?

I jerk in my seat at the sound of an incoming text.

Charles?

Hopeful nerves shake my hand, but it's not him.

Willow: Can you take some time off for lunch and last-minute holiday shopping? We three are headed to the mall.

> **Me:** Yes.

Maybe this is what I need. A girlfriend therapy session.

I drop a text to Charles, who's currently in a meeting on the other side of town.

> **Me:** I'm going to have lunch with my friends.

I grab my bag, swapping my furry slippers for heels, and march toward the elevator.

What I didn't expect was for him to text me back.

Husband aka Charles Adorable Hawthorne: Dave is waiting for you.

> **Me:** How are you texting me in the middle of a meeting?

Husband aka Charles Adorable Hawthorne: With my hands. :)

He sent me an emoji!

The elevator car arrives and the doors open, but my feet remain stuck to the landing.

> **Me:** Didn't you once say emojis are juvenile?

Husband aka Charles Adorable Hawthorne: I plead momentary insanity, my dear wife. Now, let your husband do some honest work.

I'm not even going to try lying.

I love everything about his text.

Husband aka Charles Adorable Hawthorne: And, Daisy, stay safe.

Elodie groans as we all settle in at the corner table in the food court. "God, it feels like we haven't been here in centuries."

If I can ignore the rings on my finger and a few curious glances from shoppers as they recognize me, everything feels the same as when I was just Daisy Price and Charles was my asshole boss.

Before I can hang on to that feeling for a little longer, Violet plucks a cheesy fry from my plate. "One of my journalist friends told me that the firework show everyone believed was practice for New Year's was actually a rich dude's surprise for his girl."

"Really!" Willow squeals while the delicious burger becomes hard to swallow in my mouth. "Who was it?"

"I don't know." Violet's teasing gaze fixes on me. "But whenever someone says *rich*, whose name comes to your mind?"

"Holy crap! You mean it was Charles?" Willow turns to me in her seat.

"I don't know. If it was Charles, I'm freakishly happy for Daze, but if it was someone else, I can't wait to find out about Cherrywood's new rich Romeo." Violet crosses her arms over her chest, with her grin intact and her gaze never leaving me. "So was it Charles?"

I keep my face straight.

Should I tell them? There's definitely no NDA around that. Plus, with Violet's penchant for gossip, how long can it be kept hidden anyway?

"It was. But it's no big deal."

"Uh-huh." My friends make a collective sound, clearly stating without words that they're not buying it a bit.

"I was upset about something, and he wanted to make me feel better."

"And all the florists and chocolate shops were closed?" Violet raises a brow.

"I'm with Vi on this one. Fireworks are a bit…" Willow trails off, but Violet finishes for her.

"Over the top? Unless he asked for a blow job or something kinky in return."

"Are you crazy, Vi? No!" *He was just expecting me to beg.*

"What happened after the fireworks?"

I groan. "Not you too, Elodie."

"Do you blame me for being shocked? Charles, aka the asshole boss whose actions you said are grimmer than thriller movies, is suddenly behaving like a lovesick Romeo."

"No one is behaving like anything." I feel the butterflies in my stomach taking flight once again.

"Why don't you leave the interpretation part to us? Just say what happened after the fireworks."

Before I can succumb to Violet's incessant journalistic probing, my phone vibrates on the table.

> **Dave:** All okay there, Daisy? FYI, I'm still on the ground floor, and the gentleman in the store has shown me things I didn't even know existed. How long can I look at the different shades of blue ties that actually all look the same to me?

My lips curl into a smile. After Charles made it clear

he'd appoint Dave as my personal bodyguard, I agreed on one condition—Dave can shadow me, but he can't do that in plain sight.

"Hi."

The phone slips from my hands when I feel someone right behind me.

"Oh, I'm sorry. I didn't mean to startle you, Mrs. Hawthorne," says the woman who looks around my age. "That man"—she looks behind her shoulder, but there's no one—"he was right here. But never mind, he gave me this. It's for you." She slides an envelope on the table, and a grin appears on her face while my heart thuds seeing my name written in Charles' flowing handwriting.

Daisy Hawthorne.

"Um, th-thank you," I stutter, without realizing that she's already gone. My hands and heart tremble as I open the envelope and pull out the card.

Dear wife,

I have a surprise for you. Meet me at Madison Blue, Room 215.

Your husband.

"Wow! And you guys didn't trust my jerk-boyfriend purging ritual!" Violet grins. "We asked the Supreme Goddess to send you a prince and now Charles Hawthorne is visiting malls in the middle of the day. Didn't you use to call him *workaholic supremo*? But I guess we can safely call him Daisy-aholic now."

"I…"

"You don't have to say anything. Now, let's go." Willow rises, and Violet and Elodie follow suit while I'm still stuck in my chair.

"Wait! I...I'm not done eating."

Plus, I haven't even wrapped my head around this version of Charles. Texting emojis and now this?

"Daze, what's more important?" Willow leans forward, forcing me to look up at her. "Your husband, who stopped his day's work and must have planned something romantic—"

"And filled with tons and tons of sex," Violet adds, escalating my heartbeat some more.

Is it possible Charles finally lost patience?

Haven't you?

"Thanks, Vi." Willow grins at our crazy friend before turning back to me. "And filled with tons and tons of sex. Or this mediocre burger?"

"Hey! I love the burgers here," I say.

"Daisy!" Willow holds my shoulder. "Why the heck are you still talking and not running to the hotel?"

"Because I'm nervous," I whisper, and they stare at me as if I'm speaking a foreign language. "Charles has never done anything like this before," I add.

"Shouldn't you be happy instead of nervous?" Willow asks slowly.

My heart lurches in my throat, and I wait for it all to sink in.

"What's it gonna be, Daze? You staying or leaving?"

If you follow the note, it's definitely scary but also exciting, Daisy. If you choose to stay, there's only regret. You'll never get to see this side of Charles.

"Leaving." I rise out of my chair.

A few minutes later, I step out of the elevator on the second floor of Madison Blue, which is located at the east side of the mall.

My stomach is in knots, equally nervous and excited to see what's waiting for me.

I take a right, following the direction for room 215, and come face-to-face with a man walking back and forth in the lobby, probably searching for someone.

Recognition flashes in his eyes, and after a stunned pause, I give him a polite smile. I'm still getting used to people recognizing me as Charles' wife. But when the man replies with a grin of his own, I feel like I know him from somewhere.

Stop making excuses, Daisy.

My inner self reprimands me and reminds me of Charles' words from yesterday instead.

"Is my wife ready to beg?"

If he keeps asking every day, then it won't be long before I'm saying, "Yes, sir. This girl is all set to get on her knees."

I'm still grinning like a lunatic while knocking on the door of the room. When there's no response for several moments, I turn the old-fashioned golden knob and it opens. But the moment I step inside, all the humor evaporates in an instant at the sight of the man before me.

"Jax!" I retreat instead of going forward as the door shuts behind me. "What the heck are you doing here?"

"Hi, Daisy," my ex says in a fake excited voice. "Or should I say Mrs. Hawthorne." A sinister grin takes over his face, and my stomach ties into a knot on reflex. "Does Charles

Hawthorne really think he can fool this town so easily? He got hitched up to the first available woman."

Jax takes a step closer, and my surprise finally breaks.

"You sent me that note!" I gasp. "How?"

"How difficult do you think it is to arrange a faux version of Charles Hawthorne's personal stationery?" Jax tsks, reminding me how often he used to make that annoying sound while criticizing me in the past.

"You've always been so careless, Daisy. Your boss' notes lie around the apartment *all the time*. And Charles, I don't even know where to begin with that idiot. For someone so paranoid about his privacy, he always left handwritten notes and instructions for his assistant. Has he not heard of email?"

"That's called being considerate. He knows I find it easier to read on paper. You would be aware of it, too, if in our five-year relationship, you'd have made a sincere effort to know me."

After I was diagnosed with a reading disability at a young age, my parents worked hard with me and some amazing therapists, so much that I almost feel no impact of it in my daily life. But reading and writing long notes on a screen still demands time, and I've compensated well for that by working overtime. Charles has never once been late because of my issues, and in fact, over time, he has embraced my love for paper.

But after being called out by Jax, it feels like someone just threw water over my years of hard work.

I'm unable to pull my gaze away from this man.

Is he really the one I wasted my time and tears on?

"Is that why you agreed to be his fake wife? Because he let you keep your job despite being dumb?"

"I'm not dumb, asshole. I had difficulty reading. I'm shocked I dated you!"

"And I'm shocked he married you and ruined my career for doing that interview." Jax's bloodshot eyes, fueled with rage, force me to take another step back.

"I have no idea what you're talking about, Jax. But I have no interest in spending a second longer in this room." I turn to leave, but Jax tugs on my arms and crowds me against a wall.

"Oh, no. You don't get to leave so soon, Daisy. And if you really don't know, then let me educate you. Your husband destroyed my IPO. In one night, all my investors pulled out. Everything I've worked for since years was snatched right out of my hands."

Oh my God!

I feel bad for Jax. I really do, despite the cheap trick he played with me. If there's anything in this world he genuinely cared about, it's that IPO.

But that sentiment lasts for no more than a second as he looks down at his watch.

"In fifteen minutes from now, the lobby outside this room will be filled with press and media. What do you think they'll believe when they see you and me together walking out of a hotel room?"

That's when it hits me.

"The man outside...he's the one who took your interview?"

"He sure did. It's about time Charles Hawthorne learns that he's not a god in this town."

twenty-two

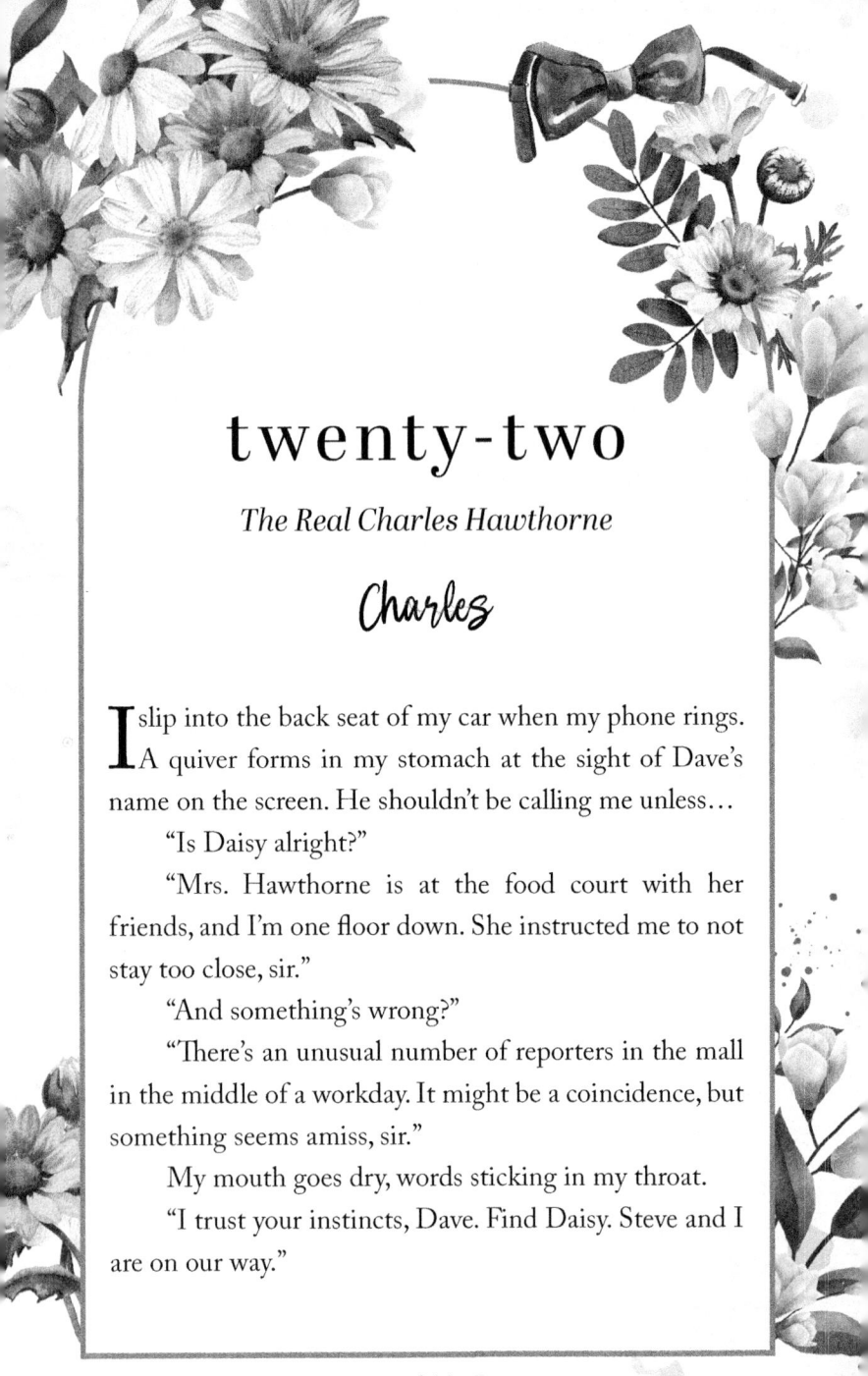

The Real Charles Hawthorne

Charles

I slip into the back seat of my car when my phone rings. A quiver forms in my stomach at the sight of Dave's name on the screen. He shouldn't be calling me unless…

"Is Daisy alright?"

"Mrs. Hawthorne is at the food court with her friends, and I'm one floor down. She instructed me to not stay too close, sir."

"And something's wrong?"

"There's an unusual number of reporters in the mall in the middle of a workday. It might be a coincidence, but something seems amiss, sir."

My mouth goes dry, words sticking in my throat.

"I trust your instincts, Dave. Find Daisy. Steve and I are on our way."

I've just ended the call when a text notification pops up on my screen.

> **Ray:** I'm in a meeting with the mayor of Cherrywood, and someone just asked him to turn on his TV. The local news is showing the mall, but I spotted Daisy's friends on the screen. Is everything under control?

My heart lurches out of my chest. All the blood drains from my face, and I let the familiar fear grip me for a second before I shoot a text to Carter King, head of Kings Security.

> **Me:** I need a small group of your best men at the Cherrywood mall. How soon can you make it happen?

I don't have to wait more than a few seconds for his reply.

> **Carter:** You can meet my five finest men at the mall's underground parking garage in ten minutes. If you want more force, it might take a while.

> **Me:** Five is good. Thanks.

"Carter King has sent additional security." I meet Steve's gaze in the rearview mirror. "Let's find them first."

My bodyguard curses before looking back at the street. In all these years, there has never been an incident when I had to call for backup security. Dave and Steve have always been enough. But this is different. This is Daisy.

My throat is dry by the time we arrive at the mall, and Dave is at the entrance.

"Please tell me you found Daisy?" My fists clench.

"Unfortunately not, Mr. Hawthorne, but her friends just told me you invited her to Madison Blue."

"I did fucking not!"

"I know that, sir. Her friends have given me a room number."

"Then let's find out who's lost their mind to think they can touch my wife and still live peacefully."

All my muscles bunch when we walk out of the elevator onto the second floor of the hotel. There're more than twenty reporters in the lobby. Their murmurs immediately come to a halt, and several camera flashes fire up as I walk farther in, flanked by my security team. The rustling of suits in the cramped space is just white noise, but it's the whooshing sound of my racing heartbeat that's deafening.

We stop outside a door with a traditional doorknob. I give a nod to the security, who immediately create a barricade between me and the media, making sure no one has a view of the room. When the knob immediately turns and the door finally opens, my heart thuds.

Daisy is crowded against the wall beside the door by her ex. Rage pulses throughout my body, but I keep my expressions flat and carefully step in. Steve and Dave follow me in, and finally, the door closes.

Daisy's eyes close in relief, and my fist tightens at the sight of a lone tear rolling down her cheeks. I look away from her and bring my gaze to her asshole ex.

"Mr. Mendes, we finally meet." I walk into the room with slow, measured steps. My voice betrays the tension burbling inside me. "But before we talk, why don't you take a step away from my wife? It's for your own safety, because right now, my brain is busy thinking of ways I can physically hurt someone and pose it as an accident."

"What are you doing here?" Jax gulps. His grip on Daisy loosens, but he's still holding her too close.

I didn't lie about thinking of hurting him, and I know I'll only be able to breathe calmly when he's out of my sight. Forever.

He releases another irritating huff, letting me know he wasn't counting on my arrival. His gaze swings between me and my bodyguards before he finally lets go of Daisy's arm.

Embarrassment flashes on my wife's face as she takes Dave's offered hand. I want to tell her that none of this was her fault and everything was staged. But before anything, I want to show her ex what it means to mess with Charles Hawthorne.

"So, what was the plan, Mr. Mendes? Invite my wife to your room and put on a show for the media? Hmm, but that's not how entrepreneurs behave, is it?" I flop down on the couch. "Oh, sorry, my bad. I must have forgotten—you're no longer an entrepreneur. How's the jobless life treating you, by the way?"

"You asshole—" Jax takes a step closer to me, but Steve steps in front of him, blocking him from coming my way and even pushing him back a step.

"I'd suggest you take your next steps very carefully, Mr. Mendes." I rise and adjust my suit sleeves before walking toward him. "You called her unfaithful when she was my girlfriend, and I ruined your career in return. What do you think I'll do when you put my wife's dignity in danger? It was a mistake to ruin *just* your career. You have twelve hours to leave this town for good or else I'll charge you with slander, libel, and defamation."

His face whitens. "You can't—"

"Do you really think I haven't encountered my fair share of assholes like you? Believe me, you're a more common breed than you think." With another step, I reach his face. "And, Mr. Mendes, next time you touch my wife or even breathe the same air as her, remember this."

My punch lands right on his jaw. Seeing the imprint of my wedding band on his skin gives me huge satisfaction.

"Clean him up before bringing him out." I don't wait for Dave and Steve to acknowledge my request, instead making a beeline for Daisy.

Her mouth is open, lips parted in a silent gasp, and when I hold her hand in mine, something I've wanted to do since I walked into this room, her skin is ice cold. "Let's go, butterfly."

"Charles." Her shock seems to finally break, and that low, quivering voice hits a nerve in my body. It's physically painful to watch her shoulders drop.

"It's okay. We'll talk at home. There's press outside. Let's handle them first and get the hell out of here."

Holding Daisy close to me, I stride outside to the waiting elevator, held by one of the Kings Security bodyguards. Just before the doors close, I jam it with my foot.

I hate lingering in this place a moment longer, but deep down, I know running away isn't the right solution. If I don't confront this now, there'll soon be another Jax Mendes threatening to disturb my life's balance and endanger Daisy. I turn to meet the gaze of the reporters.

"If you're after real news, join us in the lobby."

As the elevator doors shut, I see everyone moving toward the stairs.

"I'm sorry, Charles. Jax—" Daisy's voice is hoarse.

"Shh." I press a finger to her lips and discreetly tilt my head toward the camera on the ceiling. "As long as we're together, nothing can go wrong." My thumb traces her cheek as I hold her face.

But when I lean in and place my lips over hers, nothing else is on my mind. I'm only thinking about my wife and keeping her safe.

Bright camera flashes fire up as the door opens, and I pull away from Daisy and hold her hand in mine, standing before the reporters.

"I'm assuming you were promised gossip. Juicy news that would give your careers a kick and your newspapers or TV channels a major boost. But let me tell you something—I'm not a circus monkey, and neither is my wife. If anyone tries to put her or any other person in my family in harm's way, I'll incinerate everything. You wanted news. You wanted the real Charles Hawthorne. Here is the real me for you."

I tug Daisy closer to me.

"This is *Mrs. Charles Hawthorne*. My wife, my love, and the most important woman in my life. If anything happens to her, I'll destroy whoever supported that cause. I'll keep doing that until there isn't a single media outlet or newspaper left in this town. And that's a fucking promise."

twenty-three

Horrible Superhero

Daisy

"*This is Mrs. Charles Hawthorne. My wife, my love, and the most important woman in my life.*"

Charles' words keep echoing in my mind as I lie down in the middle of his bed. It's been hours since he dropped me home from the mall, and I'm still struggling to accept that today was real and not just a dream.

Did Charles really show up, once again abandoning his work in the middle of the day?

A knock on the door startles me, and I almost leap out of bed.

Is it him?

However, the door opens slowly, and Mrs. K peeks her head in.

"Can I make you something to eat now, Daisy?"

"Thanks, but I'm really not hungry. Have you heard from Charles?" I ask in return.

"I just got a text from Steve that they're on their way. Mr. Hawthorne should be home soon."

After she leaves, I get out of the bed. My phone is flooded with texts from Willow, Elodie, and Violet, all awaiting my response, but I'm too anxious to reply.

I opt to turn on the TV instead. The news coverage about Charles in the hotel is still playing.

I look at myself on the screen, standing beside him, my hand tightly clasped in his. I can still feel his touch, not just on my palm, but the electricity coursing throughout my entire body. On the screen, Charles clears his throat.

"*If anything happens to her, I'll destroy whoever supported that cause. I'll keep doing that until there isn't a single media outlet or newspaper remaining in this town. And that's a fucking promise.*"

His words send a swarm of butterflies fluttering in my belly.

Who exactly is this *Charles Hawthorne?*

"Mrs. Kowalski said you're not hungry, but I'm starving after playing your superhero again."

"Charles!" I turn around in a flash, my heart skipping a beat before racing wildly at the sight of him. "When did you get here?"

"When you were busy admiring me on the TV." His smile is the same one he's been giving me all week, as if nothing has happened, while I'm feeling exactly the opposite.

How is he not upset or irritated?

I had a whole apology memorized, but now…I don't think it's needed.

"I was not admiring you. Plus, you would look horrible in a cape." My mumbled words seem to cause his grin to only grow.

"I don't care. When it comes to my dear wife, I'll happily play a superhero whose power is to look horrible."

Alarm bells ring in my head. Why does his presence calm the anxiety that had gripped me tightly the entire day?

Slow down, Daisy. Don't jump to conclusions.

It's not Charles' presence but just that he's not blowing his top.

I'm just about to repeat that statement in my head once again when he leans in. I wait for his kiss. But surprisingly, it never comes. Instead, I feel a soft paper on my lips and my eyes fall open.

"What's that?"

"A precaution so no one takes advantage of us in future. Since it's widely known that my wife is a fan of stationery, this is custom-made with a barcode." He lifts the paper from my lips and turns on the camera of his phone. A second later, there's a green check mark on the screen. "Only when you see this, you can be sure that the message came from me. Otherwise, you don't have to come running for me."

"I didn't run." My rebuttal is so weak that I could have just agreed with him. After a few moments of silence, I finally ask, "Wouldn't it be easier to stop using handwritten messages and just send an official email instead?"

My palms turn clammy as I imagine myself sitting in Charles' office with my laptop, trying to keep up with his words as he dictates notes for a meeting. But before my panic engine can run at full throttle, Charles lifts my face up with his finger under my chin.

"I don't want you or any other member of my family to stop doing something they love just because there's an asshole trying to ruin it."

Our eyes connect and all the nerve endings at the back of my neck tingle. My husband, my boss, the person I used to call *asshole* is protecting me and worrying about my comfort.

"I'm so sorry about Jax, Charles," I whisper under my breath.

"I don't want you to say that asshole's name again. Jax is no longer going to be a problem in our life." Charles tucks a strand of hair behind my ear, but I'm too mesmerized by his words.

He said *our* life.

"Did you really destroy his IPO?" My heart pounds against my rib cage as I stare at him.

"Will you be upset if I did?" Charles asks, his emotions giving nothing away.

"Definitely not after what he did today."

"I ruined his fucking IPO." A vindictive smile finally stretches over his lips. "And I'll ruin him for putting you in harm's way."

Heat blooms in my stomach, spreading like wildfire across my skin at the possessive tone of his voice.

"He thought he could get to me through you. Even if he didn't mean to hurt you physically, he put you through an emotional ordeal. He has to pay a price for that."

"Because I'm a Hawthorne now?" I sound like a high school girl with my teeny-tiny voice while Charles' eyes flare with unspoken emotion.

"Yes, but also because you're my wife and you're the person I care about...a lot."

"Since when?" My voice is low and sincere, and maybe even...*hopeful*.

"Who knows?" His words hang in the air, and the butterflies in my stomach go crazy.

Before I can say anything, there's a knock on the door, and I welcome the distraction.

"Mr. Hawthorne, shall I set up the dinner table? I'm sure you and Mrs. Hawthorne are hungry." Mrs. K smiles, and suddenly, I appreciate her caring presence in Charles' home.

"You guessed right. I'm famished. Are you hungry now, my dear wife?"

I nod, and a few moments later, we're seated at the dining table. There's a nervous electricity, but looking at Charles, I'm sure it's only me who's feeling it. Because my husband, the self-proclaimed superhero of the day and the man who wouldn't smile to stop world hunger until some weeks ago, has a giant grin on his lips.

We mostly eat in silence except when our gazes connect, and in those moments, I'm the first one to break contact, ending the strange feeling, which tells me there's still a lot left in this day.

"Would you like something for dessert?" Mrs. K asks as she takes away our plates.

"I could definitely go for something sweet today," Charles replies, but he isn't looking at the housekeeper.

No, his gaze is fixed on me, causing heat to sear so deep I feel it in my bones. I up the wattage of my smile, something

I've been trying the entire week whenever he's giving me those smoldering looks.

But tonight, it doesn't seem to work.

It seems as if we've been playing around fire for too long, and now there's no escaping the inferno.

"I'll have apple pie and ice cream in a second." Unaware of the tension in the room, Mrs. K is busy arranging dessert, which is the last thing on our minds.

"On second thought, we'll eat the dessert later. I have something urgent to discuss with Daisy right now."

Only if urgent is the new word for driving your wife crazy.

When he rises from his chair and places his hand forward for me, that tiny gesture feels like the biggest moment of my life, even bigger than when I signed the marriage contract, or when Charles kissed me the first time.

His hand feels warm, unlike mine, and Charles intertwines our fingers as I get up. In a completely unhurried pace, he brings our folded hands to his mouth and kisses the back of mine.

Just a small touch and my heart is pounding in my ears. I'm in a daze, my namesake state, when he leads me in the same relaxed stride to the bedroom. But the moment the door closes, it's like a switch flips.

I squeal as Charles crowds me against the wooden door before I can walk away.

"Is my wife ready to beg tonight?"

I'd initially thought my answer to this question would be a nod, but right now, watching his smirk, it's like years of habit and I can't hold my tongue.

"Sorry, but my husband is too damn rich for me to beg for anything."

Charles' eyes widen before a laugh shoots out of him. He leans forward, his chin resting over my head as he pulls me closer.

"Damn you, butterfly." His back is still shaking with the last bits of laughter. "I never thought I'd find someone more headstrong than me, but God, you're unbelievable."

And he loves my bratty response. It's all over his face.

It's a magical feeling when you know you've left your guy speechless and in a trance just by being you. There's no effort and no race to be someone else.

He's just into the lame, silly you.

Charles pulls back, and then his thumb tugs my bottom lip down as he groans. "Since I can't take it any longer, for one night, and *just for one night*, I'm ready to beg."

Holy crap! Charles Hawthorne doesn't just say it, but he slides onto his knees. His tall frame, especially compared to mine, brings him eye level with my boobs.

"So, my dear wife, what is it gonna be?" he asks, but his hands are already moving up my legs.

I'm having a hard time believing this is the same man I've spent almost every waking moment with during the last four years, and yet he never made a comment that could remotely be labeled sexual.

"Since you asked so politely." My voice shakes as his fingers drift under the hem of my skirt, grazing the backs of my thighs.

"I seriously want you to finish that sentence in a '*hell yeah*,' Daisy."

A chill breaks out at the base of my neck, traveling down my spine until I shiver everywhere.

My teeth dig into my bottom lip, which moments ago felt his touch, and I finally nod.

"Thank fuck." Charles pulls me down to him before his face presses against my neck, and I feel his hot breath over my skin. "Do you know how torturous these days have been?"

"I'm happy I wasn't the only miserable one."

Charles chuckles and leans back, sitting on his heels.

"I've dreamed so much about it that I'm now not sure where to start."

He has dreamed about me!

Not just about me, but dreamed of us like this.

I worry I might die from this excessive dose of happy surprise, and God, that would be such a shame.

"I would be happy with anything, as long as we talk less and *do the other stuff* more."

The words have barely left my mouth when Charles' traveling fingers dip inside my underwear, and I jolt, which only makes his grin wider.

"Will you be able to control those remarks while I make you come, or should I make sure your mouth is occupied?"

Images run in my mind where my mouth is occupied with Charles' cock, and my gaze drops to his lap.

He chuckles once again. "Is my wife eager to get a taste?"

I never imagined Charles talking dirty, but God, this man could win awards for it, especially when he times it perfectly with that smile.

My eyes meet his, and I'm about to lie and shake my

head, when he unzips my skirt and lets it fall on the floor over my feet.

I gasp, and before I can react more, Charles moves the gusset of my panties aside, his mouth hot over my sex.

My brain struggles to decide whether to bend forward and take his support, which will also mean pulling away from his hot lips, or lean back against the door and push myself more into him.

I settle for something in between. My hands fist his cropped hair for support while my back arches.

My head falls against the hard wood of the door as Charles' tongue finds its way inside my sex. His hands are on my ass, squeezing my cheeks, and my moan covers any sensible word I could possibly form.

When Charles' teeth graze my clit, sparks go behind my closed eyelids.

I've never been touched this way. I've never been loved this way. And I know he's just getting started.

Like always, he hears my unsaid words, and as if to prove it, Charles pulls away only long enough to tear my silk panties, which drop down on my skirt at my feet.

His mouth sucking my clit is relentless, and his hands roam up from my hips, traveling under my silk blouse and finally over to my breasts, covered in a matching silk bra.

He starts slowly, kneading my breasts through the fabric before pushing the cups down. That only makes my boobs jut out, and Charles tweaks my nipples.

A part of my brain is trying to repeat and remember his every ministration because this is Charles *freaking* Hawthorne. A man who, until months ago, I couldn't even imagine having sex with. But here he is, holding me against his bedroom door and eating me like I'm the most delicious dessert ever known to him.

Charles Hawthorne isn't used to losing control, and I'll take everything he's giving tonight with open arms.

My eyes close. I focus on him and his touch—until the pressure builds beyond control, and I shatter into a billion pieces.

"Charles." His name from my lips is like a prayer.

"I got you, butterfly. You taste so damn good." Charles pulls away from my sex only for a second before going back in and sucking every drop.

I fold myself forward for support, physically and emotionally drained, but he pulls me closer to him. I feel him rising from the floor, and before I can make sense of it, he has me deposited on the bed, my back resting against the headboard.

"That was…" I start, unable to find the right word to fit this perfect moment.

"Just the beginning, my dear wife."

I open my eyes and press my lips against his cheek in a gentle kiss. "I can't wait."

That's the only green light he needs, and Charles' hands get to business. He pulls the blouse over my head, and with an expert move I could never imagine him doing, Charles unhooks my bra.

"That was pretty fast. How much practice do you have?"

He smirks. "Sometimes it's not about practice but motivation. And right now, my motivation to fuck you is off the charts."

While I sit naked on Charles' bed, trying to not be self-conscious, he leans back. And before I can scream at him to come back, he toes off his shoes.

My order-obsessed husband and boss kicks his shoes in different directions before removing his socks. I'm still reeling when he unbuttons his cuffs and slides his cufflinks into his pants pocket before undoing his shirt buttons and taking it off. I take in everything—his chest, broad enough to prove he's into sports but not wide like he's spending merciless hours in a gym.

My gaze moves lower to his tapered waist and the happy trail starting above his navel and hiding in his pants. But not for long, as Charles unhooks his belt, and then his pants are off. Those gray boxers I've only seen in packaging until now look mighty supreme as he saunters toward me.

His knee rests on the edge of the bed, and it dips under his weight.

"You have no idea how fucking hot you look, Daisy."

"Right back at you."

Charles chuckles, pushing down his boxers, and I need a moment to savor the sight.

"You did inherit some great family jewels."

"Have I told you how much I appreciate your running mouth?" He cocks an eyebrow as I watch him put on a condom.

I nod with a laugh, but it dies when Charles pulls on my feet and I slide down until I'm sprawled on the bed like a starfish.

His eyes shine as he looks at my sex.

"Wet and glistening, my dear wife. Is it all for me?"

"Do you really want an answer to that question?" I cock my brow, when my insides are shivering.

"I do, especially when I know it's going to be a breathy, horny yes." Charles' smirk is perfectly timed, because the moment he brings his cock against my opening and runs it over my wet lips, I can't bite back my moan—a breathy, horny moan, exactly like he expected.

"You're a vision, Daisy. Better than any of my fantasies."

I don't know what I want more, for Charles to keep talking and tell me in detail all he imagined with me, or for him to fuck me like I imagined he would.

And thank God he isn't waiting for any input from me, because in the next second, he thrusts inside me, inch by inch.

My sex, which hasn't seen any action in months, is all ready for him. But my insides need a few moments to adjust when he's fully seated.

"Tell me if it hurts," Charles grits above me.

"It will only hurt if you stop," I grit right back.

It does hurt a little, but it also feels good—real good.

"Fuck, you're big." I groan. Or is it a moan?

"I hope that isn't a complaint."

"Hell no. But can you move now, Charles?"

Before he does that, Charles grabs my left hand, which is clutching his forearm, and places it over his heart. My wedding band and daisy ring stand proud against the contrast of our skin.

My heartbeat halts at that simple act in the middle of our frenzy. I feel like this is his way of saying what we're doing is more than just sex, and I'm nervous and excited to find that meaning when Charles is buried deep inside me.

His face is serious as he continues to stare at me as if the same emotion runs through him, and his lips curl on one side.

And then Charles fucks me with long, measured thrusts. Each push seems to have a purpose, and if it's to make me forget my name, it does a damn good job.

My hand claws at his chest, and I know my nails are leaving marks on his flawless skin. But before I can apologize or form a sentence that might sound like an apology, Charles' thrusts pick up momentum, making me forget everything.

His thumb comes to play with my clit, and it takes another second before I lose it all.

He hides his face in my neck before he falls apart in one final thrust.

We breathe heavily as he drops down beside me with zero finesse.

My eyes are closed, but I hear Charles moving, possibly taking care of the condom.

"Those were some extraordinary moves," I blurt when he pulls me closer to his chest.

"Thank you so much. I'm glad you approve." His voice is breathy, and I don't miss the smile behind it. "Now sleep and you can dream about my moves when they're still fresh in your mind."

"You joke about it all you like. But believe me when I say, I'm not going to forget anything about this night, possibly ever."

twenty-four

It's a Special Holiday

Charles

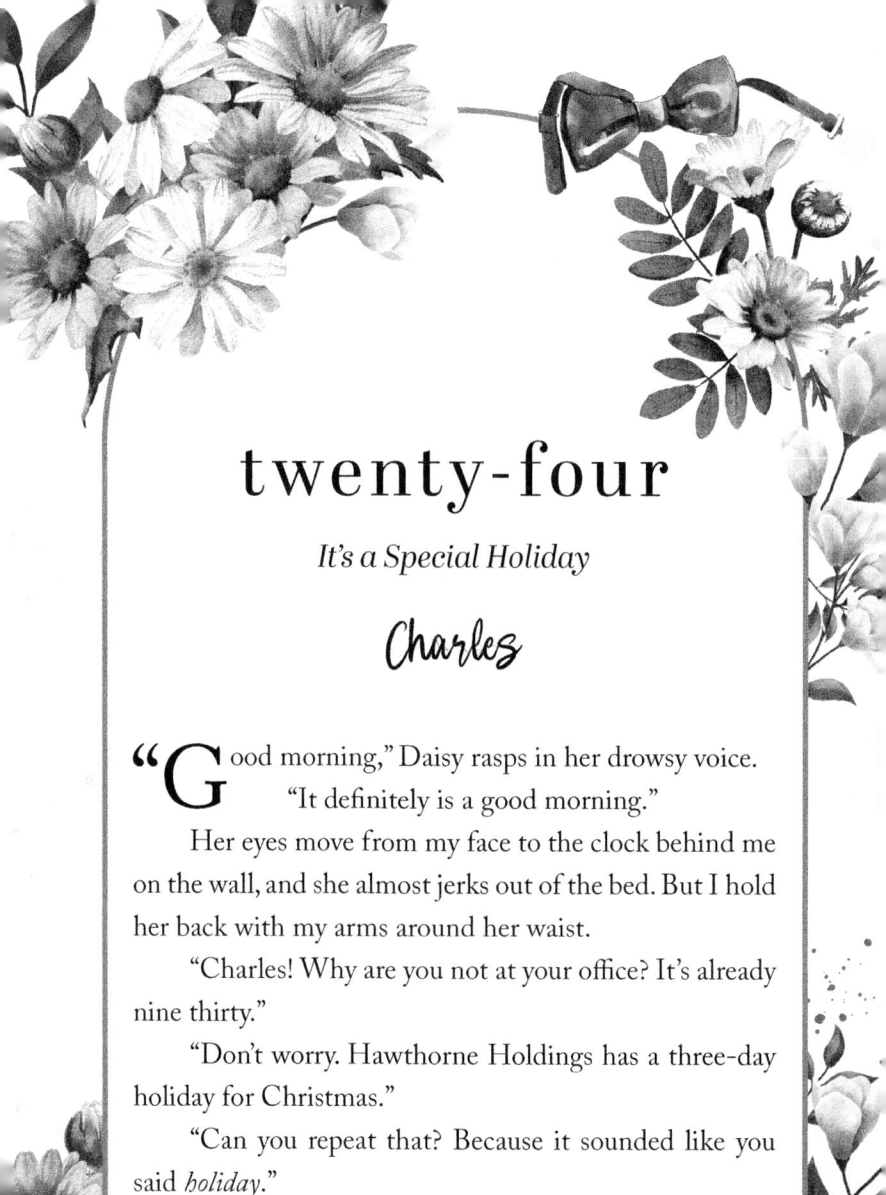

"Good morning," Daisy rasps in her drowsy voice.

"It definitely is a good morning."

Her eyes move from my face to the clock behind me on the wall, and she almost jerks out of the bed. But I hold her back with my arms around her waist.

"Charles! Why are you not at your office? It's already nine thirty."

"Don't worry. Hawthorne Holdings has a three-day holiday for Christmas."

"Can you repeat that? Because it sounded like you said *holiday*."

"And that's exactly what I said, my dear wife." Like always, whenever I call her wife, she sucks in a low breath.

"But there are no special holidays. In fact, I'm amazed

the labor department isn't knocking at your door due to the inhumane working conditions."

"Inhumane working conditions?" I throw my head back in laughter. "Every employee who works on national holidays is paid more than their fair share. It's a choice. We don't force anyone."

"I never had a choice." She pins me with her gaze.

"Because you're special." I lean forward and tuck a strand of hair behind her ear. "Do you see anyone else on this bed smelling so exquisite?"

She gasps and I love the way her eyes widen. Her face is like a canvas, so easy to read even for a dumb fuck like me who doesn't understand feelings.

"And what's the holiday about? Did you just declare Wednesday a rest day instead of Sunday?"

No one cracks me up like her. And now that I can't and don't need to hide my laughs and grins from her, I embrace the fresh burst of dopamine every time it bubbles inside me.

"As much as I'm honored that you think so much of me, unfortunately, I don't have *that* kind of power. It's a holiday because it's my wife's first Christmas as a Hawthorne. Haven't you checked your email?"

She looks at me for a second before turning around and grabbing her phone from the nightstand. The cover she's been tugging close to her neck drops, and I get a perfect view of her slender back.

Dear all,

This is my wife's first Christmas as a Hawthorne, and from this year on, I declare the next three days a man-

datory paid vacation.

I wish you and your loved ones a happy holiday season.

- Charles A. Hawthorne

CEO, Hawthorne Holdings &
Board of Directors, Elixir Inc.

Daisy reads the email out loud.

"You really declared a three-day company holiday?" She looks at me with a starry, doe-eyed expression. "Who the heck are you and where's my boss?"

I'm not going to tell her that if she keeps looking at me like this, that asshole might never appear.

"Do you even know what people do on a holiday?" Daisy asks slowly, still not over the shock.

"Don't you worry about that. I have a full day planned for both of us."

"I can't wait to listen to your great plan." She finally seems to have found her usual self and rolls her eyes. "I'm sure it involves going to museums and galleries and some highly posh restaurants."

"Don't hate it before you try it, my dear wife." I grin. "For your information, our first stop is your dad's house."

I get out of bed, and satisfaction fills my heart when she keeps staring at me. I'm only wearing track pants, which I pulled on sometime later in the night. I make a meal out of it as I saunter over to the nightstand and text Mrs. Kowalski, requesting two cups of coffee.

"Are we really going to my dad's?"

I nod. "We are going to have breakfast with him. After the news yesterday, he wants to personally make sure you're okay."

"And how would you know all that?"

"Because your dad told me so."

"You're saying that Charles Hawthorne, the man who avoids talking to people, sometimes even when there are billions of dollars at stake, talked to my dad for leisure?" Her eyebrows shoot up, nearly disappearing into her hairline.

"What can I say? He's more interesting and fun than most people in meeting rooms."

The words have just left my mouth when there's a knock on the door. Daisy pulls the sheets up to her neck, but I can't pull my gaze away from her. Sitting in the middle of my bed, wrapped in my pristine white bedcovers, she looks exquisite. Her hair is mussed from sleep. Her face is devoid of any makeup except the pink blush that makes a frequent appearance on her face these days. I could watch her like this all day, every day of my life and never get bored.

She looks thoroughly fucked, thoroughly loved, and thoroughly mine.

There's a second knock on the door and Daisy jerks. I'm relieved. It's not just me who can't focus on my surroundings these days.

I'm about to open the door when she squeals. "Stop!"

I look over my shoulder, raising an eyebrow.

"Is it Mrs. K at the door?"

I nod slowly and Daisy raises her hands up in the air in return.

"Where the heck is your shirt, Hawthorne?"

The perpetual grin on my face morphs into full-blown laughter, but I still put on a shirt.

If my wife wants me all for herself, I'm not going to complain. Ever.

When I open the door, Mrs. Kowalski is waiting patiently, holding a wooden tray with two coffee mugs that I've never seen in my house before.

One of them says Mr., and there's a black mustache and a beard under the two letters written in flowing script. The second matching one says Mrs., and there's a pink hair clip on the side.

They are too cheesy and cute.

When she finds me staring at the mugs, my housekeeper explains, "Mr. Raymond Teager's driver dropped them off this morning. He said it was a gift from your cousin."

"Of course it is." I chuckle.

After yesterday's news, my cousins must be itching to rib me, and I wouldn't be surprised if not just Ray but all four of them are behind these coffee mug gifts.

But the joke's on them. They might have thought I'd hate these cups, but I love them.

I place the tray on the bed, and Daisy sits straight.

"About last night," she starts. "So, we had sex—"

"And thank God for that, because I'd hate if it was all my imagination."

Her mouth falls open, forming a perfect *O* before she looks away and makes an annoyed sound.

"Why did I think you would make this conversation any easier?" she grumbles under her breath.

As much as I've enjoyed her annoyance over the years, I like her smiling much more.

"What's there to discuss?"

"This." She moves her hands between us before throwing them up in the air. "This was not a part of the plan, Charles. Was it?"

For the first time since I woke up today, an empty feeling hits me hard. The word *plan* surges the same feeling that has always gripped me but has been less intense since she came into my life.

"You are my wife, aren't you?"

She turns those big, tender brown eyes on me, nodding slowly. "Yes, but—"

"There is no but. The last time I checked, there's no rule that says it's a crime to sleep with your wife."

"It's not the same for us, and you know it, Charles." Her voice is low. "The contract—"

I've officially started to hate that word.

"There's nothing about us sleeping together in the contract, is there? We are like any other married couple until one of us wants to end this relationship. Do you want to end it today?"

Discomfort grips me even saying the words, but thankfully, Daisy doesn't keep my heart in pain for longer and immediately shakes her head.

"I don't. But after everything that has happened in the last week, don't you want to think more—"

"Not for a fucking second. What I want is to repeat what we did yesterday. What I really want is to finally make my wife beg. This time, possibly on her knees."

She blinks rapidly, her gaze transfixed on me, my face, my lips, and I love it.

I love that she's as attracted to me as I am to her.

"So it wasn't, like, a one-time thing?" she asks carefully, biting her lip and making me crazy.

"Do you want it to be a one-time thing, Daisy?" My heart is in my throat at that question.

Please, butterfly, don't say yes.

My prayer is answered when she once again shakes her head.

I like that I can make her speechless and throw her off-kilter for a change.

"You speak my thoughts too. So are you ready for some begging?"

"Why don't you do it, since you looked so fine doing so last night? I'll wait." She finally gives me that grin, which for years I've considered to be my good luck charm.

"It'll be the longest wait of your life, butterfly, given I don't beg."

"Really? Shall I remind you of last night?" she quips, squaring her shoulders.

"I told you it was a one-time thing." I prowl toward her. I knew expecting her not to bring up my moment of weakness was my own stupidity.

"But you looked so good on your knees, my dear husband." The title rolls between her lips with so much tease and I feel as if her mouth has a direct connection with my cock.

I place the coffee tray on the floor, and in the next breath, I pounce on her. She squeals like a madwoman, but I don't let go.

I kiss her lips, her cheeks, her neck. I kiss her everywhere I can as she thrashes and laughs.

I finally pull away the covers that hide her from me.

"You've got no fucking idea how long you've been making me crazy," I whisper in between kissing the soft skin of her neck.

Her squealing stops and she looks at me with an unfamiliar emotion. But before she can think more about the words that have slipped from my mouth by mistake, I capture her lips in mine.

I kiss her like my life depends on her touch, and it has started to feel like it does.

"You want me on my knees, Daisy? I'll be on my knees." I bring my feet down on the floor and drag hers along with me before my knees hit the ground. "But I promise you, I won't be the one who's begging today."

Her legs hang from the edge of the bed, and she gasps when I lean forward, dropping my head to her chest. A guttural groan leaves me when I suck her nipple into my mouth. She moans, and the moment I feel her writhing on the sheets, I stop.

"Feel free to say 'Please fuck me, husband,' whenever you're ready."

Her disoriented gaze meets mine, and a beat later, she realizes my game.

Yeah, I'm going to bring her to the brink of crazy. No, I'm not going to continue until she's begging me to.

Am I petty? Maybe I am.

But I also have a reputation to uphold.

I'm nicknamed *asshole*, after all. There must have been a good reason for that.

Before Daisy can move away, I drag my lips over her body. Going from one tit to another, licking those cherry nipples, sucking the valley between *her girls*, a memory of that nickname so clear in my head. A day that triggered everything.

I descend lower, skimming my teeth over her stomach, twirling my tongue over her navel. She sucks in a breath, and her body shakes and moves and quivers all at once.

"Ready to beg, wife?"

Her gritted whimpers fill the air as she grinds her teeth. "Fuck you, Hawthorne."

I chuckle and nip the flesh around her waist.

I love her curves. They accentuate her beauty.

I once again get down, resting my weight on my heels, skimming my hand along her soft, silky thighs, admiring the view.

Daisy rises on her elbows and watches me as I stare at her beautiful naked body. One I've spent years not thinking about.

But now, I can't just think about it. I have to make her beg for me to touch, kiss, and fuck it.

Talk about change.

Hell yeah, I'm suddenly a big fan of *that* c-word, among some others.

I run my thumb over her sex, gathering moisture, before I swipe all the wetness over her clit. Another favorite c-word.

She inhales sharply, but her eyes remain on my face, and I grin.

"I like knowing that I make you so fucking wet, Mrs. Hawthorne."

She sucks in another breath as I dip my head and taste that wetness.

My tongue starts slow, just perusing for a while before I really get down to work. She starts to rock against my face, and I know I need to pull back, make her beg, but that's so fucking hard.

Instead of pulling away, I spread her legs and dive in deeper with a snarl.

"Fuck, Charles. You're killing me."

I watch a shiver, and on reflex, pull away.

A cry slips out of Daisy's lips, and that's my undoing. I'll never leave her wanting for anything, and certainly not for an orgasm.

This time when I dive in to eat her sex, her fingers go through my hair, pulling on it tightly, maybe to not let me go or maybe for support. But whatever she needs, I'm gonna give it.

Making her beg is irrelevant because I can't bear her waiting for anything, especially something I want her to receive only from me.

I drop my track pants and grab the condom packet I found with a note in my laptop case the day before my wedding day.

Life can be full of surprises, and it doesn't hurt to be prepared. I'd hate for you to worry about protection with your pants down, Charlie. :)

Your overprepared brother, Ray.

That asshole.

"Charles, please. You won. I—I'm ready to—"

My hand splays over Daisy's mouth, stopping her words. Her confused gaze meets mine, but since I have no explanation for my actions, I don't provide any and instead run the head of my cock through her folds.

"It seems I don't enjoy making you beg after all." I slide

in slowly. My teeth grit as I let her adjust to my size. "You don't know how beautiful you look stuffed full of me."

Her eyes open in an instant, and my muscles tighten. Those brown pools get to me, speaking volumes.

They move from my face to where we're connected in the most basal way.

An emotion crosses her face that is so soft and pliant that I feel I'll ruin it just by watching it. She's never looked at me like that.

And it hits my chest right then like shrapnel.

From this day on, sex for me means Daisy and the way she looks right now. There's nothing else. There's nothing more.

I don't know what she sees on my face, maybe my dumbstruck emotion, but her eyes fall shut.

"You need to up your dirty talk game, Charles. This isn't working for me."

My chuckle is loud, and when her eyes open, she's grinning like a fool.

"You can't fool me right now, Daisy." I pull out and thrust inside her with more force, eliciting a moan from her. "You." Another deep thrust. "Are." Another. "Dripping." This one is accompanied by her loud moan. "All over me."

"Ch-Charles."

"I know, butterfly. If I can't make you beg, I'm going to make you cry in pleasure, and that's a fucking promise." I pull out and flip her over, ready to prove my words.

I hold her ass, raising it up before sliding my cock inside her.

"Fuck, I didn't know you'd be so deep this way." She groans and my chest cracks at the remark.

I know I'm not her first, a fact I hate but can't change, so I don't dwell on it. But I can't stop myself from grinning, knowing I gave her a first experience.

"I know, butterfly, and you look so good stretched around your husband's cock as it glides in and out." I time the words with my actions.

Her hands relax on the sheet for a beat, and she turns to look over her shoulder.

There's shock, surprise, and delight all wrapped in her face.

I know it because I feel the same.

I knew sex with Daisy would be amazing, but this is so fucking out of this world.

I feel my release right there, ready to consume me, but I don't want this moment to end.

My fingertips dig into her ass, and my strokes turn punishing. There's nothing gentle about the way I move inside her, but Daisy doesn't just moan louder but also pushes back in encouragement.

The sound of skin slapping reverberates in my room, a foreign delight for these walls, and finally Daisy gives me what I'm after.

She cries my name over and over, and that's enough for me to give in to the release and erupt inside her.

I lose balance but hold my weight on my elbows. Our ragged breathing fills the room as I place a kiss over her shoulder.

"I'm thankful I didn't know you could do that, Charles. I might have begged you long ago."

I'm unable to hold back my laughter and fall beside her. My arms drop over my eyes as I continue to laugh with abandon. Only with her could I be so carefree after such an intense experience.

I swipe the corner of my eye before turning to her and find her watching me with a smile on her face.

"You've ordered these chocolates especially for my dad?" Daisy asks, staring at the box in my hand as she slides into the limo after me.

"Yes. These are from a famous Swiss chocolatier. His family has been making chocolates for us and a few royal families across the globe. Upon my request, he prepared low-sugar, low-calorie almond chocolates for Jason."

Daisy's gaze drifts from me to the box. Her mouth opens and closes like a fish almost comically before she asks, "How do you know almond chocolates are my dad's favorites?"

"Because he told me."

"When?"

"In one of our texts."

She swallows hard. "You really talk to my dad?"

"Why are you surprised? Did you think he wouldn't want to get to know your new husband better?"

She's still hesitant but then slowly nods. "I guess he would."

I cup her face. Now that I know how she feels and reacts to my touch, I can't stop touching her. As expected, her eyes turn wide and her lips quiver.

"Why is it so surprising that I care about your dad? I can be a caring person." My thumb brushes against her soft cheek. Light shines in her eyes in a way that has always captivated me.

"Aren't you the one who told the crying receptionist to suck it up and return to work in less than two minutes or else she could find a new place to work?" She snaps her fingers, mimicking my action from the past.

I fall back against my seat, unable to hold my laughter. "You know that's not the same. She was crying over her favorite café moving less than a mile away."

She shrugs, her eyes still focused on my face. "It's a shame you don't laugh like this more often. It's beautiful."

"Maybe going forward, I will, now that I have you around me twenty-four seven." *And also because you care enough to notice my laughs.*

"I'm not your babysitter or your personal comedian." Daisy folds her arms over her chest, looking away from me. But in the tinted windows, our gazes connect, and I'm not the only one smiling.

Steve parks outside my father-in-law's home. Daisy is dressed casually today. Blue jeans. Black sweater. Canvas shoes. There's a pearl-and-rhinestone clip on her hair and minimal makeup on her face. Without trying, she's the most beautiful girl I've ever seen in my life.

I place my hand forward, and the diamond of her engagement ring digs into my palm.

I love how it feels. I love what it says.

She's mine.

We walk past the small iron gate and reach the porch. Daisy's dad is sitting on a wingback chair with his head buried in his phone, and he looks up.

"Doodles? Charles? What a surprise!"

He looks much happier and healthier since I last saw him in his home, with numerous reporters as our audience.

"Dad, why are you so dressed up?" Daisy asks hesitantly. "Did you go out?"

"No, no. Kai just took some pictures for my social media," Jason replies, leading us inside. "I'm a social media influencer now, Doodles. Do you know I've made three hundred friends in just a matter of days?"

"And what do you talk about with these new friends?"

"Cooking. Lifestyle. Alzheimer's. A lot of my online friends are patients like me who are in the early stages of the disease. We crack jokes about forgetting everything and doing stupid things like brushing our teeth multiple times a day, but also good things like forgetting our asshole ex-bosses." Jason grins.

As much as I hate everything with the word *social* in it, I'm glad Daisy's father has found something that's helping him keep his spirits high.

"Wow!" Daisy looks at him and then at me with a mix of surprise and shock.

"Your mom used to say there's a silver lining in every dark cloud, we just have to find it. I think I've finally found mine." He pats her cheek affectionately.

Of course she grew up with ample love and affection in her life. That's the reason she wants to marry for love and possibly also have kids.

Before my mood takes a turn into a dark alley, Jason slaps me on the back. "Enough about me. How's the business world?"

Daisy gasps, and I turn to look at her while her father asks, "Something the matter, Doodles?"

twenty-five

Crap. Crap. Crappity Crap.

Daisy

"He's Charles Hawthorne, Dad!" I hiss under my breath, as if that'll prevent Charles' bat-like hearing to make out my words. "You can't smack his back. I've seen him ruin people's lives for much less, like someone stepping inside his invisible personal space."

"In this house, he's your husband and my son-in-law. Right, Charlie?"

Charlie! I haven't heard anyone except Charles' family call him that.

I'm about to get between Dad and Charles to protect my lovely but stupid father, when Charles scowls—*at me*.

"Absolutely! Your daughter just enjoys imagining me as some sort of evil king."

"See? Even when he's evil, he has to be the king. Why can't you be an evil soldier?"

"You both are too cute. Fighting like cats and dogs but also unable to stay apart for longer than a minute. Daisy's mom and I were exactly the same, until this girl walked into our lives." His eyes shine the way they did when I literally walked into this house.

He then turns toward Charles.

"I have everything ready for peanut butter pancakes, Charles. After the way you protected my Doodles yesterday, I want to pass down all our special family secrets to you before I forget." He winks.

Probably for the first time since his diagnosis, Dad is smiling so wide and making a joke about his health.

"I'm ready to soak in all the secrets." Charles removes his jacket and rolls up his sleeves, making my ovaries combust.

God, I've seen the man without a shirt on, but there's something sexy and forbidden about him when he's dressed in a tailored white shirt with an expensive tie hanging from his neck, the veins of his forearms popping out and making my deep-buried fantasies come to life.

"First lesson." Dad leads my boss-husband to the kitchen. "You cannot make these pancakes for her every day or else they'll lose their impact. Only when she's upset or too angry to even listen to you."

"Dad!" I squeal. "You're my father. Instead of telling him that, you should be advising him never to do anything that would upset me."

"He's a man, Doodles, not God." Dad laughs. "Men are designed to be stupid. The key to a successful marriage is for the man to keep his stupidity in check and for the woman to be patient enough to overlook it sometimes."

My feminist brain screams at me to remind Dad that women, too, have the right to be stupid, and it's not only their job to be patient. But I don't want to ruin the perfect, dreamlike morning we're having.

Throughout the cooking, Charles hangs on to Dad's every word and instruction with the same focus that he carries in the boardroom. He even flashes a smile for the camera as Dad snaps selfies of the two of them for his social media. But when Charles slides the pancake onto a plate, his teeth grit in frustration. I can't help but chuckle when I see the reason why—instead of a perfect circle, it's turned into a soft triangle.

"You can always argue that you were going for a heart shape."

His scowl is immediately swept clean and replaced by a grin.

A grin I've started to understand.

A grin that makes my toes curl and my heart race.

He drizzles some syrup onto it before picking up a slice on the fork. His eyes dance with mischief as he mouths, "Open up."

Two simple, platonic words, yet they send heat shooting down my core.

My gaze darts toward Dad, fully engrossed on his phone with his back turned toward us. I lean forward and put the fork in my mouth, never taking my eyes off Charles. The moment my lips close around the cold steel, his nostrils flare.

"It's so sweet that I probably need to change your name again. Charles Sweet Hawthorne," I whisper.

imperfect match

"What can I do to stop your obsession with my middle name, Daisy Hazy Hawthorne?"

My legs go unsteady. "How did you—"

There's only one person who knows my official middle name, because he's the one who put it on the document.

"Dad! You told Charles my middle name! Didn't you promise me years ago that it would never come out?"

"He's your husband, Doodles. You're not supposed to have secrets from each other." He shrugs, returning to whatever he's doing on his phone.

"You can't call me that ever again." I point a finger in the air, trying to channel my strictest persona before Charles, but his grin only grows.

"I can't?" One of his eyebrows quirks up in that sexy way. "After all the heartache you've given me over the years, I think it's only fair that I tease you a little."

"No, please. I hate that name." Every childhood trauma floods back to me, where my middle name was one more reason I was bullied at school. Something that seemed harmless when Dad suggested it in this very room several years ago, became the bane of my existence as I grew up. I hate it when my throat tightens and tears well up in my eyes.

"Hey," Charles says, his thumb rubbing against my cheek. "Daisy, it's just a name."

"It was my nana's middle name." My throat chokes. "She had a blast with it with her friends. My parents wanted the same for me, but it turned into a nightmare at school. I didn't share every story with my parents, but I shiver when called by that name. I know it's silly and stupid, but—"

"I promise I'll never call you that." Charles leans forward and places a kiss on my forehead.

I nod just as Dad rejoins us. "Is it okay if I post a few of our pictures online, Charles?"

"Go ahead." My husband grins.

Is he really the same man who made a rule against opening any social media website on the company network?

"Are you sure about your private pictures being online?" I tug on Charles' sleeves when Dad is out of earshot.

"Those aren't private. But if you ever decide to share anything about what we do in the bedroom, now that's a different story." His sexy and relaxed smile makes all the butterflies go crazy in my belly.

"If I knew sex was what you needed to lighten up your cranky mood, I'd have—"

"What would you have done, Daisy?" he asks in a low, husky voice.

I can't believe it. My asshole boss, who would probably rather kill baby dolphins than learn how to make someone happy, has managed to figure out in a matter of hours how his low voice makes my heart skip a beat.

But I haven't spent years working under him in vain. I take a calming breath and purse my lips.

His gaze drops from my eyes to my lips, and his nostrils flare.

Taste your own medicine, Hawthorne.

"I'd have gifted you a special kind of massager." I wiggle my brows before motioning toward his body part a little south of his belt.

But when Charles throws his head back and laughs,

I feel like I haven't just won an argument but everything. Something hits me in the chest like Cupid's arrow as I trace the column of his neck, moving up to his curled lips, and then to his eyes, which crinkle with laugh lines.

A feeling of possessiveness burns inside me, whispering softly that I'm somehow responsible for protecting his happiness.

If earlier, as his assistant, I wanted him to scowl less, now I want him to laugh more.

If earlier I missed his snarky comments when he was out for a meeting, now I just miss him.

If earlier I hated him when he was breathing down my neck, now I love having him around me.

I just love…

Crap. Crap. Crappity Crap.

Steve parks outside the Hawthorne mansion, and before we can step out of the car, Chloe rushes to the porch.

Watching her dressed casually in red pants and a white top for a change, I feel less self-conscious about my own clothes. If I knew we were going to come straight from my dad's place to the Hawthorne mansion, I would have picked something more formal.

"Hey, Charlie. I thought we might not see you this holiday season."

"And why would you think that?" Her brother raises an eyebrow in a way I've started to find sexy.

Oh, to hell with it. There's absolutely nothing I don't find sexy about Charles these days.

"Maybe because you're always stuck to your new bride like extra strong superglue, playing her bodyguard." She grins before throwing her arms around him.

Their relationship has always been a surprise to me. For someone who avoids any show of affection as if it'll give him some communicable disease, Charles is completely different around his sister. It's like she knows a secret button that can flip her brother's mood from that of a person attending a funeral to that of a Swiftie at a Taylor Swift concert.

"But it seems you were able to pull yourself away from the task of threatening reporters, landing straight into Daisy's dad's kitchen to flip pancakes and looking so cute while doing so." Chloe winks at me before pulling me into a tight hug.

"How do you know about the pancakes?" I ask as she squeezes the hell out of me.

"Charlie is all over social media." She grins. "Did you know, until this morning, my brother hated cooking?"

"I never said that," Charles replies causally, picking some invisible lint off the sleeve of his suit jacket.

"Oh really? Then it must have been your long-lost twin who hid in the laundry room whenever I baked cookies for a bake sale and everyone pitched in except you." She pokes her tongue out.

"Weren't you like six then? Your brain was no bigger than an egg, so of course your memories are messed up."

"Please don't let him anywhere near your kids." Chloe mock groans. Completely oblivious to how her brother's jaw clenches upon her words, she grabs our hands and leads us inside. "Now come on. Grandma wouldn't let me open the presents until everyone was here."

As I step into the living room, my feet pause at the sight of a tall Christmas tree nestled in the corner, its branches nearly brushing against the ceiling. Red, gold, and white ornaments hang in every corner, so beautiful that I fear I might ruin it with just a touch. Charles' parents, grandmother, and great-gram are gathered around a grand fireplace that's casting a warm orange glow across the space. The light dances off the chandelier suspended in the center of the room, adding to the ambiance.

"Here you are, my sweethearts." GG's face lights up. She's dressed in a flowing red dress with a matching silk scarf on her hair and dangling earrings completing the ensemble. Every time I see her, I can't help but envy her confidence and zest for life.

How can someone be so in love with *everything*?

Maybe the answer lies in this room, which is plucked out of a movie set. It feels safe, warm, and happy.

"Come here, you lovebirds. It's been too long since I last saw you." GG grins, holding our faces and kissing our foreheads.

"You saw us only a few days ago, GG," Charles replies as we settle on the couch beside Chloe and are immediately handed glasses of eggnog by the staff.

"When you reach my age, *a few days* feels like an eternity."

"So, is it finally time for presents?" Chloe springs out of her seat, making me jerk in response. Charles' hand curls around my waist to help me settle as I balance my drink.

How is it that in just a few weeks, touching each other has become so spontaneous that we don't even think about it?

"You still behave like a kid, Chloe." Irene Hawthorne shakes her head in light disapproval, but that doesn't affect Chloe's smile, and finally, she motions toward the gifts. "Go ahead, take your gifts."

Chloe moves like an arrow, handing each of us a gift box beautifully wrapped with our names written on a white note card.

Crap!

"Why didn't you tell me there was going to be a gift exchange?" I tug on Charles' jacket. "I didn't bring anyone anything!"

Way to make your new family hate you, Daisy.

"We got everyone something. You'll see soon." He smiles casually while my heart gallops.

Did he just say we?

"The gifts in your hands are from Grandma, so you can all guess they will be classy and elegant, exactly like her. We'll all open them together on the count of three." Chloe makes a big show of counting, waving her fingers in the air.

My shaky hands turn cold as I remove the silver gift wrap and stare down at a beautiful pearl necklace.

"This was my mother's."

My head flies up at Charles' grandmother's voice.

"Now that you are a Hawthorne, Daisy, you will be under scrutiny twenty-four seven. Your every step will be watched, and your every word will be judged. But in between all that, you'll also have a chance to do wonderful things for this town and its people. An opportunity that comes to only a few. I hope you use your chance wisely. Consider this my blessing and best wishes."

imperfect match

I'm surprised because Irene Hawthorne isn't what someone would call soft-hearted. She's famous for being ruthless and not mincing her words. And she soon proves that I'm not wrong about her.

"You were, of course, not the girl I always imagined as my grandson's bride."

Beside me, Charles stiffens, but I don't take offense. How can I, when everything she just said is nothing but true?

I'm Charles' imperfect match, after all.

"But Charles has given up so much for this family and the Hawthorne name that I'm happy he was able to find his own happiness along the way." She leans back in her seat while guilt slithers inside me.

I close the box after thanking her and giving the necklace one last look, knowing I'm never going to wear it. Deceiving everyone is one thing, but taking something so precious that doesn't rightfully belong to me is downright stealing.

After everyone has opened their presents, Chloe goes back to the tree and returns with a new set of gifts.

"These are from the very beloved, hottest couple of Cherrywood. We can't wait to see what you both got us." Chloe waves a few envelopes in the air, grinning like a kid while the eggnog turns to acid in my stomach, ready to crawl up my esophagus.

I feel like I'm sitting in some lab's experimental chair instead of this comfy couch, where I'm bombarded with hard emotions one right after the other.

Given the envelopes and Charles' love for gift cards, I have no doubt of what he bought for his family, yet I can't help but make a tiny prayer in vain.

Oh God, please, please let it be something other than gift cards.

I really don't want the Hawthornes to think I can't carry my lazy ass to a store and buy everyone a nice present.

"What the heck is this?" Chloe's hands rest over her hips as she squints at her brother.

And suddenly I wish the opposite—for the colorful paper in her hand to be a gift card instead of whatever it is that's causing her temper to rise.

"It's a Christmas gift," Charles, on the other hand, replies calmly.

"Is this a joke? You know I'm scared of heights. I'm never going to skydive."

"You have to get over your fears if you want something in life, sis."

"I don't want anything, especially if it comes from jumping out of a plane." Chloe neatly tucks the paper back into the envelope and places it onto the table as if never wanting to touch it again.

"I have found the perfect trainer for you. You think I'd ask you to do anything that isn't safe?"

"Forget it, Charlie! I'm not going to do it." Chloe throws daggers her brother's way.

This has to be the first time I've seen her upset or angry with her beloved brother, and I worry this might ruin everyone's mood. I lean forward, about to tell Chloe that I'd be happy to get something more suited to her, when Charles places his hand over my thigh.

I glance at him and, still smiling, he shakes his head

before once again turning to Chloe, who's watching us closely with a narrowed stare.

"Oh, believe me, you will, especially when you see who else trains there."

Something unspoken passes between the two, like a secret that only they share, until Chloe's gaze drifts to my lap.

"And what about Daisy's gift? Or were you so busy planning my murder that you forgot your new wife?"

Did he?

I turn around and my eyes snap to his. Charles' lips curl as he leans forward.

What the heck is he doing?

My body is frozen in place when he places a soft kiss on my cheek. "I can never forget you. Your gift is waiting for you at home."

Silence stretches in the room except for the song of crackling fire. Charles' dad, Oscar, is the first one to break it, with a loud clap and a laugh.

"I've never been happier with a surprise. Way to go, Ace. Finally, you showed you didn't just inherit my intelligence but also my charm."

"Oh, Oscar. Our son has much more swoon than you." Kristy leans forward, placing her hand over her husband's. "You're more of a king of secret love, but Charles is really the prince of claiming possessively in public. Didn't you see him on the news yesterday? You never would have done that."

"Is the gift by any chance dirty, and that's why you couldn't give it to Daisy in front of us?" Chloe's eyes sparkle with mischief.

"That's none of your concern, sis." Charles chuckles

while I place my palms over my burning cheeks, which must be all shades of pink and red right now.

I cannot believe we're having this conversation in front of his family. But thankfully, dinner is soon announced, and we're all led to the dining room. Delicious is too small of a word to describe the four-course meal, including the exemplary French dessert mille-feuille.

I've just stepped out of the bathroom, placing my lipstick back into my bag after a quick touch-up, when I find Charles leaning against the opposite wall.

I try to step aside, thinking he wants to go in, but instead, he crowds me, holding me captive between him and the door.

"What is it?" My voice quivers without trying.

Now, every time I see him, my heart does a little flip. As much as I want to go to the doctor and receive confirmation that I have a serious heart disease, I know that's not the case. Instead, it's my fake husband giving me all these stupid, crazy feels.

"What do you want, Charles?" I ask again, and he tips his head up to the ceiling and the innocent-looking mistletoe hanging above us.

Holy shit!

"Please tell me you're not seriously suggesting what I think you are. What are you, twenty?"

That asshole in Armani continues to smile at me. Even though I hate that he's taking me by surprise at every step with that smoldering grin, my chest warms thinking I have something to do with his newfound happiness.

"You are freaking serious?" I whisper under my breath.

"Have you ever seen me not serious?"

That might be true. But this Charles A. Hawthorne is so different from the man I work for.

I'm still struggling when he leans in.

His lips touch mine, and that feeling returns in my chest. This time, he isn't rushed. No, tonight his tongue moves inside my mouth with a slow pace, like he's savoring me.

His hand moves from my face to the back of my neck, and he tugs on my hair, making me look up, which only gives Charles better access to my mouth.

My hands grab his jacket, something I've started to do without trying whenever he's kissing me, and Charles' moan gets locked in my throat.

After what feels like forever, I finally register a voice calling my name. It slowly starts to grow stronger as I pull away from Charles. It might have been one of the hardest things I've ever done in my life, especially when Charles makes a disapproving groan.

"Chloe," I whisper, licking my lips as his hot gaze traces the path of my tongue.

Chloe's singsong voice calls my name once again as we step away from the fortuitous bathroom door, which has reserved for itself a permanent spot in my memories.

But before we can further walk into the living room, where everyone is waiting for us, Charles tugs on my arm. Turning me around in a flash, he places a chaste kiss on my lips before grinning and tipping his head up toward another mistletoe.

How many did they hang in there?

"Were you the one in charge of decorations tonight, smoochmister?"

I'm torn about these green things dangling from red ribbons all over the house—they're adorable, yet potential heart-attack inducers. A part of my brain wants to just stand under them with Charles and let him do his magic, while the rational part of my brain pitter-patters and wants to run away and save me from future heartache. These moments feel riskier than actual sex.

"Finally, I found you two." Chloe releases a heavy breath. "Dad's waiting for you in his office, Charlie." She holds my hand, leading me back into the living room. "And Mom wants to talk to you."

I feel the warmth of Charles' gaze on me until I'm sitting on the couch next to his mom, and only then do I see the back of his dark suit leaving the hallway.

"How are you doing, hon?" Kristy asks as I settle beside her. Since GG and Grandma Irene retired into their rooms and Chloe is away on a phone call, it's just us.

"I'm good. Thank you."

"I remember the days following my own wedding. Being a Hawthorne bride takes a hell of a lot of adjusting. Did you know, like Charlie and you, Oscar was also my boss before we got married?" Her grin is fun, and I feel a familiar comfort in her company, as if I'm around friends.

"I didn't." My shock is genuine.

"Oh yeah, and like you two, we had to hide the relationship from everyone, including my sister," she says in a low conspiratorial voice. "For several reasons, but mostly because Oscar didn't want Charlie to get attached to someone and later realize the relationship wasn't working out."

I feel a newfound appreciation for Charles' dad. Every

kid needs to have parents who are willing to sacrifice their own happiness for their little ones. I knew how lucky I was when I found mine.

"But it's not just Oscar. All throughout his childhood, everyone around Charlie was so protective of him, and I think that safety net became a huge part of his identity, until it was pulled right out from under him. That day, our little Charlie became Charles Hawthorne. What I'm trying to say is, I'm so happy to see the long-lost carefree part of him back when he's with you. It's been years since I saw him smiling the way he is tonight."

"I don't understand. What do you mean by *that day*?" I ask before I can clamp my mouth shut.

Is this something I should have known?

"He didn't tell you?" Kristy's eyebrows furrow, making me squirm.

I slowly shake my head.

"Charlie was thirteen when there was a shooting attempt at him."

My jaw drops open, but no words make it out.

"In the end, we found out that it was the head of Hawthorne Security. That's why Charles is so paranoid about his security team. Even with Steve and Dave, who are highly trained and have Charles' complete trust, they have to undergo regular physical and psychological examinations."

I knew Charles was neurotic about his safety, and I've lost count of the number of times I've made a joke about it.

But he has a real freaking reason for it.

"Was he…hurt?" I ask, my heart thundering against my chest.

"Not physically," Kristy replies. "But someone who's close to our family was. And those months changed him forever. My sweet boy finally realized what it meant to be a Hawthorne. Until then, he had only seen the perks and benefits, but that day, he learned the darker side of being famous. And since then, he's avoided crowds, public events, and closed himself off. I used to worry all the time that he would never open up his heart to anyone again. But now, when I see him with you, I'm so relieved."

With a satisfied smile, Kristy holds my hands in between hers, but my mind is running a mile a minute.

How did I not know this?

During my initial months working for him, I did extensive research on Charles, scouring the internet, searching for anything and everything about him that would help me become the perfect assistant.

"Was this not covered by the news?" I ask, and Kristy shakes her head.

"Since it happened in London, we were able to keep it under wraps. We don't talk about it, but I know Charles can never forget that time. And it's why he's so paranoid about the safety of the people he loves."

My mind races back to the day Charles found me at Vincent's construction site. His patient voice, his affectionate words, and his worried face.

He left one of the most important meetings that day without a thought because I was in danger.

But Kristy said he's paranoid about the safety of the people *he loves.*

Does that mean he...?

No, Daisy. Don't you dare fucking go there.

"Was everything okay tonight?" Charles asks as we step out of the car and take the stone sidewalk leading up to his house. "If you're still upset about what Grandma said, I can—"

"Charles, no! Your family is amazing. And I'm not upset about anything."

"Then why are you so quiet?"

"I'm just tired." And confused. And guilty for every joke I cracked in the past about your security.

As we step into the elevator, I catch a glimpse of the lights shimmering on the giant swimming pool just before the doors slide shut. Tonight, I admire Charles' estate in a different light. He's made sure he never has to leave his sanctuary and has brought everything to him. The huge pool rivals a lake with its size. The best-in-class gym on the first floor. In addition to his living area on the second floor, he has a huge library upstairs. And let's not forget the helipad on the estate grounds.

I slide the key card into the electronic lock, but before I can take another step in, Charles tugs on my arm.

My gaze moves from his face to the doorframe. "I don't see a mistletoe here."

A lazy smile spreads on his face, swiping away the furrow lines on his forehead. "If I knew you liked kissing me so much, I'd have asked Mrs. Kowalski to place one at every corner of the house."

Oh, if only you knew, my dear husband.

"Very funny." I turn to walk in, but he once again tugs me back.

"I have something for you. A surprise." His words and the hesitation in his voice suddenly have my full attention.

"Like, a good surprise?"

"That's for you to decide." He takes out a silver silk tie from his jacket, and my eyes widen.

I gasp. "Are you going to tie me up, Charles?"

He throws his head back and laughs.

"I love the way your brain works, butterfly. I'll remember it for the future. But today, I just want to blindfold you."

I have no idea how he decides when to call me *butterfly* or *my dear wife*, but the surprise gets to me every time.

"Shall I?" Charles brings the tie forward and I nod. A second later, the soft silk fabric is covering my eyes.

"Comfortable?" he asks.

"Not as much as when I have my vision, but I guess I'll survive for a while."

His warmth is right behind me, surrounding me like a heavy cocoon. Charles gently pushes me forward, guiding me farther in. His hands are placed on my shoulders, protecting me from hurting myself.

"Careful," he says, and I stop. He guides me to the right, and I know we've walked into the living room.

"Did you turn on the fireplace?" I can hear the sound of crackling fire. Until I moved here, I didn't know I had such a love for fireplaces.

"Mrs. Kowalski did."

"Can I remove my blindfold now?" I lick my lips, suddenly equal parts curious and nervous. There's something about being blindfolded, especially when my hot husband has full control of all his faculties.

"Patience, my dear wife." I can hear the grin in his voice as he guides me. "Sit." The soft leather of the couch is at the back of my legs and the warmth of the fire on my front.

I perch down, and a second later, the low notes of soft instrumental music fill the room.

"Charles, please remove my blindfold now." I wet my dry lips once again.

"Why? Are you scared?" His voice is so low that it gives me goose bumps in its wake.

"No, I'm not scared." I grit my teeth.

What the heck, Daisy? It's a simple blindfold, and it's not that I don't trust Charles.

"Then let's keep it for a little while longer." His hot breath skates over my skin, and a second later, I feel something cold against my lips. "Drink," he whispers, pressing the glass on my quivering lips.

"Are you trying to poison me?"

He chuckles once again, and even with closed eyes, I can imagine his handsome face, his lips curling up and his eyes squinting.

"There're a lot of things I want to do with you, but killing is definitely not one of them."

Okay, then.

I take a sip and the whiskey burns my throat. Heat travels from my mouth down to my throat, and I feel it in my core.

He takes the glass away, then I'm hoisted into the air before he settles down right where I was and places me on his lap.

"I don't think this room is lacking any sitting space."

"It's not, but this is my favorite spot."

Um, okay. What can I say to that? Because truthfully, this is my favorite spot too. On his lap.

"Can I remove the blindfold now?" I've lost count of the times I've repeated this question.

But he replies with a tsking sound. "Not yet. I love having you like this. At my mercy."

"Has anyone ever told you that you're too cocky for your own good?"

"I'm sure my assistant has. Numerous times." His warm chuckle, right behind my left ear, sends a shiver down my spine.

"She sounds like a wonderful, smart woman. You should consider giving her a raise for putting up with you."

"I'll think about the raise, but for now, will a gift suffice?" His voice takes on a more sincere tone.

"Do I get to see it, or will I just hear about it from you?"

He laughs softly. As much as I love the sound of his laughter, I'm eager to see his smile. Thankfully, Charles unties the knot, and the blindfold falls away. I barely have a moment to take in the room decorated with lights and the beautiful Christmas tree before he presents a small gift box.

"Here."

My gaze shifts from the blue bow over the silver wrapping paper to the man before me. A few months ago, I would have laughed like a madwoman if anyone had suggested that I'd ever touch my boss with a ten-foot pole. Yet here I am, with no desire to be anywhere else.

"Did someone force you to get me a Christmas gift?" I ask cautiously.

"No one forces me to do anything. You know this better than anyone." He meets my gaze, his expression serious.

But wasn't he forced to marry me? The words hover on the tip of my tongue.

Shut up, Daisy. This isn't the time to win an argument.

"What is it?" I eye the box as if there's a bomb inside it, while my husband's grin only grows.

"It's something you'll absolutely love," he replies in that overly confident and cocky Charles Hawthorne style, and there's no way I can stop myself now.

"So it's a threatening device to keep asshole bosses in check?"

"Your mouth is going to get you into big trouble someday, my dear wife."

I drop my gaze away from his smiling face and carefully start to peel off the wrapping paper.

I'm *only* saving it because it's my first real Christmas gift from Charles, especially if we ignore the gift cards he sends every year to his close staff.

But my giant smile drops at the sight of a jewelry box.

Of course he got me jewelry.

After the furry slippers as the wedding gift, I was hoping for something similar. But this is Charles Hawthorne. In his world, Christmas gifts probably mean something expensive and classy.

Mustering the same excitement as before, I flip open the tiny gold latch and my heart stops.

Oh my God!

It's so not *just* jewelry.

It's a hair clip with rhinestone daisies.

Yes, it's expensive and classy, but it's so much more. It's like someone made it only for me.

I know I won't be able to stop my tears, so I don't even try as they race down my cheeks.

"Hey, you don't like it?" Charles' panicked voice doesn't help my cause.

"I love it, Charles. It's perfect. I…I can't believe you got me something so special." My hand tightens around the box.

"It's our first holiday together. I want to make it special." He shrugs, and I wait, because if I've learned something these past weeks, it's that there's always more with Charles. And he proves me right the next second.

"You told me how your dad bought these rhinestone hair clips for your mom." His fingers graze the pearl hair clip in my hair tonight. "I liked the tradition, and you definitely like wearing them, so…" He shrugs again before hesitantly looking up at me. "Why can't we continue the same tradition?"

I'm speechless. He raises his eyebrows in real confusion at my tears, and I throw my arms around him.

"Oh my God. Who knew you could be so considerate?" I say between hiccups, and I feel his chest shaking in suppressed laughter.

After a beat, he pulls me back and wipes my tears with the pads of his thumbs. His blue eyes shine with happiness as I lean forward and place a small kiss on the tip of his nose. My heart's so full and emotional right now.

"In this very moment, if there was a competition for the perfect husband, you would win it fair and square, Charles."

"So where's the Christmas gift for your perfect, extraordinary husband?"

While his smile couldn't be wider, I've lost all my happy hormones, as I'm busy panicking. My gaze moves from him to the side cupboard where, covered in gaudy yellow packaging, sits a stupid coffee mug.

It'd have been better if you didn't get him anything.

But how would I know that Charles was going to break our unspoken Christmas gift tradition this year?

He has always given me a gift card of a ridiculous amount—does it matter that I negotiated it during my first year working for him?—and I've always bought him a funny, snarky coffee mug.

A smile on his face in return for money in my bank account. This was the only way I could afford the expensive prices of last-minute holiday shopping, since I don't get any time off before that.

Win-win for all, if you ask me.

But right now, there's no room for that stupid mug next to this hair clip. This man sitting before me is not my jerk boss, but someone plucked out of every girl's dream.

Forget the white horse. Charles Hawthorne in his white Porsche is rewriting all the fairy tales.

But what Cinderella would I be if I gave him a cup that says, "You are a jerk, my dear boss-prince."

Mustering up all the courage I have, I glance up at Charles. "It's your turn to close your eyes."

"Why?" He raises an eyebrow.

"Did I ask so many questions when you blindfolded me?" I grab the tie from the front pocket of his jacket and tie it securely.

twenty-six

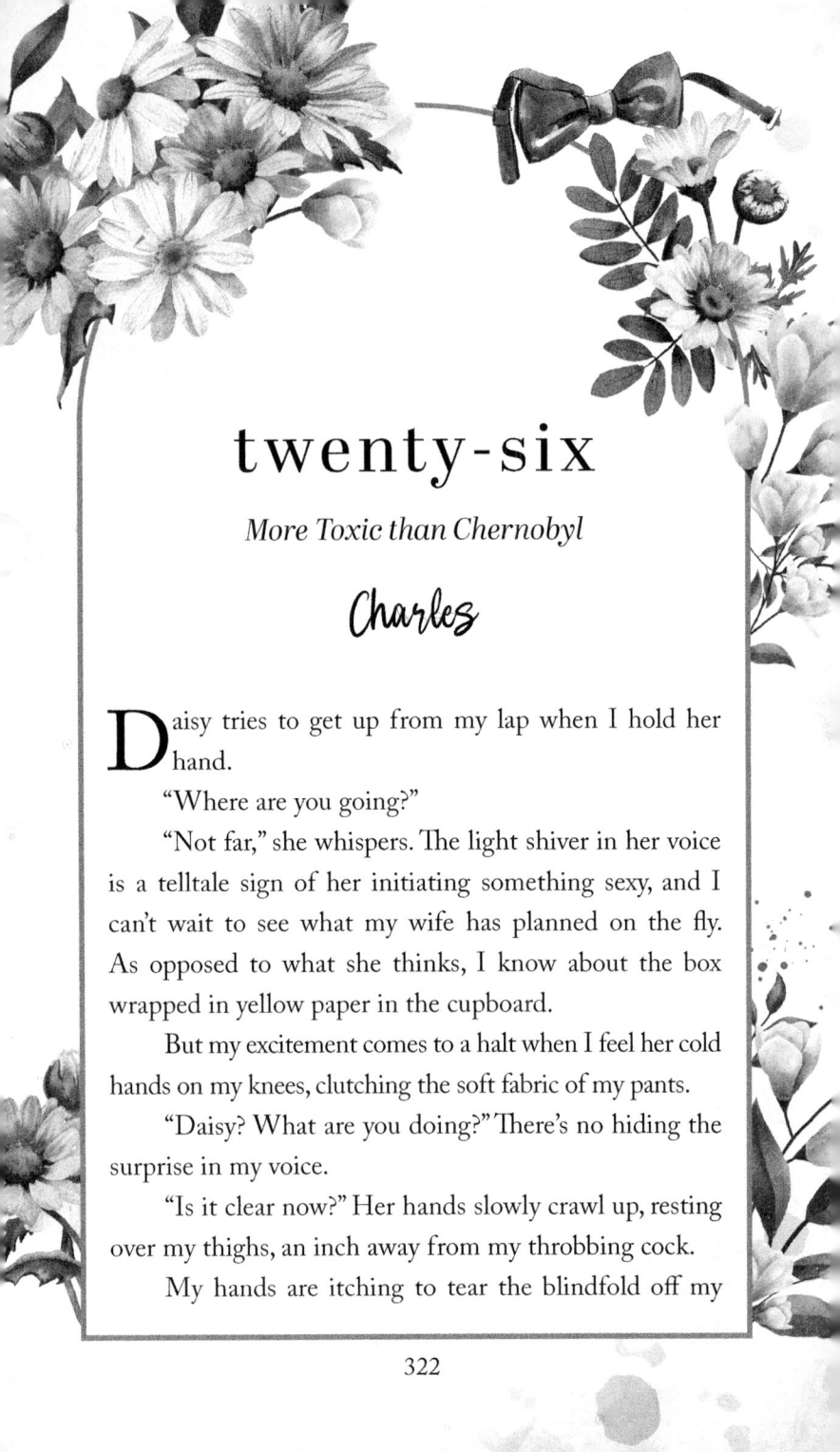

More Toxic than Chernobyl

Charles

Daisy tries to get up from my lap when I hold her hand.

"Where are you going?"

"Not far," she whispers. The light shiver in her voice is a telltale sign of her initiating something sexy, and I can't wait to see what my wife has planned on the fly. As opposed to what she thinks, I know about the box wrapped in yellow paper in the cupboard.

But my excitement comes to a halt when I feel her cold hands on my knees, clutching the soft fabric of my pants.

"Daisy? What are you doing?" There's no hiding the surprise in my voice.

"Is it clear now?" Her hands slowly crawl up, resting over my thighs, an inch away from my throbbing cock.

My hands are itching to tear the blindfold off my

face. She must be blushing so hard, the crimson spreading all over her face, down to her neck and cleavage. But there's a strange thrill in anticipating her moves when I can't see her face, which usually gives her away.

Daisy's hands move toward my belt buckle, escalating my heartbeat to the highest notch. My cock is at full mast, knowing it's in for one of the best nights of its life.

"What kind of belt is this? Where are the notches?"

There's a momentary pause in between my wild thoughts when Daisy tugs on my belt buckle too hard, eliciting a groan out of me.

"It's not a standard buckle." I place my hands above hers in an attempt to show her, when she pulls her hands away.

"Why does everything have to be so complicated with you?"

I unbuckle my belt with lightning speed. If it's making my wife cranky, especially in the middle of something so important, I'll burn my expensive belt collection and give up wearing belts altogether.

"There." I search for her in the dark, and my fingers meet her soft strands. "I'm sorry."

"You don't have to apologize. I'm just nervous." Her hands are back on my thighs, once again ready to take me to a high.

"Me too," I reply truthfully, my fingers brushing her cheek.

"Thanks for saying that. I feel better already."

My thumb drifts to her mouth, and I feel the indentation of her teeth digging into her plump bottom lip.

God, I want to kiss her right now, but I also want to experience what she's willing to show me.

It's the kind of indecision I could start to love.

"I'm happy to be of service, butterfly."

"I love when you call me that." Her voice is a whisper as she admits something I already know.

"I love calling you that."

The tiny chuckle that slips past her lips drowns out as her hands reach my cock, which stands erect through my pants like a soldier at attention.

"Someone's excited?"

"That someone has been excited since you got down on your knees. Fuck!" My words tumble over one another when Daisy unzips my pants and starts to massage me over my boxers.

The sensations become unbearable, and I place my hands over hers.

"Am I not doing it right?" she asks politely—too politely—making my cock jerk.

That tease.

If she only knew my cock is a lesser problem. It's my heart that rattles so loud that I worry I might just pass out when she speaks in that soft, honey-dipped voice.

"Not at all. But have some mercy on me and go slow."

Her hand finally stills for a beat, and she asks, "Does this mean I made you beg again?"

I never imagined I'd be laughing as hard as I am right now when there's a woman—no, not just any woman, but *Daisy*—on her knees before me with her hands inside my pants.

"Yes, my competitive wife, you made me beg again. Now, if we've done enough talking for the night, I'd like your mouth to be occupied with something other than baiting me."

"Thank you for voicing your defeat. Since you asked so nicely, I'm going to blow your mind tonight."

And God does she keep to her promise.

I rise a little in the air, helping her get my pants and boxers down past my knees, and the moment my cock is free, she whimpers.

"Holy fuck. It's so huge up close." Daisy's tone filled with wonder and amazement, has me biting my lip.

"This is not the time to act cute—" My words die on my tongue as she licks my shaft from root to tip. "Fuck, butterfly."

That's the only encouragement she needs before sucking my cock like it's a popsicle.

That's enough. I can't miss this fucking view!

"I'm taking off the blindfold." That's the only warning I give before my hands rip the tie from my eyes.

Daisy's mouth is still around my length, and when she looks up, taking me in farther, my eyes roll back.

"Damn, Daisy. I need to see you naked. Right now." I groan when my length slips past her lips.

In a state of urgency, we pull off our clothes, and I'm back in her mouth, hitting the back of her throat.

This time when she sucks me, I watch everything—the hollowing of her cheeks, the movement of her throat, and the way her beautiful tits bounce.

My hips thrust up as I cradle the back of her head.

This is one of the most beautiful sights, and when I think it can't get any more perfect, Daisy moans my name. She moans my name in an almost inaudible fashion while moving her mouth up and down my dick.

That's my undoing. Knowing it's not just me but she too

is enjoying this, I hold her hair again, her hair clip digging against my palm, making it all so real. And then I'm moving her head at a pace I ache for.

Daisy doesn't miss a beat. Like fucking always, she's with me in everything, never leaving me alone.

She cups my balls, eliciting a hissing sound as I hold back my orgasm. Just when I'm about to shoot my load down her throat, Daisy pops off me and flicks the underside of my crown.

"Daisy, don't you fucking tease me." My hips buck off the couch.

"I'm not teasing you, Charles. I want to make this so memorable that you never forget this moment." She smiles so sweetly before kissing the length of my shaft with such reverence that I almost die. I don't know if it's from my held-back release or her sweetness—probably both.

"You on your knees, naked in our living room and surrounded by Christmas lights, is the highlight of my lifetime, Daisy."

Her mischievous grin returns, and she starts to stroke me with her hand before her head dips, and Daisy is licking the sensitive skin of my balls.

There's no escape for me anymore when she sucks me into her mouth.

"Fuck, I'm about to…" I don't finish the sentence before my swollen cock jerks in her hand. White release coats her hands, my thighs, and the leather seat as she keeps stroking me.

My vision goes dark, and it becomes hard to breathe and my head falls against the cushioned headrest. I've never in my life come so fucking hard.

I'm still panting when Daisy crawls up, not worrying

about cleaning anything. My eyes open to find her licking her hand, and God, that's such a fucking erotic sight.

"I've always wanted to do that," she says in a breathy voice.

"Which part of it?"

"Doing it next to the fireplace. It was like a fantasy come true."

"Then I'm happy to be a part of your fantasy." I grin, folding my hands behind my head, trying to catch my breath.

"How often do you work out, Charles?" Daisy's gaze drifts from my face to my biceps as she wets her bottom lip.

"I'm definitely increasing my hours now that I know how wet you get watching my muscles." I flex my biceps, and she burst into giggles.

"I'm not going to apologize for admiring my husband's hard work."

"Admire away. It's only for you, my dear wife." I sit up, taking her with me, and her eyes gleam when my half-mast cock hardens under her once again. But before she can distract me with her words or just by her existence, I ask, "Not that I'm complaining, since this just might be the best gift of my whole life, but what did you really get me, Daisy?"

"What do you mean?" All the humor evaporates from her voice, and so does the color from her face.

I settle her onto the couch and arrange a throw blanket over her before pulling up my pants. The upcoming conversation definitely demands my full attention, and I can't give that when we're both naked.

I grab the gift box she's discreetly hidden in the cupboard, which I'd accidentally found this morning.

"To Charles A. Hawthorne. Merry Christmas, even though

I know you possibly don't celebrate it." I read the white note out loud before bringing it to her as she puts on my white dress shirt, looking prettier than ever.

Until right now, I never thought there'd be a day I'd share my wardrobe with anyone, yet here I am imagining her beside this fireplace in nothing but my shirt for all future Christmases.

"Charles, please don't open it." Daisy places her hand over mine, and her worried gaze moves between me and the box. "I bought this before I knew you were going to break the tradition of giving me a gift card."

"I don't think that was much of a tradition." Unlike her, I can't stop my smile. "In any case, I consider your mouth my gift tonight. This can be our secret reminder."

I unwrap the gift, and my lips twitch as I read the flowing black letters on a white cup with an illustration of a scowling man in a suit.

"Is this supposed to be me?" I raise an eyebrow before reading the words. "*Chernobyl is less toxic than my boss.*"

She plucks the cup away from my hand and hides it behind her back. "It's a joke. It has always been a joke. You know that, right?" Daisy shakes her head as she mumbles, "You possibly don't even remember all the crazy things written on the previous mugs."

If only you knew, butterfly.

twenty-seven

Too Much PDA

Charles

I'm sitting in the back seat of my car beside Jimmy, who is going nonstop about how much he loves the new version of me. Whatever the hell that means.

Every time I turn my head and look at him, I mentally curse. Why the hell am I not in the office, where I can stare at my wife through the glass separator?

I completely zone out and instead wonder what she must be doing right now. Possibly scribbling something on those colorful notepads, making lists of things and tasks.

"Are you even listening?" Jimmy shakes me.

"What?" I turn my head toward him. "What did you say?"

"Your phone is ringing, man. Where the fuck are you?"

With renewed excitement, I check my phone, hoping it's her, but that bubble breaks fast.

"Hello, Grandma. Everything okay?"

"Hello, Charles. Yes, all is fine," she replies in her usual calm tone. "I have some good news for you. I just received a call from Tim Baldwin, and it seems they've done an unofficial vote and you were unanimously voted in as the next CEO of the Hawthorne family business. The official meeting is next week. I'm very proud of you, Charles." Rare affection laces her voice, and something warm finds its home in my chest.

"Next week? But wasn't it scheduled for February?"

"It was. I guess they don't see a point in dragging this matter out further." Grandma takes a pause, and there's a hint of something akin to curiosity in her voice. "I'm sure you being on the news threatening reporters and all over social media making pancakes with Daisy's dad only strengthened your cause. Did Jimmy put you up to it?"

"You think it was staged?" My fist tightens around my cellphone. "My wife was in danger. Aren't you the one who taught me to put family and its reputation above anything else?"

But Grandma remains quiet, as if she's expecting more clarification.

"Jason Price is a good person with a terminal illness," I continue. "If spending a few hours of my time with him makes him happy, then I don't mind, especially since he might not even remember my face after a while." Just saying the words sobers me, and my stomach sinks with disappointment.

"In that case, I'm happy for you. I was worried you married Daisy to become the CEO. She's definitely extremely loyal and cares about you enough to put up with your workaholic ways."

The phone suddenly feels too heavy in my hand.

"I'm not opposed to playing fair tricks in business, especially when people on the other side of the table make such illogical demands. But mixing relationships and business is never a good idea. There are some crevices in life where business has no place, and married life is one of them."

A strange sensation like heartburn intensifies in my chest, even after the call ends.

"All good?" Jimmy asks.

"It was my grandmother. The board has unofficially voted for me as the next CEO of the Hawthorne business." There's a disconnect between my body and mind, everything moving in slow motion as I say the words out loud.

Is this fucking it?

I'm still struggling with my own thoughts when my PR manager throws himself at me and hugs me like a child hugging his favorite toy. I stiffen at the contact, but he doesn't seem to notice or care.

"Why aren't you shouting from the rooftops? Today is the day we've been fucking working for all these years. We've got to celebrate. I'll call Daisy to plan a big celebration."

"She doesn't need to do anything. She's my wife, not your assistant." My jaw clenches so tight it hurts as I pluck the phone out of his hand.

The excitement drains from him, replaced by a sheepish smile. "Sorry. Sometimes it's hard to remember she has two roles in your company now."

"She only has one role, and that's being my wife."

But instead of cowering beside the door as I had hoped, Jimmy looks at me with furrowed brows. "Is Daisy leaving the company? Is she pregnant?"

"What the fuck? Why would you even say that?"

"Why else would she stop working for you?"

"She's not quitting, dammit. What I mean is that everyone needs to stop dumping their work on her." I fix him with a scathing look. "We have a capable event management team. If you need a party, go to them. Daisy has enough on her plate." My words hang in the air as I flick the partition switch.

The tinted-black glass slides down, and Dave, seated in the passenger seat, glances over his shoulder.

"We'll be heading to work," I relay. "But first, let's drop Mr. Garcia at his office."

"Thanks for not abandoning me in the middle of nowhere. It's not like you haven't done that in the past."

"The sidewalk's looking pretty inviting right about now."

Jimmy falls silent, but the teasing grin remains. Ignoring him, I start typing a text to Daisy.

> **Me:** I'm heading back to the office. Cancel all my meetings for the day. I need to tell you something important.

My heart quickens as I lean back in my seat.

Everything I've been working for over the years is finally happening, and she's the only person I want to celebrate with right now.

She gave up everything, even her dream of marrying for love, to help me. A prick of unease hits my chest, but then I remember her delighted, rosy face from this morning as we jumped into the shower together.

No, she's happy. She's not missing out on anything.

I repeat those words in my head throughout the ride.

I practically skip out of my car when Steve parks it in the parking lot, my fingers tingling as I imagine Daisy's reaction to the news. My feet bounce, hoping the elevator will go up faster. But when I reach my office floor and enter my private office area, Daisy's chair is empty.

What the fuck? Where is she?

Frantically looking around, I check the coffee corner and conference room, but she's nowhere to be found.

The last two times I couldn't find her, she was inside a collapsing building or held hostage by her ex.

Before my thoughts can turn cynical, I send her a text.

Me: Where are you?

Daisy: I'm at the café grabbing a latte. Since you canceled all the meetings, I figured we must have some super crisis. I'm just refueling with caffeine to be most useful for you, boss.

Thank fuck she's safe. But as much as I love her sass, there are quite a few things I don't like in her text. First and foremost, I didn't know she still goes to that overly crowded ground-floor café to get herself coffee. She's my wife now, for heaven's sake.

And then she referred to me as "boss." After hearing "husband" from her sultry voice, I don't want her to call me anything else.

My fingers dig into the phone in my hand as I wait a second and then another before marching back into the elevator.

I step out in the ground-floor lobby, and for a beat, nothing changes until my staff realizes it's me.

"Good afternoon, Mr. Hawthorne."

There's a round of collective greetings, and the sound of casual conversations die away. I reply with a nod, keeping my gaze straight ahead as I make my way to the café with hurried steps.

Heads continue to turn in my direction, often accompanied by a surprised gasp. Of course they're surprised. Except for on opening day, I don't remember setting foot in this establishment. Even that day, I stayed only long enough to cut the ribbon and receive the first cup of coffee.

My eyes scan the area, and there she is. With her back toward me, Daisy is busy talking to someone. I'd recognize her anywhere since she's wearing her statement hair clip with a butterfly today.

I take a step forward to walk closer to her where she's standing in a queue. As I approach, the line starts to shorten as people make space for me, and it only takes a few more beats before Daisy takes note of the dying noise around her. She finally looks over her shoulder, and I'm right behind her.

"Charles? What are you doing *here*?" Her voice is laced with surprise and a touch of disapproval, as if I've made a huge mistake subtly reminding my staff that they're paid to work and not to squander their time.

I raise a brow, aware that we have some not-so-discreet spectators who are doing a poor job of minding their own business. For once, I don't hate it. Maybe it's because I'm in Hawthorne Tower—my territory—or maybe it's because my heart knows she's right here.

Daisy's eyes go wide as I tuck a strand of hair behind her ear. She's so still, like a statue, as if my hand drifting toward her cheeks is a bomb ready to detonate any second. I almost want to laugh.

"I have to tell you something. Let's go."

My words seem to break her stupor, and she rolls her shoulders back.

"But I haven't placed my order yet. Why don't you go ahead and I'll join you soon." She squints her eyes.

Why did I think she'd ever make it easy?

"Mrs. Hawthorne. You're leaving with me right now. I'll make sure your favorite latte is waiting for you at your desk before you're there."

"Charles, you can't—"

Her rebuttal gets trapped in her throat as I hold her face and kiss her, effectively shutting her down.

The moment my lips touch her, she stiffens, but I don't stop. I kiss her until she melts in my arms and her soft hands clutch my suit jacket.

In this very instant, I don't care that I'm standing in a room full of people. I don't care that I'm kissing my assistant-slash-wife in front of my whole staff.

When I pull back, she makes a whining sound that goes straight to my cock like a well-aimed bullet.

"Are you done being difficult?" I whisper.

"Y-you kissed me. You freaking kissed me in front of everyone." Her voice matches mine.

Knowing she'll soon find her bearings and once again make it difficult for me to take her away, I grab her hand and pull her toward the elevators. Her blazing eyes meet mine in the mirrored walls.

"You better have a really good reason to do that, otherwise I'm going to kill you."

Her anger has the opposite effect on me, and I smirk. "How are you not scared of me, my dear wife?"

But she doesn't entertain my words. Daisy places her hands over her hips. "Tell me, what's so urgent that it couldn't even wait until I had a cup of coffee?"

"I never said *urgent*. It's important. There's a difference between the two."

The elevator stops, and unease settles in my chest.

Why is it so important for me to share the news with Daisy?

She's temporary, after all, and if these past few days have taught me anything, it's that she wants things in life I can never provide—love, affection, family.

"Hey, where are you going?" she says, her steps hurried to match mine, as I don't stop at her desk but walk inside my office. "So what's this non-urgent, yet important news?"

"The board has unanimously agreed to make me CEO." The excitement coursing through my veins minutes ago has vanished, and I have no clue why.

The irritated creases on Daisy's forehead soften. Her mouth opens and closes as if she's trying to say something, but no words come out. And then she rushes into my arms with such speed that I have to take two steps back to find my balance.

She finally gasps. "Is it really true?"

All my previous anxiety evaporates in an instant in the wake of her happiness. I nod and her hands loop behind my neck, her bottom resting against my forearms as she sticks to me like a koala bear with a giant smile.

"You did it, Charles. You finally got those stupid old men to see that there's no one more deserving than you to lead your family's business."

I've heard those words numerous times, but from her mouth, I know they're not merely words. They're truth.

"It's not I, but we. We did it together. I couldn't have done any of this without you, and I'm not just talking about now." I motion to the tiny space between us. "I'm referring to all the work you've done all the previous years."

When her pink lips curl up, I feel like someone has hit my heart with a gong.

She has no fucking idea how precious she is to me.

And then a teasing, knowing smile returns to her face. "Who knew you were such a softie at heart."

"In case you've forgotten, I can once again get you accustomed to the hardest part of me."

And I'm not kidding. I've never been so fucking hard.

Everything I've wanted is right in front of me, and the woman in my arms is the most important among all.

A blush creeps up on Daisy's face like every other time I say something dirty to her. The pink hue starts from her cheeks, crawling down to her chin and neck. I love knowing I'm the reason behind her flustered state.

She makes an attempt to get away from my hold, but I don't let her.

"Charles!" She squeals as I walk farther into my office. "Put me down."

"Nope. You might have jumped into my arms on your

own, but I'm the one who decides when you leave, Mrs. Hawthorne."

"What do you mean?" She squeals once again as I settle her down on *my* chair behind my desk and lean forward.

"I want to thank you." I push her curl behind her ear, and my hands drift to her hair clip.

"Charles, I cannot accept another damn expensive gift."

"Good. Because I'm not planning on giving you anything. I just have words today."

Her irritated brows relax as her lips curl into a smile. "Now this will be a change. Charles A. Hawthorne has words."

"Don't worry, this is exclusively for my wife." For some reason, the words that sit right on my tongue don't find their way out, and I'm about to say some nonsense when Daisy holds my face in her hands.

"Charles, if you ever need a person to share something with, I'm always here."

My hands rest above hers. I'm really fucking in her debt for her unconditional support, even when it comes with a heavy dose of craziness. "I usually do such talking with my cousins. But it's not just about me today. I couldn't have done this without you. Thanks for never leaving my side and for sticking with me."

She smiles, so soft, so genuine. "I'm happy you think so. But you've spent all your life working toward this. I can't say the same. I'm sure there're many people who have done bigger things than handling your calls and preparing for your meetings."

"You do much more than that. You and I both know it." I pin her with my gaze. "But today, I want to celebrate." I remove my suit jacket and deliberately place it onto the desk before unfastening my cufflinks.

Daisy has this strange fascination with my forearms. In the early years, I thought she was intimidated by me, like my past assistants, avoiding direct eye contact. But now I know how much they turn her on.

She bites her lip, her chest rising and falling with labored breaths. "Celebrating? Like with wine?" Her gaze shifts from me to the bar cabinet.

"Oh, I have something stronger in mind." I grin before dropping to my knees in front of her.

She gasps. "Charles, what are you doing?"

"Just wait. Not everything needs to be told in words."

"Are you insane? The door is unlocked. Anyone could walk in!"

Even though it's not that easy for just anyone to walk up to my private floor, I flick the button under my desk and the office door locks.

"Happy? No one is going to disturb us now."

"B-but this is your office." Her words quiver as my hands graze her legs, slowly skating upward, tracing the goose bumps at the back of her knees, then crawling up to her thighs and under her skirt.

"And you are my wife. I have the right to do whatever I want. Don't I?" I tap my ring finger where my wedding band sits snugly over her silk panties.

"Holy freaking shit! This is not a dream." Daisy's jaw drops as I tug the side zipper of her skirt lower.

"Dream about getting fucked in my office often,

butterfly?" I smirk, helping her get up just enough so her skirt drops over her feet and those towering heels.

I know I have.

"I wouldn't say often." Her words turn into a moan as I pull her forward before drawing her panties to the side and placing my lips right over her sex.

Fuck, she tastes good.

"So do you have any objections to me making you come so hard, you see stars during the day, my dear wife?"

She's quiet for a second and then slowly shakes her head.

"Good answer." I kiss my way up to her stomach, covered in a silk blouse. My single aim is to map every inch of her body with my mouth. My tongue swirls around the clothed, peaked indentation of her nipple before taking it into my mouth while pinching the other with my thumb and forefinger.

She moans loudly, and a groan rumbles in my chest.

I kiss her neck, then finally reach her lips. Our mouths crash. Her arms wrap around my neck, and I don't see anything other than her right now.

I am guided by desire and nothing else, with one goal—her pleasure.

My tongue strokes against her closed lips, seeking, demanding entry, and as always, she yields.

In an attempt to deepen the kiss, I cup the back of her head, and she tugs on my hair.

I kiss her like I'm drowning and she's the harbor. She kisses me like she's in a desert, and I'm a lake surrounded by the shade of green trees.

We are desperate. We are wild.

In this moment, we are a *perfect match*.

But nothing has been enough with Daisy.

I need more. I need everything with her.

When I pull away, she moans my name in protest. "Charles."

"You keep at it, butterfly. I'm not stopping until you're crying my name so hard that you're heard in the café downstairs."

"Fuck, Charles. You really upped your dirty talk game."

This girl makes me smile in the most unlikely times. I'm back at eye level with her sex and look up to find her head rolled back against the headrest.

"I had to, since it makes you so fucking wet, my dear wife." I suck her through her panties before tugging them down, and once again, the sight of her naked sex, soaking wet and ready for me, is like a needed shot of adrenaline.

Her grip tightens on my hair as I push her legs further apart, her knees touching the two armrests.

"Holy crap." She groans, her eyes closed as I delve in.

My focus is her swollen clit as I lick and suck until Daisy is writhing and bucking in my chair. In my office. The place that has witnessed so many of our interactions. But this is the most memorable— her chanting my name, begging me to not stop.

Doesn't she know I would rather die than stop?

My tongue buries inside her, my broad shoulders keeping her legs pushed open, and her back arches before she comes with a loud wail.

But I'm still not satisfied.

Will I ever be when it comes to her?

My tongue once again touches her clit, and Daisy lets go of my hair.

"No, Charles. No…I can't anymore." Her hands, about to come between me and her sex, halt when I slide a finger inside her. My mouth is back on her clit as I pull out before pushing back in.

In and out, until I find a pace that gets her hands back in my hair and my name back on her lips in that moaning tone.

Her wetness coats my hands and my jaw, and her cries fill the space between the walls of my office. My cock is throbbing painfully behind my zipper when I rise.

Daisy doesn't make any moves, as if she's too boneless to even lift a limb. She stares up at me, cheeks flushed with that rosy-pink color. There's a light sheen of sweat on her forehead, causing some of her hair to stick to her skin.

In all, she looks breathtaking.

"That was the best kind of celebration," she whispers in a breathy voice.

My lips curl up as I unbuckle my belt. "What made you think it was over, butterfly?"

twenty-eight

Dangling in Your Arms

Charles

It's been a week since I got *the* call from Grandma. During this time, I've received emails from almost every board member expressing their confidence in me and my leadership, congratulating me even before the final voting is executed a month from now.

Despite it all, I sometimes struggle to believe that everything that seemed so out of reach just a few months ago is now right in front of me.

My train of thought breaks as I step into the kitchen and find Daisy standing behind the counter, beating what looks like pancake batter in a glass bowl. Dressed in one of my old college T-shirts, which hangs from one side of her neck, with her hair pulled up in a messy bun, she sways to the sound of the latest indie soft pop song.

All the Christmas decorations are still up in the

house, as she clearly instructed Mrs. Kowalski that everything would stay as is until spring. And if that makes her happy, why the hell would I change anything?

She drops a big dollop of butter into the pan, and it sizzles.

"Good morning." I walk closer and kiss her exposed neck. "Why are you in the kitchen and not Mrs. Kowalski?"

"Because Mrs. K also deserves a break, especially on weekends. I sometimes can't believe the authorities aren't knocking on your door for exploiting your staff."

"I don't exploit. I pay—"

"Mrs. K doesn't work on weekends for the extra pay, Charles. It's because she worries about your paranoid ass. She knows you'll never let anyone else step foot into your house, and I'm sure she doesn't want you eating out two days in a row."

I'm about to give some lame excuse, but she keeps staring at me with that *you better not lie to me, Hawthorne* look.

"All weekend?" My anxiety can't be tamed. My housekeeper has been with me since I moved out of the Hawthorne mansion.

Unlike me, Daisy starts to laugh before patting my chest. Her engagement ring and wedding band shine against my black T-shirt. "Don't worry, I'll make sure you survive well, my dear husband."

Her breathy, playful words help in slowly releasing the uncomfortable feeling clawing at my chest.

"Does that mean we have the whole house to ourselves?" I raise a brow, and she grins before nodding.

"Yes. What are you going to do about it?"

"Oh, I can think of a lot of possibilities." I lean down to kiss her, but she swiftly turns around.

"Not here, mister. Sex and cooking when mixed together only leads to one thing—accidents." She removes the pan from the heat and, with practiced finesse, slides a pancake onto a plate and drizzles on some fresh syrup before placing two strawberries on top.

As I'm now looking forward to this accident-free alone time with her, I circle the counter and flop down on the barstool.

"You need any help?"

She shakes her head. "No. You just sit and eat." Daisy places a cup of coffee before me, and after I've taken the first bite, she slides her iPad in front of me. "There's an email from Jimmy."

The tasty breakfast immediately loses its flavor in my mouth. Nothing good follows Jimmy's name.

"He wants us to attend a New Year's charity function." Daisy opens her email.

"I'm not—"

"Just hear me out, Charles. I know you don't like these events, and now that you're almost appointed the CEO, I'm sure Jimmy won't hassle you like before. But"—she leans in, her expression sincere and serious—"I think you should still attend at least one annual event. Let the town know you're here for them, and despite you disliking stuffy parties, you're making an effort for them."

The familiar anxiety knocks on my chest just imagining it all.

"You can prepare yourself ahead of time, work with your security. For this"—she taps on the screen—"I've already talked to the organizers. They are more than happy to accommodate our requests if your presence is what they get in exchange."

"This is important to you."

Surprise flares in her eyes. Of course she's surprised!

It must be the first time I'm not throwing a tantrum because an invitation matters to someone. Daisy slides in between me and the granite counter.

"It isn't about me, Charles. It's about you and this town. I hate that despite all the amazing work you do, you still have to prove yourself to everyone. But the thing is, the people of this town don't get to see your daily struggle and challenges. Why not give them an up-close view of Charles Hawthorne? Not the one the media talks about, but the real you."

Her finger rests above my heart, and instead of feeling dread, her touch, her words, her care, works like the best security I've ever had. They even threaten my inner demons.

"You can do just one annual event and then return back to your hermit tower."

"Hermit tower?" I raise an eyebrow and she smiles. Unlike all the other times, I don't feel the urge to storm out of the room when someone points out my lack of participation in social events.

And it's all because of her.

"Okay, let's call it the top floor of Hawthorne Tower. Better?"

"Much." I hold her hand, flattening it against my chest once again. "I'll go, but only if you come with me."

"Of course I'm coming. You think I'd leave my boss alone at a party? I can't even imagine how many murder charges would be reported in just one night."

imperfect match

"Very funny. Anyway, I'm not planning to take my assistant, but my wife."

"Then I'll be dangling on your arm like a dutiful wife." She bats her lashes, and the grin that lights up her face hits straight into my heart.

"Dutiful? Do you even know the meaning of that word, my dear wife?" My fingers stroke her flushed cheeks. How did I survive all these years without this? "But, in any case, I can't wait to be the hanger from which you *dangle*."

This time her laughter is out of control. She throws her head back, and the sound, the laugh lines on her face and the way it makes me feel…I already want a repeat of it all.

"What are you planning to do today?" I ask when she's finally recovered from her giggling fit.

Everything about this moment is so domestic and so mundane, yet I've never been more calm.

"I'm going for a spa day with my friends. We'll drink wine, eat too much sugar, and talk about boys."

"Should I be worried?" I lean in, stroking the soft skin of her neck and shoulders with my nose, breathing in the floral scent of her body wash.

"You're the only boy on my mind these days."

I'll have to work extra hard to be the only boy on her mind all the time.

"What about you? What's your plan for the day?"

"I'll go to Elixir. I'm sure I'll find at least Alex working, if not all of them, even on a Sunday."

I tap lightly on Alex's office door. The deep furrows on his forehead remain as he glances up from his computer.

"Rough start to your weekend?" I settle into the chair across from him.

"Not everyone is living on the Sunshine Street these days."

"Thanks for the warm welcome, brother."

"Sorry." He sighs. "Just a bit on edge."

"What happened? I thought your Sunday skydiving sessions were supposed to be meditative and peaceful," I say carefully, testing the waters.

But his jaw tightens, confirming my suspicions. My lips struggle to twitch, but I keep them flat. My sister must have made her appearance at the field.

"Everything is fine. You don't have to worry."

And before I can probe deeper into Alex's hollow response, the door swings open and Ray and Archer stride inside.

"Why can't we find another piece of land?" Archer's voice is tight with frustration, as if he's been having this conversation with Ray for some time.

"Because the one we have now is perfect," Ray replies in a relaxed, laid-back tone.

"We don't have anything. I told you they're not selling. What will you do now? Kill them?" Archer's tone is sharp.

"I don't need to kill anyone. I'm a businessman. I negotiate."

"What's going on?" I ask as Ray and Archer settle on the corner couch, finally finding a gap between their rapid fire.

"Do you remember the land I picked for the next Elixir

hotel?" Ray prompts, and I nod. "Well, someone in the owner's family is having last-minute cold feet."

"Why? Are we not paying to their expectations?"

Ray shakes his head at my question. "They'd prefer to expand the family inn on the same land."

"Is the inn competition for Elixir?" I lean forward, raising a brow.

"Nah. We don't do cute and cozy. But they're definitely throwing a wrench into our plans. I should—"

"You should just look for another option," Archer cuts right through Ray's words. "It's not like Cherrywood is short on commercial land."

"Calm down, Archie. I'm not going to blackmail them. Everybody has a price. I just need to figure out what I need to pay here. What's wrong with that?"

"The capitalist has spoken." Disapproval paints Archer's face.

"News flash, bro, we're all capitalists. The moment we step into the business world, we sell a part of our soul, and unlike you, I don't fake it."

"I'm not faking anything," Archer hisses in Ray's direction. "I'm just telling you to be a little more human." When Ray just shrugs in response, Archer shakes his head. "I hope someday someone comes into your life and shows you that this business can also be done equally well with a little compassion."

"You mean like Charlie?" Ray's laugh couldn't be more staged. "If only Donna was young. Unfortunately, she's already married and happy with her husband."

His funny remark about his assistant doesn't sit right

with me. A cold feeling seeps through my chest, chilling my veins.

"I think you've been enough of an asshole for today, Ray." My molars grind together, not liking that he's pulling Daisy into their stupid argument.

"Say, how long are you going to continue with this marriage charade anyway?" Ray raises his eyebrow. "Didn't you already get what you needed out of this marriage?"

I know he's trying to get a rise out of me and divert Archer's attention away from him. And I hate to admit it, but he's doing a damn good job of it.

I take a deep breath. "The official decision hasn't been announced."

"Mm-hmm, so you mean there's still a few weeks' time before you both go your separate ways?" Ray crosses his arms.

"It'll probably be longer. I don't want anyone to think I married only to become the CEO." The sentence and the thought leave a strong distaste in my mouth. As much as I try to forget it, the words keep running in a loop in my head, ruining my entire day.

twenty-nine

Completely, Insanely, Irrevocably Irresistible

Charles

"Can you zip me up?" Daisy stands before me, dressed in a silk champagne-colored cocktail dress. Her hair is elegantly swept up in a loose bun, secured by the rhinestone daisy clip I gifted her for Christmas.

Warmth floods my chest at the sight of it. I fell in love with that clip the moment I laid eyes on it on the jeweler's website.

"How does it look?" She glances over her shoulder with a smile on her lips.

"You always make it look beautiful." The words tumble from my lips instinctively, causing her smile to falter.

She turns around, her hand over her chest, holding her unzipped dress in place. "Do you even know how sweet you are sometimes?"

"Does that mean my plan is working?" I pull her closer, my hands finding home on her waist.

"And what plan would that be?"

"To make myself irresistible to you," I state and she grins.

"Definitely. You are completely, insanely, irrevocably irresistible to me, dear husband."

"Mission accomplished." I lean in, but before I can ravish her lips like I want to, she places her hand over my mouth.

When I raise an eyebrow, she gives me an air-kiss and smiles. "Sorry, but I've spent a lot of time on my makeup tonight, and I'm not going to let you ruin it."

I gently remove her hand from my mouth before tucking a loose curl behind her ear. "You look beautiful, and I agree to not touch your makeup right now. But once we're back home, your makeup, your dress, everything will be ruined if I don't find you on our bed, begging for my cock."

She blushes, as always when I talk dirty to her. And lately, I've made a habit of it just to see that adorable color on her cheeks.

My hands, which are resting on her hips, slide upward to the small of her back. Without losing eye contact, I slowly zip up her dress, stopping midway.

"Are you seriously going to a public event without a bra?" My gaze drops from her face to her chest before returning to meet her eyes, watching her lips curve into a smile.

"Actually, I am. The dress has a built-in bra."

"I love it." I run my hand along the silky fabric. "It means I have one less thing to take off."

"Who knew you could have such a one-track mind, my

dear husband. But there are hundreds of people waiting for you at the ballroom, so be a gentleman." She grins, adjusting my pocket square before stepping out of my arms.

I help Daisy drape a shawl over her shoulders. "By the way, what's the charity for?"

"It's for kids who've lost their parents."

As we arrive at the venue, I feel a surge of anxiety watching the press outside, their cameras aimed at every car passing through the gates. I'm still in the middle of my routine of breathing in, breathing out, and repeating when Daisy places her hand on my thigh, intertwining our fingers.

"It's going to be great." She ups the wattage of her smile, though I'm not sure if I'm doing a good job of masking my nerves.

Once again catching me off guard, Daisy leans in and plants a kiss on the corner of my mouth. With her thumb, she smudges any lipstick she might have left behind. My grip tightens around hers.

"What happened to your makeup getting ruined?"

Any lingering anxiety dissipates as she shoots me a sassy look and winks. "Fuck the makeup. You look absolutely delicious, my dear husband."

I'm still grinning when Steve opens my door, and before my lips can flatten at the sight of the multitude of cameras pointed at me, Daisy is by my side. She loops her arm through mine, clinging to me as if she needs support, when the reality is quite the opposite.

The burning sensation in my chest intensifies. I know

I'll never find anyone else quite like her. Someone who knows my insecurities. And even if she extracts great joy in making fun of me in private, in public, she's determined to ensure I appear the strongest, bravest, and simply the best, period.

"That went well. What do you say?" she asks as we make our way to the carpeted entryway of the building.

"Everything goes well when I have a charm like you sticking to me like superglue."

She laughs up to the ceiling as the doors open and a venue staff member runs forward. "This way, Mr. and Mrs. Hawthorne."

As Daisy and I step inside the main reception hall, which is at its maximum capacity, all heads turn toward us, and my familiar anxiety starts to make its appearance.

She's about to take another step forward when I lightly tug her back. "Don't you dare leave my side." The word *ever* remains lost in my throat.

Her brows knit together in surprise before she slowly nods and whispers, "I'll stick to you like a parasite, husband."

I can't stop my lips curling into a grin. It's definitely a first that I'm smiling instead of furiously searching for the exit in the middle of a social event.

The night progresses better than I expected. Perhaps it's because of the woman who hasn't left my side for a single second.

She maintains a constant smile, even as she fields detailed questions about our work and love life—not my words but those of a woman whose name I've forgotten. Daisy makes excuses on my behalf when she sees my patience wearing thin, especially as one man after another tries to broker a deal.

What did they expect? That I'd shake hands with them after hearing their pitch for five seconds and say, "Let's become best business buddies"?

Conference rooms are meant for that, not stuffy parties.

But this old man before us is proving to be difficult, as he fails to pick up on Daisy's polite hints. I'm a breath away from throttling him for giving my wife such a hard time.

"Mr. Hart, you'll hear from us soon," Daisy repeats in her same patient voice. "I have your business card. In fact, I have three." She waves those blue-and-white cards in the air. "But if you'll please excuse us, I have to show Charles something."

The man, who appears to be in his late sixties, places his half-full champagne glass on the side table. "Oh, maybe I can tag along."

No, you cannot.

I'm about to take a step forward and tell him that we've had enough, when Daisy holds my hand, once again intertwining our fingers.

"I'm sorry, but I have to say no. It's actually something romantic, and I'd like to show it to Charles alone." Daisy whispers the last sentence as if letting him in on some secret.

Confusion paints Mr. Hart's face, and I'm about to put my foot down because there's no way this man is accompanying us. My wife has something romantic planned and no one sees it but me.

"Of course. You lovebirds go away." He shoos us like pigeons, something no one has dared to do to me before.

But I'm too happy to care about anything. Daisy and I skip out of the room like arrows shot from a taut string. I don't know who pulled whom out first. We step into a lobby that is thankfully vacant, and Daisy leads me down the left corridor flanked by several rooms on either side.

"It's here?" I raise an eyebrow. I thought it would have been on the top terrace.

She places a finger over her lips and motions for me to follow. We finally stop at one of the last doors, and she takes out a key card from her purse.

As we step inside the room, my gaze traces the walls, which have olive-green wood panels. There are several paintings hung on them, but nothing says "romantic" to me.

"It's here? The romantic thing?" My hands slide into my pants pockets as I scan the room once again.

"I'm sorry, there's nothing. I booked this room for you in case it became too overwhelming in the ballroom. But you're doing so great." Daisy steps forward and pats my tie. Her hand lingers over my chest. "I still wanted to tell you about it. You can come here anytime, under the pretense of an urgent phone call."

My heart is about to burst out of my rib cage.

She's taken care of everything.

But why am I surprised? It's not the first time she's done such a thing. There's a reason Daisy is the absolute best assistant I've ever had. She knows what I want without me saying it, and she delivers it without fuss.

My heartbeat escalates, whispering slowly that she's more than an assistant, but I ignore the voice, which has slowly started to grow louder and louder.

I take a step forward, and her eyes go wide as she steps back until I have her captive against the wall.

"Don't you dare look at me like that, Charles!" She tries to move away, but I circle my arm around her waist, pulling her closer to my chest.

"Like what?"

"Like you do when you're turned on." Her hands on my chest make a lame attempt at pushing me away.

"What can I say? We're alone in a room that you arranged for us, and you're looking so beautiful. I wonder if you imagined us like this." I tuck a curl of her hair behind her ear with my free hand. "You against the wall, your dress bunched around your waist, my hands pushing the zipper down."

"Wh-what? I did not!" She gulps hard, and I almost want to laugh.

"But you don't hate the idea," I quip, drawing circles over the column of her neck with my thumb.

"I—I…" she stammers, then closes her eyes. I clamp down on my laughter, watching her breathe deeply and mumble something inaudible before she opens her eyes again. "Charles, we cannot have sex here!"

"Why not?"

"Because there's a party going on less than fifty feet away, and I'm not going to walk into that room after having sex with you. People will know!"

"Nobody will know. I'll make sure of that. You just keep your screams under control." I dip my head lower. Even though she's wearing those killer heels, she only reaches my chest.

"My screams? What about you?" Her chest rises and falls in sync with mine as I kiss the column of her neck.

But before I can do or say anything more, a loud noise comes from right outside the door, as if somebody just dropped a tray full of cocktail glasses. Daisy pushes against my chest and slips out of my hold.

"Don't you dare put me under your spell, Hawthorne," she says, fixing her hair before opening the door and storming out.

I follow her back into the ballroom with a grin on my face. The night is once again looking up.

"I was searching for a scowling face among the crowd, yet here you are, grinning like this is your favorite spot." I hear Ray's voice before he slaps my back.

"And I didn't know I should be looking for you here. Have you secretly become a fan of such events, brother?"

He smirks. "I like them just as much as you do. Of course, unlike you, I'm not here to flaunt my wife or marriage, but for business."

My molars smash together, and right then I spot Daisy returning from the powder room. Her gaze immediately finds me, and she gives me a soft smile.

"You control your tongue around her, Ray." I speak in a low voice, which only makes my cousin grin more.

"Hello, Raymond." Daisy slides up beside me, and reflexively, my arm goes around her waist, pulling her closer.

My cousin's astute gaze follows my move, but thankfully, he keeps his mouth shut.

"Since you have someone to protect you, I'll be back in a second." Unaware of the silent tension between Ray and me, Daisy grins and tries to pull away. But my grip around her waist only tightens.

"Where are you going?" The words slip past my lips easily.

"Um, I want to let the organizers know that we'll be leaving soon." Her eyes dart to Ray before settling back on me. "I'll be back in a sec, I promise."

"Don't worry, Daisy. Go ahead. I'll keep your husband safe." Ray winks at my wife. I know he means no harm to her, but protectiveness surges inside me.

When she finally leaves, he coughs, but before he can throw a jab my way, I give him a stern stare. "Don't you fucking say a thing."

Ray shows me his hands in mock surrender and then grins. "I was about to say that it's good to see you like this."

"And what's the reason for your unexpected presence here?"

"Would you believe it if I said I didn't come to ruin your lovely evening, Charlie? I just came to have a few words with the mayor." Ray tips his head toward the mayor of Cherrywood at the other end of the room, surrounded by her army of personal assistants. "I hear she's a fan of such events."

"And why are you stalking her? She's been married to a good man for almost twenty years, for your information."

"Very funny." He laughs softly. "But I'm here to talk about the land for the hotel."

"I thought you were going to negotiate with the owners."

"That's still in the works." There's a tic in his jaw for the first time this evening.

"Looks like someone's plans aren't panning out."

"But why don't you worry about your wife? Her one second seems to have stretched out for several minutes."

Those several minutes continue to stretch. Ray is already with the mayor, laughing and charming the woman, while I'm left unguarded, ready for anyone to come up to me. And they do. I'm drawing these men like moths.

I entertained the first man who approached me, but it quickly became apparent why I avoid such events. I despise small talk.

I'm about to storm out of the room when I hear my name in her cooing, soft voice.

"Charles." Daisy stands by the door and beckons me over with a curl of her hand.

Her smile, the curl of her lips pulled to one side, is enough to bring my fast-beating heart to its normal pace.

Without thought, I reach her in two long steps.

"Where were you? I was wait—"

"I know. I'm sorry. But I met someone, and I want you to meet them too." Her smile hasn't slipped an inch. "Come with me." She once again tugs me toward the hallway, but this time I'm not feeling the same excitement like the last time she led me in this direction.

"Who did you meet, Daisy?" My feet stop, bringing hers to a halt as well.

The shine in her eyes drops but wasn't she the one who promised to stick to me like a parasite?

"You remember I told you this function is for homeless and orphaned kids and a few were invited?" She holds my hands in between hers, her eyes sparkling with enthusiasm. "They are the sweetest bunch, Charles. I promised them a meeting with a prince, so are you ready, my dear husband?" She bites her lip, her excitement barely contained.

While I was experiencing one of the most uncomfortable moments of my adult life, waiting for her like a lovesick puppy, she's busy making new friends?

But Daisy isn't waiting for a response or reaction from me. No, she's too pumped, for whatever damn reason. That's how, moments later, I find myself standing outside a room while my wife walks in, straight to a group of kids seated around a fireplace and holding neatly wrapped gifts.

"Hey, kids, this is Charles. He's the prince of Cherrywood." She grins conspiratorially with all the tiny humans, while an uncomfortable feeling claws at my chest, begging to be released.

I'm about to insist that we need to leave this place right now, when someone tugs on my pant legs. I look down to see a little girl barely reaching my knees, with a toothy grin and pigtails. "Would you like to join our tea party?"

Tea party? What's happening tonight?

I'm Charles Hawthorne, the man who has avoided every social interaction for the last decade with the same intensity a supermodel avoids carbs.

Yet here I stand.

I don't reply to her, because all the ways that come up in my head to decline the invitation aren't polite or suited for a young girl's ears.

Everyone keeps staring at me for a while, including my wife, as if expecting a response. But I continue to stand there like a statue with my arms crossed over my chest. Daisy must have finally become attuned to my feelings, as she slowly turns to the kids away from me.

But not before I catch her smile losing its shine. As

always, her face speaks volumes. She's disappointed, but right now, so am I.

"Okay, kids, it's time for me to leave, but I wish you all the very best. And, Max, when we meet next time, I hope you can teach me how to play chess." She fusses with the hair of a little boy who's holding a chess set close to his chest.

Daisy doesn't wait for me and marches right out of the room.

"Do you know these kids?" I ask, catching up with her.

"I don't have to know everyone to be polite to them." Her lips press into a thin line.

"You're upset?"

"And you're very perceptive," she replies flatly.

I run a hand over my jaw as the vision of a little girl's crestfallen face swims before me, and a twinge of guilt tightens around my heart like a lasso. "I'm not an asshole in general, Daisy. But I've just had enough of this place."

"Of course you have. When can anyone or anything be bigger than you?" Before I can tell her that's not true, Daisy stops under the sign pointing toward the restrooms. "Can you tell Steve or Dave that we're ready to leave, and I'll meet you in the parking lot in a few minutes?"

She doesn't wait for my reply and walks away from me. My feet remain stuck for a beat as I watch her leave, and once she's no longer in my sight, I turn around.

My breath skitters as I find myself back at the same doorway of the room, watching the kids lost in their own world.

"Can I help you, Mr. Hawthorne?" A middle-aged woman approaches me from behind. "My name is Greta Day. I'm the head supervisor at the local orphanage."

I swallow the lump in my throat before words find their way. "I was invited to a tea party a few minutes ago."

The woman's brows rise.

"I didn't properly reply to the invitation. Unfortunately, I cannot attend, but could you please arrange for a proper party tomorrow nevertheless? Please send all the invoices to my office."

Her eyes crinkle at the corners, sparkling with joy and surprise. "That's…very generous of you, Mr. Hawthorne. The kids would love that."

The burden of my guilt lessens a tiny bit, and I stride toward the parking lot, where Dave is waiting for me, holding an umbrella against the unexpected rain. Daisy is already seated in the car, and as I slip in beside her, no words are exchanged between us.

How did this evening turn out like this? So many promises were made for later, but now it's like something broke between us. Eventually, her silence becomes unbearable.

"Why are you still so upset?"

In response, she folds her arms over her chest, looking out the window as if she can't hear me.

"Is it not enough that I've given more money to this charity in one night than they would otherwise see in a decade?"

I hate every word that comes out of my mouth, but it's like my tongue is possessed.

When Daisy turns around, her eyes are blazing with untapped anger. I have seen her in a lot of different moods, but the emotions on her face right now are new—raw and personal, as if she's silently warning me to choose my next words carefully.

"You can't fix this problem by humoring those children for a few minutes, Daisy." I lower my voice and try to keep it light, hoping to put this behind us.

"They're not a problem. They're kids. And I'm really worried about your future little ones, Charles." She rips away the bandage I was just trying to apply.

"No need. I already told you I don't want any of those."

"You don't want one of *those*?" She repeats my words as if that's the craziest thing she's ever heard. "You realize if everyone thought like you did, there wouldn't be you, me, or all the other people in this world?"

Why is she so surprised? I thought I made myself clear already on how I feel about kids.

"I don't have a problem with the general idea of procreation, but it's not for me. I don't want to make decisions for someone who doesn't even realize how much effort you're putting in. I would rather do something where I have a clear understanding of the return I'm getting."

"A child is not an investment!" She throws her hands up in the air. "It's an emotion, a feeling."

"Good for those who want to experience it, but that's not me."

She looks at me with wide eyes as if she can't believe what she's hearing and then lets out a bitter laugh. "Why am I surprised?"

I hate the way she says it.

It feels like everything we shared these past months has vanished in the wake of this evening. She's once again just my assistant, who equally admires and hates me.

But what she's arguing against is wrong. As much as

I'm pleased Daisy had a loving childhood, her extreme anger toward my behavior is unwarranted.

"You think you can change the lives of those kids by simply talking to them? They don't need to be pampered but made aware that no one is going to come and help them. They'll have to work harder than other kids their age. So instead of asking Max to practice chess, you should have asked him to study hard so he can find a job. You—"

I'm still in the middle of my monologue when she flips the button and the privacy screen comes down.

"Dave, can you please stop the car here?"

My driver looks at me and then toward the heavy downpour through my window.

"You want something?" I ask carefully, but my suspicion is already rising.

"Yes, I want fresh air." Her chin lifts in defiance. "The air in this car has become too suffocating for me."

"Don't be stupid, Daisy. It's cold and raining outside. You'll get sick."

"I would rather get sick than sit with you right now, Charles."

"Why? Because I'm telling the truth?"

"Because you're being an asshole!"

My bodyguard's cough lightly reminds us of their innocent presence.

"Just stop the freaking car."

When Dave looks at me again, all her anger gets transferred to my driver.

"I'm not Charles' property. If you don't stop the car, then I'm going to jump out." Her hand is already at the door, and her face says she'll do it—jump out of the fast-moving car just to get away from me.

This time, Dave doesn't wait to see my nod, and the car comes to a screeching halt. Daisy wastes no time, and before I can say anything, she's out.

"Fuck!" I follow her as she strides down the street. Fast-falling raindrops are almost blinding, and my tux is soaking wet in a few seconds.

"That's enough show for one day." I grit my teeth. "Get back in the car, Daisy."

She doesn't listen to me. Her wet dress clings to her as she marches away like a woman on a mission. A mission I don't understand.

She'd get fucking sick if we continue this ill-timed walk. I grab her arm and tug her back. Daisy loses her balance but I'm here to catch her.

My hands stay on her waist, and I take a moment to calm the loud thumping in my heart. "Why are you so upset?"

When she looks up at me, there's fire in her eyes.

"Daisy, what am I missing here?" I ask her in my softest voice.

She's not one to flip without reason—that's me.

"Because I was one of those kids not many years ago."

What? My mouth dries in the middle of the rain.

"I don't understand."

"My dad and mom adopted me, Charles. I'm not their biological kid. I was just a homeless girl who made her way to their place on a rainy night like this." Her hands grip the lapels of my jacket, and the fire fades from her eyes.

"Fuck, butterfly. I…I didn't know."

"It doesn't freaking matter." Her words come out in a staccato rhythm due to her teeth chattering in the cold. "Just so you know, as much as those kids need someone to remind them about their tough life ahead, what they really crave is love." She pushes her wet hair away from her face and her slowly turning-blue lips.

"Daisy, I—"

"No. You don't get to say anything, Charles, because you don't know, but I do. I know I'm not going to change their life by 'smiling and humoring them for thirty minutes.'" She makes air quotes, repeating my words, filling me with more regret. "But what I also know is that in these thirty minutes, I've given them a reminder that not everyone in this world is waiting for them to fail. There are good people out there, like my mom and dad. People who believe in them. People who think these kids deserve fun as much as any other kid. And when random assholes try to knock these angels down, they can look back to these thirty minutes, and maybe it'll give them strength and hope."

Every word from her mouth, every tear from her eye mixing with the rain, hits straight into my heart.

"I'm sorry for making a scene, but when I said I couldn't sit in the car with your words hanging in the air and reminding me of every crappy comment I've ever heard in my life, I really couldn't."

Daisy doesn't wait for my response or an apology, marching back to the car, while I stay stunned at my spot.

How did I not know this about her?

thirty

Heart or a Jerk-Off

Daisy

I swipe my key card and stride into Charles' house, making a beeline for the left wing and the guest bedroom. I don't stop until I've reached the bathroom.

Struggling with the soaked dress, I wrestle with the zipper until it finally gives way, and I peel it off. I'm shivering and my teeth chatter nonstop as I get inside the shower. Even when I hate admitting it, Charles was right about one thing tonight—there's a high chance I'll be sick tomorrow. Adjusting the water to a slightly too-hot temperature, I let it cascade over me, closing my eyes and taking a deep breath.

Why does my heart ache as though someone has ripped out a part of it?

Since we got married, every time the topic of babies and families came up, Charles made it perfectly clear—both in words and actions—that he wants no part of it.

So why does it hurt so much?

Perhaps because you foolishly hoped these past weeks might change his mind.

My inner voice chooses the worst moment to chime in.

"No, I didn't."

My job was never to change Charles, only to ensure he gets the CEO position he deserves. And as always, I've done my job.

But isn't he the same man who gave you that rhinestone daisy hair clip? A piece of jewelry that was the greatest expression of love between your parents?

He never used the word love.

Right now, I feel like a three-headed monster. My two inner voices clamor for attention, each with its own argument, until it all becomes too much and a fresh headache blooms.

"Enough."

I shut off the water and step out of the shower, only to realize that none of my toiletries are here. For the first time since arriving in this house, I'm not sharing the same space as Charles.

My eyes close, and memories from just a few hours ago flood my mind. While getting ready for the event, Charles and I were in perfect sync. I brushed my teeth while he shaved at the sink. As I applied makeup, he stood behind me, tying his tie and casting smoldering glances my way. He zipped up my dress as I adjusted his pocket square. We looked every bit the perfect couple, ready for an amazing evening and looking forward to a memorable night.

But that was all an illusion.

It's my mistake that I forgot the reality of our marriage.

I'm here on a job, and hiding out in the guest room isn't just childish—it's jeopardizing everything Charles and I have worked for.

I slip on a bathrobe and leave the bathroom, but my legs hesitate to carry me to the door. It's a dance of one step forward, two steps back, until I finally sink onto the bed.

I'll worry about the world and Charles tomorrow.

Turning from one side to the other, something feels off. The Egyptian cotton sheets scratch against my skin, as though this is the most uncomfortable bed I've ever slept in.

How did everything shift so drastically in such a short time?

Before our marriage, I used to hate thinking about Charles more than necessary, but now when he's not near me, I miss him like he's a soldier away on deployment and I'm the wife who hasn't seen her husband in months.

When I finally fall asleep, I dream about seahorses. In their world, the male seahorse carries the eggs until they hatch. If any father has a right to complain about babies being too much work, it should be a seahorse dad.

The bed dips beside me and I whisper, "Don't disturb the dad."

"Hush, go back to sleep," he whispers, enfolding me in his arms.

My heart flutters with the realization that this isn't a dream. He's come to me after an argument. "Charles? What are you doing here?"

In this simple gesture lies the answer to why his words cut me so deep.

Beneath Charles' unyielding, invincible businessman

exterior beats a heart full of worry, care, fear, and love—all human emotions, even when he wants everyone to believe he's some sort of robot.

"The bed feels too big and too empty without you," he murmurs against my hair. "I'm sorry for hurting you, Daisy. I'm sorry for everything I said. Fuck, how did I not know about your parents?"

I turn toward him, my face brushing against the curve of his neck. He holds me so tightly, as if afraid I'll slip away again.

If only he knew how hard these few hours have been for me.

"I don't often talk about it," I confess, wanting to share a part of my past with him. "I was Daisy Hazy Price, daughter of Jason and Penny Price. I couldn't have asked for more loving parents. I may not have been born in their house, but it was always my home."

Charles strokes my hair, and I lean into his soft touch.

"Within a year of my arrival, Mom and Dad made sure everything around me felt like mine. My drawings hung up on the fridge, clinging to magnets from our various trips. They replaced all the photos of just the two of them with ones including me in every corner. Honestly, most of the time I forget I don't share the same genetics as my parents. But then moments like these, when I meet kids like me, I'm reminded of a part of my life I've unconsciously forgotten. I realize how fortunate I am to have such parents." My throat tightens, and Charles kisses the top of my head.

"I'm so fucking sorry. I know words will never be enough for all the nonsense I said and did tonight, but please accept my apology."

My head rests against his heart, which always seems to beat a little too fast.

Is it only when I'm around him, or is it always like this?

"You hate kids, don't you?"

Charles stiffens beside me, and several moments pass in silence. Just when I think I won't get a reply, he answers, "I don't hate kids, Daisy. I hate the idea of being a father because I know I'll fail, and I hate failing."

What? That's...something I never imagined.

"How can you speak with such certainty about something you've never experienced before? Maybe you'll be an amazing dad." Hope swells within me as I picture Charles cradling a baby in his arms.

"Please." He gently holds my face in his hands. "I really don't want to talk about this anymore. I know it's not for me." His expression softens, and I don't know what he sees on my face when he adds, "Do you know how much damage bad parenting can cause, even unintentionally? I don't want someone to grow up believing they'd have been better off never being born."

"Charles!" I gasp. "Why would you say something like that?"

"I was not a product of love, Daisy." His grip tightens, almost painfully, but the emotional intensity swirling in his eyes silences me. "I was a pawn in my birth mother's scheme to take over the Hawthorne business. I'm fortunate to have had Dad and, later, Kristy in my life. But an unloved childhood leaves its scars. I know I'm flawed and could never risk passing on these fears to someone, knowing a lifetime wouldn't be enough to heal them."

A pang of pain shoots through me.

How did I never see this side of him?

I should have.

I understand the feeling of being unwanted by your own parents. The same emotion that fueled my desire to have my own family had an opposite effect on Charles.

He doesn't want kids, to spare them the pain we both endured.

How could I even hold it against him?

He has every right to feel the way he does.

I place a kiss over his dry lips. "Thank you for opening up to me, and I'm so sorry you had to go through all those emotions as a kid."

Charles returns my kiss with one on my forehead and asks, "So are we good?"

I nod after a beat.

But are we really good?

Yes, we've resolved what happened this evening, but tonight also made something painfully clear.

Charles and I are like two corners of a river. We may flow in the same direction and experience the same waves of emotions, but we can never merge.

While I long for the warmth of a big family, he wants no part of it.

We are undeniably an imperfect match.

I wake up feeling as though a drummer is pounding away inside my head. Shifting to my side, I release a groan, my throat feeling as if it's been rubbed raw with sandpaper.

Geez! How sick am I?

I place my palm on my forehead, only to have it replaced by Charles' large, warm hand.

"I knew you'd get sick."

"I'll be fine soon," I mutter before succumbing to a coughing fit.

"Yeah, I can see that. I'm going to ask Mrs. Kowalski to make you a warm drink."

My eyes shut as Charles leaves the bed. God, I need something for this pounding headache.

My fingers are pressed against my forehead when a squeal rips out of my throat. My eyes shoot open as I'm lifted into the air.

"Charles! What on earth are you trying to do, kill me?"

"Don't be so dramatic! I'm taking you back to where you belong."

Moments later, he settles me onto *his* bed beneath the soft silk covers. His face is mere inches from mine.

"Promise me you'll never leave this room after an argument. If something bothers you, talk to me. I don't want us to be the kind of couple who can't resolve issues through talking."

Oh, Charles!

"Are you the same guy who has branded himself an *anti-conversationalist*?"

His lips twitch and his blue eyes crinkle. "Not when it comes to my dear wife. For her, I can be a chatterbox."

"If I wasn't feeling so sick, I'd pounce on you right now."

How can he be this freaking sweet?

"Easy there, tiger." He grins and leans closer, planting a

gentle kiss on my forehead. "You'll have plenty of opportunities to pounce on me later. For now, please just rest."

He hands me two white pills and a glass of water, and I take them without question.

Sometime later, when I blink my eyes open, the medicine has started to show its effect. My headache has dulled slightly, but unfortunately, my throat still throbs just the same. Adjusting the pillows, I attempt to sit up as the door swings open and Charles steps in, phone pressed to his ear.

"That sounds good, Doc." He's once again impeccably dressed in a crisp white shirt and a silk tie, though today, he's missing a matching pocket square. Worry lines crease his forehead as he settles beside me. "How are you feeling now?"

"Much better." I place my hand on his cheek, my heart fluttering as he leans in and, without caring about the germs, places a quick kiss on my fevered lips.

Isn't he the same man who had the cleaning staff sanitize his entire office floor after Jimmy once went into a coughing fit?

"The doctor will be here in fifteen minutes." Charles glances down at his watch. "I'll wait until he arrives."

I grab his wrist and look down at the time. Even disoriented, my practiced brain remembers his schedule by heart.

"Charles, you have a meeting with Vincent Beaumont in person in an hour. I'm perfectly capable of talking to the doctor myself."

He makes no move to get up, but his gentle fingers tuck a strand of hair behind my ear.

I must look horrible, with a red nose, puffy eyes, and

sweaty hair plastered to my forehead, yet he gazes at me as if I'm the most beautiful woman he's ever seen.

"You certainly know how to make a girl feel special, my dear husband." I touch his freshly trimmed jaw, and he playfully boops my nose in response.

"You are no ordinary girl, my dear wife." A smile finally graces his lips.

"Please go to the meeting. I'll text you as soon as the doctor leaves."

Silence hangs between us, and I watch various emotions flicker across his face before he reluctantly nods. "Okay. But if you forget to text me—"

"I won't," I reply fast, pushing the covers aside.

"Whoa. Where do you think you're going?" Charles grabs my waist, putting me back in place. "You stay right in this bed until the doctor says you're perfectly fine."

"I appreciate your concern, but I'm sure you'd prefer that I meet the doctor wearing more than just a bathrobe." I nod toward my body, and Charles' gaze follows.

His eyes flare before he quickly shakes his head.

"Definitely!" His response is clipped while I bite my lip to stop my grin. Charles slowly rises up. "But just stay here." A second later, he returns with a pair of my underwear and a pajama set that has cupcakes all over them. "Change here."

"I'm not changing in front of you, Charles. I don't look sexy at all right now."

He grabs my shoulders, locking eyes with me.

"You difficult, difficult girl. I'm not a perv. I was going to give you your privacy and go out of the room, but you don't leave the bed unless you have to use the bathroom. Got it?"

imperfect match

I nod more than a few times. "How can I disobey my husband's orders?"

He chuckles, kissing my forehead again. "You're the least obedient person, Daisy. Now get changed and remember to take it easy today."

I'm still smiling even after Charles leaves.

Lately, my mood swings like a pendulum, shifting from one extreme to the other. Right now, I'm riding high on happiness.

Exactly twenty minutes later, the Hawthorne family doctor pays me a visit. After taking a blood sample, he prescribes some antibiotics and advises me to take it easy for the entire week.

Once the doctor leaves, I shoot a text to Charles.

> **Me:** Following doctor's orders, I'm off duty for the week, Mr. Hawthorne. Hope you can manage without me. ~ Your obedient assistant.

His reply is immediate.

> **Husband aka Charles Adorable Hawthorne:** Working without my competent assistant will be a challenge, no doubt, but I'd rather have my wife get some rest and get well soon. So I'll try to manage. ~ Your loving husband.

> **Me:** Awwww, who knew you could be so cute, hubby.

> **Husband aka Charles Adorable Hawthorne:** I love the new

nickname, but what are those hands doing? Is it some kind of hint that you want to jerk me off?

I burst into laughter.

> **Me:** You and your one-track mind. They're hands making heart signs. 🖤🖤

The cutest thing happens next. My emoji-despising husband replies to me with a kiss.

Husband aka Charles Adorable Hawthorne: 💋

If getting sick is the price to pay to see this sweet and cute side of Charles, I'll be praying for rain every week.

Husband aka Charles Adorable Hawthorne: Enough texting for now, my dear wife. I don't want you getting another headache.

> **Me:** You're no fun.

Husband aka Charles Adorable Hawthorne: I'll be fun in person this evening.

I glance around the empty room and then down at my phone, hesitating before typing another message to Charles.

> **Me:** Is it okay if I invite my friends over?

My teeth sink into my bottom lip. I know Charles doesn't like people invading his private space.

Husband aka Charles Adorable Hawthorne: That's your home too, Daisy. You can invite anyone you like.

Reading his response, I let out a squeal so loud that Mrs. K rushes from the kitchen to check on me. She looks at me with a mix of surprise and concern.

"Sorry, my friend just sent me a picture of a cute kitten."

It takes a moment before she smiles and leaves, and I grab my phone.

> **Me:** You are the cutest. Can't wait to see you this evening.
>
> **Husband aka Charles Adorable**
> **Hawthorne:** Have fun. Now let your husband get some honest work done.

About an hour later, my friends are gathered in Charles' kitchen while Mrs. K prepares her mouth-watering pierogi. I'm perched between Elodie and Violet on the barstools, sipping ginger-orange tea. Willow is behind the counter, bombarding our chef with questions like a third grader.

"Why don't you all sit in the living room, and I'll bring the food as soon as it's ready? I'm worried you'll overexert yourself, Daisy," Mrs. K suggests kindly.

Before I can respond, Willow hides her hands behind her back, which were moments ago chopping herbs. "Am I bothering you too much with my questions?"

Mrs. K smiles. "Not at all, dear. I love having company in the kitchen."

"Oh, thank goodness, because I'm having a blast." Willow throws her arms around Charles' housekeeper, who looks momentarily surprised before patting my friend's back affectionately.

Her smiling gaze meets mine. "You girls go. I'm sure

Mr. Hawthorne wouldn't be thrilled to hear that you spent the whole day with me in the kitchen, Daisy."

"Okay," I agree, more so because my headache is slowly starting to make a grand appearance.

Once the three of us are settled on the couch, Elodie surprises me. "When you said you were sick, I really thought you were pregnant."

"What? Why would you think that?" My hand reaching for my tea on the table freezes midair.

"Daze, even when we were kids, your biggest dream was to have your own family. It was natural for me to think so, now that you're married to a man you love."

"And not just any man, but Charles Hawthorne," Violet adds.

"You thought the same?" I ask cautiously.

"Of course. Haven't you read any gossip columns recently?" Violet nods.

"No, why?"

"There's an article about you and Charles almost every week speculating if you guys got married because you were pregnant, or better yet, when the next Hawthorne will be born. So, believe me, there are a lot of people waiting to see your little one!" Violet grins, filling my chest with equal parts warmth and despair. It's the feeling that comes when you wake up after dreaming about your biggest wish coming true. You feel the skin-tingling euphoria about something that's just a figment of your imagination.

I shake my head slowly and take a sip of my warm drink. "Thank you for keeping me updated on the town gossip, but enough about me. What's new with you guys? I feel like I haven't seen you for so long."

"You'll be pleased to hear that I'm joining the local news as their newest local reporter." Violet beams.

"You are? Oh my God, that's such great news, Vi!" Elodie and I throw ourselves over Vi, laughing and tumbling onto the floor until my senses remind me of any potential germs I might transfer to my friends.

"I only got the confirmation two days ago—"

"And you waited two days to tell us about your dream coming true? That's so cool, Vi!" I playfully smack her hand before settling back on the couch.

"Sorry." Violet holds her ears with a sheepish smile. "But the dream is to someday work for the *Elite Gazette*, but yeah, this is a good start." There's unmissable glee on her face as she claps her hands together. "I can't wait to cover all the amazing gossip in town."

"You know you have to publish real news and not just gossip, right?" I raise an eyebrow.

"Of course." She waves her hand dismissively. Elodie and I probably don't look convinced, because Violet straightens up. "If you must know, I'm very ethical when it comes to journalism."

Before I can ask her if there's a journalist oath, Willow enters the room, wiping her hands on a kitchen towel.

"Why were you all squealing as if you just found out that Minnie King is performing in town and we just got front-row tickets?"

Minnie King, aka Dreamcatcher, is one of the most famous pop soul and ballad singers, and she has fans from all age groups, nine to ninety.

"About my new job." Violet shrugs, then looks at me and Elodie. "I told her this morning."

"Since when are you interested in cooking, by the way?" Elodie flicks her eyes toward Willow.

"What, because I cook badly, I'm not allowed to enter anyone's kitchen?" Willow flops onto the floor, sitting cross-legged. When she pushes the sleeves of her pullover up, the vines of her tattoos peek out. "Since you sound so interested, I'm trying to rope in a new chef at the inn."

"That's amazing, Willow. Does that mean business is going well?" Elodie asks, but Willow's expression darkens.

"What is it?" I tilt my head to the side.

An irritated look crosses her face. "Remember my grandfather's land, the one he inherited from his parents?"

"The one you're supposed to inherit next?"

Willow's mouth twists into a thin line at my words. "I was supposed to, but now someone else is claiming ownership. He's a distant second cousin and claims the land was gifted to his father several years ago. After the initial shock, I thought maybe it'd be for the good. What's better than having a business partner who's also family?"

"But he isn't on board with your plans?" Elodie leans forward.

"No, he wants to sell it to some big hotel chain. I don't know who the buyer is, but I know he has deep pockets and big connections."

"Oh, Wills! I'm so sorry. Is there anything we can do to help? Maybe I can talk to Charles." There's no one in town with deeper pockets and bigger connections than him.

Willow finally smiles and shakes her head. "Thank you

so much, but not yet. I have a plan. Maybe I can turn this around to my advantage." The spark returns to her eyes. "I have an appointment scheduled with the big-shot hotelier. I'm going to pitch my plans for the land—extending our inn to a rustic, charming wedding location. Apart from the Butterfly Inn, there's no other proper wedding venue in Cherrywood, but we host so many weddings each year."

"That's so true!" I find myself nodding along with Elodie and Vi.

"So, you all think it's interesting and he might agree to investing in my idea instead of establishing a huge hotel that no one wants in Cherrywood?"

"Of course!" I give her a high five. "That's very smart, Wills." But I'm not entirely surprised, Willow has always been the one with the most business acumen.

"Thanks, but now everything rides on the mystery man, my potential investor." Willow leans back. "So what about you, Daze? When are you starting on your plan for that big family?"

And for once, I have no response.

All my friends are working toward their dreams. They have a plan, but here I am, holding something beautiful in my hands that I never dreamed of.

What am I supposed to do now? Live this life and forget my dreams? Or leave this and chase what I've always wanted?

Because as badly as I want them to, these two things will never be the same.

It's been five days since my friends visited me. I'm feeling much better now and, truth be told, eager to dive back into work. However, Charles has been adamant that I take the entire week off.

I'm sitting in the sunroom with a cup of hot cocoa. After last night's snow, Cherrywood is draped in a beautiful white blanket, and through the clear glass, I have a picturesque view of the town—the frozen lake, snow-capped peaks, and a scattering of red and pink decorations as the town gears up for Valentine's Day.

Despite seeing the sight all my life, my lips instinctively curl into a smile.

Our townsfolk certainly know how to celebrate.

The last few Valentine's Days have been nothing short of dreadful for me. I'd spent weeks planning every little thing, only to end up alone since Jax was too busy with something important at work.

But this year, I'm scared to even make a single plan, knowing that the man I'd make plans for would perhaps exceed all my expectations.

If you have to plan, plan your exit, Daisy. Your work here is done. Staying any longer is only going to cause heartache.

That voice in my head grows louder with each passing day spent in this house. But that's not the only change.

Every moment I'm with Charles, this feeling to just crawl inside him and never leave wells inside me with no end in sight.

I can't even pinpoint the exact moment my insufferable boss transformed into the man I've fallen so deeply for.

You really lived up to your name this time, Daisy Hazy.

Love and family were never a part of this deal.

Shaking my head to silence the inner monologue, I reach for my laptop on the nearby table. I must return to work before I lose my mind.

I sift through my inbox to see if anything unusual jumps out, but every project seems to be on track. Until my eyes lock on an email from an unfamiliar address and my heart nearly leaps from my chest as I read the words.

> Dear Mr. Hawthorne,
>
> I trust this email finds you in good health. I'm pleased to share some photographs from the tea party you graciously sponsored for the kids. They loved everything—the clothes, the food, and the gifts. Furthermore, Max has started his sessions with his private chess instructor. Thank you for arranging that.
>
> Best Regards,
>
> Greta Day
> Supervisor at Cherrywood Orphanage

My hands tremble as I open the attachments.

Lulu! The little girl who invited Charles to her tea party during the charity event is dressed in a delicate tutu skirt. It takes a moment for me to realize that it's from Chloe's last fall collection. But it's not just Lulu, every child is wearing vibrant, chic clothes, and their radiant smiles are the most beautiful accessory.

The door to the room swings open. My laptop still rests on my lap when Charles strides in, his smile faltering as he makes a beeline toward me, dropping his laptop bag at the foot of the couch.

thirty-one

Like Stars Looking Good Together

Charles

"Hey, what's wrong?" I run my fingers over Daisy's cheeks. She's much better now, even the red on her face has returned.

"Did you pay for Lulu's tea party?" Daisy asks instead, her voice almost a hiccup.

"Um, Lulu?" The furrow between my brows deepens.

"The girl at the charity event."

My entire frame goes rock solid. "How do you know about that?"

"I was going through the emails." She points toward her laptop on her lap. My official email is open, and there's a picture of kids sitting in a park wearing my sister's latest collection. "Did you do it all because of me?" Daisy asks carefully, and my head jerks up.

There's so much hope and affection in her eyes that

I can't even think of lying. It was by coincidence that Chloe visited me in my office when I was browsing the net for kids' designer clothes. Any other day, I'd have forwarded such a task to Daisy, but not this time, when I'd caused her pain with my attitude.

It was Chloe's idea to send her designs for the kids. She even organized a big photoshoot for them. But I only agreed to everything because I haven't been able to erase the image of Daisy's hurt face soaked in rain from my memory.

"I don't know. Maybe I did it because I knew you didn't like how I behaved. Or maybe I did it because I didn't like how I behaved." I glance away from her, grabbing the laptop from her lap and placing it on the floor.

"You're so sweet sometimes that I can't believe you're a real human being, let alone a businessman, Charles."

"Why did businessmen become unpopular?"

Daisy's eyes narrow an inch, as they always do whenever she's trying to make sense of my mood. And it's not long before she takes a hint. She knows I don't want to talk any more about the pictures, because they speak about the part of me I usually keep hidden from everyone.

But not her.

Her expression slowly changes, and she removes the thin throw blanket placed over her. A blush takes over her face as she sits cross-legged before me.

"The doctor okayed me for work." She rolls her shoulders, and I have to bite back my smile. A sexy comment is soon coming my way. "And other things too."

"Other things, you say." I can feel my lips stretching.

The office has been no fun without her. I'm never going

to admit it out loud, but post-lunch, I've spent all my meetings in a distracted state of mind, more interested in the clock as the minutes ticked by one after another, nearing the time I could leave without getting raised eyebrows from my staff.

I lean forward, my nose brushing against hers. "What other things do you have in mind, my dear wife?"

"I thought I'd have to persuade you some more, given you showed no interest in me this last week." Her low voice is barely above a whisper.

"There can never be a time when I would not want you, butterfly. Do you know how hard these days have been? My hand is chafed and my dick on the verge of falling off from the treatment I've given myself in the shower since you're off-limits. I'm counting the seconds for you to get better."

Daisy's jaw drops before she throws her head back in laughter. "I can't believe you just said that," she says in between her giggles.

"It's true." I pounce on her, taking her with me to the carpeted floor of the bright sunroom. My thumb trails down her jaw before sliding against her lower lip. "I've missed you. I've missed your mouth. I've missed your kisses. I really like kissing you, Daisy."

Even though my intention is to keep it light and fun, when I kiss her, I'm not thinking about sex. I am thinking about heart and feeling and all those emotions which I have kept at an arm's distance until now.

"Me too, Charles. But right now, I'm hoping for something more than just a kiss." She rolls her pelvis against my cock, thankfully making me forget all the deep-shit feelings.

"Is that so, butterfly?" I grin, my fingers tracing a path from her back to her waist, reaching her stomach, and finally resting on the waistband of her shorts. "Are you saying you want me to fuck you and remind you to whom you belong, Mrs. Hawthorne?"

A little moan escapes her at the name, and she nods frantically, her thighs rubbing together as I tug her shorts down.

When the tip of my little finger slips under the waistband of her panties, skimming the warm skin, she groans. "Holy fuck, Charles."

I never hear Daisy curse except when we're like this and she's turned on. I can't be more proud knowing that I make her forget her manners.

"How are you so fucking wet so soon, Daisy? What were you thinking about?" She's dripping on my fingers already.

"You, always you." When I push her silk blue panties down, she eagerly helps me, kicking them off with her feet.

Her eyes gleam when she tugs on my belt. Now, with a practiced finesse and not missing a beat, she takes off my notchless belt before unzipping my pants. My boxers come down next, and this time it's my turn to groan when my cock gets the much-needed space.

She pumps my already hard cock a few times before lining it against her clit and we both moan together.

"Fuck, you're heaven, butterfly."

But the next second, when I slip inside her, I go rock solid and she does too. It's as if we both recognize at the same time why this feels so goddamn good and amazing.

"I don't have a condom on me." I groan, my head hitting

against her shoulder, and I pull back and slip out. My cock almost protests and weeps, pre-cum landing on her thigh.

"You mean, not even one?" Daisy's voice is shaky, and I shake my head.

I'd thought the absence of condoms in my home would be another reminder that I can't fuck her until she's perfectly fine. If only I knew that she's not just fine but in need of me.

"Charles." Daisy's voice is soft, while I'm still cursing my luck. Talk about missed opportunities. "I'm on the pill and I'm clean. I've never done this… I mean, without a condom."

My brain seems to freeze, incapable of forming coherent thoughts.

Do I want to experience everything with Daisy?

Fuck yeah.

Do I want to give her an experience she's never had before?

Without a doubt.

But this…this is so much more than that. This is about trust and so many more emotions I'm scared to name right now.

"Me too," I reply, confirming my status. "So, this is it?" My mind buzzes with excitement in anticipation of another unforgettable life moment.

"Are you nervous, Charles?" Daisy bites her bottom lip before a giggle shoots out of her.

But soon those turn into a gasp when I turn her over on her stomach, bring her knees up on the soft Persian carpet, and then push them apart with my own to give me better access. I push inside her once again, inch by inch, and God my eyes roll back.

"You're so goddamn tight, Daisy. Do you feel me? My skin, my cock moving inside you, butterfly. Tell me you feel it."

"Fuck, Charles. I do." She moans, pressing herself back into me, encouraging me to thrust inside her, and I'm all too happy to oblige.

My hands slide up from her perfect hips, inside her silk top, and reach her boobs covered in a silk bra. I push it down, and those full tits fall into my hands.

"You are so perfect everywhere, and so mine, Mrs. Hawthorne," I whisper, my breath skating over her earlobe, and she lets go of the sexiest moan.

"You like hearing that, don't you?" I ask, even when I know her response. "You like hearing that you're mine. You like hearing that all those reporters who are eager to see any personal side of my personality are now dying to know how I fuck my wife when we're alone."

"God, Hawthorne." She exhales. "Are you trying to kill me?"

"Never." My one arm tightens around her chest and pulls her up a little, while my other goes for her clit, fingering that nub in a fast tempo.

"Charles, I'm—" she cries, but I already know she's coming as an orgasm racks through her.

I pick up speed as she shudders and mutters indecipherable words in a moan. Her sex squeezes me, my breathing turning labored as her warmth chokes me.

"Fuck, Daisy." I grip her hips, and in two punishing thrusts, I empty my load inside her.

Inside her and not a condom.

That fact doesn't escape me, especially when I pull out

and see the evidence of what we did dripping from her sex onto the carpet.

It's established right then.

Forget porn.

Daisy on her knees, wrung out on pleasure with my come leaking out of her pussy, is my biggest turn-on.

It's been a few days since the most amazing sex of my life, and so many things have changed since.

"For someone who just got what he's always wanted, you look pretty glum," Ray comments as I tear my gaze away from Daisy and her friend Willow across the hall.

The board cast their votes, and as of last night, I'm officially the new CEO of the Hawthorne business empire.

Right now, we're at a party arranged by Jimmy, and everyone who's someone in Cherrywood is in this room, drinking expensive champagne on my tab.

Like Ray said, this moment is everything I've dreamed of since forever, yet instead of feeling relief and excitement, my skin itches as if I'm dressed in tattered rags.

And it seems I'm doing a shitty job at hiding my feelings.

"For someone who complains about social events, you're being seen an awful lot here these days. Is your land deal still not through?"

My cousin's jaw pulses, and I follow his gaze as he throws daggers toward Daisy.

"Why the hell are you glaring at my wife like she's broken your favorite toy?"

His flared nostrils relax at my sharp tone, but I don't miss the tightness around his eyes.

"I'm not staring at anyone. I zoned out. And don't worry about my business. I have it under control. Speaking of your wife, why is she so far away? Isn't acting like she's completely smitten with you part of her job?"

His grin is all Lucifer, and I'm glad Ray is my cousin and not just some business associate. Because suddenly the title of murder convict isn't looking that appalling.

"Something wrong?" His smile fades. Once Ray has his eyes on something, it's hard to escape his trap—a trait I appreciate in business, but not so much in this moment.

"Nothing's wrong. If anything, everything's just perfect." I nod toward the yellow banner proudly displaying my name and CEO title.

"You and I have been friends even before we became cousins, Charlie. I can read you better than our favorite well-worn comic book, dog-eared and all." He sets his untouched whiskey glass onto the corner table.

How long has it been since he drank at social events?

A simple moment once again changing lives.

Yeah, you're one to talk, Hawthorne.

I steal another glance at Daisy, who's looking stunning in a bright red off-shoulder dress, matching heels, and a crimson bow in her hair. Lately, I find myself doing this often—admiring her from a distance.

It didn't take me long to notice she's been avoiding me since our mind-blowing adventure in the sunroom. She spends a lot of evenings at her dad's place, and her lunch hours are often spent in training new assistants.

But last night, during the official announcement, I caught a glimpse of the Daisy I've known all these years. She jumped into my arms without caring that we were in the living room and Mrs. Kowalski was right there changing flowers. But before things could escalate beyond a kiss, she stepped out of my grip, and then until I fell asleep, she was on a phone call with Willow.

"Come with me." Ray tucks his hands into his pockets and strides away without waiting for my response. I'm so fucking tempted to blow him off and stay put. But knowing Ray, he'll return and drag me until he's at the root of my troubles.

When it comes to family, everything is personal for him.

With one last look at Daisy, her teeth sinking into her bottom lip as she listens to her friend's animated chatter, hands flailing and all, I make my way toward the door Ray just exited.

I find him standing on the dark balcony, illuminated only by the faint glow of streetlamps and the tip of his lit cigar.

"So she can smell booze on you but not tobacco?" I hate my irritated words as soon as they leave my mouth.

"Does that make you feel better?" He takes another drag before flicking the butt into a glass of water he must have picked up on the way, the lingering aroma of spent tobacco subtly filling the air.

"Sorry. It was an asshole thing to say."

"It was, but also not like you, not when it comes to Quill. So tell me what the fuck is going on with you and Daisy."

"She wants kids," I blurt. The tension has been simmering inside me for so long.

I'm not stupid. I know why she's pulling away.

"Was that also part of the contract?" Ray crosses his arms over his chest.

"Can you stop bringing up the contract every time we talk about Daisy?" My teeth clench painfully. "She's my wife, for God's sake, not some business deal."

"I thought her becoming your wife was part of a deal."

"I don't know why I thought talking to you was a good idea." I turn around to storm off, but he grabs my arm.

"I'm not trying to get a rise out of you, Charlie. I'm genuinely trying to understand what has changed between you two."

How can I explain that not one thing, but everything has changed? I've started yearning for things that had no place in my life.

Like making her smile.

Or waiting in bed to watch her sleep until she opens her eyes because I want to be the first thing she sees every day.

"You like her?" he asks cautiously, devoid of humor or emotion.

If it weren't about me, I'd find the situation laughable—two big-shot businessmen hiding from everyone and talking about a girl like a pair of high schoolers.

"I...I don't know." *How long are you going to hide from the truth, Hawthorne?* "But what I do know is we want opposite things in life."

"So she wants kids and you want...?"

"Not to have kids." Every muscle in my body tenses.

"Why?"

"Because she wants her own family."

"I was asking about you, smartass. What she wants is a natural thing."

"I can't bear the responsibility for someone. Keeping them safe, watching them twenty-four seven." A tightness grips my chest. "I don't want to mess up anyone's life even by mistake."

"How do you have such strong feelings about something you haven't experienced?" His calm voice is judgment-free as if we're talking about the weather and not my marriage, which is on the verge of failing.

"She says the same thing, but I don't have to eat poison to know I'll hate dying."

"Please tell me you didn't compare having kids to eating poison in front of her?" Ray glares at me, my words finally breaking his poise.

"I didn't. Not because I feel differently, but because she's barely spoken to me in days." I tug on my tie, the knot feeling too tight. "I think she's planning something."

"What do you mean?"

My mouth dries up, voicing my biggest worry. "Once I become the CEO, she can ask for a divorce. We'll pretend to be married in public for a few more months, but unofficially, we won't necessarily have to live in the same house, the same room."

Ray's brows rise. "And that's in the contract?"

I nod. "It is."

He's quiet for several beats as he grabs the wrought-iron railing. "When you both want different things in life, isn't it better this way, to split up soon? Or are you having a change of heart?"

Am I? No fucking way.

"Not on this matter. But I don't like that she's drifting away like this. Life was good until now."

"For whom? You or her? You can't have it all, brother. You can't choose to enjoy the rain but also not want to get wet. If you don't want the life she does, you have to let her go. That's the only fair thing."

A weird scratchiness settles in my throat, making it hard to swallow as I imagine my home without her. Life will once again become bland, save for the occasional burst of color she brings into my office. And like dried leaves yearning for the first gentle touch of an autumn breeze, I'll wait for those moments.

But what if she no longer wants to work for me?

She's receiving enough money in return for the marriage, and didn't I offer to buy her a house in any city she desires?

Fuck, what was I thinking?

No, Daisy won't leave her dad. She'll stay for him, if not for me.

"Let's go. We've been away for too long. Plus, I need a few minutes with the mayor before she leaves." Ray pulls away, breaking the silence.

As we reenter the ballroom, the atmosphere has shifted. There's more chatter, the music pulses louder, and there's a noticeable increase in servers darting around with empty glasses.

"Are we in the right room?" Ray scans the area, but my focus is fixed on one person—Daisy.

"Absolutely."

The worry lines on her face have melted away, replaced

by a soft rosy glow that paints her cheeks, making her look stunning.

"Great. I just spotted the mayor." Ray pats on my arm. "You keep in mind what I said, Charlie."

I only half listen to his words as I make my way toward my wife.

"Thank goodness you're here, Charles. Can you please take Daisy home? She's had a bit too much to drink." Willow guides a tipsy Daisy to my side.

"What happened here?" I draw Daisy closer, her hand clinging to mine around her waist.

"Mayor Coggeshall happened." Willow tightens her bun as a few red strands spill out. "She was convinced Daisy was pregnant because, apparently, old women have X-ray vision and all." Her words hit me like a sledgehammer.

"And?" I force the words out, hiding my rising panic as best I can.

"And what?" Willow looks at me like I'm insane.

Doesn't she realize the bombshell she's just dropped on me?

"Don't worry, Charles. I showed her she's way off base. If me gulping down six champagne glasses in a row isn't enough to prove her wrong, I don't know what else is." Daisy winks at me lazily, her eyelids drooping.

She looks so breathtakingly beautiful that I can't tear my gaze away from her.

"You can gawk at your wife at home, Charles. For now, please leave. If you stay another minute, I guarantee she'll either pass out or get sick."

"Daisy, we're home." I gently shake her shoulders as she lies sprawled over me in the back seat of my Porsche. "Let's get you into bed."

"Which one?" She slowly opens her eyes, her chin resting on my chest.

But my heart lurches at her question.

Why would she ask that?

Except for one night, she's never slept anywhere else but in my bedroom, including the last few days, when she either pretended to be asleep before I joined her or waited for me to doze off before slipping in beside me.

"You have always belonged in my bed, butterfly." I stroke her cheek, and only when she leans into my touch before closing her eyes does my heart settle back into its normal rhythm.

I place Daisy on the bed and untie the straps of her heels. My gaze stays on her pink toenails for a beat too long before I pull the covers up to her neck.

"I missed you. I missed us." The tiny quiver in her voice knocks the wind out of me.

Fuck, butterfly.

"I missed you too," I whisper, and her eyes widen. "Too much."

Miss doesn't even cover how I feel these days.

Daisy's fingers trail up to my forehead, then down the corner of my face before running through my hair.

"You, Charles Ashcroft Hawthorne, are a dream I never even dared to dream. I never thought I'd marry someone like you, someone who would show me things I didn't dare to wish for. Even if it's only temporary." She wets her lips while

I'm frozen in place. "I wish this was real and we weren't like stars that look good together but in reality are light-years apart."

Her voice cracks, and a single tear slips from her eye before she falls unconscious, her head resting on my chest.

I don't know if there's a word for the emotion I'm feeling right now. The tear tracing down her cheek, seeping into my jacket, feels like acid ready to burn me.

She wants me.

She doesn't think she can have me.

"I wish I was enough to make all your dreams come true, butterfly."

thirty-two

The Secrecy Pact

Daisy

"Daisy." I hear a voice that sounds like my mom's from someplace far away.

"Mom? Is this a dream?"

"It's me, honey. Mrs. Kowalski."

I slowly open my eyes, and after the initial blur, her face comes into focus, along with a smile.

"How are you feeling now?"

A groan escapes my lips as I try to sit up, holding my aching head between my hands. "God, how much did I drink last night?"

"Mr. Hawthorne told me what happened. You definitely proved the mayor wrong."

"Oh gosh! Mayor Coggeshall was being her usual small-town gossip diva, which I usually adore. But last night—God, what will everyone think of me?" I unceremoniously flop back down on the pillow, trying to recall how much of a fool I made of myself, and by association, of Charles.

He must be so freaking angry.

"Don't worry. From what I heard, others were in no better shape. Plus, it's a party. That's one place you're allowed to let loose."

I feel the bed dip next to my head as Mrs. K places something cold onto my forehead, immediately dulling my headache.

"Sometimes I feel like you're my mom." I sigh without opening my eyes.

"I might not be your mom, honey, but I'm mom-like." I hear a smile in her voice, which makes my own lips curl. "Plus, I care about you and Mr. Hawthorne as much as I care about my own kids."

"Thank you so much." I open my eyes and grasp her soft, cold hand on my head. "Was Charles upset?"

This time, her laughter fills the air. "He loves you too much to be upset with you."

I sit upright in a flash, headache be damned. There's something more urgent here.

"Did he say this to you? Like in those words? Did he say that *he loves me*?"

Her eyebrows furrow, and a second later, I realize my mistake.

Crap!

Aren't I playing the part of the girl he's head over heels in love with?

"I mean, Charles rarely shows his feelings, so I thought

if he ever said something to you… I know it's stupid." I try to play cool, while my heart races wild.

Mrs. K thankfully smiles. "It's not stupid at all, sweetheart. We girls love to hear if our men talk about us. I know the feeling. But you know Mr. Hawthorne better than anyone. He never says how he feels. He shows it. And you, my dear, are so good at noticing all his small gestures. That's what makes you two perfect for each other."

My gaze drifts from her face to the nightstand, where there's a bottle of Advil and a small note card.

You're sleeping so peacefully, I don't want to wake you. I've already called the doctor to make a visit whenever you're up.

Take care, butterfly. I'll see you in the evening.

Mrs. K is right. Charles has always spoken in tiny gestures—cooking with Dad, fireworks for me, a tea party for Lulu.

The housekeeper places two white tablets in my palm and hands me a glass of water.

"You get ready now. I've texted the doctor, and in the meantime, I'm going to make you my personal remedy for such situations."

She's almost at the door when I call her. "Mrs. K, thank you for being here for Charles and me."

"You never have to mention it, sweetheart."

Half an hour later, I'm sitting in the living room, nursing a glass of something green that surprisingly doesn't taste as awful as it looks, when the doorbell rings.

"Mrs. Hawthorne, how are you doing this morning?" The family doctor enters, followed by Mrs. K.

"I'm hoping in a few hours I can respond with a 'perfectly well' to that question."

He chuckles, settling into an armchair beside me. "I heard you gave our mayor some well-mannered alcohol-fueled comebacks."

"Oh God! Please don't tell me I've already made the news." I lean forward, burying my head against the pillow on my lap.

"Mr. Hawthorne would never let that happen." Mrs. K grins when I finally look up.

"So, are you experiencing any nausea, headache?"

"Just a headache, but I already took two Advil and they seem to be slowly doing their job."

I'm still not sure why someone would need to see a doctor for a hangover. It's not medical but a behavioral situation, isn't it?

"Since I'm here, what do you say we run some blood work and check your vitamin and iron levels?" The doctor opens his bag and begins preparing a syringe. "Is there any chance you could be pregnant?"

"No! I'm not pregnant." The words spill out of my mouth.

A few years back, I always thought whenever a doctor would ask me this, I'd be ecstatic and maybe a little nervous, but never this terrified.

But if Charles' last reaction has confirmed anything, it's that this question is his worst nightmare.

"I can't be."

The doctor coughs lightly, and Mrs. Kowalski's brow furrows. They both continue to stare at me in confusion.

Of course they're confused.

We pose as the happiest and most in-love couple in public, and here I am, freaking out at the prospect of a baby like someone just handed me a manual to a crashing aircraft in a language I can't read. Panic level: the highest.

"I mean, Charles and I want to have a few more years to ourselves before we start a family. I'm very, *very* careful and always take my pill on time."

The doc and Mrs. K exchange a look as something unspoken passes between them.

"What is it?" I ask, dread slowly knocking at the door.

"Do you use any other form of contraception, Mrs. Hawthorne?" the doctor asks carefully.

My mind immediately goes to the sunroom. That was the one and only time we did it without a condom.

But you know one time is all it takes, Daisy.

"Not always," I reply slowly. "But isn't the pill one of the most effective ways?"

"It normally is. But you were on antibiotics for a long time because of the flu, and those medicines are known to reduce the effectiveness of hormonal contraceptives."

"Wh-what? How…how did I not know this?" My hands instinctively curl around my stomach before I look down.

I know it's silly and stupid, but I swear I feel like my belly has grown a little, and there's a warm sensation inside me.

Yeah, that's the booze from last night, Ms. Daisy Hazy.

"I'd recommend that we run a test, Mrs. Hawthorne." The good, patient doctor gets up.

"Can you—I mean, can *we* not tell Charles anything right now? I—I don't want his hopes to be up for nothing. And if it does happen"—the shiver that courses through me is equal parts worry and hope—"I'd like to tell him myself."

"Of course. That's totally understandable." The doctor places a tight band around my arm as I sit there feeling confused.

It feels like an important moment, like I should wish for something, but what? A positive or a negative?

I'm still holding the cotton ball on my arm when the doc finishes packing his bag. He's about to leave when he turns to me. "I see this is probably coming as a shock, but if you want a faster result, you can always take a pregnancy test, Mrs. Hawthorne."

My heart leaps out of my chest. Suddenly, peeing sounds like the most dangerous activity.

The doctor leaves while I'm stuck in place. My friends were right the other day. My dream has always been to start my own big family. I'd imagined the moment I'd miss a period and would take a pregnancy test. It was supposed to be magical.

My husband, who never had a face in those fantasies, would hold me in his arms. We would count each other's heartbeats while the clock hands moved too slowly. And finally, I'd ask him to check because I would be too freaking scared. He'd turn to me with a huge smile and show me the stick with a pink line, which would just be the starting line of our happiness.

Tears race down my cheeks, dropping onto my hands. My pounding heart is filled to the brim with feelings and emotions of unlived dreams. But maybe this is my chance.

How can you be so cruel, Mrs. Hawthorne?

Your husband, a man who always aims to do what's right, doesn't want kids. What do you think will happen when he finds out? Do you expect him to say, "Okay, now you're pregnant, so let's live like a happy family"?

When did your dreams become bigger than his fears?

You were never so selfish, Daisy.

Okay, enough! You can't accuse me of something I haven't even done.

I push away my inner critic, currently scaling the ladder of morality, and grab my phone.

> **Me:** I need to invoke our childhood secrecy pact. You have to do something for me without asking questions.

The reply comes immediately.

Willow: Shoot.

> **Me:** Are you home?

Willow: I'm at the inn, but I can be home in twenty minutes.

Right now, I'm grateful for that summer evening when, sitting on my parents' porch, Violet proposed a secrecy pact. Once in our lives, each of us gets to ask the other three to do something, and no questions will be asked. We finished with a pinky swear and blew over our linked hands, sending our pact to the fairies for authorization.

> **Me:** Okay, I'll see you in 20. Can you also bring a pregnancy test?

The phone trembles in my hand as I see her typing and deleting. I almost feel sorry for Willow. She must have so many questions, especially after witnessing my drunken antics last night at the party.

Willow: Got it. But you know I'll have to tell Vi and El about it, right? The pact only works when all of us are involved.

Me: I know. You do that.

Twenty minutes later, Steve drops me off at Willow's place. Three untouched pregnancy tests sit ominously on the table. No one speaks for several moments, and in the quiet room, the hum of the fridge booms like a distant drum.

"So are we just going to stare at them or do something?" Vi, sitting cross-legged on the floor, breaks the silence.

"Why do we have three?" I turn to Willow instead.

"I thought you might want to be completely sure."

"But I don't know if I can pee three times." I grab the water bottle I brought along. It's already half-empty.

"You don't have to pee multiple times, Daze." Elodie gently places her hand over my shoulder. "Once will be enough." She hands me a disposable plastic cup and takes away the bottle. "But do you not want to talk about it first?"

"That's not how the pact works," Vi immediately jumps in, and for once, I appreciate her general sense of overenthusiasm. "Plus, what kind of question is that? Daze is definitely pregnant. Duh."

"And would you rather not take the test with Charles? I'm sure he'd prefer knowing about it before us, especially if the tests come out positive."

"I wouldn't be so sure," I whisper while my friends stare at me, their gazes filled with unasked questions. "I need to do this on my own." My hands tremble as I pick up the tests from the table.

Moments later, I place the three sticks on the edge of the basin, waiting for the chemicals to do their work and predict my future. When I walk out of the bathroom, I'm met with the anxious faces of my friends.

"And?" Willow runs her hands over her arms.

"There are still a few minutes." I show them the timer on my phone. "But I'm too nervous. Can one of you please check it for me?"

"You got it." Violet takes my phone and heads toward the bathroom, walking past me.

As I stand between Willow and Elodie, the timer goes off. The otherwise gentle sound of church bells feels like war music to my ears.

"It's negative." Violet shrugs, glancing up from the tests.

All the anxiety of the last hour washes away, leaving an unexpected feeling of bereavement and disappointment in its wake. It's as if I just lost something very precious.

"Negative on all three?" My eyes betray me, and I repeatedly blink to get rid of the wetness.

"Not exactly. You're pregnant. All three tests are positive." Vi's downturned expression slowly morphs into a grin.

"What? Why would you do that?" My heart ricochets against my rib cage with relief, feeling as though I've just accidentally met a long-lost friend.

"So you could truly understand how you feel about this." Violet points in the general direction of my belly. "You seemed confused before."

"Vi! That's insanely cruel." Willow smacks Vi's shoulder, eliciting a groan.

"What? Haven't you seen *Friends*? When Phoebe did it, Rachel thanked her, but I get shoulder hits. No point in doing good these days."

"You're crazy, do you know that?" I tug on Violet's arm before she can walk away. "But your craziness is good sometimes. Thank you. It really helped clarify things."

"And?" Violet raises an eyebrow.

"I'm having a baby. You're all gonna be aunts soon." Saying it out loud makes it extra real.

"Yay!" My best friends take me into a group hug, and I don't bother hiding my tears.

"Are we finally going to talk about the rest of this? Like why you're doing this here and not with Charles?" Elodie tips her head to the side when we pull back.

My heart thumps like a drumroll in my chest. My secret has grown too large to keep from my friends any longer. "Can we sit down first?"

Around half an hour later, I'm back in the same spot on the couch, with my three best friends staring at me, mouths wide open. I'm not surprised, since I just broke their long-held belief about my boss being in love with me.

They're aware that Charles proposed to me because he was cornered, but after seeing Charles on TV asking for my dad's permission, like everyone else, they were convinced this was the most epic love story of the century. And I know deep down they think this thing between Charles and me isn't one-sided.

I never had the courage until today to say the truth, that my marriage came with an end date.

imperfect match

The silence becomes heavy and suffocating, and I'm the first to break it.

"You can judge me. I won't mind."

"We're not judging you, Daze." Elodie fidgets nervously. "But this sounds like something out of a movie. A contract marriage."

"I still can't believe you guys managed to even fool me." Violet's brow furrows in disbelief. "Are you absolutely sure you don't love each other?"

She places her phone onto the table, and there's a candid photo of Charles and me on the screen. My heart skips a beat watching his beautiful smile as I brush snow from his woolen coat.

"How could you fake that look?" Violet asks, and I'm not sure if she's referring to me or Charles.

"Vi is right, Daze. We've all seen how Charles looks at you and how much he's changed since your wedding." Elodie's voice is soft, filled with hope and concern.

"It doesn't matter. He doesn't want kids." I nervously rub my clammy palms against my thighs.

"What does that mean? This is his kid, right? He must have done something to get you pregnant." Willow balls her hands into fists.

My teeth dig into my bottom lip. Was it something he did or was it my own lack of knowledge?

"Do you know birth control pills are as effective as a Tic Tac if you're on antibiotics?"

"What?" My friends let out a collective gasp, which is oddly comforting.

Since this morning, I've been wondering if this information

was something I should have known already. Maybe they taught it in sex-ed class while I was dozing off on the back bench. But thankfully, it's news even for my friends.

"So what now?" Elodie's words pull me out of the brain fog.

"I can't impose this on Charles, especially after knowing how he feels about kids. I'm going to tell him he can be as involved as he wants, and I'm not expecting him to be running for the Best Dad Award. I—"

Elodie's hand on my knee stops me mid-sentence. "I'm not asking what you're going to do, Daze, but what do you really want?"

I close my eyes, and an image of a childhood dream dances before me—my own family, and this time my partner has a face. Charles. My heart races, my body trembling at the sight of the image before everything dissipates like smoke.

"You know you can tell us anything, Daze. This is a judgment-free place, even without the secrecy pact."

My eyes open at hearing Willow's voice.

"It seems like everything in my life comes with a 'but.' Parents who brought me into this world *but* can't love me. Jax, who claims to love me *but* can't stop fucking around with the whole town. Charles"—my voice cracks—"who can't be more perfect *but* despises the thought of family and kids. Why can't I have a relationship where I have it all, just for once?"

"Maybe you do have it now, Daze." Willow tips her head toward my stomach.

I wrap my hands around my waist, and there's a click in my chest as if something broken has found a tiny fix.

"Maybe I do."

thirty-three

Space for Dreams

Charles

My mind is completely distracted as the head of finance at Elixir goes over quarterly profits. His presentation slides with numbers and pie charts in green, red, and blue blend into a blur on my computer screen.

I pick up my phone once again and reread the text from the doctor this morning.

> **Doc:** There's nothing to worry about, Mr. Hawthorne. Mrs. Hawthorne doesn't have any deficiencies. I suggested she take it easy in the coming days, and although you don't need any instructions, a part of my job is to remind you to make sure your wife is happy.

What does he mean by that?

Does he think she's unhappy?

I'm almost tempted to ask, but what kind of husband would that make me? Shouldn't I already know if my wife is happy or not?

Stop pretending like you don't.

Out of habit, I glance out the glass wall and nearly spill my coffee over the keyboard when I find her seated at her desk.

How long has she been there?

"Fuck!"

"Do you have a question, Charles?" Ray asks, and I realize I've interrupted the entire meeting.

"No, everything sounds good so far. Please continue."

This time, I remember to mute myself before turning my attention back to my wife. Unlike other days, she hasn't turned on her PC, going through her emails and making a task list. Instead, today she's simply staring at the monitor, her status on the company network still unavailable on my screen.

I watch as she bites her lip, looks down at something on her lap for a long moment before her gaze flicks toward me.

My heart catapults out of my body when our eyes meet.

That's insane. She can't see me, but I can see everything. Every trace of worry, every line of panic etched on her face digs into my heart.

Daisy closes her eyes, squares her shoulders, and then returns her attention to the monitor. The arrow of my mouse hovers over the blue icon, the one I've never used until now. It was just for security reasons when Nick, the head of IT, installed software on my PC allowing me live access to any screen on the company network.

I push away the guilt, making room for worry, and type Daisy Price-Hawthorne into the search bar of the app.

She's looking at my calendar.

Not just looking, but trying to find an open slot. But fuck, I'm booked solid until eight PM.

She's my wife. She should never have to check my calendar just to talk to me.

"Sorry, gentlemen, but I need to step out," I announce, interrupting Ray mid-question.

There's a moment of silence. No one leaves a quarterly financial review, at least not unless someone's dying or bleeding.

"Is there something more urgent than this?" Ray's tone is clipped.

"Believe me, there is." I hit the red button and exit the meeting.

My rapid heartbeat is in sync with my footsteps as I walk out of my office.

"Charles." Daisy jerks in her seat when I stop next to her desk. Her gaze flies from my face to the monitor. "The meeting ended early?"

"I stepped out."

"You stepped out of Elixir's quarterly financial review? Why?" Her jaw falls open.

Say something.

Fast.

Say anything, dammit.

"How are you feeling now?"

"Charles, I was hammered, not sick." She tucks her hair behind her ear. "If anything, I should be embarrassed. I'm so sorry for the previous night."

"I'd say you did a good job at shutting down the mayor and the whole being-pregnant rumor mill."

But her face falls at my lighthearted comment, not just in worry but in sheer panic.

I thought I was becoming an expert at reading her, but right now, her emotions are like a pop quiz for a subject I didn't study.

She leans in to grab something from her desk—a plain white notepad—when I spot something wrong. She isn't wearing a hair clip today!

"You sure you're okay?"

"Can we talk?" she asks instead, circling her desk and nodding toward my office. The rare serious cadence of her tone doesn't help in calming my nerves.

A few moments later, we both settle on the leather couch, which has been a witness to so many unforgettable conversations.

Today might be another of such days. I can already feel the shift in the air to something heavy and ominous.

"Is it about work?" I don't even fucking care about the hopeful tone of my voice.

Daisy slowly shakes her head, plunging my heartbeat to the lowest notch. When I think something dreadful is coming my way, her lips curl into a smile. I follow her gaze to the golden desk plaque that my cousins gifted me.

Charles Hawthorne.

CEO of the Hawthorne Empire. Fucking Finally!

"I'm so happy you finally got what you deserved, Charles. Congratulations once again."

Her words are like an olive branch, and I grab it with both hands.

"You are the one person who doesn't need to congratulate me, Daisy. This wouldn't have been possible without you."

"So your plan worked. We both got what we wanted out of this arrangement."

"We did." I steel my spine, ignoring the voice in my head that is screaming at me to put an immediate stop to this conversation.

"In that case, how soon can we end this and go our separate ways?"

There's a deafening silence in the room followed by her low but controlled words. There's a pain in my chest, as if someone is crushing my heart into tiny, sharp pieces. It takes me several beats to find my voice.

"What's the rush?"

When I proposed this crazy idea to her months back, I'd thought this would be just like any other business deal. Then why does it feel like I've lost everything when on paper, I have everything I've ever wanted.

"I can't do this anymore, Charles."

"Do *what* exactly?" This strange emotion in my chest finds escape in the most unsuitable form. She's the last person I should snap at.

But this is Daisy Price-Hawthorne. A girl who has never taken shit from me.

"To name a few things—cheating everyone, lying to our families and friends. I'm slowly forgetting what's real and what's fake. I'm sorry, I thought I could, but I can't do it anymore, Charles." Her hands quiver as she grips the notepad tightly on her lap, but it's her voice that scares me. There's a finality in it.

"What if it's not fake?"

Daisy's brown eyes widen and lock with mine. I feel like I'm reaching her, reminding her of all the moments since the day I made the proposal, until she jerks herself back.

"Fooling ourselves will only lead to more pain, Charles. You and I can never be real together. We are too different, and so are our aspirations in life. But it's *my* responsibility to make sure that my dreams have the space and chance they deserve."

I hate that I understand her every word. I fucking married her for my dreams, so how can I ignore hers?

"I don't know how this works with a contract marriage. Do we sign some papers, or do we officially apply for a divorce?" She glances up at me from the table. "In any case, let's get it over with fast so we both can move forward with our lives."

But she doesn't know there is no forward for me without her. Unknowingly, she's become my beacon of happiness, and once she's gone, my life will once again become a circular monotonicity. I'll be living the same loop again and again.

"I need this, Charles." There's a quiver in her voice when I don't say anything for several minutes, but I find myself nodding in response.

For the first time since we got married, she's asked for something for herself.

How can I say no to that?

I tap away all the emotions bursting inside me that want me to pull her closer and whisper in her ear that I'm never letting her go and I don't care about any law.

"I'll have the papers ready in the next couple of days. You'll no longer be tied to me." Those are the hardest words I've uttered in a long while. "But can I ask you not to make the news about our divorce public for now, and if possible, wait for a while before you go out…on any dates." My fists clench as I imagine her with someone else. Someone who would make her happier. It's as if all my nightmares have suddenly come alive right in front of my eyes.

Daisy looks up at me with a horrified expression.

"I'll never do any such thing, Charles. Until you're ready to make the announcement, I'll be Daisy Price-Hawthorne."

Her gaze drops from my face back to the table. We both remain seated in silence. I try to fill it with words, but suddenly I have nothing to say—no plans for a common future, no excitement for the present.

Finally, she rises, her heels clicking in my office. The sound used to be exciting, but now it tightens a noose of pain around me with every beat. But before she can leave, I call her name, and Daisy looks over her shoulder.

"What are you planning to do now?" She's definitely no longer staying as my assistant. There's no point in even asking that.

"I don't know." Daisy shrugs. "Do you remember when you first offered me the marriage contract, you suggested I could see the world? Maybe I'll do that. I can leave Dad alone for a while, since Kai is taking such good care of him."

I've never seen anyone sadder than her while talking about world travel.

"If you need time, take it, Daisy. We don't have to decide anything right now." I don't even bother hiding the pathetic hope behind my voice, but she simply shakes her head in response.

"All I need is a divorce, Charles. And as soon as possible." She leaves my office while I'm fixed in place.

All my lifelong fears have come true.

I've never been enough to make anyone happy. Why did I think Daisy would be an exception?

thirty-four

You Handle Your Baby and I'll Handle Mine

Daisy

I slip into the back seat of the car, and the dam of tears I've been holding finally bursts free.

Every moment since I walked out of Charles' office after signing those marriage papers rushes back to me. In these months, my life changed in such a way that I'll never be the same person I was before.

"We've arrived at the hospital, Daisy." Dave's voice breaks through the speakers before he opens the door. "Is everything alright?" His movements stall as he finds me sniffling.

"Yes, everything's fine." I look at the tissues strewn around on the leather seat beside me. "I…I just got a text from Dad and got a bit emotional. He's waiting for me in the waiting room."

What have you become, Daisy?

A wife who lies and a daughter who profits off her father's illness.

"I'll walk with you to reception." Dave begins to turn away, but I grasp his wrist, halting his steps.

"Sorry, but my dad gets anxious around too many people."

Understanding flashes in Dave's eyes, mingled with concern, before he says, "Mr. Hawthorne asked me to ensure you and your dad see the doctor immediately, Daisy. He won't be pleased otherwise."

My feet falter. Did Charles call Dave before or after I asked for a divorce?

As if nature wants me to have an answer to my question, Dave's phone rings.

"It's Charles, isn't it?" I ask as he retrieves it from his pocket.

The bodyguard nods.

"May I speak with him, please?" I extend my hand, and without hesitation, Dave places the phone on my waiting palm.

"Has Daisy met with the doctor yet?" Charles' no-nonsense business tone hits me like a shock. It's been months since I heard him speak this way. How much has changed between us?

"Charles, it's me," I respond slowly.

"Daisy?" There's the sound of something crashing in the background before he curses softly. "Fuck. Sorry, I just knocked over a paperweight onto my coffee mug. Is everything okay?"

"I don't want Dave to accompany me to the hospital."

There's a tense silence for a few heartbeats before Charles clears his throat. "I didn't mean to intrude—"

"No! That's not what I meant." My throat clogs with emotion. How did we become almost strangers in such a short time? "Dad gets anxious in hospitals, especially when there are a lot of people." My tongue feels like lead as I recite the lie.

"Dammit." I can imagine Charles tugging on his hair. "Sorry, Daisy. I didn't consider that." His voice tightens the knot of guilt around my throat some more, making it hard to swallow. "Of course. You go ahead. Dave will wait for you in the parking lot."

"Thank you."

I hand the phone back to Dave before striding away, dragging along my aching heart.

As planned, Willow is already waiting for me in the hospital lobby, which is thankfully empty.

"Thank God you're finally here! I thought you got last-minute cold feet." My best friend's fingers, tapping away on her phone, pause as she looks up at me. She places a baseball cap on my head and pink sunglasses, which threaten to engulf my entire face, over my nose.

"Can you recognize me?"

"I'd recognize you in a room full of masquerade masks, Daze." She gives me a *duh* look, but before my master plan completely loses its spirit, she hands me a bag. "But that's because we're besties. Change into these, and no one will know it's you."

We slip into the ladies' bathroom, and I promptly duck into a stall to shed my lavender skirt and white silk blouse.

"How do I look?" I walk to her in baggy jeans so ripped

up, they look more shredded than stylish. Her red crop top shows my midriff in a tasteful and not indecent way. I feel like an adult trying to pass as a high schooler.

"You look smoking hot!"

"The point is to make me invisible and not stand out."

"Trust me, everyone will be too busy admiring your curves to notice your face. Now, let's go, I've already booked the appointment for you."

"Under your name?"

"Yep. We'll tell the receptionist I'm the patient, and then hopefully the doctor will understand why you want to keep it a secret, with you being Mrs. Daisy Price-Hawthorne and all."

Not for much longer.

We settle in at the OB-GYN and pediatric unit waiting room. The metal legs of the chair groan under my nervous fidgeting legs, but they still as Willow's phone goes off. Her annoyed expression could carve ice as she lets it go to voicemail.

The incessant ringing persists, and her expression turns murderous. "Stop calling me, Gus. I'm not having this conversation on the phone."

The other voice is muffled by her sharp inhale.

"Did you hear a word I said this morning? I'm not signing anything. And if it comes to it, I'll drag you and your greedy billionaire friend through court. You're a fraud, and I won't let you touch my grandfather's land—"

Mid-sentence, she springs up from her seat, eliciting a squeal out of me.

"That's private property, you jerk! If you don't leave now, I'll sue you for trespassing."

She ends the call but doesn't return to her seat. She's like a human pressure cooker right now, and I can practically hear the lid rattling as she paces the floor. We've been friends since kindergarten, and I know her every move. She needs to be somewhere else right now.

"Go." I stand before her, bringing her marching to a stop.

"What? No. I'm not going anywhere."

"We've already done the hard part together." I jerk my head toward my clothes. "I'll be okay from here."

"Stop it, Daisy. I'm not leaving you alone. Your husband should be here with you, dammit. But if that stupid guy is too busy or too scared to be a father, you don't need him anyway. But I'm not going anywhere."

Oh, Wills.

Who would know the importance of a dad more than her?

A tingling sensation runs down my spine, like a gentle electric current swirling with gratitude.

"Do you know how lucky I feel to have you in my life? You're the best friend a girl could ask for." I feel the anxiety rolling out of her as I hug her tight. "If I'm thinking of doing this alone, it's only because of my friends. I know I can count on you all."

"We're here every step of the way. You—" Her words are once again cut short by her ringing phone. The soft lyrics about a first love don't sound so peaceful right now.

"Go, Willow. Please." I don't know what exactly is happening in her life, but soon I'll get to the bottom of it.

Indecision flickers in her eyes as I gently nudge her toward the door.

"I'll be fine, I promise."

"You call me the moment you're done or if you need anything, Daze."

When Willow's phone rings for the millionth time, she finally leaves.

In the eerie silence of the waiting room, a tightness grows in my chest. To calm myself, I get up from the chair and pass by the numerous posters on the wall.

Can I do this alone? Not just today's appointment but this journey—

My anxiety doesn't even get to see the full light, because it's soon replaced by *pure fear*.

A familiar voice, loud and clear, booms from the hospital lobby. Mayor Gretel Coggeshall.

What the hell is *she* doing here?

It hasn't been long since I gave my uncensored drunk performance to prove I'm not pregnant, yet here I am.

Crap! That woman has X-ray eyes. If she could correctly judge I was pregnant even before I knew, how could she not recognize me?

I skip out of the waiting area, aiming for the ladies' room where I changed, but that's not going to happen. She's already headed my way.

I look around and spot a door. The shining metal doorknob to my right calls my name, and without a second thought, I turn it open.

The moment I step inside, my whole world tips at the sight before me.

Ray sits across from a female doctor, cradling in his arms the most adorable little girl, about five or six years old. She hides her face in his chest and wraps her tiny arms around his neck at my unexpected appearance.

Is this some sort of portal to a parallel universe?

Because the corporate shark Raymond Teager, who's equally revered and feared among his competitors, doesn't do cute. And for the love of God, I can't imagine anyone using him as a protective shield. But right now, he's the picture of cuddliness, except for the murderous expression on his face that shifts to confusion as he looks at me from head to toe.

"Daisy?"

So much for the disguise.

"Sorry. I got lost."

The doctor rises from her chair. "You're in the OB-GYN and pediatric wing right now, Mrs. Hawthorne. Where exactly were you trying to go? Perhaps I can assist you."

My palms turn clammy under her well-intentioned probing. Nervous, my gaze jumps to Ray, who continues to regard me with the same trust level a grizzly bear has for strangers approaching her cubs.

But his hands…

I can't pull my gaze away from them. His large palms, which are strong enough to throttle anyone and do serious harm, are stroking the little girl's back with featherlight touches.

The doctor clears her throat, making me jump.

"I…I was here to talk to my dad's doctor." The lie slips out of my mouth again.

"It'll be the news of the year if the media spots you in this swing. You know that, right?" Ray smirks as if he's the one who'll be benefiting the most out of that horrible situation.

The little girl releases her arms from around his neck. Pushing her bangs out of her eyes, she looks at me. Her untidy ponytail shifts in the air as she moves her head like a puppy, while Ray's hold around her stays firm.

"You have a daughter?" I ask. After watching them for a few moments, I have zero doubts about their relationship.

Nobody replies until the girl nods excitedly.

She doesn't say a word and just grins at him, and my heart melts.

"Yes," Ray replies with his lips curling.

Holy crap! In all the years I've known Ray, I've never seen him smile so wide, and ladies and gentlemen, that man has a seriously beautiful smile.

While I stand there stunned, Ray does the honors of introductions. "Daisy, meet my daughter, Quill." He then looks down. "She's Uncle Charlie's wife, your aunt Daisy."

Quill's forehead puckers as if solving some serious algebra equation, until she leaps out of her father's lap and dashes to stop right before me. Before I can make sense of her overenthusiasm, she hugs my legs, squishing me in the cutest and softest shackles ever.

My pregnancy hormones start to kick in when this sweet bundle presses her face to my thighs and I hear destiny whispering, *"Get ready for a whole new kind of love, Daze."*

"I'm so happy to meet you, Quill." I crouch down, getting at her eye level.

But she doesn't say anything, instead showing me her toothy grin once again.

"Okay, Quills. Back to Dad." Ray's voice is soft, but there's an unmissable underlying tension.

Quill immediately returns, situating herself right back on her dad's lap.

Before I can turn around and give these three their privacy, which I ruined by my sudden arrival, Ray tips his head to the side.

"That disguise is absolute shit, Daisy. I'm sorry to say, but the person who loaned you the clothes either has bad eyesight or doesn't care about you enough."

I'm about to remind him that I never asked for his advice, but Ray shakes his head.

"If even one picture of you in this wing goes public, it'll create a massive PR headache for Charles, you, and Jimmy. Unless that's the intention? To attract media attention?"

"What? Crap!" *Does that mean I'll have to camp out here for eternity?*

"No, Mrs. Hawthorne. That'd just be too cruel of us." The doctor smiles, making me realize I've once again spoken the words out loud.

"We will see you next week, Doc." Ray gets up from his seat, and my heart squeezes when he waits for Quill to grab his index finger in her tiny hand, and only then does he turn to me. "You'll leave with us."

The hell I will!

I immediately step away from the door, but so does Ray.

Instead of walking to the door behind me, he saunters in the other direction toward a PRIVATE sign on the wooden-paneled wall. My curious gaze follows as he flips the light switch and the door opens to an elevator car.

"What in God's name is that?"

"This is a secret elevator that will lead you to a private

parking lot, Mrs. Hawthorne. It's built for cases exactly like these, to ensure privacy for some of our well-known patients."

I'm still reeling at the sight of such James Bond technology in our sweet small town, where all the innocent grandmas think they know everything about everyone.

"I hope you and Mr. Hawthorne will be using this elevator together soon." The doctor winks as I follow Ray and Quill inside.

"I've already texted Dave that I'll be giving you a ride home."

My gaze continues to move between Ray and Quill, who's sleeping peacefully on her father's chest, her breaths soft and even.

"How come no one knows about her?"

"Who says no one does? All the relevant people do." His omnipresent cocky smirk is right there on his face. But when I don't look away, Ray makes himself busy brushing invisible lint from his pants—the only sign of unease.

"Then let me ask again. Why are you keeping her hidden from irrelevant people like me? And where's her mother?" I whisper, careful not to disturb Quill.

But Ray is done playing nice.

"Why don't you worry about your own secrets, sis? Because if my sources are correct, your dad didn't have an appointment at the hospital today."

I gasp. "Are you spying on my dad?"

"Don't be dramatic. Jason texted me about going on a hike with Kai and invited me along." Ray pushes his phone toward me, revealing a picture my father sent just an hour ago of him and Kai having a picnic in the forest.

Ray had replied with a thumbs-up emoji. I'm about to scroll up, but before I can read anything further, he snatches his phone back.

"You talk to my dad? How did he even get your number?"

"He asked at the last Christmas party." Ray shrugs as if it's no big deal.

But don't I know how seriously these men take their privacy? Charles' private number is shared with fewer than ten people, and I'm sure the same is true for Ray.

"Why would you do that?"

"He's a good, genuine person, unlike most people these days." He raises an eyebrow. "So, are you going to tell me why you're hanging around the OB-GYN department dressed like a teenager?"

Within the next second, my brain has crafted lies ranging from meeting a friend who just had a baby to picking up some stuff from a neighbor, who's a doctor in that wing. But for some reason, the words remain trapped in my throat.

Looks like I've finally consumed my daily quota of lying.

"I had my first appointment…at the OB-GYN."

"Does Charlie know?" Unlike my pounding heart, Ray's voice is calmer than an instructor on a meditation app.

"He doesn't need to." I shake my head. Do I care about him telling Charles? Maybe a little, but it will come out eventually. It's not like I can hide this from Charles forever.

"May I ask how you reached that conclusion?"

"Can you stop doing that? Speaking in that ice-cold

voice," I blurt, running my hands over my arms involuntarily. "It's giving me chills over here."

Ray finally loses his stoic expression and runs a hand over his face.

"What's going on, Daisy? Why isn't Charlie with you?"

"He doesn't know," I whisper. "He doesn't want kids."

"Isn't it a bit late for that?"

"It was a mistake," I whisper slowly.

If I thought I knew how Raymond Teager looks when he's angry, I was horribly mistaken.

If looks could kill, I'd be burning in flames right now.

"I expected a better answer from you, Daisy, at least on this matter. Coming from someone who was taken in by strangers, the word *mistake* sounds a bit harsh, wouldn't you agree?"

I stiffen at his venomous tone.

"Charles told you about my childhood?" My words are low, embarrassed and annoyed, but he shakes his head.

"You really think we wouldn't do a background check on the girl our cousin marries?"

"If you know everything, then don't you know how Charles feels about babies?"

So many emotions fly across Ray's face, yet he remembers to cover Quill's visible ear with his hand.

"How does that fucking matter now? You're pregnant. He's going to be a father. With all due respect, his feelings can go fuck themselves."

Watching Ray fight for his cousin's unborn child tightens my throat.

"Charles never hid his feelings about being a dad, and I respect that. And who am I to judge someone's fears?"

"You're his wife, aren't you?" Ray nods toward my wedding ring.

"Since you know so much, I'm sure the reality of our marriage isn't a secret to you and your brothers."

He's about to say something when I bring my hand forward. "Please. I can't talk about this anymore. I'm grateful for your help at the hospital, but this"—I motion toward my belly—"doesn't concern you."

Isn't he the one who doesn't even consider me relevant enough to know about his daughter?

thirty-five

What About Pets and Plants?

Charles

My hurried steps grind to a halt as I spot Ray on his living room carpet with his sleeves rolled up and a scrunchie dangling from his teeth. Quill is nestled between his outstretched legs and the father-daughter duo is engrossed in a braiding tutorial on Ray's laptop.

They don't even look up at my arrival until I call Quill.

Ray's hands still as he's grabbing Quill's wild golden locks, and for a second, I forget my worries and snap a picture of the scene.

"Very mature." Ray lets the baby-blue scrunchie fall to the ground and then smirks. "What took you so long?"

My irritation is cut short when his daughter crawls from her father's lap onto mine.

"Hello, Uncle Charlie. I met your wife today. She's so pretty, like a princess." She signs with her small fingers, making only a few mistakes. She's still learning sign language, and I know Rowan will make sure she's well versed in no time.

I can't believe the coincidence.

Selective mutism is such a rare condition, and yet we have two people in the family struggling with it.

"I think so too, Quillbug."

Quill falls into laughter when I tickle her belly.

"Time for a bedtime story, Miss Quill." William, who prefers to still be called a butler at an age approaching ninety, appears from inside the house.

"Grandpa Will. How are you doing?" I rise up to give the old man a hug.

"I'm doing very well, Master Charles. How are you and your lovely wife?"

"Oh, let me first check with Ray, since he kidnapped her." I throw my brother an irritated look, which only makes his grin wider.

"You boys will never change. Come on, Miss Quill, let's see if the princess in your book is still asleep."

Once it's just us in the room, I turn to my cousin, who's now by the bar.

"Where the fuck is Daisy, Ray?"

I felt her absence in my house the moment I stepped inside this evening. A minute later, my heart catapulted out of my body when Mrs. Kowalski confirmed that Daisy came in with Ray, packed a bag, and left.

"She asked me to drop her at her friend's place."

I never imagined this sight—Ray pouring Diet Coke over ice in two glasses and then pushing one toward me.

I throw it back as if it's a whiskey neat and miss the sting. "And you didn't bother asking me?"

"She's your wife, not your property. If you think otherwise, feel free to take your male chauvinistic ass out of my house and return when you're back to your senses."

If there's one thing that calls out the deep-buried, forgotten humanitarian in Raymond Teager, it's even the slightest implication of a woman being undervalued.

"Don't you fucking know me? You think I treat her like my property?"

We stare at each other for a while like two dogs forced to fight, until he shakes his head.

"She looked upset and I realized things might not be going as smoothly as stated in the contract. Or am I mistaken?"

I can't believe this asshole, who knows I hate that word *contract* and yet continues to use it, is the same man who moments ago was learning how to braid his daughter's hair.

"She wants a divorce."

I'd have appreciated if there was a glint of surprise on his face, but he's definitely not here to please me tonight.

"And you don't?" he finally asks, after taking a satisfying sip of his Diet Coke. "You got what you wanted, and I'm guessing you've ensured her father's care is covered even after you split. Isn't this a win-win since you never wanted to get married in the first place?"

My grip tightens around the glass. "I like having her around." The confession slips out of my mouth, and I hate it. Not the admission, but the fact that I'm still lying.

Like.

Such a weak word for what I feel for Daisy.

"Are you telling me you've fallen for your fake wife, Charlie?" Ray chuckles, but when I don't join him in his stupid laugh or flick his head like I want to, he sobers fast.

"Holy shit! I had too much faith in you, brother. Do you know you just cost me a Ferrari?"

"What the fuck does that mean?"

"It means I owe Rowan a Ferrari. On your wedding day, I said this sacred union wouldn't last for more than six months, but he was convinced you would fall in love with your bride and end up in a Disney happily ever after. I'm so disappointed, Charles! I thought I knew you the best among us all."

"That's such an asshole thing to do! Do you think I feel better hearing about it?"

"And you think I care how you feel? I just lost a quarter of a million dollars. Anyway, you're wasting your time here, especially now that I know how you feel about her."

Ray takes my empty glass from my hand and gets up, silently asking me to do the same.

"Daisy is at her friend's place. The obnoxious one with red hair. Willow—that's her name, right? I think you better go run and talk to your wife, especially if you plan to woo her back into your life." That bastard grins before grabbing a rose stem from the vase on the bar and securing it in my suit pocket, even tapping on it.

I wish with every fiber of my being that someday soon he's in a similar situation and I'm the one telling him to go run and woo a girl.

I'll see your smile that day, Ray.

As Steve drives me from Ray's to Willow's place, I let my mind run wild.

She left.

She fucking left.

Why am I surprised?

She told me this morning she wanted a divorce as early as possible.

What I hadn't realized was that it would be so cathartic. As the car takes me closer to her, the burning ache starts to slowly morph into resolution.

When have you ever given up so easily, Charles?

All your life you've been trained to turn things around in your favor.

I can't give up until she's back where she belongs.

In my home. In my heart.

"Charles." Willow opens the door.

There's no surprise on her face, as if she was expecting me all along. Instead of inviting me in, she grabs her coat from the coat hanger and steps out, forcing me to retreat.

"Daisy will be right back. You can take a seat on the couch." She motions her head to the side but doesn't make a move to let me pass.

I'm about to walk around her and finally cross the wooden door that's keeping me away from my wife, when Willow grabs my arm.

"Don't break my friend's heart, Charles. You might be the

prince of Cherrywood, but she's a very important person in my life. I'll come after you with everything I've got."

I raise an eyebrow, looking between her and where she's holding me. I've ruined people for much less. And if our interests weren't so aligned in this moment, I might have shown her what it means to threaten Charles Hawthorne.

"Believe me, that's not why I'm here." I pluck her fingers off my suit one at a time and step around her, walking inside.

My gaze scans the empty room, landing on Daisy's still-unpacked duffel bag in the corner.

Good. We can leave as soon as I share what I need to say.

I hear the water running in the bathroom, and a second later, she stands at the doorway.

"Charles! What—what are you doing here?" Daisy's shock is apparent in those wide eyes.

You can fucking do this, Hawthorne.

"There's something I have to say." The air suddenly thins, making it harder to breathe, as if a weight is pressed against my chest. "Hear me out before you make a decision, Daisy."

"Charles, don't do this. Please." Her eyes fall shut as her fingers tightly clutch the sides of her skirt.

How can she look so haggard within just a few hours?

Ignoring her plea, I approach.

"My room, my home—it doesn't feel the same without you, my dear wife. Come home. I want you there."

A gasp escapes her lips as my fingers trace a gentle path from her forehead down to her cheeks.

"But you and I—"

I place a finger over her lips, halting her words.

"How about we compromise? Work with me, Daisy.

Please." I lean in, pressing my forehead against hers. I feel her shaky breath on my skin, tickling my five o'clock shadow. "Help me find a middle ground."

She removes my finger from her mouth and takes a step back. I immediately miss the contact.

"How can we compromise on something like this, Charles? This isn't a business deal you can negotiate."

"I know that." I run a hand over my hair. "I wouldn't be feeling so scared if it were a business deal. I know how to handle those. But this"—I wave my hand at the space between us—"this is so new and damn difficult. Despite that, I know I don't want to live without you." My voice softens. "I want us to be together, Daisy. I'm happiest with you. And looking at you right now, I think you're happiest with me too." My fists clench tight. "Correct me if I'm just being delusional and selfish. Am I not enough?"

Her jaw drops at my outburst.

You've never sounded more pathetic in your life, Hawthorne.

But then she takes a step forward. Hope surges like a helium balloon in my chest when Daisy places her hand over my cheek.

"The time I've spent with you in your home has been the best part of my life. I know I'll never experience such happiness again."

"Daisy—"

This time, she puts a hand over my mouth.

"You are enough. You're so damn more than enough, Charles. You are a dream husband, exactly like a prince. But unfortunately, I'm not a Cinderella. I'm a normal girl who wants a simple life."

"Then come back home with me. We'll make our own simple life with everything you want."

"Not everything," she whispers, deflating my excitement.

"Everything except that. I promise you won't regret this, Daisy. You'll miss nothing in life. I'll make sure of it. We can have a pet." My mind runs wild with the possibilities, all with the single aim of getting her home. I've been trained to think on my toes, and even though I denied it before, this feels like the biggest deal of my life. "A dog, maybe two. Even a few cats, and some cool plants."

Yes, pets and plants, I can tolerate.

I wait for her to join my excitement and say yes to all that, but instead it's like she's waiting for me to join her on the other side, the non-excitement zone.

Everything with this girl has been a challenge. Why did I think today would be different?

"I love you, dammit."

Instead of being shell-shocked or surprised, she once again closes her eyes. She didn't avoid looking at me this much even on the days I was my grumpiest self at the office.

"You heard me say I love you? I don't expect you to say it back, but some acknowledgment would be good, Daisy." My words are flat, devoid of the nervousness that's building up every second inside me.

Tears spill from her eyes, cracking a piece of my heart in their wake.

Fuck it.

"Say yes, Daisy, and we'll figure out the rest." I grab her shoulders and pull her closer, trying to knock some sense into her. The life I'm showing her isn't bad; some might even say it's fabulous. But she's too blinded by some childhood fantasy of having her own family.

Blood relations mean shit. Doesn't she know that?

"I can't." Her lip wobbles.

"Why the fuck not?"

"Because I'm pregnant!"

It takes a second for me to register the meaning behind her words.

P-pregnant…

She's…pregnant!

My hands drop from her shoulders, and my thoughts spiral into a chaotic whirlwind. I take a shaky step back.

Daisy's lips move, but I fail to register the meaning, even if I hear them alright.

"I—I'm sorry. I just found out, but you don't have to worry about it. I'm going to leave Cherrywood. I know how you feel about this."

Her arms wrap around her stomach protectively, tightening the grip of the invisible cold hand around my chest.

"I hope there are no hard feelings, Charles. I'm already looking for jobs outside the state. If you prefer, the baby won't even have your name. You don't have to be involved in anything."

She continues to say many things, but I can't make any fucking sense of them.

She's pregnant with my kid. There's a tiny heartbeat inside her right now that is a part of me, and in nine months, it will turn into a person.

My child.

My hands tremble at my sides as I turn around and leave.

Dave drives the car through the gates of Hawthorne mansion. I've spent the majority of my childhood in this place. A vast compound, huge gardens that the whole town can't stop raving about, the koi pond, evergreen water lilies that sleep in winter.

Everything is familiar and should give me peace. Yet every time I'm here, anxiety creeps into my chest, reminding me of my pathetic childhood self, the one who was so fucking needy. I cringe at the memory of that boy who craved the attention and affection of his mother.

When I step out of the car, there are two night guards stationed at the main entrance. Responding to their greeting with a nod, I walk inside.

"Mr. Hawthorne, everyone just retired to bed. Shall I wake up—"

I interrupt the housekeeper with a shake of my head. "No. I'll just be in my room for a second and be gone in the next. Please don't worry. You can go back to sleep."

Even though she nods and steps back, I know she'll be waiting in the kitchen until I'm gone, in case I do need something. That's the night service protocol at the Hawthorne mansion. We're not called "Cherrywood royalty" without reason.

My feet shake like a toddler who just learned to walk as I step inside my childhood room. Everything is exactly as it was when I left for college.

On one wall are pictures of Chloe and me over the

years, starting from the day she was born, the happiest day of my life, until she and I packed my stuff the night before my departure.

They also include the major milestones of our lives.

Her first step. Her first birthday. Her first day of school as she held my hand.

The smile that tugs on my lips while remembering my sister slips the moment my gaze falls on the closet.

I dig out the metal box with a tiny golden lock buried in the back. I told my family it was a time capsule and nobody touched it. My hands shake as I take out the tiny key from my wallet.

Don't do it, Charles!

A part of my brain screams at me to leave the room and finally burn this box. I don't know why I even have it in the first place. Unlike Chloe's pictures, this isn't something I want to revisit.

At what point in my childhood did I become so damn sadistic?

This is nothing but self-torture.

But there's a second voice I've spent the majority of my life ignoring, and today it has finally found a microphone.

I stored this box and its contents for a day like today.

There's a reason I don't want to have a family, and that reason is in this box.

But Daisy *is* pregnant.

I don't allow any other sentiment to replace the fear that's harboring in my chest right now and flip the latch open.

Colorful envelopes are carefully stacked one over the other.

imperfect match

Some plain, some with hand-drawn flowers, and some with stickers of whatever was my favorite that month.

I tried everything in hopes that someday one of them wouldn't be returned unopened.

That never happened.

I pick up the first letter from the heap and my hands shake as I tear the corner of the envelope, which was sealed when I was only five and hasn't been opened since. The address was written by my nanny at that time. I had asked the middle-aged woman to pinky swear she wouldn't tell my dad that I was writing letters to my mother.

But I don't believe now that she would have kept that promise. I'm sure my dad knew exactly how I was spending every moment when he wasn't around. He sacrificed his own happiness to give me the best life, despite the fact that the woman who gave birth to me dumped me on his doorstep without a second glance.

I open the pages and look at my block handwriting. The letters are all twisted, and I've butchered several of them. My Ds look more like Os, and my Ts like Js.

Dear Mom,

I miss you.

Will you come to see me on the 12th of May? My school is celebrating Mother's Day. Usually it's Grandma Irene or Aunt Clem or Aunt Florence who come. But I'd really love if you are there someday.

Your loving son,
Charlie.

The next one must have been written when I was eight, because I was into superheroes at that time. I put colorful stickers of men in tight suits all over the margin of the paper.

Dear Mom,

I miss you.

Today is my birthday. I'm sure you remember. If you are not too busy, can you come to see me?

Aunt Clem is throwing a big party.

Dad asked me what I wanted, and I told him I wanted a mom.

Will you please come home, Mom? You can also send me your picture until then. I want to show it to my friends. I'm sure you are very very pretty.

Waiting to meet you someday.

Your loving son,
Charlie.

It's not just the words, but also the memories of those moments when I wrote them. There's evidence of my tears on these pages, along with my anger when I pressed the pencil too hard as I begged my mother to come home and love me.

And as much as I hate that I'm her offspring, how can I be trusted to provide affection to a little one when my blood is the same as the woman who has given the words "absent parent" a new meaning?

So what are you going to do now?

There's already a kid in line, and I can't send it back.

My pulse pounds as I imagine a kid with my blond hair and blue eyes writing such letters.

No. Fucking no.

I'll do what I do the best. I'll provide for Daisy and our kid, everything they need. She won't have to work a second and all her time, all her attention will be for our kid. She can attend all the soccer matches, school plays and picnics. They both will want for nothing.

I'll make sure this child has the affection of a mother throughout his childhood unlike me.

Determination fills my lungs, and I dial my lawyer.

"Charles." Troy's voice is raspy from sleep. "Everything alright?"

"I want you to do something for me."

"Right now?"

"Yes, this is urgent."

"Okay. Give me a sec," he whispers before I hear the rustling of sheets and then his heavy footsteps. "Okay, I'm in my office now. Tell me what you need."

"I want you to make a deed. Effective immediately, Daisy will have one hundred percent ownership of my current and future wealth."

"Wh-what? Did you have too much to drink tonight?"

"I'm fully conscious. Do what you are asked," I snap back, which is met by a pause, and then I hear a loud sigh from Troy's side.

"You're not making sense, Charles. As your lawyer, it's my duty to tell you that this is insane. When you got married, you were adamant about not having a prenup. What is this now? Some sort of anti-prenup. Are you and Daisy getting a divorce?"

"I don't pay you to ask questions. I pay you to do what I tell you to do. Have the papers ready by the morning. I'm sending you an address via text. Make sure they go out by first post."

"I hope you know what you're doing, Charles."

I can't even be upset with the man. He's just looking out for me.

"Just do what I ask, Troy."

I end the call and close the metal box, but the ghost of horrid memories is already out. Instead of shoving it back into the closet, I grab my coat from the bed and leave the room, holding the self-fulfilling prophecy as to why I'm not suited to be anyone's parent.

thirty-six

For All the Daddies

Daisy

I open my eyes to find Willow sitting cross-legged on the other side of the bed. Her red hair is tied up with a pen hanging from the loose messy bun, while her fingers tap rhythmically on the laptop before her.

"Is there any coffee left or did you drink it all?" I jerk my head toward the empty coffee pot on the nightstand.

"Don't worry, there's plenty. Plus, shouldn't you be the last person to care about coffee right now?" Her furrowed brows slowly settle down.

"I care about you." I loop my arm around hers. "So, tell me whose murder my bestie is planning this morning."

"I'm not there yet. But if things don't go the way I'd like, killing is definitely not off the table." The serious, murderous look on her face has me laughing.

"I was joking, Wills!"

"I'm not." She then abandons her laptop and fully turns toward me. "So? Anything?" She tilts her head in the direction of my tummy.

I'm not sure who out of the two of us is more eager for my morning sickness to kick in.

"Nothing." I shake my head, a tad disappointed.

"Really? I thought pregnancy was supposed to be more dramatic." And then she leans forward, eye level at my tummy. "You listen to me, champ. Your stuck-up dad, whose idea of a laugh is tilting his mouth to one side, has already ruined fifty percent of your chances of being a cool kid. But this aunt wants all the tantrums, so don't be too shy in there."

"You make that request when you're having one of your own." I laugh, pushing her away.

"That day is never coming. Don't you know me at all?"

"How are we friends again?" A laugh slips past my lips at the sight of her serious face. "Me, a girl who couldn't wait to have her own family, and you, who hates kids."

"I don't hate kids. I just don't plan to have my own."

"Uh-huh. We'll see someday."

Willow grins. "That's what I'm saying. We won't be seeing anything, any day."

The doorbell chimes, and we both turn our heads toward the wall clock in sync.

"These two. Total clockwork these days." Willow springs out of bed, pirouetting out of the room with a mischievous grin.

My gaze slants to the wall calendar, and the smile drops.

A week has passed since I sort of moved in with Willow because I had nowhere else to go. When I married Charles, I had to give up the lease on my old apartment. Keeping it would have meant leaving bait for the media and reporters who are always after Charles. And now, moving in with Dad was out of the question, since that would mean too much risk and explanation, especially when I have to keep my move under wraps.

It's also been a week's time to the day I broke the news of my pregnancy to Charles.

Also the day he walked out after saying *I love you*.

That date would be bold and highlighted in the brightest color if I wrote a daily journal.

Yet nothing has changed.

The divorce papers I requested are still MIA.

I remain employed at Hawthorne Holdings, even though I haven't set foot inside the building for seven days and am completely oblivious to any potential corporate fires.

In the grand scheme, we're living like strangers, and officially, we're still bound together.

"Daisy! You coming?" Violet's loud holler jerks me out of my mental freight train.

When I reach the living room, there's a colorful and healthy spread of breakfast on the table like every other day this week. My friends have taken the notion of "they're with me in this" to a whole new level. At least one of them, if not all, is constantly by my side.

We haven't had this much girl time since our school days.

I plop down on the couch, and a familiar face stares back at me from Willow's laptop screen.

"Why are you checking out Raymond Teager's professional profile?"

Willow's lips press together and eyes squint, but she doesn't say anything.

"You are giving that look, Wills." I raise an eyebrow.

"What *look*?" she deflects, avoiding eye contact.

"The one that says you're mentally cursing the guy without a filter," Violet chimes in from her spot on the floor.

"Exactly that one!" I exclaim.

"Oh, hello, Mr. Teager. You look pretty hot in this picture." Violet shifts the laptop for a better view, waggling her brows.

The Teagers and Elixir Inc. are as well-known in Cherrywood as the Hawthornes.

"Really? I thought he looked more like Satan or one of his demons." Willow snags a piece of cheese from the platter Elodie is still arranging.

"And all the cute videos of puppies and kittens were unavailable this morning, so you were entertaining yourself with demonic men?" Elodie doesn't break a smile, and I purse my lips to hold back my own.

Willow responds with a deep exhale, puffing out a heavy breath.

"Are you sure you're not developing some secret crush on Daisy's brother-in-law? No one would blame you if you are. Raymond is the hottest of them all." Violet folds her arms over the edge of the table before resting her face on top.

Not from where I'm sitting. There's never been anyone more handsome than Charles for me.

"Vi, give your gossipy journalist brain a break! Since you all seem to be so wrong, let me tell you. I'm searching for his weakness, okay?"

"What did that handsome man do to you?" Violet pushes a grape into her mouth.

"That Lucifer hiding behind an *apparently* pretty face is the man backing my cousin Gus to take away my grandfather's land from me."

"What?" Three gasps blend into one another.

"Why didn't you tell me sooner? I…I could have helped you." I turn to face Willow properly now.

"All's under control, girls. I'm already talking to a lawyer. I'm not going to let those assholes steal what's mine."

There's an absolute determination in Willow's face, and as much as I admire her self-confidence, I'm worried about her. Ray is notorious in the industry. If he's locked his eyes on any real estate property, there's a minus one percent chance that it doesn't get acquired by Elixir Estates.

I lay my hand on her arm. "I can still try something, Wills."

"No! Not at all." There's a horrified look on her face at my suggestion. "You and Charles have more important things to discuss *when* you're both ready to talk."

My heart sinks a little, because that day is slowly getting farther and farther away.

"I wasn't talking about Charles. I can try talking to Ray and explain what this land means to you."

I've witnessed Ray's softer side with his daughter. Perhaps I can appeal to that humane part of his personality.

"Absolutely not! Can you believe what that jerk asked me in the first meeting? He wanted to know if I'd be calling Charles, in tears, begging him to talk to his cousin."

"He actually said that?" I wince as Willow nods.

"That man is a pompous ass."

"I bet he's also got a nice ass, especially when it's not hidden behind those tight pants." Violet raises an eyebrow.

"I've seen much better-looking men."

None of us are convinced, but we all nod, watching the deadly expression on our friend's face.

"Can we discuss something else? The thought of Ray Teager's bare ass is enough to make me want to throw up."

"How's the prep for tonight shaping up, Daisy? Need any help?" Elodie asks, as if the topic has been on the tip of her tongue all along.

"Nope. Aunt Mel, Kai, and Dad won't let me near the preparations. It's like it's my birthday, not Dad's." I smile, appreciating this day with Dad, where, despite his memory lapses, he still remembers enough to celebrate.

Who knows if I'll be here next year.

"Did you try to keep it a surprise from Jason?" Violet interrupts my thoughts before they can completely get swamped by worries of the future, and I shake my head.

"No. I want Dad to enjoy every moment of today, including the preparations."

"And what about *him*? Is…he coming?"

It doesn't take a genius to know who Willow is asking about.

"I don't know." I shrug. "But Dad personally called everyone last month."

"I have a feeling Charles will be there." Elodie settles next to me on the couch, carrying two cups of her Yogi tea and handing one to me.

Someday soon, I'll have to break the truth to her. This tea might just do the opposite of its intended effect. Instead of calming my absent morning sickness, it might just provoke it.

"Charles is the kind of guy who always does the right thing," Elodie continues.

"Always?" Violet raises an eyebrow toward my flat stomach. "Since when does leaving your pregnant wife become the right thing?"

"Vi!" I exclaim. "Can you be a little less dramatic? I asked Charles for a divorce, not the other way around." I ignore the gnawing voice in my head, reminding me yet again that he never stopped me. "And I'm not some helpless woman."

"Since Willow and Vi have already picked their 'man I plan to hate the most today,' can I ask something else?" Elodie takes a sip of her tea and asks in an even tone, "Your dad doesn't know about you two not living together, but what about his family?" Her gaze points at my finger, where my wedding band and engagement ring are still sitting snugly.

The right thing would be to take them off, at least when I'm in the house, away from the public eye.

My mind reminds me of that at least once a day, but I've yet to heed. Parting with these rings would mean snapping off the last thread binding me to Charles.

"I don't think they know either. I received a text from Chloe last night. She was at Charles' place, and he told her I was staying with Willow because she's going through some crisis." I pause and turn to Wills. "Is it possible that he was talking about this?" I jerk my head toward Ray's photo on her laptop.

"How would I know?" Annoyance paints her face. "But would you be surprised if his asshole cousin told your husband himself?"

"Are you okay with this? Pretending in front of your dad," Elodie cuts through Willow's irritation.

"I have to be because I'm not telling Dad, especially not today." I close my eyes, imagining the moment my dad learns the truth. *Oh, Daddy.* "He loves Charles too much." My heart pounds in a painful rhythm, and by the look of concern on my friends' faces, they're not missing anything. "I also fear that he'll forget, and then I'll have to tell him again every day. Or worse, he forgets that this has to be kept under wraps and tells someone."

"Talk about a crisis." Willow groans. "Charles Hawthorne should sort out his crisis first and then poke his nose into others' business."

It's six in the evening and Dad's living room buzzes with relatives, ex-colleagues, and friends from the neighborhood who have been witnesses to every twist and turn of our lives.

Kai manages the drink table, tactfully limiting the champagne intake of our geriatric guests and discreetly checking on their current medications before handing anyone anything.

"Wow! This turned out so much bigger than what I expected!" Aunt Mel fans her face with both hands.

"You've outdone yourself tonight. Dad is so lucky to have a sister like you."

Her smile grows as my arms encircle her.

"I don't know what I'd do without you, especially with Dad's condition." My throat tightens.

"Hey, Doodles." She rubs my back with her usual motherly touch before stepping back. "Jason and you are my family. You never have to thank me for anything. Plus, your husband's family just added more spark and zing to our evening. Did you see the cake Charles' great-grandmother brought?"

Her eyes shine as her head slants toward the side table, where there's a huge birthday cake with Dad's name on top that Chloe and GG personally delivered. Right now, they're both with Dad, and Chloe is busy taking pictures for their social media profiles.

I nod. "That's really sweet of them."

"It is. I'm so happy you found a loving family for yourself, kiddo. I must confess, when I first heard about you and Charles, I was skeptical. Everything was perfectly timed. He was pressured to marry, and a minute later, he conveniently announced you as his girlfriend. For a long time, I thought that man was blackmailing you."

I freeze in my spot, the ball of nerves tightening around my throat like a too-tight necklace.

"But now I see you two together, and I feel so stupid to even doubt for a sec. That man loves you like crazy." She pats my cheek affectionately, completely oblivious that I'm a second away from passing out. "Where is Charles anyway?"

I swallow hard a few times, my voice a bit shaky. "He should be here soon."

In truth, I have no clue where he is or if he's even coming.

She nods, giving me a warm smile, and then slips away to greet her friends as Violet and Elodie join us.

"Looks like we might get to see the only thing missing from this kick-ass party!" Violet grins before tipping her head toward the dark corner of the room. "Murder! Willow is one second away from ripping Raymond Teager's head off, don't you think?"

My mouth goes dry when I find Willow rising on her toes, her hands reaching for Raymond's neck. Judging by her feelings toward the man, she's definitely not trying to caress his face.

"Gosh! Are you crazy, Vi? Let's go and stop them!" I'm all ready to intervene and prevent Willow from spending a night in jail, because I doubt Raymond will look the other way and not press assault charges if even Willow's finger makes contact with him.

"You stay and see after the guests. I'll check on Willow." Elodie stops me from walking away. "And you, little quarrel connoisseur, help me, will you?"

My eyes are fixed on my friends as they pull Willow away from Ray, when a throat clears behind me.

"Hi."

My heart catapults out of my body at the familiar voice—one that used to drive me crazy for four years, but now, after not hearing it for a week, I'm not sure how I survived these past few days.

I turn around slowly, my pulse beating at the highest rhythm.

Charles stands before me, looking more handsome than ever. His hair is slicked back, and he's dressed in a sharp black suit, white shirt, a purple tie, and his signature Hawthorne crest cufflinks.

There's an unmissable tightness on his face that I haven't seen in a long time.

Since you moved in with him, you mean.

His gaze lingers on my face for a moment before dropping lower. Instinctively, my hands curl around my flat stomach.

Charles' head snaps up, his eyebrows shooting high.

"Look who showed up at last!" Chloe's playful jab draws my attention, and I find her standing between Charles and me. "Being fashionably late is practically a crime on your father-in-law's birthday, you know."

"I'll keep that in mind for next year, sis." Charles gives his sister a small smile.

Next year! Will we even be here like this next year?

"This is for Jason." He presents a silver-wrapped box to me.

"Uh-huh. In case you forgot, it's Jason's birthday, not Daisy's. If you want to gift your wife without reason, do that at your own home." Chloe grins, as she links her one arm around her brother's and the other with mine. "And FYI, the birthday boy is waiting for you, so you can eye-fuck each other later."

My dad's face lights up at the sight of Charles, and for just a second, I forget everything as my heart swells with happiness for my father.

There hasn't been a single face he failed to recognize this evening.

I'm sure he's feeling proud of himself.

"Hey, everyone, that's my son-in-law." My dad's friends make room for Charles on the couch. "You all know him as one of the best businessmen in the country, but let me share a secret about Charlie—he's the best son a man can ask for. I don't worry about my Doodles." Dad's gaze finds me, and he beckons me over. "Hey, kiddo, what are you doing over there? Come here."

He extends his hand, and in a heartbeat, I'm nestled between him and Charles.

"As I was saying, I no longer worry about my Doodles. I know this guy will take care of my daughter, her happiness, and her dreams even after I'm gone."

"Dad!" I release a heavy breath, my lungs burning and my body trembling with overwhelming emotions. I'm on the verge of crying like a child when Charles' hand gently rests against the small of my back.

When did his presence, his touch, become my anchor? The entire last week was a blur, going through the motions of life without much thought. Yet in this moment, my brain is acutely aware of everything.

His warm hand, the subtle circles he traces on my back—I missed him. I missed us.

"You're making my wife emotional, Jason. I don't like it," Charles says in a lighthearted tone, but I catch the underlying seriousness.

Laughter ripples through everyone, even Dad, who affectionately pats my cheeks. "That's why I love him so much. He'd fight for your happiness even with your own damn dad."

"Did someone call for champagne?" Like a lifesaver, Kai appears, holding a huge tray of drinks.

Thank God, my poor heart can't take any more of these emotional hits.

"A special drink for the most special man tonight." He hands Dad a martini glass with clear soda and an olive. They share a wink. Before I can appreciate Kai's presence in my parents' home once more, he hands me a champagne glass like everyone else.

So much for being a lifesaver, Kai.

So far, I've managed to avoid drinks, either by discreetly leaving them on the table or surreptitiously tossing them into various indoor potted plants. I'd planned to apologize to all the flora for their imminent hangover later.

But right now, with all these people facing me, I have no clue how to get out of this.

"Cheers!" someone says, and before I know it, there's a clinking of glasses, including mine.

"Hey, Daisy. You don't like it?" Kai raises his eyebrow as I sit with my untouched drink.

Gosh, he's watching too.

I'm about to bring it closer to my lips when Charles gets up, placing his empty glass on the table.

"Awesome, Kai. Can't wait to have another one, my man." He gives our temporary bartender a friendly pat on the back before extending his hand. "Mind if I steal Daisy for a moment?" he asks, but his tone is final. He's not expecting anyone to interrupt him.

My breath stutters at the unexpected interruption. I rise on shaky legs, my brain debating for a second whether to stay or follow him, but ignoring Charles is not something I can ever do.

Charles stops in a corner behind a heavy beam, away from prying eyes.

Without a word, he snags my glass and throws back the drink.

"Let's go." He takes my hand, leading me away.

What in God's name just happened?

I can't tear my gaze away from the back of my husband's

head as he guides me back to my dad before settling down beside me.

I don't get too much time to think, as the next round of drinks is served quickly.

Throughout the night, by one excuse or another, Charles manages to pry away the alcohol from my hand and empty it into his own mouth.

"Now that's a pretty sight." Ray snaps a picture of Charles leaning against the porch wall. One arm is thrown over my shoulders, keeping him upright.

"Go away," Charles mumbles, eliciting another laugh out of Ray.

I've never ever seen Charles drink irresponsibly. Knowing there's a slim chance of a repeat performance, Ray's enthusiasm makes complete sense.

"Did you just figure out tonight that party drinks are free and decided to make up for all the missed opportunities, brother?"

"Some dads quit drinking, and some get drunk for their babies. You should feel guilty for making fun of me, Daddy I-don't-drink-anymore," Charles slurs, head thrown back, eyes shut.

His hearing must be impaired too, because there's no way he missed my loud, untamed gasp. All I can do is gape at him, struggling to find the words to express the strange feeling in my chest.

Did he just indirectly refer to himself as a dad?

"Do we both agree your husband is more intelligent when drunk, Daze?" Ray smirks, tipping his lips to one side.

"Stop bothering my wife, and by the way, her name is Daisy. D-A-I-S-Y," Charles enunciates before growling, and his hand tightens around my shoulder as he pulls me closer. "You're not allowed to call her by any other nickname."

If I had the power to freeze one moment of my life, it would possibly be this. On my dad's special day, my husband is not just defending me but also our unborn baby.

A shiver races down my spine, and my skin prickles with a mix of heat and cold. It's as if every nerve ending is on high alert, desperate to remember this rare moment for eternity.

"If I didn't love you, Charlie, I'd have shot a video of you and shown it to everyone." Ray holds his cousin's head with both hands and places a kiss on top.

Am I freaking dreaming or did Raymond Teager, real estate shark, just kissed his cousin's forehead?

His cheeks flush as he tucks his hands back into his pockets, stealing a glance at me. "I just got carried away. Don't mention this to him or anyone. Please."

"I don't think anyone would believe me if I did. I'm having a hard time believing what just happened wasn't a dream."

He grins before motioning toward Charles. "Good. Do you need any help?"

I shake my head. "Steve and Dave will swing by Charles' place. Once he's settled in bed, they will drop me off at my friend's. If we leave separately, my dad will get suspicious."

Ray's chest heaves as he releases a weighty breath. "I hope my dumbass brother realizes fast that he's losing the most amazing time of his life." He turns to leave, pausing on the first porch step. "You take care, Daisy. I look forward to meeting my nephew or niece in a few months, and I can't wait to see my Quillbug play with a little brother or sister."

"You and me both, Ray." My voice cracks at his genuine smile.

With a final nod, he leaves. I can't pull my gaze away from the man whose vulnerability for his daughter echoes that of any other dad, when in every other sense, vulnerable is not a word one would use for Ray.

"Daisy. Charles. Are you two still here?" Dad steps out of the door, now dressed in his nightclothes.

"Yes, I wanted to wish you a good night before leaving."

The conversation seems to wake up Charles, who encircles Dad in a hug. "It was a freaking awesome party, Jason."

Dad's eyes crinkle with suppressed laughter. "You take care of him tonight, Doodles. I'm sure he's going to regret it in the morning."

"I will." Pulling Charles back and settling him against the wall, I hug my dad. "Happy birthday, Daddy. I'm already looking forward to next year."

"Me too, kiddo."

"Me three," Charles slurs.

Charles is almost asleep as I guide him to his bed. Leaning him against the headboard, I remove his shoes and gently place his feet on the bed.

"Help me a little, Charles," I groan, struggling with the task of removing his jacket.

"Are you trying to take advantage of me, my dear wife?" he mumbles, eyes closed, a grin playing on his face that can only be described as cute.

I've always loved it when he called me those three words, *my dear wife*.

I belong to him. I'm dear to him.

After I untie his tie, my hands move to his collar, and I unbutton it. His eyes open, and our gazes meet, his blue irises locking with my browns. The nerve endings at the back of my neck tingle.

I break the contact first, putting an end to the growing sense of longing that consumes me the longer I spend in this room.

"This week was horrible. I fucking missed you, butterfly. I lo…" Charles' voice trails off as my eyes flutter open to find his head hanging low.

Oh, Charles.

Gently, I help him lie down and cover him with the comforter. As he begins to breathe deeply, my gaze drifts from his calm face to the other nightstand, exactly as I left it a week ago. The entire room feels unchanged—my purple towel still hangs on the vanity chair, and my makeup and skincare that I left behind in my rush are neatly arranged on the table alongside Charles' cologne and accessories. Why hasn't he thrown my things out yet?

Something heavy clogs in my throat, giving me false hope. I look away and pour him a glass of water, placing a pack of Advil next to it.

I know I should go, but my legs won't move. My brain continuously screams at me that I'm being foolish to leave Charles and this place that has started to feel like mine.

"Take care." Leaning in, I plant a kiss on his forehead. I turn around again, ready to take a determined step away from the man who's completely stolen my heart, but he snags my hand.

"Stay, butterfly," he whispers, his eyes closed, yet his grip on my hand is tight. "I wish I was enough for you." His words linger in the air.

"Charles," I whisper back, my voice breaking. "Please don't do this." A hiccup escapes me as his eyes slowly open.

"Do you know how much I fucking love you?"

It's the second time he's said those words, and a tear spills from my eyes at the raw vulnerability on his face.

"Does that not count for anything?"

"It means everything to me and so much more, Charles." I get down on my knees, our faces merely inches apart. Leaning in, I whisper against his lips, "I love you too. I love you so much it hurts sometimes." My lips touch his, causing him to inhale sharply.

"I missed you."

"Me too. But our situation still hasn't changed, or has it?" I keep the annoying hope that starts to build away from my voice.

For the first time tonight, it's Charles who makes the first move to pull away. He rests his head against the pillow.

"I can't do this, Daisy." There's sheer pain in his voice, as if something inside him is tearing him apart.

"Why? Is it all because of your mom?" I blurt, not

expecting a response, but he opens the nightstand drawer and takes out a metal box. He hands it to me before closing his eyes.

"Good night, Daisy."

I step into the living room with the box tucked under my arm to find Mrs. K sitting at the dining table.

"These are date cookies I made a few days back. If you have a craving for sweets, these are healthy." She hands me a paper bag.

"Thank you so much." My voice cracks, and she cups my cheek with her hand.

"Everything is going to be all right, dear. He loves you too much to let you go."

I nod, knowing Charles does love me, but there's something else that is much stronger pulling him away from me.

When I arrive at Willow's place, she's perched on the floor in the middle of her living room, surrounded by her laptop and a stack of papers.

"How did it go with Charles?" she asks, setting aside her work.

I shrug, hanging my coat on the rack and avoiding eye contact. "He was passed out most of the time."

"And what about you? How are you?" She studies me closely as I turn around.

"I'll be okay."

"Do you want to talk?"

I shake my head. "No, I think I want to be alone for a while."

"Gotcha. But if you need anything, like a pair of ears to hear you out, just holler, okay?"

"Thanks, Wills." I smile, then motion to the stack before her. "Um, and I wish you the best of luck with whatever you have planned for tonight."

"Thanks. The perfect plan would have been to murder Raymond Teager, but since I heard the jails are fully booked these days, I'll settle for doing serious damage to his reputation and a body part he's so proud of."

"Be careful, Wills. Ray has a reputation for being ruthless."

She waves a carefree hand at my concern. "We'll see who's more ruthless between the two of us. And, Daze, this came for you a few days back." She grabs an envelope from her stack of unopened letters. "Sorry. In all the stress, I missed checking the mailbox."

My hands shake as I grab the white cover that has a Hawthorne seal on the back.

Did Charles finally send me the divorce papers?

Looking at the metal box and the unopened envelope placed on the bed, I know I can't ignore them any longer. I've already changed out of the dress and into my pajamas and done more skincare tonight than I did the whole week.

My hands shake and my eyes betray me as I repeatedly blink, but the wetness never disappears.

Fuck it.

This is what you asked for, Daisy. Now face it.

I grab the envelope and tear it open without pause. Brushing a hand over my cheeks and wiping away the tears, I read the text.

What the heck?

I reread it as my lungs start to burn. The words make no freaking sense.

Charles Hawthorne transfers 100% of his current and future wealth to Daisy Price-Hawthorne.

Oh, Charles! What have you done?

But why are you surprised, Daisy?

Charles has always been *fair* in business, but when it comes to relationships and family, he's *unprecedented*. He's the same man who cooked with my dad, threatened reporters for me, and destroyed Jax's business.

So, of course, when it comes to his own child, how would he make any exception?

But he never wanted to be a dad!

I drop the pages onto the bed and open the latch on the metal box, hoping it'll have an answer to why Charles' lawyer is playing such a bad joke on me.

There are envelopes—fifty, maybe even more—in various sizes and colors, and all addressed to the same name. Monica. I turn the first one around and take out the letter. My gaze immediately drops to the bottom of the page.

Your loving son, Charlie.

My heart sits back so deep in my chest that I fear it'll stay there forever.

These are letters from Charles to his birth mother!

I sift through the envelopes, which seem to be carefully

chosen, and based on Charles' writing, I make an assumption about his age for each one.

My hands stop when I find the one that seems to be the oldest of all.

Dear Mom,
I miss you. A lot.
Your loving son,
Charlie.

The words are written on a lined paper in a child's broken writing. Knowing the confident man that Charles has grown into, it's almost impossible to imagine him as a kid. Someone who would make simple mistakes, like write his letters wrong. But these letters are proof that behind the unflappable exterior beats a heart that once pined for affection.

My eyes burn as I put all the letters back into their envelopes and bring the box close to my heart. Tears spill from the sides of my eyes, getting lost in my hair, and slowly things start to piece themselves together.

He's scared.

thirty-seven

What I Can Give You

Charles

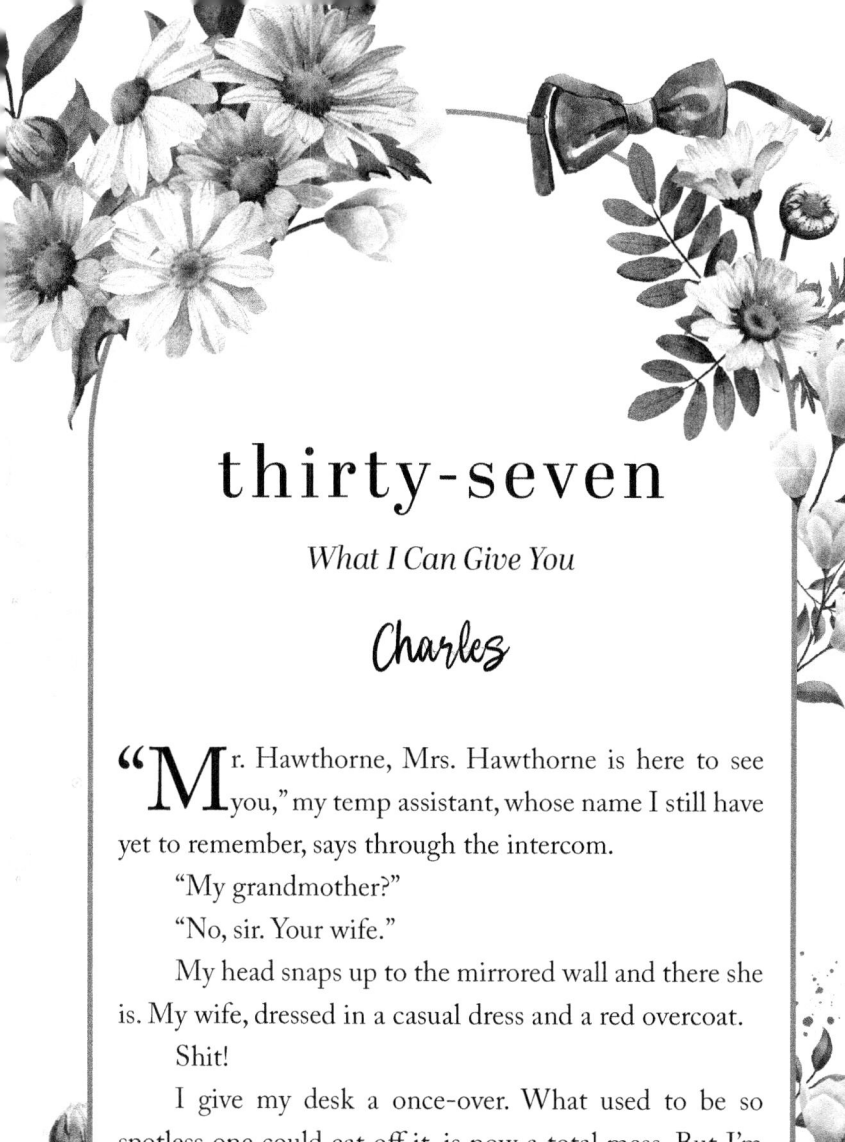

"Mr. Hawthorne, Mrs. Hawthorne is here to see you," my temp assistant, whose name I still have yet to remember, says through the intercom.

"My grandmother?"

"No, sir. Your wife."

My head snaps up to the mirrored wall and there she is. My wife, dressed in a casual dress and a red overcoat.

Shit!

I give my desk a once-over. What used to be so spotless one could eat off it, is now a total mess. But I'm not going to keep Daisy waiting by tidying it up now.

"Send her in." My stomach rolls as I wait, and it doesn't take long before there's a knock on the door and she steps inside.

Memories of last night, which I'd ignored until now,

surround me like a shroud at the sight of her. My office walls dissolve away, leaving only her and me in our bedroom, as she whispers, "I love you, Charles," and kisses me.

I've replayed this scene so many times in my head since this morning. I have no clue if it was real or a remnant of some drunken dream. And what would I give to confirm it?

"How are you feeling?" she whispers, still several feet away from where I'm standing behind my desk.

"Like my head is going to explode any minute now," I reply honestly. "Thanks for leaving the meds out. About last night—"

"I have to return something to you," Daisy interrupts me midsentence, stepping farther in and placing a shopping bag on the table.

Surprise flashes on her face as she looks at my desk. But the girl who used to make fun of me and lived for opportunities to call me a neat freak doesn't comment, and instead takes out a manila-colored envelope.

"I missed it last week." She slides the papers right in front of me.

Ownership papers.

"I don't need your money, Charles." Our eyes meet and she looks as tired as I feel.

Shouldn't she be the happiest these days?

I look away, unable to look at her and say the words at the same time. "I can't give you anything else, Daisy."

As if I needed any proof to confirm I'm already failing at this dad thing.

"I never asked for anything else. I once made the mistake of keeping a man's wishes above mine, but I can't do it anymore. It's no longer just me." She then places the metal box on the table. "But if it's fear stopping you, then I can assure you I don't plan to be like your birth mother, Charles."

What? She took that from these letters?

"It's not you I doubt." My jaw clenches, and her eyes widen to an alarming degree.

Why the fuck is she surprised?

I'm the son of that woman. How can she trust me with her kid?

"You think you won't be a good dad because of your mom?" She gapes at me, and it takes her a few seconds to find her voice and bring her eyebrows down her forehead. "Do you realize what you did last night? You hate losing control or anyone having an upper hand on you. Yet last night, for my dad, for us"—her hands splay over her flat stomach—"you got drunk." Her voice softens as she whispers, "You told Ray that some dads stop drinking for their kids, while some get drunk."

I fucking said that?

"I don't have a single doubt you'll be an awesome dad, Charles. Your kid would be so lucky to have you."

Her words start to replace the darkness in my chest with something else, something bright, but I blow out that feeling, which has no place inside me.

"My track record says otherwise."

"Yours or someone else's?" She shoots me a withering look, taking me by surprise.

I'd expected her to be upset, not this livid.

"How can you be so dense to judge your parenting skills based on your mother's behavior? I…I can't believe it." Daisy takes a step back and throws her hands up in the air. As much as I hate seeing her irritated, especially when I know she needs to be happy right now more than ever, I can't lie that I don't derive a minuscule amount of pleasure from watching her act as she used to when she was just my assistant.

"I'm sure every new parent worries how they'll do. Heck, I'm a nervous wreck most days myself. But do you think I worry for a second that I won't love my baby?" Daisy shakes her head, glaring at me. "Despite the fact that I don't even know who my birth parents are, I don't have a trace of doubt that I'll love my child unconditionally. I've seen love in the eyes of the people who raised me, and so have you. Your dad, your grandmother, Gigi, your stepmom, your aunts, Chloe—everyone has shaped your personality."

She sucks in a breath, and I'm tempted to offer her some water. But I also don't want to encourage her words more. She's completely mistaken this time.

"Nothing you say can change my mind, Daisy." My throat tightens uncomfortably, and I look away to avoid her gaze.

A long stretch of silence lingers between us until she slices it with a deep sigh.

"I cannot walk this path for you, Charles. This can only be your journey. You have to believe that you'll be enough. But if you're ever willing to step out of this zone of fear, I'm here to walk with you. You won't just be enough, you'll be an awesome dad. I know it."

I keep my eyes fixed on the table, afraid she'll see the hope her words give me.

How much would I like to be enough?

She slides the metal box forward.

"Thank you for sharing this part of your life with me. I know how hard it must have been for you. Take care, Charles." Just when I think Daisy is about to turn around and leave, she steps forward and places a kiss on my cheek.

Before she can step away, I grip her arm, and her eyes flicker over my face as I grab the envelope from the table. "This is yours. Please take it."

Her gaze drops to the envelope. "I thought these were divorce papers."

Something in my chest twinges at the thought, and it takes me a second to find my voice again. "If that's what you want."

"That's the only way forward."

Unlike the silence in the room, there's a voice screaming inside my head.

How is this moving forward when my life has returned back to where it was before her?

"Goodbye, Charles."

An uncomfortable feeling claws at my chest, begging to be released as I watch her leave.

"Daisy?" I call out her name right when she reaches the door.

She looks at me over her shoulder, eyebrows raised.

"Did you say last night that you loved me, or…was that a dream?"

Her brows pull together. "I love you, Charles A. Hawthorne."

thirty-eight

A New Pregnancy Expert in Town

Charles

"What do you think about this for the spring catalog, Mr. Hawthorne?"

One of the PR interns aims his laser pointer at the projector screen, but my gaze is fixed on the date on the bottom of the screen.

It's been exactly two months today since Daisy walked out of my office.

Two months since she confessed her love for me.

And two months since we last spoke.

"Charles, the team is waiting for your opinion." Jimmy clears his throat, tapping lightly on the wooden table.

"Sorry, guys, but something urgent just came up and I have to be somewhere. I trust your judgment in picking the best fit for the company." I'm already up from my seat. "Can't wait to see what you decide."

I can feel all the eyes tracking my moves as I step out of the room, but what's the point of sitting in a meeting when my mind is elsewhere—with that far more important thing that's waiting at my desk.

Sometime later, a knock breaks my concentration. I've just tucked the book into the top desk drawer when Jimmy enters my office.

"What the fuck is happening, Charles? You leave every meeting abruptly with one or the other lame excuse. If you don't have time, inform my team beforehand, will you?"

"I did apologize before leaving, didn't I?" My gaze narrows.

I'm the CEO, for fuck's sake.

But Jimmy's concern for my irritated mood lasts less than five seconds before he pushes another set of my buttons.

"Where is Daisy, by the way?"

"Can you stop repeating the same question every fucking day?"

"I will. The day you give me an answer that makes fucking sense. What's going on between you two?"

"Everything is perfect between us. I told you she's taking care of her dad, who's gravely sick, by the way," I almost snap at him, my voice sharp and cutting, but over the years, Jimmy has developed a thick skin against my attitude.

"Uh-huh. You mean the man who posts on social media five times a day about his cooking, fashion, and life?"

God, Jason.

"And unlike you, Daisy is not being a jackass."

"You spoke with her?" The words scrape against my

tongue like sandpaper as I clutch on to the armrests. "What did she say?"

"Why don't you ask your damn wife, if everything between the two of you is so perfect?"

Without giving me another glance, he storms out of my office. I wait for the door to click shut before retrieving the book. After a deep, calming breath, I turn to the page where my bookmark rests.

Chapter 3: Foods to Eat in Your First Trimester.

It's way past dinnertime when I reach my home, and my feet hesitate at the landing at the sound of a feminine voice talking to Mrs. Kowalski.

Daisy?

That can't be right. I just saw her.

"Look who finally showed up." Chloe, perched at the kitchen counter, raises her head from a fashion magazine.

"Why are you here so late?" I approach my sister, dropping my laptop bag onto the couch.

"I was right on time for dinner. Hate to break it to you, big brother, but you're the latecomer here."

Shit! Did we plan something and I forgot?

"Relax! I'm just an unannounced guest." My sister grins, snagging another cookie from the half-empty plate in front of her.

"Sorry, had too much work." I ruffle her hair before settling onto the barstool beside her.

She makes an annoyed sound, swatting my hand away.

"Really? Because I checked with your temp assistant,

and he said you left work at six. Where've you been for the last three hours?" My little sister sits up, swiveling in her seat to face me.

She's like a bloodhound when it comes to digging up info. I usually enjoy her talent, but not today, when it's directed at me.

Though she's out of luck.

There's no way I'm confessing that I've been spending my evenings parked outside Daisy's friend's apartment with one of the pregnancy books in hand, just to catch a glimpse of my wife.

Was it really three hours today?

Who cares? It was well worth it.

Daisy came out for a walk with Willow. And bless the spring weather, I was able to catch a glimpse of her pregnant belly in that crop top she paired with her joggers.

Chloe snaps her fingers before my face, pulling my attention back to her.

"I was in a meeting at a client's office." The lie slips past my lips effortlessly.

"Uh-huh," my sister mutters under her breath, as if she already knows my bullshit. But otherwise, she's quiet, and that can only mean one thing. She's got bigger fish to fry tonight.

"Why did you say you're here?" I ask to know the reason for her unexpected arrival.

"I wanted to have dinner with my brother." She gives me that smile that means mischief half the time.

"Got it." As soon as I place my hands on the counter, like clockwork, Mrs. Kowalski enters the kitchen.

Efficient doesn't begin to describe my housekeeper—

she sets out placemats on the counter and arranges a colorful cheese, fruit, and cracker platter and two wineglasses before leaving us alone.

Meanwhile, Chloe grabs a bottle of pinot from the rack. After uncorking it, she fills my glass to the brim and then hers.

"Are we celebrating something or just getting drunk?"

"I don't know and I don't care." My sister giggles before clinking her glass with mine.

We're barely two minutes into this suspicious dinner, and I have taken one sip of my drink, when Chloe taps on the counter.

"You know we know, right?"

Talk about taking something head-on.

"I don't know what you're talking about," I reply, avoiding eye contact and focusing on my drink.

My sister is just warming up.

"Charlie, I've had enough of your nonsense. Tell me exactly what happened between you and Daisy."

"Nothing happened. She's taking care of her dad, and since we don't want to confuse Jason, she's staying with Willow. It's closer—less traffic, easier commute."

The excuse I'm repeatedly giving to Jimmy takes full, concrete form.

Chloe doesn't say anything for a moment, but I can practically see steam coming out of her ears.

She gnaws at the inside of her cheeks, and that's how I know she's repeating the counting routine our mom forced her to learn to control her temper.

I'm actually impressed to see her practice it in real life.

"So you're saying that Charles Ashcroft Hawthorne, the

man who has the power to halt the entire town's traffic with a single phone call, prefers his wife staying away because of commute time? How dumb do you think we are?"

Her words hit a nerve deep in my heart. *What's the use of all this power, if I'm still unable to win my wife back?*

"Not enough, it seems, because I expected you not to pry into my personal life." I slam my glass down a bit too hard, surprised it doesn't shatter. "I love you, Chloe, but God, you can be so irritating sometimes. Learn to read the room and heed when someone's subtly telling you to mind your own business."

Am I the dumb fuck to think my sister will cower and back away?

Definitely, because as opposed to my liking, Chloe only sits tall in her seat.

"This is every bit of my business. My brother's acting like an idiot, and I want to know why."

"There are things you don't know here, Chloe," I mutter under my breath, words of frustration escaping past my lips.

"Like Daisy being pregnant and you being an asshole to send her away when she needs you the most?"

Her reply is like an unexpected whip, sharp and firm, and a chill runs down my spine.

If Chloe knows, that means everyone in my family is aware of it.

"I didn't send anyone anywhere. She left on her own."

"And did you lose your voice or your ability to stop her?" Chloe doesn't pause for a reply. "It's because of your mom, isn't it?"

Silence lingers between us for a few moments.

"What do you mean?" I ask, shocked not just because of her accurate conclusion but also because Chloe and I have never talked about my birth mother. In fact, for years, she didn't even know we were stepsiblings, and when she did find out, that word became the most hated word in her dictionary.

"You've got some crazy, stupid idea that you won't be a good dad because of how your mom treated you." Her eyes lock with mine as if she can read every insecurity, every fear, inside me.

Even though she's pushing all my buttons, frustrating the hell out of me, I'm so grateful to have her in my life. Fighting with me for my happiness and what she believes is right.

But tonight, she's wrong.

"So now you're an expert on the woman you haven't even met?"

"I don't need to know anything except that she left her little boy behind." Chloe takes a breath, placing her hand over my clenched fist on the counter. "Remember when I was little, I used to ask if you could be my protector forever? Let us be that for you for once, Charlie. I know you're scared, but please let us in. Let Daisy in."

The hopeful gleam in her eyes dies when I pull my hand out from under hers.

"I know you mean well, but I don't want to discuss this. Not now, not ever." My jaw clenches to the point of pain. "But since I also know how hard it is for you to give up once you've set your mind on something, let me be clear. Yes, everything you said is true. *Maybe* my belief is misplaced. But no one, including you, can change how I feel about this. This is for Daisy and me to figure out how we want to move forward."

"But you're not talking to her, dammit. Or are you making plans in your sleep?"

"That's enough."

I don't know if it's my raised voice or that my housekeeper knows I've never taken that tone with my little sister, but she hurries into the kitchen.

"Don't worry, Mrs. K. Everything's fine. My brother's just being his usual dumbass self." Chloe's lips curl, but her eyes shoot daggers at me until she turns her gaze away. "Since you're here, can I ask you something? Daisy's been having morning sickness and can't keep anything down. Even though Willow's excited that the baby is finally making its presence known, which to be honest, everyone thought would be a miracle in itself given its Charles' kid, Daisy's diet is taking a serious hit. She mentioned craving your pierogi yesterday. Could you make some, and I'll take it over to Willow's?"

Mrs. Kowalski's already tying her apron, while I'm stuck on her words. People are having fun at the expense of my baby. What the fuck?

"Sure. I'll also make a big batch tomorrow. Daisy can freeze it."

"Thank you so much. You're seriously my last hope. Everything GG sent has been rejected by Daisy's stomach, and our great-gram's only a few recipes away from taking it as a personal offense."

What in the hell is happening behind my back? Here I thought my family had no clue Daisy was pregnant, but not only do they know, they're also dispatching food and are more up-to-date on her present state than me.

"If you know so much, shouldn't that have been the first thing you asked Mrs. Kowalski when you came here?"

It's as if my words don't even reach my sister. She waves her hand, swatting my concerned words like a fly.

"Who the hell are you to worry about her?"

A seething storm churns inside me, a tempest of fury and frustration as she dismisses me so easily on such an important matter.

"She's still my wife, in case you've forgotten, sis."

But my low, threatening voice has no impact on Chloe. "Go away, Charlie. Take your grumpy macho act elsewhere." She shoves me out of the chair before turning back to my housekeeper. "Mrs. K, do you want to see the baby? Daisy had her ultrasound this morning. I can't believe my little blip of a niece is already ten weeks old."

A possessive pang hits me like a tornado as Chloe pulls out her phone and slides it across the counter to my housekeeper. I reach for it, but my sister snatches it away, while Mrs. Kowalski freezes, her hands in the air.

"You come to my house uninvited, drink my wine, ruin my evening with your nonsense talk, and yet you keep such a big thing from me? Give me that phone, Chloe."

"I'd die before I let you see my niece. Only those who care about Daisy and my little princess have the right to see her pic. Since you care about neither, you can fuck off."

My blood rushes in my ears, a roar that drowns out everything else but her words and the desire to see the picture.

"Your niece wouldn't even be here if not for me. If

anything, I have the first right to her before anyone else, and especially you."

"Oh, really! Your *contribution* in her making means shit, Charlie. You need care and compassion to be a real dad or mom. And you've shown neither to my niece."

If I weren't burning in frustration, I'd have laughed at her use of the word *contribution*, but her one word seems to pinch deeper and deeper inside me.

Niece. Again.

My muscles tense.

Until now, every time I thought of my baby, I imagined a five-year-old boy having the time of his life with his mom. She comes to his school events, playdates, and soccer matches. But what if it's a girl—missing her dad?

Fuck no.

"Who said anything about a girl? It takes at least twelve weeks to find out the gender of the baby?"

"So what are you, the new pregnancy expert in town?" My sister raises an eyebrow.

At least I hope to be expert enough for my baby.

When I just stare at her, Chloe shrugs. "I have a feeling it's a girl."

Before I can stay with that warm feeling gripping my chest a second longer, my sister turns to the housekeeper.

"Mrs. K, how was it when you were pregnant? Did you guess if it'd be a boy or a girl, and were you right?" Unlike when she's talking to me, Chloe's beaming at my housekeeper. "I ask Daisy every day. But all she says is, 'I just want a healthy baby.' What kind of boring answer is that?"

Mrs. Kowalski laughs, her hands pausing over the rolling pin before she resumes flattening the dough.

"Some women say they do have a feeling. In my case, my husband and I made a bet. I wanted a girl, but he was sure it'd be a boy. And he was right both times."

"That's so cool! I can't wait to go betting war with Willow, Elodie, and Violet."

Chloe keeps talking about *my baby*, and for the first time, my heart isn't gripped with fear.

There's something like pink hope filling my insides with a promise of a never-ending adventure.

thirty-nine

Oh, My Tiny Blip

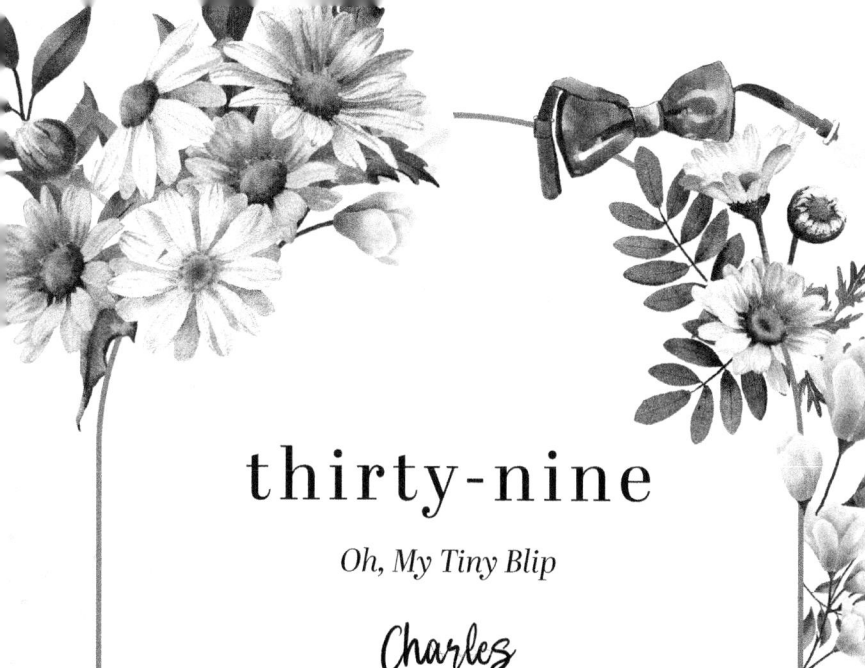

Charles

"Mr. Hawthorne."

Before I can step into the elevator, Dave calls my name in a low voice, and I turn around.

"I went to drop off apple pancakes at Miss Willow's apartment, sir. Since Mrs. Hawthorne is unable to keep anything down, including the famous pierogi, Mrs. K is trying some new recipes." His forehead creases as if my baby's unacceptance of food is a personal offense toward him.

Looks like not just my family but even my staff has tagged along in Daisy's pregnancy journey.

Am I the only one uninformed of her these days?

I'm about to tell Dave to stick to his job description and nothing more, when he places a white envelope forward.

"Daisy gave it to me this morning, and Mrs. K and I both believe it was meant for you."

I continue to stare at him, making no attempt to pick up the envelope, because I fear what it might contain. I've yet to send her the divorce papers.

Has she taken matters into her own hands?

"It's the picture of her ultrasound," Dave whispers, and I snatch the white paper from his hand and tuck it safely into the inside pocket of my jacket, close to my heart.

My legs feel heavy throughout the entire elevator ride from the parking lot to my office. My one hand is holding my laptop case, but the other is pressed close to my chest, where I can still feel the envelope.

My temporary assistant rises from his seat to greet me.

"Cancel my next meeting. I'm busy for the next hour."

I don't wait for his nod or any verbal confirmation before heading straight to my office. Sliding the laptop bag onto the desk, I perch on my chair.

My hands quiver with curiosity and nerves as I open the envelope and, with gentle care, slide the photo into my hand.

And there it is. My tiny blip.

Thanks to my books, I'm well versed at reading ultrasounds.

My hand halts above the image when a throat clears, and I jerk in my seat.

"Fucking hell."

My head snaps to find my dad seated on the corner couch, with his Hawthorne crest lighter dangling from his index finger and a cake box from Hawthorne Bakery on the table before him.

"What are you doing here?"

"I was waiting for my son. But there must be something really captivating in there, since it's the first time you didn't scan the room before walking in."

His lips twitch, and his head cocks to one side before he leaves his spot and walks to me, bringing along the cake box.

Those few beats give me time to bring my racing heartbeat back to normal.

"Is it just my imagination or has my family suddenly started to miss me too much?"

Dad chuckles, dropping down into the chair across from me.

"We always miss you, Ace. Kristy and Chloe went to see Daisy, so I thought it's only fair I come to see my boy."

I snort, not because of him calling me a boy, but because Dad could be standing on trial and he still wouldn't be able to lie properly. There's no way he came for fun on a Wednesday morning. He's here to talk, something he deems more important than my morning meetings.

"Uh-huh. Aren't we all bored sitting at our own homes these days?"

"Can you blame us? Our first grandchild is on the line. If your mom and sister could, they would live with Daisy." Dad opens the cake box and passes my childhood favorite toward me—chocolate mousse cake. "I even offered for her to move into the Hawthorne mansion, but she declined."

I can't push the plastic fork hanging in the air into my mouth.

Since when has everyone started making plans for Daisy?

"And you didn't think to run it by me once?" My lips

press into a thin line, trembling with the effort to contain all my feelings on the matter.

"Did you ask me before you sent your wife away?" Despite his words, his tone is calmer than mine.

"How many times do I need to say that I didn't send her away? She left on her own." My left eye twitches as I press my lips together. "Plus, I'm not going to have this conversation with you too. Chloe has already given me enough heat."

"You should listen to your sister. She can be very wise sometimes. Let me also tell you that she's very protective of her little niece."

My heart thuds at his words, and it takes a beat to find my natural voice.

"Not you too."

"You know Chloe always gets what she wants." Dad smirks. "Plus, I can already imagine myself humming to my little princess wrapped in a pink blanket."

I'm not stupid. I know what everyone is doing—they're trying to show me the life that lies on the other side of my fear.

And God are they persistent and damn good at this.

"Chloe only gets what she wants because everyone goes above and beyond to make that happen. So unless someone has the power to convince Mother Nature, I'd suggest we put a lid on the niece talk."

"You're no fun." Dad dabs his mouth with a paper napkin before leaning back in the chair. "Since you're only interested in serious talks, I wanted to confirm that you've taken care of security for Daisy."

I nod, finally happy to have a sane conversation. "There

are undercover bodyguards from Kings Security stationed outside Willow's apartment. They make sure she's never left alone, including the times she's at the hospital."

"Wouldn't it have been easier if she were with you?"

"Dad—"

"It's because of Monica, isn't it?" Dad's voice lowers.

I don't remember the last time we talked about the woman, but there's an unusual heaviness in my father's otherwise warm voice.

"We don't have to talk about this, Dad."

"But we do, especially when I see that not having talked in the past is perhaps the reason you're giving up on one of the biggest happinesses of your life. Despite how your mother's and my relationship went, I never regretted having you, Ace."

"I know, Dad. I also know that woman was just too greedy and too selfish." And I carry those genes in me.

A sad smile tugs on his lips. "An abundance of money comes with its own set of problems, Charles. Since you could learn, you were taught to differentiate between its power and pitfalls. But what about those who see the other side of it every day? The side where there's only less of everything— opportunities, money, safety. Do you blame Monica for wanting an easy pass when she saw wealth that could change her whole life?"

Before I can nod and scream, *"Hell yeah, I do,"* Dad sighs.

"I don't. Not anymore. Because I've realized I was also at fault somewhere in our relationship. I should have been clearer that I wanted nothing to do with the family business and the money that comes with the Hawthorne name. We weren't the right match, and I should have seen it sooner."

My dad takes the blame for something that isn't his fault, and my respect only grows for the man.

He leans forward. "But nothing makes a father more sad than knowing his kid is missing life's happiness because of his faults."

"It's no one's fault. I'm just not cut out for this." I look away to escape the look of disappointment on his face.

"Nobody is cut out for being a dad, Ace. This is not a skill you can learn by taking a course. But someday, after hours of waiting, a nurse places a small crying bundle in your arms wrapped in a white towel. That kid looks back at you and holds your finger in its tiny fist. And it's just you and the baby while everything else around you dissolves."

Dad places his hand over mine. "That's when you know you'll do everything for that little person, and your life will never be the same. Being a dad is not a task. It's a feeling, and you don't feel it until that moment."

Something heavy clogs in my chest as I imagine being in the hospital and holding *my baby*. One part Daisy and one part me.

"I might not understand all your fears, Charlie, but I know you. You're my kid, and you don't give up."

Dad straightens up and circles my desk. "So even if you think you're not cut out for it, you'll work to become what you have to in order to give all the happiness in this life to your wife and your kid. And you will not stop until you're the most awesome dad in the world." His voice is no longer soft but filled with energy, and I can't deny that I feel it inside me as well.

"I think that title is already taken."

He grins and slaps my back. It only takes a few more seconds for my lips to curl up the same way.

"That's what I'm talking about. You're the best fucking son, Charles. And I'd hate to see you give up on one of the greatest happinesses in life just because you're scared."

My father's words hang in my office even after he leaves, and I find myself too restless to settle down. I leave my seat and walk toward the glass wall where I've observed Daisy from afar for four years.

But today, everything is different.

There are no pink Post-its in my office any longer.

There're no sparkly napkins at the bar.

And even though the maintenance staff is asked to check up on her plants, they're turning dry, one leaf at a time.

I had someone from the local nursery check up on them last week, but if that doesn't work, I'll be sending them to the state's best botanist.

But they don't need an expert.
They just need her. Exactly like you.

"Can I ask for some help?"

Mrs. Kowalski immediately turns to face me from where she's watering the plants in the sunroom. The same place where our tiny blip was conceived. I don't think he or she would appreciate knowing that fact when they grow up.

Yeah, I've started to wonder if my blip is a girl and not a boy.

Damn, Chloe and her convincing superpowers!

"Mr. Hawthorne, I didn't know you were coming early.

Sorry, I'll get your coffee ready right now." My housekeeper sets down the plastic watering can that reminds me of Daisy's elephant-shaped one now staying untouched in the office.

"No, it's not coffee, but...I'd like your help with something else." My palms go clammy, and I have the sudden urge to rub them over my pants.

God, why is this so damn hard?

My housekeeper patiently waits for my instructions, while my tongue seems to have gotten stuck at the base of my mouth.

Fuck it, Charles.

This is your home.

If you want to cook, you cook, period. No one can stop you.

Putting my hands inside my pants pockets, I stand tall.

"Can you show me around the kitchen and help me cook?"

Her eyebrows shoot up as if I've just asked her to sell national secrets to our enemies. "If you'd like to eat something special, I can make it for you, Mr. Hawthorne."

"It's not for me." I swallow hard, shifting my weight from one foot to the other. "I had a meeting with one of the most expert nutritionists in the country, and I want to try a recipe for Daisy. But I've never cooked before."

Her face lights up as if I've just told her our nation is going tax-free.

Moments later, I'm standing in the kitchen, following Mrs. Kowalski's instructions. I've ditched my jacket, and my shirt sleeves are rolled over my forearms. A white apron hangs from my neck, and I'm holding the long waist ties in each hand as if they're bombs.

"Shall I help you?" my housekeeper asks softly, and I look over my shoulder to see her all ready.

I nod, and with expert hands, she ties a knot that is neither too tight nor too loose.

"Do you want to show me the recipe, and I can check if we have everything here?"

"What if we don't? Aren't grocery stores closing soon?" I look down at my watch and mentally curse.

I'm failing at a task before I've even begun.

This must be a new record for you, Hawthorne.

"I'm very proud of my pantry, Mr. Hawthorne." Mrs. Kowalski, on the other hand, couldn't be any calmer. I must have that freaked-out expression on my face, because she adds, "In any case, twenty-four-hour shops are always open."

Thank fucking God.

"I just want to follow the recipe exactly as mentioned." I finally take out the printout from the inside pocket of my jacket.

"I wouldn't expect anything less, sir." There's no humor in her voice as she looks down at the recipe. "And good news, we have everything."

"Even the cast iron pan?"

"Only the best one." She winks and places the skillet over the stove before producing a bag of oat flour on the counter. "But first, we need to knead the dough for the tortillas."

It takes forty minutes and multiple failed tortillas that don't even get a chance to land on the pan, because I roll so hard that either they stick on the pin or there are big holes in the flat dough. Finally, we have two tortillas that look barely professional, but Mrs. Kowalski is convinced they will taste very good.

"Now, let's chop the veggies."

It takes another hour before there are two cheese quesadillas, a mango smoothie, and a small batch of apple peanut butter cupcakes.

Everything has finally been packed. Mrs. Kowalski is about to throw a plain white paper napkin into the bag, when I interject.

"Can you put this in?"

Her gaze lands on the pink napkin with golden letters stating, *Have a day that's as magical as a unicorn*, and just smiles.

A no-nonsense comment and definitely no making fun of me.

I knew she was the best person to ask for this help.

Daisy's words from some weeks ago ring in my ear.

"Mrs. K doesn't work on weekends for the extra pay, Charles. It's because she worries about your paranoid ass."

"Shall I call Dave or Steve, and they can take it to Daisy?" My housekeeper's hand is poised to lift the bag from the counter when I intercept, extending my palm.

"I'll take it to them." I take hold of the bag in one hand while reaching for my jacket with the other.

Before exiting, I glance back to see her tidying up the mess I left behind.

"Mrs. K?" I call, using the nickname my sister coined years ago and everyone opts to use except me. "Thank you so much. Not just for this"—I tip my head toward the bag—"but for looking after me all these years."

Surprise gleams in her eyes, but only for a second. Her lips once again curl into her usual motherly, soft smile. She knows I don't like making a big fuss of things.

Maybe I've been too fast in dismissing my luck when it comes to people around me and their care.

"It's always been my pleasure, Mr. Hawthorne. I hope the happiness you deserve finds its way back to you."

I nod in appreciation before heading off to locate my bodyguard.

"Do you want me to do something more than hand over the bag, sir?" Dave asks as we stand across from Willow's apartment for several minutes. I haven't asked him to leave, nor have I let go of my deadly grip on the bag.

"How will we know if she's able to eat this?"

"She'll text Mrs. K, sir. Don't worry."

But what if she doesn't? What if Daisy thinks she's caused enough problems for everyone, and she just starts lying?

I know her. If her imminent desire to please everyone hasn't reared its head by now, it'll do so soon.

"That's not enough." I rake a hand through my hair. "Can you ask her to try it and stay there until she's done?"

My grip on the bag tightens as I imagine my bodyguard sitting before Daisy and watching her eat.

It should be me, for fuck's sake.

"Mr. Hawthorne, would you like to join me?" Dave asks slowly, as if he has a telepathic connection to my thoughts.

"I can't." My voice has no bite at all as I finally hand the bag to him.

With worrying about her diet and then cooking, I'm fucking drained to even snap at people.

I don't know what Dave sees on my face, but he takes out his phone and dials someone. Immediately, my phone vibrates in my pocket.

The moment I pick up, he turns around and skids into Willow's place.

Holy fuck, that's genius.

forty

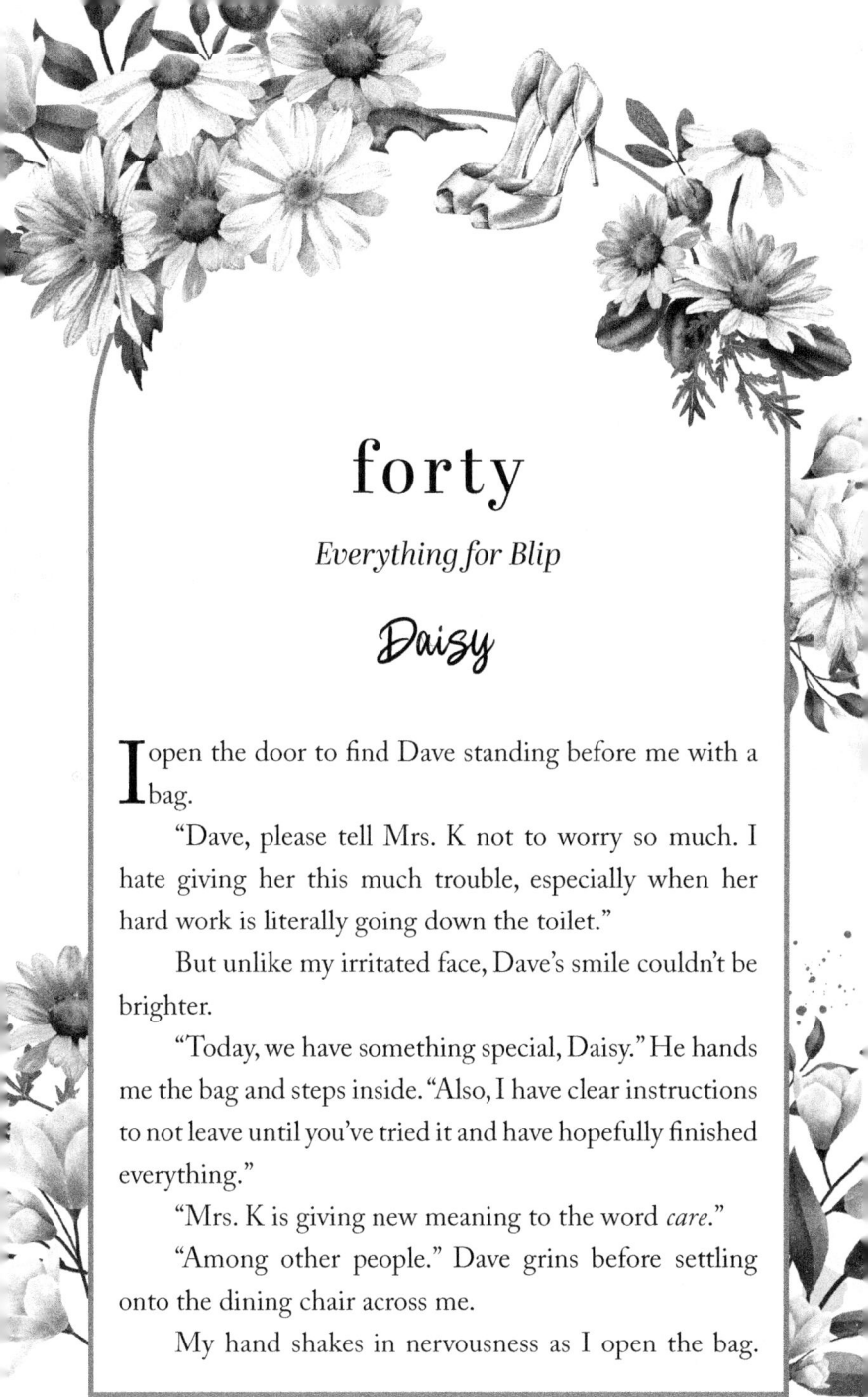

Everything for Blip

Daisy

I open the door to find Dave standing before me with a bag.

"Dave, please tell Mrs. K not to worry so much. I hate giving her this much trouble, especially when her hard work is literally going down the toilet."

But unlike my irritated face, Dave's smile couldn't be brighter.

"Today, we have something special, Daisy." He hands me the bag and steps inside. "Also, I have clear instructions to not leave until you've tried it and have hopefully finished everything."

"Mrs. K is giving new meaning to the word *care*."

"Among other people." Dave grins before settling onto the dining chair across me.

My hand shakes in nervousness as I open the bag.

As much as I'm loving the care and affection I've received the past few weeks, I hate to be the biggest disappointment.

So much wonderful food has gone to waste that I worry I might have volunteers fighting against world hunger at my doorstep soon.

Please, my little blip, be a good champ and let's not disappoint Mrs. K once again.

But every thought evaporates from my mind at the sight of the pink paper napkin I'd ordered for Charles months ago.

How?

Before my shock can find an audible voice, Dave places his phone face-first onto the table. The green light indicating a live call blinks a few times. I look up at him and he gives me a smile, the same one he used to show whenever I would say something mean about Charles before we got married.

Charles!

Oh my God. Did he help Mrs. K pack this?

I remember Dave's words from five seconds before. He's been instructed to not leave until I've tried the food.

By whom? Charles?

My anxiety is at full throttle as I take out the food.

I grab the cutlery Mrs. K always packs with the meals and open the glass box.

For the first time this week, the warm smell of cheese and veggies is appetizing, but it's not just the smell. Unlike the other meals, there's no special garnish. The tasty food is placed in a simple fashion. In fact, too simple.

I cut the quesadilla, only to realize it's not perfectly round.

This is not Mrs. K's work.

My gaze snaps back to Dave, who's waiting in anticipation, and then to the phone that is still intermittently blinking.

What in God's name?

Charles A. Hawthorne stepped into his kitchen and cooked! For me!

"So how is it?" Dave asks, and I'm sure it's more for Charles' benefit so he knows the call is still running.

I take a bite, and for a second, I forget everything because it's heavenly. I don't wait to reply and take another bite.

"How did that miracle happen?" Willow squeals as she enters the room.

Charles' bodyguard subtly turns the phone upside down.

"Dave, can you please tell our cook that Blip and I both agree this is the best food we've eaten ever."

"Blip?" Dave grins, raising an eyebrow.

"Yes, in one of the numerous pregnancy books Daisy's reading, the baby is referred to as a blip." Willow slips onto the chair beside me. "So that's the nickname for now. But don't worry, Dave, Chloe and I are starting a petition to change it to something more interesting. You and Steve will also get to sign."

"I don't know." Dave grins. "I kind of like it."

I finish the entire meal, including the mango smoothie that still has a few chunks of the fruit, and the cupcakes that are once again not perfectly shaped.

But there's never been a meal more perfect.

Dave places all the empty containers back into the bag and tips his head to the side.

"I'll see you tomorrow morning, Daisy. Let's see if we can keep up with what we started today."

My heart is so full knowing how many people have come into my life since my marriage to Charles. People who care about my and Blip's happiness.

Mrs. K, who made sure I knew Charles was the one to cook tonight.

Dave, who gave Charles and me a moment to share, despite us being apart.

"Dave, thank you so much for tonight." My throat is full of emotion as I hug the man.

"You never have to thank us, Daisy. We want you, Mr. Hawthorne, and your little *blip* to be happy and healthy always."

Instead of walking to the door, Dave leads me to the side window and subtly tilts his head to the glass. I follow his motion and spot Charles' limo.

It's not the first time I've seen it here. But it's the first time I've seen Charles leaning against the car with his phone to his ear while looking down at his shoes.

"Take care of yourself, Daisy, and I'll see you soon."

Dave leaves while I remain stuck in place, hiding behind the curtains.

"What was all that about?" Willow, who has thankfully been quiet so far, joins me.

"Charles cooked and came with Dave to make sure I ate."

What she doesn't know is that he even came up to her home—at least his ears did.

"And little blip agreed to his dad's cooking out of all the

amazing chefs? So not cool, kid. *So not cool.*" Willow shakes her head, but her smile says it all.

She's not just surprised, but immensely impressed.

The next morning, Dave comes with breakfast and a bouquet of wild daisies with a small white card that reads: *For you and tiny blip.*

There's no signature, but I've spent the past four years seeing Charles' handwriting every day.

I can recognize his wavy letters in my sleep. Not to mention, it's on the same thick paper with barcodes he specially issued for me after the whole debacle with Jax.

Once again, the fruit platter and avocado toast is met with full agreement by my taste buds and my stomach.

Dave's phone remains on the table throughout breakfast. And later, I watch my husband, dressed in a navy-blue suit all ready for work, standing outside his car with his phone pressed against his ear.

"Haven't you started looking forward to these meals with Dave?" Willow raises an eyebrow as, on the third day, I place the numerous books I've been reading on the dining table.

"I thought I'd share some of the things I'm doing these days with Dave. Just watching me eat must be so boring for him."

"You mean for Charles to just hear you eat?" Willow's eyes narrow slightly and her lips twitch.

"You knew?" I gasp.

"Daze, I'm not *that* stupid or romantically challenged. Every time Dave is here, his phone is on the table and Charles has his pressed against his ear." My friend leaves her spot on the couch and joins me by the table. "It's actually romantic, though a bit psycho, if you ask me."

"I think he knows I know."

"Of course he does. Who in their sane mind talks to their bodyguard for one full hour about how hard it is to sleep these days? Charles must have given Dave a nice raise. That bodyguard is playing the best Cupid one could ask for." Willow has just said the words when the doorbell rings. "And here comes our Cupid extraordinaire now."

"Hi, Dave." Willow opens the door, waving at the bodyguard before settling on the chair across from me at the table. "What do we have for Daisy today?"

Dave's smile only widens as he takes a seat beside me. "In addition to breakfast, some books." He hoists a shopping bag from my favorite local bookstore.

"Great minds think alike." Willow grins. "Daisy brought out her pregnancy books to show you."

Smooth, girl. Now I don't even need an introduction.

"Just a few books I'm reading these days." As I go around, reading to Dave (in reality to Charles) some of my favorite highlighted passages from my favorite books, Dave's phone vibrates and I go silent.

Is it Charles?

But he has always been a quiet participant of our meetings.

"Have you read Emily Oster's books, Daisy?" Dave

doesn't even hide his broad grin or the text from Charles as he places his phone on the table.

How does Charles know about pregnancy books? Is he reading them as well?

Before my heart can explode with emotion and I turn into a blubbering idiot, I reply, "Of course. Right now, I'm reading *Expecting Better*."

Dave doesn't reply and stares at his phone, like me and Willow.

"That's a good choice." He repeats Charles' words like a parrot. *The best parrot in a black suit.*

My emotions take a new flight, hope surging inside me after being absent for so long.

"Have you by any chance heard of Adam Camp?" I ask in a quivering voice, but when Dave and Willow stare at me in confusion, I explain. "He writes pregnancy books for dads."

This time when Dave's phone chimes, he grabs it fast.

"I'm reading *We're Pregnant*," he replies in shock as if he can't hear his own words.

But could anyone blame him?

Charles Hawthorne is reading a pregnancy handbook for first-time dads.

My mind is still swirling with thoughts.

Charles, the man who can have Michelin-star chefs cook for him every day, going into the kitchen and cooking—that I can imagine.

Charles, the man who thinks there's no bigger currency than time, sitting in a car, listening to me go on and on about the pain in my back and feet—that I can *maybe* get on board with.

But Charles, someone who has forever been scared of the idea of being a dad, reading pregnancy dad books—that's everything I need to break the dam of my emotions.

Maybe Dave sees the emotion on my face, because he slowly shakes his head and says instead, "Before I leave, I have to give you something."

I nod as he slides a small lavender-colored bedtime storybook onto the table. My hands tremble as I flip over the hardcover and my heart once again ricochets at the sight of Charles' handwriting.

Our tiny blip.

forty-one

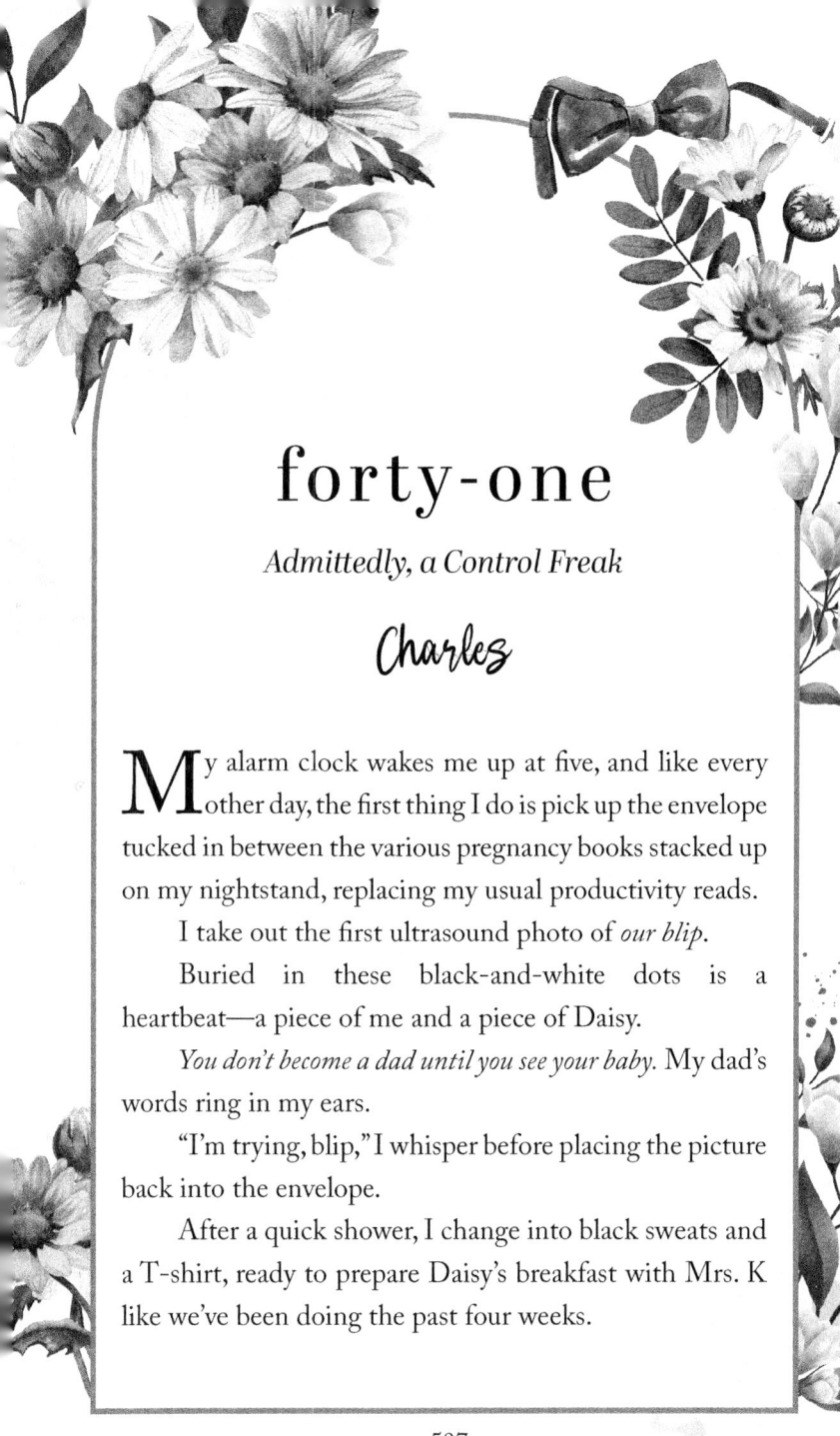

Admittedly, a Control Freak

Charles

My alarm clock wakes me up at five, and like every other day, the first thing I do is pick up the envelope tucked in between the various pregnancy books stacked up on my nightstand, replacing my usual productivity reads.

I take out the first ultrasound photo of *our blip*.

Buried in these black-and-white dots is a heartbeat—a piece of me and a piece of Daisy.

You don't become a dad until you see your baby. My dad's words ring in my ears.

"I'm trying, blip," I whisper before placing the picture back into the envelope.

After a quick shower, I change into black sweats and a T-shirt, ready to prepare Daisy's breakfast with Mrs. K like we've been doing the past four weeks.

I run a hand through my hair, hesitantly going for my phone.

There's no point in dancing around it. Every fucking day, Chloe sends me a text reminding me how much of a jerk I've been to her niece, and I have to remind her to mind her own business.

Filled with forced determination, I reach for my phone.

Now what?

Did my little sister come back to her senses?

That doesn't sound like Chloe.

I check my phone again in case there's some problem with the network, but everything seems okay.

Maybe she stayed up late working or watching a movie.

Yeah, that has to be it.

I'm so lost in my thoughts that I didn't even see Mrs. Kowalski in the kitchen.

"We're ready, Mr. Hawthorne. As per the recipe you sent me last night, I got fresh raspberries."

When I snap my head up to her from my phone, her smile drops.

"Is everything okay?"

I shrug, taking the apron from her hands and tying it effortlessly.

"I receive a text from Chloe every morning without fail. But today, she's silent. It feels weird. I guess I just miss her." I smile, trying to shake the ominous feeling slowly finding space in my chest.

"Your sister loves you a lot." Mrs. Kowalski places a cup of coffee before me as I start to read the recipe printout I handed her yesterday.

First thing, eggs.

I'm about to grab the mixing bowl when the doorbell rings, followed by a beep alerting us that someone has walked in.

A cold sweat breaks out on my forehead, chilling my skin.

Apart from Mrs. Kowalski, there are only two staff members who have direct access to my house. Dave and Steve. But they wouldn't be here without reason.

And I don't have to wait long, because moments later, both of my bodyguards fill my living room, harrowed expressions on their faces.

"You need to see this, sir." Dave doesn't say more and grabs the remote from the counter.

My stomach clenches with a nauseating twist of dread.

The TV monitor in the kitchen comes to life, putting my chest in a chokehold.

"This is live," Steve confirms, as I'm unable to look anywhere but at Daisy on the screen.

Dressed in a yellow summer dress and a long cardigan, flats on her feet, her hands clutched in front of her, she stands in the middle of a sea of reporters outside Cherrywood Memorial Hospital. She blinks on the screen, and my stupor breaks.

"Where the fuck is her security?" I grab my phone from the counter, my grip painfully tight as I dial Carter King, but the call goes straight to voicemail.

"They were two cars behind, as always, Mr. Hawthorne, but as soon as Daisy stepped out of her car, the press surrounded her and now there are cameras everywhere. Her bodyguards are trying to get to her."

I'm still processing Steve's words when I hear a reporter's voice on the screen.

"Mrs. Hawthorne, congratulations on the good news. But where's Mr. Hawthorne? We heard you're no longer staying at his residence. Is this true?"

I pull my gaze from Daisy's face to the headlines running at the bottom of the screen.

Is the local fairy-tale love story coming to an end?

Or was it a marriage of convenience that has finally come to its planned ending?

"I need his name!" My growl roars in my living room. "I need the name of this dumbfuck reporter who thought he could ask these fucking questions to my wife." I turn to face my bodyguards, who nod furiously before I speed-dial the chief of police.

"Mr. Hawthorne, I'm seeing the news. We are—"

I don't waste time in pleasantries and interrupt whatever he's about to say.

"I need the streets from my estate to the hospital all clear, Chief. Not a single vehicle, not a single soul." My chopper could have been faster for the distance, but not when it's impromptu.

"You got it, Mr. Hawthorne."

"Let's go." I'm already striding toward the door, when Mrs. K gasps my name.

"Mr. Hawthorne, you should take it off!" She points toward the apron still tied to my front as shock and worry consumes her features.

I tear the material away from me, swallowing the wince when the neck strap bites my skin. Without caring where it lands, I march down the stairs, forgoing the elevator, with Dave and Steve on my heels.

The minutes-long ride to the hospital feels like hours, while my gaze stays on the live newsfeed running on my iPad.

She's still there, in the midst of the crowd.

Nervous and worried, facing questions no one should have dared to ask her. It should have been my task, protecting her, protecting our blip.

But I'm coming, butterfly.

We finally fucking arrive, and I don't care whose collar I grab as I make my way toward my wife.

The annoyed looks around me morph into shock as I'm recognized by the swarm of men holding cameras and mics. I don't give a damn about the flashes that go off, as the attention only makes it easier for me to reach Daisy.

Five months.

It's been almost five fucking months since I last saw her in person, breathed the same air as her.

And she looks more beautiful than in any of my fantasies and dreams.

My heart pounds violently in my chest, each beat like a drum roll. "You do like to attract a crowd, my dear wife," I finally whisper, my mouth almost dry, words sticking in my throat.

I'm not thinking about the cameras or reporters when I caress her cheek, soft as always, and right now, red in nervousness.

She sucks in a breath, her lips quivering and her eyes

closed as she leans into my touch, filling my chest with relief and happiness.

"I'm sorry for being late, Daisy." *Five fucking months late.*

Before I can apologize for my absence, my failures in being a better husband and a decent father, someone hollers, pulling me right out of this heaven.

"Mr. Hawthorne, are you saying you and Mrs. Hawthorne are still together? Our sources have confirmed that she's staying with her friend."

Even when I hate doing it, I turn my head toward the man who said those words.

"You certainly need better sources, because the ones you rely on are doing a shit job." A fire burns in my chest, spreading outward in a wave of heat as I pin the reporter with a steely gaze. "Does your wife never stay with her friends?"

"I'm not married." He squirms, giving me a huge satisfaction.

Of course you're not. Fucking loser.

"Many months back, in a situation similar to this, I said in very clear words…" I pause, making sure I have everyone's attention. "If ever my wife's safety and her comfort are threatened, you'll get to see the real me. But today, you didn't just make her uncomfortable, you also put her and my baby at risk."

My arms go around Daisy's waist, and I gently pull her close. My heart jolts at an unbridled intensity as it registers the changes in her body. Something I've observed only from afar until now. There's relief at having her close after so long beneath the nervousness as the reality of us becoming parents becomes starkly clear.

When my palm rests over her hip, I feel a shiver run through Daisy before she further slumps against my chest.

How did I manage to stay away from her, knowing she's needed me?

Not any longer, butterfly.

But first things first.

I turn to face the media with more determination.

"Tomorrow is definitely not looking good for a lot of you. You can expect suspensions and termination letters at your desks." I don't stop, even when a collective gasp fills the air and the bright camera flashes suddenly stop. "And for all those who are scheming at publishing their last piece, labeling me a control freak and a tyrant, let me confirm—yeah, I gladly accept those titles. I'm the control freak who will do everything to protect his wife and his baby. And now, if you would excuse us, we have an important appointment to keep."

I turn away from my stunned audience. Dave, Steve, and Daisy's bodyguards create a barricade until we reach the steps of the hospital.

"Charles," she whispers, finally finding her voice.

There's so much I have to say, so much I want to hear, but not here.

"Everything's okay, butterfly."

There's a flock of people waiting for us just inside the glass sliding doors, including the two security guards of the hospital.

"Thank God you're safe, Daisy." The head of the OB-GYN department steps forward. "We called the police, and they should be here any minute. But of course, your husband's way was much more effective." The woman doesn't hide her smile, reminding me of her picture from the hospital website. I've had her résumé and personal background memorized since she started checking my wife.

"Okay, people, let's get back to work. Show's over." She waves the pink file in her hand and shoos around the crowd before turning to the two security guards. "And you two, for Christ's sake, be better at your job. I don't want a repeat of this."

There'll be no repeat. I'll make sure of that.

I'm definitely not counting on anyone else when it comes to Daisy's safety.

"Daisy, Mr. Hawthorne, this way. I'm all ready for you." The doctor saunters toward the hallway, and I don't get to ask Daisy anything—not even how she's feeling—because we're immediately ushered into the examination room.

The soothing pastel walls have framed prints of babies. Daisy goes behind the privacy screen while I'm rooted in my spot next to an examination table, covered with a crisp white disposable sheet.

"Is this your first ultrasound, Mr. Hawthorne?" the doctor asks casually while I suppress the urge to shake under her scrutiny.

As the adrenaline starts to cool, my anxiety at being in a completely unfamiliar place starts to make its grand appearance. There was no time to prepare myself for all of this. I become aware of my tight fists and clenched jaw when Daisy's cold hand rests over mine.

She's right beside me, and once again her touch takes away all my anxiety until it's just hope that's left behind.

I help her as she lies down, and not taking my eyes off her encouraging face, I hum a yes to the doctor.

"Then I must warn you, it's an unforgettable experience."

I don't tell her that everything has been unforgettable since our little blip made an appearance. But nothing could have prepared me for the loud thumping sound that fills the room.

My pulse thunders in my ears as I look between Daisy and the doc, who grins widely.

"That's right. This is your baby's heartbeat, Mr. Hawthorne."

"So strong?" The words slip out of my mouth in equal parts wonder and amazement.

How can something so tiny be so strong?

Daisy's grip tightens around my hand, and I watch a single teardrop rolls down her cheeks.

"It's beautiful, isn't it?" The doctor's gaze is focused on the screen before her, while I'm unable to look anywhere else but at my wife.

Beautiful is a weak word to describe what I'm feeling right now.

This moment is breathtaking. Divine.

It's the promise of a happy lifetime.

forty-two

Always an Exception

Daisy

Right beside me, seated in the back seat of his car, Charles keeps patting the pocket of his sweats as if to ensure the flash drive that holds multiple images of our baby is safe.

Yes, that's right, in his sweatpants!

My order-obsessed husband who would not leave his house if his socks didn't match his tie and shirt is right now dressed in black sweats and a matching T-shirt that stretches over his chest. It would have been a social media story in itself if he hadn't threatened everyone.

"Are you really going to take their jobs?" I ask, catching Charles once again checking his pocket.

His gaze drops from my face to my hands resting on my belly, and he lets out a shaky breath. "I can't let this go so easily, Daisy. Especially now, when there's so much at stake."

"But you know this will happen again. Maybe not tomorrow, but these people consider keeping up with your personal life their job."

An icy grip of terror squeezes my heart as I remember the moment when, all of a sudden, I was surrounded by the sea of loud questions and flashing camera lights. I thought I'd never escape. But then, once again, Charles was there for me. And he's still here.

"My main job is to protect my wife and my kid. So they can try all they want."

My breath hitches as his lips press into a thin line, trembling as if in effort to contain the bulk of his emotions.

Like he can physically see the emotions swirling inside me, Charles leans forward. "*Come home*, Daisy, where I can keep you both safe."

My eyes close, more because he's making it so hard to deny him. But *his place* was never *my home*. It was a temporary stay, a fact I was foolish enough to forget.

"I can't do this, Charles. Leaving your home once was difficult enough, so walking out again would be so, so hard." Tears burn the backs of my eyes, threatening to spill over any second.

"Who said you ever have to leave? Come back to *our home* to stay forever. You, me, and our blip."

My eyes open, those tears finally skating down my cheeks, but this time they're made of unexpected hope and not despair.

"It's the first time we've spoken about the baby," I whisper.

"That's not true. We talk about our blip every day, don't

we?" The smile that pulls on his lips goes straight to my heart. And then his eyes descend from my face to my belly, covered behind a billowy dress that shows only a little bit, but I guess it's enough to bring all his emotions home.

"I wasn't sure you were aware that I knew about Dave's phone," I whisper.

Yes, we've talked in the last few weeks, but there's a difference in watching different emotions take over his entire face one second after another than just imagining how he's reacting to my voice.

"Your breath hitched when you opened the bag the first evening. I knew you'd seen the unicorn napkins. I'm aware of Mrs. K's food presentation skills, butterfly. I'm not that dense. And I also saw how she made sure all the food that went to you looked simple and plain, leaving no doubt in your mind that she wasn't the one who'd prepared it. I knew you'd connect the dots, and then your voice changed to that tone it only ever takes with me. I fucking loved every second of it, knowing your every word was for me." His hand covers mine, effectively making contact with our blip through the fabric of my dress.

Charles gulps before bringing those beautiful blue eyes from my belly to my face. "May I?"

I slowly nod, and after a few heart-attack-inducing seconds, his palm flattens and he once again continues in a soft voice.

"But now I worry our blip will start to associate Dave's voice as his dad's. And if that happens, Dave will have to leave, not just the town but the damn country."

Oh my God!

Did he really just say *our blip* and *his dad?*

"I'd hate to let go of a such a good bodyguard, Daisy."

I can't help that my lips curl upward. "Our blip is very lucky to have so many people who care about him. But most of all, to have you as his dad, Charles." I twine my fingers with his, still splayed over my belly. "But you don't have to change yourself for this. You can be in Blip's life as much as you want, even without us getting back together. Me and Blip are not a package deal."

"That's what you don't understand. You are important not because of Blip but because you are you, my dear wife."

Hearing those three words tightens my throat. "Those are the words of a man who wants to do everything right, Charles. But soon you'll itch to have that quiet normalcy in your life."

My words halt when the car comes to a stop, and I look out the window, scanning the all-too-familiar parking space. "Why are we at the office?"

"Because I had a feeling our conversation would go this way. Come with me. I have to show you something." He steps out as Dave opens his door, while I remain seated.

"Charles, I'm not signing any new papers."

Damn, if he came up with a new proposition or contract to keep us tied to him…

"Good, because I'm not asking you to." Charles throws me a grin and steps into the elevator, waiting for me.

And a few beats later, I'm standing next to him as the elevator doors close. How can I not?

I, too, want all that Charles is offering, but I also don't want him to do so out of fear.

And that's how, with a hope-filled heart, I ride the elevator with him.

The temp assistant rises from his seat, a flash of surprise in his gaze. I'm sure it's because of Charles' uncharacteristic attire. I give him a small wave while my husband's hands are safely tucked inside his pockets until we enter his office.

His first task is to unlock the top drawer of his desk, the only part in this office, and possibly in his life, that has been off-limits to me. My feet won't take me inside as I watch Charles safely retrieving the flash drive from his pocket and placing it in there. To my surprise, he doesn't shut the drawer, but with a forced tug, pulls it out completely.

"Can you come here?" There's an unusual trepidation in his face, which makes me nervous but also curious.

I take a few steps, looking down, not knowing that I'll never be able to unsee this ever again.

"W-what is all this, Charles?" My heart skips a beat before racing wildly.

Why? Because my boss, my husband, has a drawer full of things that I purchased to annoy the crap out of him? But that's not it. The wooden drawer is filled up to the top with colorful Post-its with *my handwriting*.

I grab one of the notes and realize it's about a project we did almost three years ago.

"These are the to-do notes I stick on the wall." If my shock could convert into a physical being, it would consume the whole room.

"Every single one of them from the last four years," he confirms.

"But I—"

"You remove the old ones every morning and throw them into the trash can." Charles' grin is still in place as he points toward the tiny plastic bin that magically appeared in his office four years ago exclusively for my paper waste.

"And you're saving them like some sort of homage to me?" A shock-laced tingling sensation spreads from my core to my fingertips.

What does this even fucking mean?

"Among other things," Charles replies casually—a bit too casually—once again dropping his gaze to the open drawer, and I catch sight of the coffee mugs I've given him on various holidays, each one with a crazy drawing and a crazier phrase.

I pick up the one that was the start of this tradition.

Not today, Satan! I mean, yes, boss...

There's a bat-like figure complete with wings and a tail dressed in a suit, breathing fire.

"So what does this mean? Did you have a crush on me, Charles?" I ask carefully.

All these years?

While my hands fly to my chest, Charles' cheeks turn red.

Oh my freaking God!

I know cute is the last word one would use for Charles, but dear Lord, he has never looked cuter than right now.

And before I can roast him further, because it's been so long that I've talked to him like this, said whatever is on my mind, Charles takes a step in my direction.

"I don't know why I started storing them. Maybe because I thought someday you'd need a reminder of how hard you've worked. Or maybe it was just impossible to throw away something created by you, even if it was just a Post-it." He's right before me now. "What I'm saying is, you've always been an exception. The one anomaly, the one burst of color I've always wanted, always craved, in my otherwise perfect, orderly, and bland life."

He holds my face between his hands, and I look up at him like a girl with stars in her eyes.

"I have something more powerful than just a *crush* on you, my dear wife. If you're not convinced even now, give me a chance and I'll prove to you that you and Blip are all I need. Not just for a few months, but for my entire lifetime."

As much as I want to jump up and down and grab everything I've dreamed of—real love, a real family—there's something between Charles and me that's still keeping it from being real.

"But what about the contract? There's something legal on paper that says this marriage isn't real."

Charles grabs the back of his neck before I hear him mutter under his breath. "This can be the biggest romantic moment, or she might hurl the glass paperweight at you, Hawthorne."

"What did you just say?"

"What if it isn't?" he asks in return.

"What isn't what?"

The way Charles avoids my gaze makes me nervous. This man makes others uncomfortable. He is always perfectly composed.

"What if the marriage contract was never notarized? What if the only legal document binding us together is our marriage license?" he finally says.

"But…"

What is he saying? That my marriage was a real one, after all?

"It wasn't how I'd planned, Daisy. I swear. After the marriage ceremony, the contract papers were supposed to go to my lawyer. But then you came to my home, and I liked you in my space, in my bed, more than I thought I would. I'm not saying I did the right thing, but even though we were imperfect on paper, it felt like I'd found my perfect match. And it seemed you felt the same."

"This is so…" My brain struggles to find the right words.

"Romantic?" Charles supplies with a hesitant smile.

"Not the first thought in my mind, Mr. Hawthorne." I cross my arms over my chest. "You could have at least told me."

"I tried. Not once, but many times. And later, I started to worry that you might not see it the way I did."

My brain wants to be upset with him, at least for a short while, for keeping me in the dark and for making me constantly worry about that word—*contract*—but my heart is too busy interpreting what this really freaking means.

"So what was your plan? Keep this from me forever?"

"Not forever." Charles places his hands in his pockets, and that act pushes his broad chest forward. Before I can get distracted by that, his slow smile captures my attention. "I was thinking I'd give the contract papers to you on our fiftieth anniversary and we could make paper lanterns with our kids and grandkids."

Kids? Grandkids?

Am I in a weird, crazy dream?

"Fifty years! You would wait fifty years?"

"I'd take secrets to my deathbed if it means keeping you in my life, Daisy."

Charles' lips hover over mine, as if silently asking if we're good, not just for now, but really, for forever.

"Are you sure? Because my dream is a big, happy family, Charles." My voice shakes, but his lips curl into a heart-stopping smile

"I can't wait to give Blip a brother or a sister in a few years."

"You're killing me, Hawthorne." I rise on my toes, pressing my lips to his. I clutch the front of his T-shirt, only to drop it the next second as I take a step back.

"Holy crap! Blip kicked! Blip freaking kicked for the first time, Charles!"

And then, it happens again.

I bring Charles' hand under mine, flattening it against my stomach, and a second later I feel a tremor pass through him.

"That's…a solid kick." He's in awe.

"Talk about picking favorites, Blip. You don't let me eat until your daddy is doing the cooking, and now this." My gaze swings to Charles. "I've been asking Blip every day to give me a reaction, but no, nada. You were worried you might not love your kid, but I don't think our blip will stop until she has all your love, Charles."

"She?" He still hasn't come out of the shock.

"Chloe can be very convincing." I bite my lip as Charles shakes his head.

"I would love my bratty sister to be right once again."

epilogue

Charles

The inn is decorated in nontraditional Christmas décor, with pink streamers and balloons. There's a huge Douglas fir that's almost hidden in silver tinsel and white and pink bulb ornaments, with pink bows in every visible corner.

For someone who fell in love with the color pink two months ago, exactly when our daughter made an early arrival into this world, even *I* think it's a tad too much. But this party is run by Chloe and Daisy's friends, who have made it a personal mission to ensure my daughter's first Christmas is nothing short of the biggest event this town has seen.

And I'm fucking grateful for this life, these people who make every day feel like it's a celebration, and most of all, for this woman under my arms, holding my baby.

Yes, my sister once again got what she wanted, and I am the happiest man on the face of the earth.

Our blip now has a beautiful name, exactly like her.

Penny Georgina Hawthorne, named after two amazing women who have played a big role in my and Daisy's life—Daisy's mom and my great-gram.

"You know Penny isn't going to remember anything, right?" Daisy raises an eyebrow as Willow and Chloe bring in another box of decorations and place them on the next table.

"There's something called photographs, Daze." My sister makes her *duh* face. "Plus, we will remember, and I don't want to ever feel like I could have done something more for my favorite niece's first Christmas." Chloe visibly shudders, and Willow nods her head furiously.

"Ditto."

"How do you know she's your favorite niece? We could have another daughter, who you might love more," I say, even when it seems impossible.

I don't think I could love anyone more than I love Penny. Okay, maybe one person.

My dear wife.

But that's only because she's the one who brought all this happiness into my life.

A warm, soothing feeling spreads throughout my chest, filling me with a sense of peace as I pull Daisy a bit closer and her gaze flies up to me.

"What?" she whispers for only my ears, and I shake my head.

"I'm just…happy." When I smile, her lips curl further.

"Me too."

"For someone who used to be so scared and a total jerk about babies, look at you now. Already talking about baby number two." Willow wiggles her brows.

These past two months, I've grown closer to Daisy's friends, and not by choice. These women are at my house to see Penny almost every day.

Neither of the girls wait for my answer and are already marching toward the door, where they meet Daisy's dad. Jason Price strolls in, dressed in a red suede coat over a white turtleneck. His long white hair is loose today and not in the statement ponytail, reaching almost to his shoulders.

He's followed by Kai, who has become more like family to all of us, but mostly to Jason.

"There are my favorite girls." Jason immediately reaches us.

The days of his memory lapses are still there, and when all of a sudden this sweet man looks at me like a stranger, it kills me. I can only imagine how it must affect Daisy. But not today.

I hug my father-in-law before shaking hands with Kai.

"Dad, you're early." Daisy hugs her father before placing Penny in his arms.

"I know, Doodles. But I didn't want to wait until the evening to give my daughter and granddaughter their presents."

"You being here with us is the greatest gift of all." Daisy's voice gets heavy, and when I pull her closer, she leans into my touch as we both watch Jason look down and smile at his granddaughter. "You don't have to give us anything more, Dad."

"It's my right to spoil my granddaughter and any other future grandkids. Isn't it, Charlie?"

"Absolutely." I nod.

Jason grins at me before kissing Penny's forehead and giving her back to Daisy.

He pulls a small jewelry box from his pocket and opens it for us.

Wow. It's the smallest hair clip I've ever seen, with a bow and two pearls.

"Oh my God, Dad! It's so beautiful, but you really didn't have to buy anything for her."

"I didn't buy it, Doodles."

I take Penny from Daisy's arms. It seems whatever Jason is going to say next, they won't be just words.

"Many, many years ago—a year after our marriage to be exact—your mom was pregnant for a very short while. It was her birthday, and I saw this at a jewelry shop." Jason places the box into Daisy's quivering hands.

"Why did you and Mom never tell me…about the baby?" Daisy's voice trembles.

"Before you came into our lives, we never talked about it. After Penny's miscarriage, doctors confirmed we could never have kids. But then you walked into our lives, and it was as if we all were meant to be. Just the three of us." Jason brushes away the tears rolling down Daisy's cheeks. "Your mom didn't give this to you, simply because you were too old for this when you first started wearing her clips, and that's the only reason, Doodles."

"I'm sure of that, Dad. But I'd have loved to know that I had an angel sister or brother."

imperfect match

My chest tightens as waves of emotion crash over me, and I secure Penny closer to my heart.

"Then someday we'll talk about it. But today, I want to give this to my granddaughter. I found it while cleaning out your mom's drawers some months back and gave it to Kai in case I forgot." Jason grins, cocking his head toward his nurse. "And when I was talking to him about Penny's first Christmas gift, he reminded me of this. So, this is from him too."

"Thank you so much, man." I give Kai a nod.

"You can thank me for reminding Jason, but I'm not piggybacking on his gift. I have my own gift for Penny, and it might not be as emotional as Jason's, but it's still pretty cool."

"I'm sure she's gonna love it." Daisy gives Kai a hug before standing next to me. "It's like Penny got Mom's blessings today."

"You gave your daughter your mom's name, Doodles. Her blessings are always with Penny, with all of you. And before I forget, this is for you, my sweet daughter." Jason pulls out a pair of keys from his pocket.

"Dad! Why are you giving me your house keys?"

"They're more symbolic right now, and I'm going to take them back because these are Kai's set." Jason grins, shaking his head. "The lawyer couldn't get the papers ready, so we had this idea that I could share the news with the keys."

"What…news?"

"I'm transferring the house into your name, Doodles. It has always been yours."

"Dad, I don't—"

"I know you don't need it." Jason looks at me before looking back at his daughter, making my pulse pound. I hate that my wealth has made this sweet moment awkward. Thankfully, Jason doesn't hold on to it for long. "But it was my and your mom's dream to pass the house on to the next generation when we built it. After I'm gone, you can do whatever you'd like with the place, Doodles. Keep it as your parents' house with their memories, turn it into a B and B or a library…"

"Those are all amazing ideas, Dad. But I don't want to think about it now. I want you to live there so I can visit you often. I want Penny to crawl on those wooden floors I never got to crawl on. I want my kids to have picnics on your porch like I did with my friends while you watch over them like you and Mom watched over me."

Surprise marks Jason's features as if he hadn't thought of it.

"And, Dad, there will never be something of you and Mom that I won't need. I am honored and so will my kids be when I pass it to them."

"Was it too much for her?" I ask Daisy as she places Penny in her crib next to our bed.

"She was napping for most of the evening, Charles. I feel bad for all the work our friends and families put in for her, while she ignored everyone like a diva." Daisy slides beside me on the bed and I immediately pull her closer, right under me where she looks the prettiest.

"She's Charles Hawthorne's daughter. She was born with a license to be a diva in Cherrywood, butterfly." I tuck a curl behind her ear before following the path with my lips.

Daisy's laugh turns into a moan, and I immediately pull

back. We haven't had sex in a long time, and to be honest, my dick has started to hate my own hand. But after watching Daisy endure that long labor, I'm gonna give her all the time she needs, even if it means my body parts might go to war with each other.

"Are you practicing to be a saint?" Daisy's hands cup my face. "Or have you lost interest in me?" There's a mischievous grin on her face.

"Didn't I once tell you there would never be a time when I wouldn't want you, butterfly?"

"I remember clearly, since it was the day we made that." She juts her chin toward Penny's crib.

"Gosh." My head falls over her shoulder. "I sometimes can't believe I had something to do with the making of something so precious and delicate."

"You always undermine yourself, my dear husband." Daisy's hands bring my face closer to hers, and as always, I give in to her every command, silent or otherwise.

She gives me that siren look that turns me on like a teenager who's just hit puberty.

She hasn't looked at me like that in a long, long time.

"The doctor okayed me for…sex," she whispers, confirming my suspicion. "I mean, only if you want."

"Want? I'm dying for you—to be inside you, to be above you, to be under you—but…" I pause, my mouth dry. My dick's screaming in protest, ready to dull any rational thoughts. "I'll die if I ever hurt you, especially when we make love."

"But I want—"

My lips crush over hers, her words getting lost in our breaths. She never has to ask.

Daisy moans when our tongues make contact, and that sound, that touch, has a direct line with my cock, which is now at full attention. And it's his Christmas when Daisy rubs her legs up and down, occasionally brushing her sex covered in silk shorts against my hardening dick.

Before I can lose all sense and start to think with my little head, I pull away. "Fuck, butterfly."

"Charles!" Her cry and protest are the ultimate test of my patience.

"I know." I move down until my face is on level with her core and then tug the waistband of her shorts lower. Before I can repeat the move with her panties, she places her hands over mine.

"I…I'm not the same down there."

"Of course you aren't, butterfly. You've become a mother. You've made me a dad. You're more beautiful and more precious to me in every way." I place a kiss on the stretch mark near her belly button before placing a kiss on her sex through the cotton of her panties.

"God, I missed your mouth." Her head falls back against the pillow.

"Good, because I'm determined to show you such a good time, you'll not even miss my cock."

"What does that mean?" Daisy's smile drops as she stares at me with wide eyes.

"We're not going to have sex, but I'm gonna blow your mind with my hands and my mouth. So are you ready, Mrs. Hawthorne?"

acknowledgments

They say it takes a village to raise a child, and you need some super awesome ladies to release a book. :)

As always, this book wouldn't have been possible without the support of so many amazing people, and I'm grateful to each and every one of them from the bottom of my heart.

My editing team—Dawn Alexander, Amanda Cuff, and proofreaders Judy & Michelle—tirelessly made sure you're getting the best version of this book.

The Qamber Designs team has my heart. The stunning covers from Najla and the interior paperback formatting from Nada are absolutely fantastic.

I partnered with The Author Agency for this release. Shauna & Becca have been amazing and have truly been on top of the promo game.

To my ARC readers, thank you for reading and loving my characters, and for spreading the word about them. I appreciate every edit and every post you make about my books.

And most of all, a huge thank you to every reader who has picked up any of my books. Thank you so much for giving my writing a chance.

also by vikki jay

Elixir Billionaires
Beautiful Rose (Zander & Rose)
Chasing Sophia (Asher & Sophia) novella
Marrying Hope (Zach & Hope)
Saving Vienna (Zane & Vienna)

The Kings World
Second True Love (Keith & Clementine)
Promised Love (Lukas & Autumn)
Protected Love (Gavin & Minnie)
Forever Love (Carter & Merida)

Elixir Bachelor Billionaires
Imperfect Match (Charles & Daisy)

about the author

In those early morning hours when I'm alone, my imaginations run wild and I pen down the lives of people living in my head. All my life, I have lived in small towns in different parts of the world. The friendships, the camaraderie that people share around me inspired me to create Cherrywood and St. Peppers, the two towns where all my stories take place.

I write about beautiful coincidences, finding love in unexpected places and times, and fighting hard to get that happily ever after. My characters are sexy yet shy, strong yet reserved, willing to do anything to find their soulmate.

You can find me on the different social media websites or stay connected by subscribing to my newsletter via www.vikkijay.com

Printed in Great Britain
by Amazon